WORTH EVERY
Penny

HAWKSTON BILLIONAIRES
RAE RYDER

Worth Every Penny

Book One of the Hawkston Billionaires

Copyright © 2024 by Rae Ryder

The right of RAE RYDER to be identified as the author of this work has been asserted by her in accordance with the Copyright, Designs and Patents Act 1988.

All rights reserved. No part of this publication may be reproduced, transmitted, or stored in a retrieval system in any form or by any means without permission in writing from the copyright owner, nor otherwise circulated in any form of binding or cover other than that in which it is published and without a similar condition being imposed on the subsequent purchaser.

This is a work of fiction. All characters in this publication are fictitious, and any resemblance to real people, alive or dead, is purely coincidental.

PB ISBN: 978-1-915286-04-8

www.raeryder.com

Cover by GetCovers

Editor: Sarah Baker

To all the girls who ever wanted someone they couldn't have.
From this page on, imagine you can.

Author's Note

Please note this book is written in British English and will include British variations on spelling and vocab where applicable.

You'll find pavements, lifts, tubes (as in metro/subway), boots (of the car), a lot of S instead of Z, and an extra U in places you might not expect. Sometimes an E for an A, too.

You'll also find a toy boy rather than a boy toy.

Trigger warnings can be found on my website at www.raeryder.com/content-warnings.

This book contains mature content and is intended for those over 18.

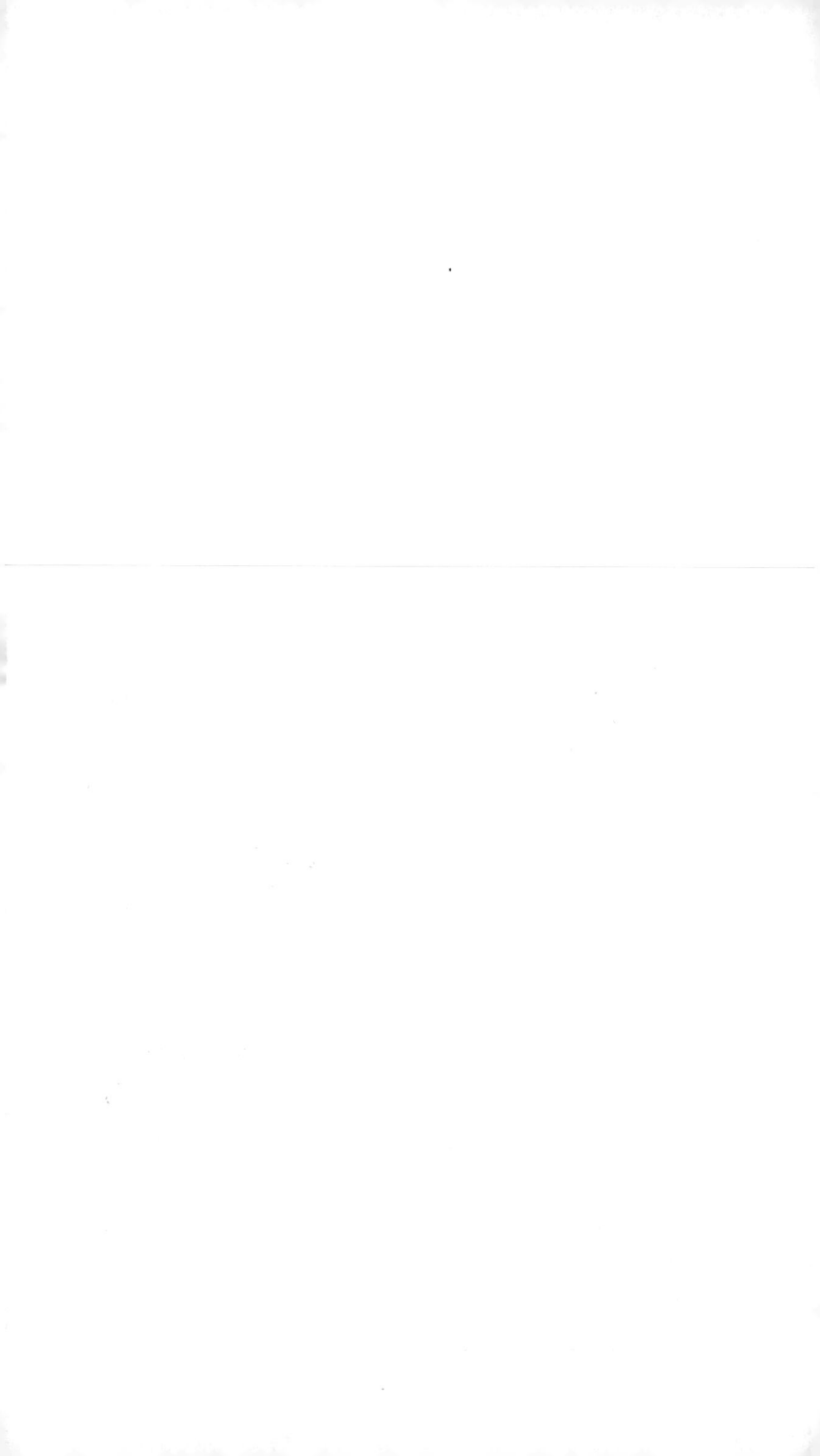

1
NICO

The blonde from last night is still half-asleep, or pretending to be, as she drapes her leg over my hip and squeezes. *Fuck's sake.* We might have slept together, but morning cuddles are definitely not on the agenda.

She grinds against me and gives a little moan. It's a lot quieter than the screaming she was doing when her fifth orgasm hit, but there's no way she's asleep. I grit my teeth and shove her leg off.

Her eyes flutter open and she lets out a sultry yawn like I didn't nearly push her off the bed. "Hey, handsome."

"Morning." I flick back the sheets, exposing us both to the chill.

Her smile disappears and the seductive look in her eye flattens. She knows what this is. She knew last night because I must have said it about a hundred times.

One night only.

I'm not looking for something serious.

This is just a casual fuck, okay? Nothing more.

She agreed; enthusiastically, too. But they always look bitter in the morning, no matter how explicit I've been.

I get up and head to the shower, hoping she's gone by the time I get back.

She isn't.

I have a towel wrapped around my waist, but she's still naked on the bed, one knee raised, running her hand up and down her leg like it might tempt me back into the sheets. Her pussy splays open like the centerfold in an anatomy textbook as she slides her fingers towards it and raises an eyebrow at me; a clear invitation if ever I saw one.

But I have a strict rule about these things. Once the sun comes up, it's over. No point encouraging them if there's no future. It's not fair to anyone.

The moment she reads the wordless rejection on my face, she pulls her legs together and sits up. "Can I take a shower too?" she asks.

On the scale of 1 to *bitter*, I'd put her about a 3. Maybe this one's a realist.

I nod my head towards the ensuite. She disappears, but the sound of running water doesn't follow, and a moment later she's back, holding up the tiny bottles of hotel toiletries. "Can I keep these?"

I resist the urge to roll my eyes. "Knock yourself out."

She grins and cuddles them to her chest. "Thanks. These are lush. You have such good stuff at Hawkston Hotels. I love the shampoo."

"You've stayed here before?" I don't know why I'm asking because I don't give a fuck, but she chatters away, oblivious to my disinterest.

"Not this exact hotel. I stayed in the one in Istanbul on a business trip. And the Hawkston New York with my sister last Christmas. That one's fab. Such luxury. The Christmas tree in the lobby—it must be thirty feet tall. It's like the one at Rockefeller Center."

"Not quite."

Ignoring my dismissive response, she returns to cradling the toiletries like she's just given birth to them before her expression brightens with an idea. "Hey, I don't suppose I could get a room discount in the future? You know, like, as a thank you?"

I shutter my eyes for a second. *Unbelievable*. This woman needs to disappear. Even my chivalry has limits. "Sorry, we don't do that."

She whistles a sigh. "Shame. Really do love these places."

Truth be told, I've never been a huge fan of Hawkston Hotels. Not that I'd ever admit that to my father. He built the hotel chain from the ground up to become the largest in the world. Corporate luxury—large, soulless and functional.

I prefer a little boutique place, like the Lansen Luxury hotel chain I'm about to buy. But given that I just returned from the US and my brothers wanted to celebrate, we met at the Hawkston Mayfair. Slap bang in the middle of London's West End. Crown jewel in the portfolio.

"I've never slept with an actual Hawkston though." Her vivacious tone cuts through my thoughts, sending a spark of irritation up my spine. She looks excited enough to explode. "What did you say your name was?"

I would've given a fake name last night, but Seb, my youngest brother, was intent on seducing every attractive woman in the bar downstairs by telling them we owned the place.

Fucking idiot.

I make a mental note not to pick up women in one of our hotels again, and quickly calculate the risks of telling her my real name. She could Google it in thirty seconds, so I figure I might as well.

"Nico."

"Nico." She clicks the consonants like she's tasting it. "Nice name."

"Thanks." I don't ask for hers. I don't need it.

She heads back into the bathroom, and the water starts running this time. I take the opportunity to get dressed. I hate putting on last night's clothes, but at least I had the presence of mind to hang up my suit and fold my shirt.

The hotel phone rings and I pick it up. "Yes?"

My brother speaks. "Breakfast? I hear the full English is good here." Seb sniggers at his own joke.

I don't return his amusement. "How many people are in your room?"

"I'm alone."

"You're shitting me."

He laughs, and I can picture that one-sided dimple on his cheek that women seem to love. It's the ultimate contrast to the strong Hawkston jaw we all share.

"They just left," Seb admits. "I'm pretty sure one of them nicked a hand towel. Took the fucking toiletries too. What's up with that?"

"Token of a great night?"

Seb laughs again.

"Or maybe," I say, "You made them feel so filthy they needed the extra soap."

"Both. Definitely both." He chuckles, then his tone changes. "So, food?"

"I can't. I've got a breakfast meeting with Jack Lansen."

"About their boutique hotel chain?" Seb perks up at this.

"Yup. We've got to thrash out the details, but we're close to agreeing on a figure."

I pin the phone between my ear and shoulder so I can brush a hand down my crumpled sleeve. *Damn*. Looks like I slept in it. Thank God it's only Jack I'm meeting. He's my best friend and won't care if I turn up hungover and in last night's clothes, but my pride isn't keen on the idea.

"Rather you than me." Seb groans. "I'm so hungover, I couldn't negotiate shit right now. Is Kate coming?"

An odd contraction occurs around my heart. *Kate*. Jack's little sister. "No," I say, dissociating from whatever the fuck is happening inside my chest. "She's not involved."

Seb makes a contemplative hmm-ing sound, but before I can wonder what he means by it, the woman reappears from the bathroom, swathed in a plush, white towel. I hang up on my brother without saying goodbye.

She gives me the once over. "Goddamn, you look good in a suit. I think you might be the hottest man I've ever fucked."

Heard that before. "I'm blushing," I deadpan.

She giggles. "Are you sure you don't wanna do this again?"

"Once is more than enough." My voice is completely neutral, but I imbue the words with just enough respect to placate her. "But thank you."

Her brow creases, like she's unsure if I've insulted her. She must decide I haven't because she drops the towel, props one foot on the end of the unmade bed, and starts massaging the Hawkston Hotel's body lotion into her thigh in long, lingering swipes.

She's in no hurry to get out of here.

The phone rings.

"Me again," Seb says when I answer. "The sober Hawkston just turned up at my room."

My eyes widen. "Matt came back?"

"Probably couldn't wait to get the fuck away from Gemma," Seb whispers, all levity gone from his voice.

Matt, our middle brother, ditched us early last night when it was clear where the evening was headed. He'd never cheat on his wife, but everyone knows his marriage is fucked. I'd take these empty one night stands over that shit any day.

There's a fumbling noise on the other end of the line, and when Matt's deep voice sounds, I realise they've passed the handset between them. "I've got you a clean suit," he says. "And shirt."

"Really?"

"Yes, really."

A relieved chuckle escapes me. "You'd make a great PA if you want to quit the hotel business."

He grunts. "Figured you wouldn't have the foresight to think about your clothes, beyond how quickly you could get out of them."

I wasn't that fucking desperate. "I'll have you know I folded my shirt last night."

Matt scoffs. "Course you did." I can almost hear him rolling his eyes. "I called your housekeeper. She sent it all over in a car."

"Tell me she sent boxers."

"And socks. There's even a bottle of cologne in here. They're at reception. I was going to bring them up, but Seb suspected you might have company."

I side-eye the woman, who's squeezing back into the little black dress she was wearing last night. She notices me looking and turns on the sultry eyes again.

"She's leaving," I say pointedly.

The woman pouts like a dejected toddler, blinking rapidly at me, but I'm immune to the act. I put my hand over the phone and hold it away from my mouth, so there's no doubt I'm talking to her.

"Thanks for a great night, but I've got back-to-back meetings all day." Her expression doesn't change and I sigh. "You need to get out of this hotel room in the next five minutes or I'm calling security."

She scowls and flaps a pair of black nylon tights in my direction. "Jesus. Fuck. All right, all right." She pulls the tights on so fast that a ladder appears all the way up the back of her leg and she glances down to inspect the damage, cursing under her breath. Her eyes flash at me like it's my fault.

She picks up her shoes and flips me the middle finger before striding into the corridor barefoot.

The door slams and I bring the phone back to my ear. "Coast's clear. Can you bring the stuff up to my room?"

Matt's laughter blows a harsh breath down the phone. "Only you, Nico. Only you."

2
KATE

I check my watch. Mum is twenty minutes late, and she hasn't contacted me to explain why. I wouldn't stand for this from anyone else, but because Mum might carve my heart out and eat it if I abandon her, I'm still waiting outside Oxford Street Tube station during rush hour, freezing my tits off.

Maybe something's wrong, and here I am thinking bad things about the woman who brought me into the world. Anxiety swirls in my stomach, and when my phone buzzes, I feel a flush of relief. Maybe that's her now, contacting me to explain her tardiness.

I open my phone to find three messages from my brother, Jack.

Jack: Where are you?

Jack: I told you to get here early.

Jack: I've got news! Big news. Huge-fucking-news. We're celebrating! I want to have a toast before anyone else gets here.

Ooh. What's he so excited about?

If Mum gets here soon, I won't have to wait long to find out. I'm only minutes from the venue. I can see it from here: a rooftop cocktail bar on Regent Street, Union Jack flag rippling proudly from the balcony of the six-storey Portland stone building.

I fire back a message.

Me: Patience, birthday boy. I'm waiting for Mum. Are we celebrating something other than your descent into old age? You're not getting engaged, are you?

He responds instantly.

Jack*: Fuck no. Just get up here.*

My brother is the eternal bachelor. There's always a woman in his life, but he treats them like disposable contact lenses. In, out, and onto the next. I don't think he's ever had a serious relationship, and he's turning thirty-five. Then again, I haven't either, but not for the same reasons. My work is my priority, not men.

I put my phone away just as my mother appears through the crowd of London commuters. She's wearing a fuchsia evening gown with a matching coat, and she stands out like a flamingo in a field of penguins.

"Kate, darling." My vertebrae contract at the way she shrieks the word '*darling*'. Only Mum could make a term of endearment sound like a reprimand.

When she reaches me, she air kisses me on both cheeks. Commuters part around us like the Red Sea, casting irritated glances our way. It's poor form to stop in the middle of the pavement, but Mum doesn't care and I can't escape her now.

I step back and cast an exaggeratedly admiring glance over my mother. "Wow. You look sensational." It's not a lie—for a woman of sixty-two, she looks fabulous—but it's also expected, like throwing money into the offering bowl at church. If you don't compliment Mum as soon as you see her, you're going straight to hell.

She strokes a bejewelled hand down her dress before primping her coiffed ash blonde hair. "I do, don't I?" She smiles, but it drops as she looks me up and down. "Your dress is very plain. Did you come from the office?"

Sadly, the compliment giving is a one-way street. I glance down at my dress. It's sleek, black, with a touch of lace at the neck and sleeves. Subtle, but I thought it worked. Now I'm doubting myself and wishing I'd worn something else. "I did, but I got changed for the party."

"Poor choice, Kate. You look like a crow. It's a birthday party, not a funeral." Mum pauses in her admonishments to inspect me again, making my stomach tighten. "Did you even fix your make-up? What kept you so long in the office, anyway?"

At this last question, a frisson of excitement bursts through me and I forget to be annoyed by her insults. I've made huge strides on my project today, and although I'd rather Jack was the first person I shared my news with, Mum is standing right here, asking why I've been working late, and my enthusiasm has it all spilling out.

"The Knightsbridge Spa project." My voice is feverish with delight. "I've finally convinced David Webster at Argentum to partner with Lansen."

Mum looks at me blankly, and I feel like a boat with a leak slowly sinking to the bottom of the ocean. She doesn't care about my work; she cares that my focus on it prevented me looking my best tonight, as though my lack of freshly applied make-up might reflect badly on her.

It was stupid to think she'd care enough to remember that the Knightsbridge Spa project was Dad's last project before he died. He was obsessed with it, and although he left the family business—Lansen Luxury Hotels, the best boutique hotel chain in the UK—to my brother, the spa project is all mine. My shrine to a beloved father, who I miss every single day. I've toiled on it for years, so the news I got today is a huge win.

"It was Dad's last project," I remind Mum, but she's still staring at me as though I'm speaking a language she doesn't understand. Any hope I had of gaining some recognition for all my hard work is quickly seeping away. "His dream. He was always jotting down notes about it on napkins around the house. Don't you remember?"

Mum flaps a hand. "That ridiculous scheme to build a luxury spa in the style of ancient Roman baths?"

Her words wound me. The project is *not* ridiculous. "Yes, and Scandinavian hot pools, right in the centre of London."

Mum lets out a dismissive laugh. "Your father was always a dreamer. He ought to have stuck to hotels." A flash of understanding crosses her face, and she rolls her eyes. "Don't tell me that's why you look like this?"

I bristle. She doesn't care about my attempt to fulfil Dad's dream. And she doesn't care that I love my job, either.

Mum, failing to notice that she has offended me, hooks her arm into the crook of my elbow, and together we make our way towards the party venue like we're the best of friends, all while I repress the urge to shove her into the middle of the road and leave her there.

She gives my arm a squeeze and leans conspiratorially close. I can sense anticipation wafting off her, and I know she's about to gossip. "Speaking of the hotel business, did you hear that Nico Hawkston's back in town?"

Butterflies erupt in my lower abdomen at the mention of his name. I mentally climb down there and snap their wings off. My feelings for my brother's best friend are complicated, but I would rather die than share any of them with my mother. "I did."

Of course, I knew Nico was back in London. I couldn't have missed it. Not only is he all over the business pages, but Elly, my best friend and flatmate, has taken to leaving glossy magazines all over our flat with the society pages flicked open to pictures of Nico exiting a club or a limo, some gorgeous woman hanging off his arm. I don't know if she's trying to torture me or tempt me.

Britain's Most Eligible Bachelor Returns to the UK, and this time he's here to stay.

Mum, in an unusual moment of awareness, seems to have noticed that my thoughts have drifted, because she shakes my arm. "There was a spread on him in *The Sunday Times*. Hawkston's the biggest corporate hotel chain in the world, and Nico's here to grow their presence in the UK." Mum lets out a wistful sigh. "And he's looking so handsome. I don't know what the Americans have been doing to him, but... dear Lord, he's quite something. Not that he wasn't before, but he's"—she puckers her lips and puts her fingertips to them, making a lip-smacking kissing sound—"like a movie star. The absolute epitome of a real man."

I cannot stomach the way Mum worships him, especially after how he treated my father. Just before he died, Dad struck a deal with Nico to sell him our family company. Dad was so excited. Desperate for Lansen Luxury Hotels to become part of the Hawkston Hotels Group. Then, with no explanation, and for no discernible reason, Nico pulled the plug.

The stress and humiliation drove my father right to the edge. He was beyond devastated, and Nico being his godson made it worse. It makes my blood boil to even think about it, but I play it down. "He's not that great, Mum."

Mum cackles. "Not that great? We used to laugh about the crush you had on him. It was terribly funny how you'd blush right to the tips of your ears whenever Jack brought him to the house. It's been forever since he came to stay. I don't think he's visited since your father died."

Thank goodness, because if he had turned up, I'd have thrown him out. I always thought it was strange that Jack didn't harbour the same resentment I did. He and Nico continued to see each other as if nothing had changed. Whenever I asked Jack about it, he gave some flimsy response about forgiveness. At any rate, in the intervening years Nico and I have never crossed paths, which is just as well because, as far as I was concerned, after Dad died, Nico was no longer welcome in our home.

Or my heart.

But Mum's not wrong about that crush. As a teenager, I'd been completely obsessed with him. When he came to stay, I'd linger by the tennis court and watch him and Jack play, or I'd sit by the window in my bedroom so I could see him swimming in the pool. And then, when I was alone, I'd sketch his face. His body. I had Nico Hawkston memorised; every line of his being learnt by rote, carved into my mind like words on a tombstone.

Other girls might have cut posters of their favourite boy band members from magazines and stuck them on the walls, but I drew my brother's best friend and kept the sketches hidden away so no one would find them.

I can't think of it now without cringing, but eventually I drew him naked, daring to imagine what he looked like beneath his clothes. That shift marked the end of my innocence. Teenage hormones gone wild, with no outlet but pen and paper.

The first time I ever pleasured myself, it was Nico I thought of, just the way I'd drawn him. And I did it over and over again.

It was my shameful secret.

But in real life, Nico never touched me. And why would he? I was only ever Jack's little sister, who blushed and stuttered in his presence. When I gathered the courage to make my feelings known, the results were disastrous. It was late one evening, after most people had gone home from one of Jack's parties, when I found Nico alone in my parents' hot tub. Determined to convince him I was old enough for him, I slid into the water and removed my bikini top. I was so nervous I was trembling. Nico was horrified, yelling at me to get dressed and go back to the house.

The shame still blisters beneath my skin when I think of it, but it got easier to bear once I really saw him for the ruthless bastard he is.

Mum halts, dragging me to a standstill beside her whilst she digs into her handbag and pulls out a copy of The Sunday Times Magazine with Nico's face on the front. "Look at this." She shakes it at me. "I defy you to say this man isn't spectacular." Her severe expression softens as she swoons over Nico's picture. "We might get to see him in the flesh tonight. Jack would have invited him, I'm sure."

A rip-roaring panic tears through me. Knowing Nico is back in London is not the same as potentially spending an evening in the same room as him.

I snatch the magazine from Mum's hand. "Why are you carrying this around?" I march towards the nearest litter bin, but Mum is quick to catch up to me, grabbing my wrist before I can toss the magazine.

"Don't you dare throw that away," she snaps. "I'm keeping it to show Curtis."

I pause, still holding the magazine. "Who's Curtis?"

Mum scowls, as if me not knowing who Curtis is proves my uselessness. "If you ever called me, you would know about him. Your brother speaks to me every Sunday."

I blink extendedly, holding back the surge of emotion that assails me at yet another comparison to Jack. Mum's golden child. She has always adored him, but when he started making serious money through all his side-businesses and investments, it got even worse. I never stood a chance.

At least when we were kids I had Dad in my corner, always ready to give me a hug and plant a kiss on the top of my head, telling me he loved me, which made up for the millions of times Mum dismissed me. A hollow ache sets up in my chest at the thought of Dad and I push it away as fast as I can.

"How long have you known this new man?" I ask.

Mum gapes at me. "New man? You make me sound like a hussy. It's been six months since Jeff and I ended things, and my bedroom has been quite empty, I can assure you."

This is why I don't call home. Every comment I make gets twisted into something vile. "Really, Mum, I didn't mean to imply—"

"A month," Mum snaps. "I've known him a month."

I inhale through my nose and hold my breath for a moment as I debate what to say next. Despite our awkward relationship, I want her to find happiness now that Dad is gone. "Are you happy?"

"Oh, yes. When you know, you know." Mum grins, but her smile vanishes when she looks at me. "Although I suppose you don't know. How's the love life? Still as arid as the Sahara?"

Nico's handsome face flashes in my mind before a wave of irritation pushes it aside. *Why does she always have to be so cruel?* I'm about to put my foot down and tell her she's being mean when she lets out an excited squeal and jumps an inch in the air. "He's over there. How's my lippy?"

She puckers her bright pink lips but doesn't wait for my reply before she grabs my hand and tugs me across the road, dodging through bumper-to-bumper black cabs and red double-decker buses, to where a man is leaning against the wall of Jack's party venue. At first, I don't think this can be the man Mum means, because he's barely older than me.

He's tall and skinny, with lank dark hair that falls almost to his jaw. His black trousers are tight, tapering into gold trainers, and a white bow tie hangs limp and unfastened under the collar of a black shirt. He looks like he's been partying all night and is ready to go home.

"That's Curtis?" I ask. "He's very... young."

Mum coos like I've just delivered the world's best compliment. "He is. Only thirty-three. I haven't been with such a youthful man since I married your father. I'm a new woman. Better than a facelift." She winks at me like I'm one of her friends and conversations about facelifts and sex with younger men are normal between us.

"Oh. That's great. Good for you. Definitely better than plastic surgery," I reply flatly.

"I'm so glad you agree, because"—she takes a deep breath and for a moment I think she's going to tell me she's getting married—"he's moving in with me."

What? She's only known him a month. He's younger than Jack. What does he want with her? I don't have time to process this bombshell before Curtis notices Mum and bounds towards us as though his gold trainers have springs in the soles.

"You must be Kate," he purrs against my cheek when he reaches me. He's leaning in far too close, one hand snaking round the small of my back. Saliva makes a wet click in my ear as he whispers, "Aren't you a beauty?"

I'm too stunned to speak, and immediately after Curtis slides his hand off my back, something touches my bum. Gentle... no more than a misplaced stroke. *Did he fondle my arse?*

Maybe I imagined it. I *must* have imagined it.

He's grinning when he steps back, but his gaze lingers on my tits. I cross my arms as a barrier.

I have no idea what to do or say. My mother has a toy-boy who felt me up and is currently staring at me as though I'm a piece of meat.

Tearing his gaze from me, Curtis tugs Mum against him. "Shall we have a drink before the party, just you and me? A quickie?" He waggles his eyebrows, and bile rises up my throat.

"Oh yes, let's," Mum chirps, before turning to me, "You don't mind, do you? Tell Jack we'll be there soon." She gives my arm a squeeze and leans in, her head slightly tilted towards Curtis as she whispers in my ear, "Isn't he a delight?"

A delight? No, Mum. He makes my skin crawl.

She turns away, focusing on Curtis before I can respond. "One quick tipple," she announces. "After that, you must meet Jack. He's absolutely my pride and joy. Apple of my eye. No mother could wish for a better child. He's a real self-made man. Worth a fortune. And he's so sweet to me. I don't know what I would do without him."

Mum and Curtis drift away, arm in arm. Neither of them looks back and I'm sure Mum has already forgotten I was standing beside her and that we were supposed to arrive at Jack's party together.

I expect to feel deflated, but I don't. Maybe the pain of having a mother who constantly finds me lacking is wearing off, or perhaps I've repressed it so long that I can't feel it anymore.

I nod to the doorman and pass through the grand entryway to the bar. It's calm in here compared to the bustle outside, and the tension falls from my shoulders. I head towards the lift, which opens as soon as I press the button. I step inside, but right before the doors close and seal me in, they jerk to a standstill and begin to open again.

A tall man, at least six foot two, maybe three, appears in the gap. He's in a tailored suit, broad shoulders swathed in a cashmere overcoat that's so perfectly cut it looks like he was born in it.

But it's the sight of his ridiculously handsome face that hits me like a sucker punch. Seeing those cheekbones and smoldering dark eyes in print is one thing, but when the man himself is within touching distance, it's quite another.

He drags his gaze up my body, causing tingles to erupt over my skin, and when his eyes lock onto mine, my lungs turn to concrete.

Nico fucking Hawkston.

Jack's best friend. One of the richest men in the world.

And the man who caused my father's death.

3

KATE

Nico hesitates on the threshold of the lift, as if wondering whether being sealed in this small space with me is a good idea. But the flash of indecision disappears almost instantly, and he strides in, clearly realising there is no socially acceptable way to back out of this scenario.

I can't stop staring. While he was breath-taking at twenty-six, at thirty-four he's exactly as Mum described. *Spectacular*. And yet the word isn't enough to encapsulate the power emanating from him as he steps towards me. A ruggedness has replaced his boyish good looks, and he's broader than he used to be.

As he takes his position beside me, I'm still struggling to catch a full breath. *Damn it*. The last thing I want is to be physically affected by him, but old habits die hard, and his sudden proximity is asphyxiating.

I remind myself that his actions caused my father's death. I cannot have feelings for him. Not anymore. I will never forgive him for what he did.

We stand in silence as the lift closes and begins to rise, and I'm not sure I've ever experienced a more awkward moment in all my life.

Nico is the one to break the stand-off.

"It's been a long time, Little K."

Little K. I haven't heard my childhood nickname for years. Rolling off Nico's tongue, in his deep, resonant voice, it sounds a lot less innocent than it used to. My heart is racing.

He's so close to me I can smell his cologne. An expensive mix of bergamot and leather. It's the same scent he's always worn, and a hit of nostalgia twists my insides. All my teenage longing rushes through me like a summer heatwave, and a wave of dizziness assaults me.

I reach out to steady myself against the wall, and Nico's dark eyes flash with awareness, landing on the spot my hand meets the metal. He lifts a brow.

This is unbearable. I can't stand this man, and yet he has my mind and body spinning like a carousel.

"Kate. My name is Kate." My voice sounds unnatural and forced.

"I know what your name is."

Then why does he insist on my nickname? Does he still see me as a child? Irritated, I suck air through my nose before I speak. "It's been eight years. Why are you back now?"

A beat of awkward silence passes, and Nico examines me, eyes narrowing as if he suspects there's another meaning behind my question. His voice is quiet when he finally responds. "I've been back many times. I just haven't seen you."

His words carry a weight I can't make sense of, and there's a glimmer of something that looks like regret in his expression. But then it's gone, and I wonder if I imagined it. His gaze darts downward, and for a brief second I think he's checking me out, but when his brow creases, I realise he's staring at the magazine I'm holding. The one Mum gave me that displays a full-size image of his face.

I'd forgotten I was holding it. My body heats uncomfortably as embarrassment floods me. When his eyes flick back up, I blurt, "It's not mine."

Nico stifles his smile and clears his throat. "Of course not." He pauses, deliberately scanning the empty lift, a knowing look in his eye. "Whose is it?"

The space seems to shrink, and his body feels even closer to mine than before. Admitting that my mother gave me the magazine doesn't strike me as any better than it belonging to me. With Nico's gaze fixed on me, the back of my neck turns hot and sticky. I want to use the magazine to fan my face, but I check the impulse. Thankfully, I'm saved from replying by the opening of the doors, and Nico puts his arm out to allow me to exit first.

He follows me to the cloakroom, where we check our coats. Once the attendant, a young woman in her twenties, has hung them up, I put the magazine face upward on the desk. The attendant stares at it, then up at Nico and back again, her eyes widening.

I tap the magazine between the image of Nico's eyes. "Could you put this in the bin for me, please?"

Beside me, Nico's jaw tightens, firming angles already so sharp they could draw blood, but he makes no comment.

The girl doesn't move, as though she's waiting for me to change my mind, or perhaps wondering why I'm doing something so rude. She looks at Nico, glances back at the picture of his face then up again, and states, "This is you."

"It is," he agrees, his voice low and unmistakably sensual, although it doesn't strike me as deliberate. It's just the way he is. *Unintentionally sexy.*

"Are you famous?" She sounds breathless, and a red rash is spreading upwards from beneath the collar of her shirt.

Nico huffs a laugh, a deep and mellow sound that I feel in places I shouldn't, and from the look of the rising blush on the girl's skin, I'm not the only one. "In some circles."

She licks her bottom lip. "Would I know you? Have I seen you in anything?"

Please. She thinks he's an actual movie star? This is ridiculous. "No," Nico confirms. "I'm not in the entertainment industry."

The girl looks up at him adoringly. "You should be."

Oh, come on. Could she be any more obvious? I'm getting more and more irate, not only because my attempt at throwing the magazine away has fallen flat, but because I'm witnessing another woman wilt in Nico's presence. I'm about to grab the magazine off the desk and chuck it towards the bin I can see over the girl's shoulder, when she pushes it towards Nico and asks him to sign it.

I can't believe it. I've been completely thwarted. This is a nightmare. I let out a disapproving sigh.

Nico gives me a cocky sideways glance as he takes his pen from his jacket pocket and signs the magazine with a flourish. Even his signature is sexy. The girl looks delighted, whereas I'm about to burst into flames of rage.

"She doesn't even know who you are," I hiss.

"No." Nico tilts his head in subtle agreement with my point, then undermines it entirely as he adds, "but she wants to."

I can't disagree, which only makes the flickering flames of rage in my belly burn brighter. *So arrogant.* I do not have time for this nonsense. "Can I get a token?" I ask the attendant.

She blinks at me, completely disoriented. "What?"

"For my coat," I explain.

She shifts into action, realising she's let Nico knock her off her job. "Oh, yes. Sorry. Here you go." She slides two tokens across the desk, one for me and one for Nico.

I snatch mine and move away, giving myself a shake as I go. I refuse to let Nico Hawkston ruin my night.

He calls my name but I keep walking, breathing a sigh of relief when his phone rings and he stops to answer it, allowing me to continue towards the bar alone.

4
KATE

My body is still buzzing with adrenaline as I push open the doors to the bar. I need to ground myself, or I won't be able to focus on Jack, his birthday, and whatever his great surprise is.

Amazingly, I'm still early. The bar is almost empty and soft music filters through hidden speakers. The lighting is dim, and the floor is dark stone. On one side, the wall is entirely glass, leading out to the balcony and the glittering lights of London beyond. It's glamorous without being too showy.

I spot Jack at the bar, perched on a red velvet stool. He's flirting with one of the waitresses, who's filling glasses of champagne. She stops what she's doing and leans across to help him fix his bow tie. I want to laugh; I've seen that move before. He's incorrigible.

"Happy birthday!" I cry as I cross the room towards him.

Jack spins to face me and his lips part in a huge, cheeky grin. He pushes off the stool, dwarfing the small waitress, who gawks as if his stature is both impressive and shocking. Even I can't deny that he's looking pretty damn handsome in his tux this evening—sleek lines and good tailoring accentuate his pale blue eyes, dark hair, and the slight cleft in his chin. I feel a burst of pride that this man is my brother.

Warmth spreads through me as he pulls me into a massive hug, like my nervous system is being dipped in a bath. It's just what I need. My brother is eight years older than me, and being hugged by him is one of the most comforting things in my life, not least because it reminds me of Dad. They even smell the same; clean, like fresh laundry, but with a smokier element too, as though their jacket was hanging next to a wood-fire moments before they put it on.

Jack releases me and stands back to look me over, his lips tipping up at the corners, when suddenly his attention shifts to something over my shoulder.

"Nico!" he yells. "Get over here."

My body goes haywire, every nerve ending firing off at high speed. *So much for grounding myself.*

I look back towards the door to see Nico pacing towards us, closing the distance with a few long strides. There isn't a hint of hesitation in his graceful movement.

"Happy Birthday," Nico says to Jack, and they clutch one another's hands for a second, before drawing into one of those manly hugs that ends with a thump on the shoulder blade as they separate. They're both grinning, pleased to see each other, and they exchange a few pleasantries.

"Little K," Nico says to me with a respectful nod of the head, as if we haven't already done this.

A brief silence follows, and Jack looks between us, his gaze settling on me. He's expecting me to say something, but I'm too preoccupied trying to make sense of the way my body is reacting to Nico's presence.

"It's Nico," Jack tells me, as if my silence means I've forgotten who he is. "Nico Hawkston."

"I know." My tone is cool, even though I'm fizzing beneath the skin.

"We spoke in the lift," Nico explains to Jack. "And now we've exhausted all conversation."

I can't tell if he's joking, but it's a fair assessment of the situation. I'm not about to make small talk with Nico fucking Hawkston if I don't have to. Jack's perturbed gaze bounces between us.

"Don't tell me this is your big news?" I ask my brother. "Nico Hawkston's back in town?"

In my peripheral vision, Nico flinches. It's not a bodily flinch, but a tightening of the muscles around his dark eyes. Maybe I sounded more sarcastic than I meant to, but I'm still wondering what Jack's '*huge-fucking news'* is, and hoping this isn't it.

Jack swipes a glass of champagne from the bar and hands it to me like nothing's wrong, but when he smiles, his lips pull away awkwardly from his teeth. Nothing about it is natural.

It sets me on edge.

Jack hands Nico a champagne glass too. Nico takes it, a slight crease marring the space between his dark brows.

We stand—an awkward circle of three—until Jack thrusts his hand into the middle and raises his glass in a toast.

"To us," he says.

I don't move. Why is Jack toasting 'us' like we're all best of friends when Nico screwed over our dad, disappeared off to America, and has avoided me for eight years?

Nico hasn't raised his glass either. His eyes dart to Jack, an accusatory glint in them. "You didn't tell her," he says.

"Tell me what?" I ask, confused.

The light in Jack's eyes dies. "Well, fuck," he mutters.

I look between the two of them. "What's going on? Can one of you spit it out, please?"

Nico makes a throaty noise, which could be a laugh, could be a groan. Whatever it is, he's deferring this one to Jack.

Jack takes a great, heaving inhalation, then blows the words out like a confession. "I've had an offer for the company."

Air stalls in my lungs. *An offer? To sell the company? What the hell?* I haven't been working my arse off at Dad's company for the last five years so we can sell it. I put my champagne glass back on the bar, straining to keep my voice level when I say, "I wasn't aware you were thinking of selling."

A flicker of uncertainty darts across Jack's face. "I should have told you, but I wanted to sort through the details first. The offer's a good one. Really fucking good."

A vicious heat burns in my chest. I can't believe he's making a decision like this without consulting me. I try to hide my shock, but I'm sure Jack can see it. He sips his drink, eyes wary as he waits for me to recover.

I dare a glance at Nico, whose gaze is flicking between me and Jack, and my skin prickles, my intuition giving me a warning. *Please, no.*

Focusing on my brother, I ask, "Who's the buyer?"

"I am," Nico says.

My stomach drops.

No. It *plummets*.

I swing to face Nico, forgetting about Jack entirely, and hold my palm up. "Oh, no. Not fucking you. We are not selling Dad's company to you."

"Kate, please," Jack reprimands, but I ignore him. He should've known I would never go for this.

Nico, whose composure has barely faltered in the face of my outburst, bows his head. "I'll let the two of you discuss this in private." He takes a step back. It's such a dignified response compared to mine that a hot rush of shame blasts through me.

Jack reaches out to him. "No, Nico. Stay."

Nico shakes his head, mahogany hair flopping over his forehead. "Talk this out. Then come back to me."

Jack opens his mouth to speak, but Nico's already turning away. I don't know where he's going, and right now I don't care.

Jack puts his champagne next to mine on the bar. "That was... fuck, Kate." He clenches a fist and lets out a frustrated groan. "That was rude. I know you're angry, but—"

"You cannot sell Lansen to Nico." My jaw is so tight the words scrape out.

Jack stands taller. "I bloody can. No one else is going to give us an offer like this. And Nico's practically family."

"He's not my family," I fire back. "He'll *never* be my family."

Jack sighs. "Don't you even want to know how much he's laid on the table?"

"No!" I slam my hand on the bar.

The waitress' eyes widen and she shoots a hand out to steady the nearby champagne glasses. At the same moment, Jack rears back, hands raised like I'm pointing a gun at his chest.

"Woah. I didn't do this to upset you. I hope you know that. I've been running this company for nearly a decade. I know what I'm doing. And selling it to Nico makes sense."

I slide my hand off the bar. My palm stings like a bitch, but I pretend it doesn't.

"I don't know how you can even contemplate this." I'm trying to keep my voice calm, but my words have a hoarse, raw edge. "Nico had his chance to buy the company and he fucked it up—"

"It's different now."

"How? How is it different? He's still the same ambitious bastard he was back then. He completely screwed Dad over." The pitch of my voice is rising, but I can't stop. "He might as well have murdered him with his own hands—"

"Kate, please. I don't want to fight about this. Be reasonable."

Be reasonable? I might not own the company like Jack does, but I am his sister. Doing the deal behind my back feels like a betrayal. And doing it with Nico Hawkston? That's the worst.

I cross my arms to contain the heat expanding in my chest.

"I'm not denying that this is hard." Jack reaches out to touch me, then decides against it and lets his arm fall. "He was my father too. But if there's one thing I know about Nico, it's that he's incredibly loyal—"

"Are you joking? Because I don't see that at all."

Jack's eyes swivel to the door, where the first guests are trickling in. I can tell he wants to tell me to keep it down, but instead he steps closer and lowers his voice. "Can you just trust me on this?"

"Is it about the money? Because—"

"No. It's not the money, although I'd be lying if I said it didn't matter. The money represents what we've done. What we've achieved. We aren't in opposition here. Can't you see that? This is how we honour Dad. You with the spa project, and me with the sale. Dad wanted both of those things. You know he did."

I take a moment to consider this. Dad did want the sale, but if he had known how it would play out, I doubt he would have pursued it. "The spa project didn't fucking kill him, though, did it?" Bitterness spills from my words.

Jack lowers his head, rubs the back of his neck, then looks back at me. "Let's discuss this later. When you've had time to digest it."

"I don't need time," I snap. "Do not sign the company over to that man."

"I'm not asking your permission." *Of course, he isn't.* "Here." He takes a rolled up sheaf of papers out of his pocket and holds it out to me. "Take a look at the contract."

There's already a contract? I stare at it but make no move to take it. "How long have you been in negotiations?"

"A few weeks."

An unpleasant sensation throbs at my solar plexus. *They've left me out.* "Why didn't you tell me? Didn't you trust me?"

A tiny muscle on Jack's jaw clenches and relaxes. "I had to make the best choice for the company, and Nico is it. This is business, and I knew you'd get personal."

It *is* personal. Not telling me until the last minute feels calculated... but I don't want to ruin Jack's party by throwing a full-on tantrum.

The crowd of people by the entrance has grown. They're spilling into the room. We've got seconds to bring this conversation to a close before the swarm of well-wishers reaches us.

Jack forces the contract into my hand. "Read it over. It's a lot of money. Too much to say no to. We won't get better than this."

My fingers cinch around the paper, crumpling it. I'd tear the damn thing up if I dared, but as much as I would love to deny it, I want to know how much money Nico's laying on the line for the business.

"What about my spa project?" I breathe. "I had news to tell you about it." I'd been so happy about my progress, but what with Mum dismissing it and now Jack telling me he's selling the company, I feel foolish. Childish, even. Out of nowhere, my throat gets a little choked up.

Jack leans towards me, looking concerned. "What news? Tell me?" His voice is gentle.

The urge to cry is so fierce that I'm sure my eyes must be wet, but when I wipe them with my fingertips, they come away dry. "I'm finally getting traction. I had a meeting with David Webster earlier and he's agreed to do it. We're building Dad's spa."

Jack's face breaks into a smile of genuine warmth. "Oh, Kate. That's incredible. Well done."

I swallow back the lump that's sprouted in my throat. "Does it even matter now that you're selling everything?"

Jack pulls me into another hug, and for a few moments, I soak it up. "Of course it matters. This is huge." He squeezes me, then pushes me away, his hands clamped to my upper arms. "You've worked hard for this. Dad would be so proud."

This is the recognition I wanted when I told Mum earlier, and finally hearing it from Jack only intensifies my emotions, which are already running riot tonight. By the time I extract myself from his hold, my throat is completely choked up. "Thanks," I croak.

"You'll get to keep the project," Jack adds. "Nico will let you manage it."

He's talking as though the sale is a done deal, and my annoyance rises again. I can't take much more of this emotional yo-yoing.

Arms wrap around me from behind and squeeze my waist. I yelp just as my best friend Elly releases me and steps into view. She's grinning, but she takes one look at my teary face and squares up to Jack.

"What did you do to her?" She snarls, and the expression, paired with her wild mane of blonde curls, makes her look like a furious lioness.

I tuck the contract into my bag, knowing it's confidential and even if I wanted to explain it to Elly, I couldn't. "Honestly, it's nothing."

She raises an eyebrow at me, then glares at Jack, but her hostility doesn't find its mark as his admiring gaze sweeps over her in return. She looks gorgeous in her white mini dress and cowboy boots, but

Jack would look at anyone that way. He's the biggest flirt there is. "Hey there, El," he says, his voice velvety smooth.

She rolls her eyes and focuses on me. "You okay?"

"Yeah. I'm just sad Dad can't be here."

Elly's bottom lip turns downward, her blue eyes full of compassion. "Oh, Kate. I'm sure he's watching you both."

Her comment hovers undisturbed for a few seconds, and then she hugs me again. "This'll cheer you up," she whispers before releasing me and turning to Jack. "I got you something." She pulls a small tissue wrapped parcel from her bag. Her eyes twinkle, mouth slanting into a smile as she hands it to him. "Happy birthday."

With a bemused look, Jack unwraps the gift. It's a tiny statue of a naked man with an engorged penis that rises level with his head.

"Wow." Jack twists the statue around on his palm, examining it from every angle before his gaze flicks to Elly. "Didn't realise you saw me this way. Not bad at all. I'm flattered. Truly."

Elly huffs, and her expression turns serious. "It's Priapus, the Greek God of fertility, not you. I thought you could put him outside Kate's spa when it's up and built. You could have two lifesize versions at the door, like the Beefeaters at the Tower of London, but with enormous dicks and no clothes."

Laughter splutters from my mouth for the first time this evening. "That sounds terrifying," I squeak. "It's definitely not what Dad intended."

"Yeah, El," Jack adds, the amusement clear in his voice. "It's not a brothel."

"Fine," Elly snarks. "I'll leave the creative details to you two." She smirks. "But when it's finished, I'm going to be the first one getting naked in the sauna."

Jack whistles. "I'll be second."

She gasps and playfully slaps his arm, and he recoils, pretending to be in pain. Elly bursts out laughing and I can't resist joining in, a wave of gratitude assailing me that she's here to lighten the mood. We continue giggling as Jack aborts his play-acting and slips his hands in his pockets, smiling at both of us.

The room is filling up, and when our laughter eases, Elly glances around. "Come on," she says to me. "There's a very handsome waiter over there who looks like he needs entertaining."

A small frown mars Jack's forehead as he watches my best friend flounce across the room. "I think she likes me," he announces, nodding to himself.

I snort. "Definitely not."

"She gave me an erect penis," he says, as though this confirms it.

"For the spa."

Jack rolls his eyes. "Whatever."

I smile. Jack's ego is spectacular; I'd never be able to convince him he wasn't universally irresistible, even though Elly is walking away from him to chat up someone else.

He blinks as though he needs to clear her from his vision, then rubs a hand over his mouth and shakes his head before looking up at me, his eyes full of apology. "I shouldn't have sprung the news of the sale on you like that. I'm sorry. Really."

His words cause pressure in my chest. I don't want to be angry with him, especially not on his birthday. I give him a smile that's half-happy, half-sad. "Happy Birthday, big brother. I still love you."

He blows out a breath and his shoulders sag. He was more tense than I'd realised. Maybe he didn't expect me to forgive him at all.

"Thanks," he whispers, holding my gaze for a meaningful second or two before forcing a glass of champagne into my hand. "Try to enjoy yourself, won't you?"

"Yeah, yeah," I reply dismissively.

Jack's friends surround us, eager for his attention, and I push my way through the crowd, leaving him to it.

I down the glass of champagne, followed in quick succession by a second I grab from the bar. I wouldn't call this enjoying myself, but it's the next best thing.

I move towards Elly, who must sense me coming because she scurries over and grabs my arm. "Oh, by the way," she says in a conspiratorial whisper. "The cloakroom attendant is out there reading a magazine with Nico Hawkston's face on it. How weird is that?"

5
NICO

Kate fucking Lansen.

I thought I had this deal done. Now, I'm wondering how much of a fuss she's going to kick up. When I admitted I was the purchaser, the look on her face was pure wrath. But even with her eyes flashing loathing, she was stunning. And if that kind of passion is anything to go by, she'd be wild in bed.

Talk about an intrusive thought.

Until tonight, I hadn't seen Kate since she was eighteen. She's just as beautiful, but her features are more mature. That naivety she had when she was younger is gone, and what remains is more alluring.

But as attractive as Kate is, I can't let her get in the way of a good deal.

If I can find her in the crowd, talk to her one to one... convince her the purchase of the company isn't a bad thing... that *I'm* not a bad thing...

I glance around the room, sweeping the crowd for her. Fuck, it's busy in here. From the looks of it, Jack invited half the London society pages. There are at least three guys I went to school with, a woman my mother tried to set me up with when I was twenty-two, and Henry Banville, the youngest (and possibly the richest) Duke in the UK.

But no sign of Kate.

A nudge to my elbow brings me back to the present moment. Champagne slops out of my glass at the impact.

"Watch it!"

My brother, Seb, chuckles. That little dimple appears on his left cheek and his blue eyes dance with amusement.

"It's not as if you're drinking the stuff," Seb argues, clinking his champagne glass against mine. "Shouldn't you be celebrating?"

"Jack hasn't signed the contract yet. Couple of small details left to finalise."

"Nothing serious? No roadblocks?"

"No." I'm not about to tell Seb that Jack's little sister could derail the whole thing. "But I won't celebrate until it's official."

"Fair enough." Seb props his elbows on the bar behind him as he looks out into the party. He's thoughtful for a moment. "I was hoping you might bring Erica tonight."

"She was busy."

Erica Lefroy is the UK's top runway model, and she's a long-time friend of mine. We went on a couple of dates a few years ago, but didn't hit it off romantically. We've been friendly ever since, and whenever we're seen together, the press goes crazy for it. The attention is a tedium I could well do without, but I enjoy her company enough to bear it.

I can tell that Seb wants to talk about her, but I'm too distracted. If I don't secure this deal tonight, I won't be able to sleep.

"What the fuck?" Seb mutters, hooking my attention. "Is that Matt?"

I follow Seb's gaze. Our middle brother, scowling deeply, is barreling through the crowd. He's intently focused on something on the other side of the room. I swing to check what, and my stomach falls as I catch sight of his wife, Gemma, and teenage son, Charlie.

Gemma's sleek blonde hair frames her Grace Kelly face, but she's far from the poised, aloof woman I'm used to seeing. Charlie, a gangly fifteen-year-old, is clinging to her arm, stumbling along beside her, his feet catching on the hem of her pale blue evening dress. He's so drunk he can barely stand up and Gemma looks like she wants to push him to the gutter.

Charlie's hair is a shocking electric blue. It's as eccentric as his black tie suit is conformist. Mother and son are drawing horrified glances from other guests.

"This can't be good," Seb says under his breath, throwing a wary look at me. "Charlie's gone *Sonic the Hedgehog*."

"If Sonic downed half a bottle of vodka before he went out."

"Fuuuuck," Seb breathes.

Charlie is my only nephew. The teenage pregnancy that nearly gave my mother a coronary. I'm pretty sure the only reason it didn't is because Gemma is part of the Von Arsworz family—one of the largest diamond suppliers in the world—so it was unlikely Matt had been trapped by a gold-digger. He was just a foolish teenager who didn't wear a condom.

Small mercies.

"He's going to kill them," Seb mutters.

Without another word, I rush towards the imminent collision of husband and wife, hoping I can prevent the ensuing marital battle from erupting on the dance floor. Seb skids along behind me.

"What the hell is going on?" Matt is whisper-yelling when we get there, his anger bubbling beneath the surface. "Why is our son so drunk he looks like he's about to wet himself?"

Gemma huffs as she props Charlie up. "This is as much your fault as mine, Matthew."

Matt's eyes pop wide, but I suspect she may have a point. Not that I'd ever say that to Matt, but he works fucking hard. How can he also be there for his kids?

"How is it my fault?" he growls.

Seb catches my eye, slicing his throat with his fingers like being here is going to kill *us*. Then he jerks his thumb, signaling we should leave them to it.

I shake my head, refusing to desert Matt with this mess. I hook Charlie's arm around my shoulder, taking his weight from Gemma.

Fuck, this kid smells like booze and sweat. His full weight leans on me until Seb, with a subtle eye-roll, takes his other side.

Without acknowledging me or Seb, Gemma fixes the sleeves of her dress and flicks a sheet of blonde hair over her shoulder before her icy glare fixes on Matt.

"You left without me. I didn't want to come alone, so I brought him as my plus one." She wafts one hand lazily in the air. "I may have lost sight of him for a while."

Matt's eyes dart to me. The frustration in his gaze is painful to see. If we weren't standing in the middle of a bar, he'd probably yell. But he doesn't. Instead, a contained fury rumbles in his voice when he asks, "And his hair. When did that happen?"

Gemma performs a half-hearted shrug, her left hand still wafting in the air.

"Hey, Dad," Charlie slurs, head lolling. "Did the hair myself. This morning. Got a tongue piercing too. Thought you'd like it."

With his eyes barely open, Charlie lets his tongue hang out. A silver ball sits right in the fold. He's so drunk there's no chance of having a reasonable conversation with him, but the piercing doesn't look new.

Above the dark scruff that covers his jaw, Matt's cheeks turn red. He hoists Charlie from between me and Seb and shoulders his weight alone. He forces his son to stand as upright as possible, but Charlie immediately slumps, eyes shut. The kid is well and truly fucked.

"I'm taking him home," Matt announces, turning towards the exit before Gemma can object. She teeters behind him on her heels.

"But I've only had one drink," she wails.

Seb's expression mirrors my disbelief.

"Then stay here," Matt spits out over his shoulder. Gemma pauses as if contemplating doing the right thing, before peeling off towards the bar and leaving Matt to manage a drunken Charlie alone.

When they're out of earshot, Seb says, "If he doesn't divorce her soon, I'm gonna do it for him."

If the situation wasn't so messed up, I'd laugh. "They're miserable."

"Yup." Seb swipes a champagne from a passing tray and takes a long swig. An attractive woman in her early twenties walks past. She pauses mid-step to run her gaze over Seb, whose eyes bug out like a cartoon.

"I'm going..." he begins.

"Yeah. Fuck off."

Left alone, I heave a sigh of relief. I love my brothers, but if I have to deal with anymore family dysfunction this evening, I'll need to swallow a packet of migraine pills before midnight.

I don't get long to appreciate the breathing space, because Jack Lansen is cleaving a path towards me. He smiles and shakes hands as he goes, kissing women on the cheek like he's some kind of celebrity, but when he reaches me, his smile disappears.

"Thank God you're still here," he says. "I thought Kate might have run you off the premises."

My gut pinches at the mention of his sister. "It would take more than that to get rid of me," I tell him, before draining the remains of my champagne glass. A waitress appears and tops it up immediately. She flutters in my peripheral vision, lingering longer than her job requires. Mildly irritated, I give her a smile, which she returns with gusto.

I focus on Jack, and the waitress finally gets the message, drifting away to attend to the other guests.

"I should have told her before," Jack admits. "But I wanted to surprise her. I didn't think she'd take it that badly. She has this weird obsession with the company being her last link to Dad. And if we no longer own it, then we're finally burying him."

"Is that what she said?"

Jack scratches his cheek, not meeting my eye. "More or less."

"Come off it. It was clear as fucking daylight that selling isn't the main issue. It's selling to *me*."

Jack's brow furrows, and he stares at the ceiling like there's something interesting up there. I glance up to check: there isn't.

"It's complicated," he mutters. "She thinks you had your chance, and you blew it."

Fuck this bullshit. "Don't you think we ought to tell her the truth?"

Jack stiffens, and this time his eyes latch onto mine. "No. It would absolutely destroy her, and I'd rather save her the pain." He must see the disagreement on my face because he's quick to continue. "You know how she worshiped our father. The man could do no wrong. I can't take that away from her." Jack sighs. "It's kinder she thinks you're the problem than Dad was."

The problem.

It's better than *The Grim Reaper*, at least. That's what they called me in the press. Fuck, it was horrendous. The papers running headlines like, *Ruthless Nico Hawkston backs out of deal that kills Gerard Lansen,* as if my actions could cause someone's heart to give out.

Like I said, *bullshit*. All of it. But back then, we were grateful for the distraction because it hid the real, dirty truth of it.

Kate was as clueless as the rest of them. *No wonder she hates me.*

Something tugs awkwardly in my chest, and the physical discomfort of it reminds me why I've spent all these years trying not to think of her.

I fix Jack with a hard stare. "We should tell her. She's not a child anymore. I'm not sure she was a child at the time, either."

Jack gives me a pained smile. "Honestly, there's no need. No point in opening up old wounds. Plus, we promised my father we'd hide it from her." An image of Gerard Lansen on his death-bed, his face haggard and drawn, flashes in my mind. Jack leans in and whispers a reminder, "His dying wish, Nico."

My jaw locks. I wish I'd never agreed to it. "She never asked about what happened?"

"No. By the time she joined the company, I'd stabilised everything. No small thanks to you." Jack rubs his hand over his forehead. "She might be annoyed now, but she'll come round. She's soft underneath it all."

Soft underneath?

I'm immediately assaulted by images of Kate sliding her bikini top off in the hot tub, breasts full, nipples peaked... the scene blurred through the steam and the passage of time.

Shit. This is a woman I haven't encountered for nearly a decade, but at the slightest suggestion, I'm seeing her without her clothes.

Jack keeps talking, but I'm not listening, too engrossed in thoughts of Kate.

"Nico?" Jack's voice penetrates, and I refocus to find him staring at me with concern. *Fuck's sake.* This woman is already distracting me from more important things. "Sorry, what?" I manage.

"Kate," Jack clarifies. "She's got a big heart. It'll work out. Reckon she always had a thing for you anyway, when she was a kid." I frown and Jack observes my confusion for a moment, then grins and elbows me in the ribs. "Don't go getting any ideas. She's too good for you."

"Right. Of course," I say, and Jack gives me a puzzled look, probably because I gave a serious answer to what must have been a joke. *Damn*. If he ever suspected I'd thought about Kate in any way other than as his little sister, I'd lose my dick to whatever rabid dog he set upon me.

When we were in our mid-twenties, one of our mutual friends tried it on with her at a bonfire night party. Fireworks, marshmallows, and a sneaky grope of her arse.

Jack punched him so hard he lost a tooth.

None of us ever went near her after that. Jack was so overprotective, he would have followed her to university to barricade her into her room if he wasn't already working overtime trying to salvage the wreck of his father's company.

And I certainly never told Jack about the hot-tub. How she straddled me in there at his birthday party. *Fuck, that was probably on this exact day... ten years ago?* She was only a kid; maybe sixteen or seventeen. There was no way I wasn't pushing her away, telling her to go back inside, but she'd made short work of the bikini top before I got the words out. I can still remember how her white bikini bottoms were almost see-through as she grabbed a towel and made a run for it.

Jack lays a hand firmly on my shoulder. "I've got to go work the room. Do you know how many women I'll disappoint if I don't give them a moment of my time tonight?"

I grant Jack the expected chuckle and he moves away, leaving me alone at the bar.

A waitress—a different one this time—fills my glass. I watch the bubbles rise for a few moments, but all I can think of is Kate and I decide I can't leave here tonight without at least trying to talk to her about the deal.

Taking my freshly filled glass, I wander the room for a few minutes. When I finally catch sight of her, she's laughing like she hasn't a care in the world, and I get the unnerving sense that I'm seeing a version of her I'm not supposed to see. A party I'm not fucking invited to. A knot of emotion forms at the base of my throat, throbbing behind my collarbone. *What the fuck?*

I swallow it down just as Kate swipes a hand through her long, dark hair, pushing it over her shoulder so the glossy veil falls down her back. I instantly want to wrap it around my fist and force her to her knees.

The crowd swells and shifts and I lose her, but I'm pretty sure if I closed my eyes she'd still be there—those long, toned legs and the perfect curve of her arse—imprinted on my retinas.

Fuck me.

I need to find her. *Now.*

6
KATE

Jack has too many friends. The party is in full swing, and the bar is absolutely heaving with people. I lost Elly half an hour ago, after she left me to use the bathroom.

It's probably just as well she's not here, because the effort not to tell her about Nico and the deal is wearing me out, and the contract is burning a hole in my handbag. I need to read it.

I haven't been able to think of anything else since Nico walked away earlier. He's floating in the dark corners of my mind like a ghost. I keep expecting to turn and find him staring at me, but I haven't caught so much as a glimpse. Maybe he left. Something that feels disconcertingly like disappointment settles low in my belly, and it's confusing as hell.

What I need is a moment to myself, and a breath of fresh air.

I dodge through the partygoers and escape to the rooftop balcony. On a warm evening, the place would be bustling with bodies, but tonight there's a chill in the air. Not even the smokers dare to come out. I'm alone.

Perfect.

The only problem is that I checked my coat into the cloakroom, and didn't bother to pick it up to come outside. I'm woefully underdressed.

Lights sparkle across the city, twinkling like stars. It's beautiful out here, but I can't enjoy it. My conversation with Jack and Nico earlier dampened my mood, and without Elly to distract me, I replay it in my mind.

Jack wants to sell Dad's company and there's nothing I can do about it.

I rest my champagne glass on the wall so I can pull the contract out of my handbag and scan it. It's a skeleton contract—only a couple of sheets—but it highlights the main details of the deal. I reach the bottom of the page, but there's no sign of the proposed price. I'm about to flip the page when—

"Little K."

My heart comes to a jarring stop and I grip the railing that runs around the balcony, the metal so cold it bites.

Nico Hawkston is standing somewhere behind me, and even though I've been thinking of him, the reality of his presence is more intense than I imagined. His energy pulses at my back like an electromagnetic force. I don't dare turn around.

I lift my glass, tipping back the rest of my champagne, hoping the alcohol might quench my body's unruly reaction to the sound of his voice. Unfortunately, it only stokes the fire.

I let out a slow breath as he approaches, each click of his shoes hitting my heart like a bullet. His silhouette appears in my peripheral vision until he's standing right beside me and a coil of heat in my lower belly turns red hot.

In another reality, this situation might be romantic: the two of us alone in the darkness, the rest of the world oblivious to our intimacy. It pains me we're so far away from that.

Reluctantly, I turn.

The lines of his face are harsh out here in the darkness, brutal shadows cast beneath his cheekbones like they've been aggressively chiseled from stone. Thick, dark hair falls across his forehead, and the only suggestion of emotion on his face is the smallest crease between his brows.

He leans against the balcony wall, one hand tucked into the pocket of his trousers, hitching up the side of his dinner jacket. He's all casual elegance and sophistication, oozing sex appeal as naturally as the rest of us exhale carbon dioxide.

We stare at one another for a few moments, his eyes so intense it feels like he's trying to swallow me with them. White teeth rake over his full bottom lip and it's sexy as hell. All the blood drains from my brain, pooling indecently between my legs.

How many seconds pass like this? Five? Ten? Or is it only one long drawn out second? I have no idea. On an intellectual level, I know I should say or do something, but my twenty-six-year-old body has been hijacked by teenage me, who's desperate to bolt out of the starting blocks and straight into Nico's arms.

And that absolutely cannot happen.

"I take it you're not keen on the deal?"

His words bring me back, and coarse laughter cracks from my lips. "What could possibly have given you that idea?"

"Swearing in my face rather gave the game away." He strokes the underside of his jaw with two fingers, a glimmer of amusement in his eyes.

A powerful gust of bitter wind blows down the length of the balcony and my whole body shivers.

"It's too cold to be out here without a jacket," he tells me. "Take mine."

It's not a question. Typical Nico, hiding his control with the pretense of kindness.

The scent of his cologne wafts towards me as he shrugs out of his jacket, and my body hums with arousal. It doesn't feel like a memory of the past. It feels very present day. *Present moment.*

I've been silent too long because Nico, still holding out his jacket, repeats, "Little K?"

"I told you, it's just Kate. And no, thank you. I'd prefer to freeze than take anything from you."

His gaze narrows, but he doesn't query my statement as he retracts the jacket and puts it back on.

"Jack showed you the contract," he confirms, nodding at the sheet of paper in my hand. "Serious reading for a party."

His casual tone has me seething. "As if I could enjoy the party now that you're here," I mutter. I'm not even sure I want him to hear it, but I don't want him to think his presence is welcome. It's not. *Definitely not.*

Nico stiffens. "Christ, Kate. You're as cold as the weather. What's going on? Is this about me buying Lansen?"

This is my opportunity. If I don't address it head on, I'll lose my nerve. "I'm surprised you dared come anywhere near us, after what you did to my father." My voice is tight with the effort of restraining my anger.

He stills a moment that stretches interminably long. Then, finally, "Ah."

Scowling, I step closer to him. "Is that it? Is that all you have to say?"

"What exactly do you think I did, Little K?" His voice is silk, his upper class accent like crystal in the dark night.

"Stop fucking calling me that," I snap.

Nico's only response is to raise a brow, his attention not wavering from me for a second. He waits, and the need to answer his question overtakes my irritation. "You killed my father."

A beat passes before he replies. "How did you reach that conclusion?"

His voice is calm but curious, making doubt flail in my gut like a dying beast. But I know I'm right. *Why won't he just admit it?* My fingers tighten on the stem of my glass.

"The timing. Two weeks after you refused to go through with the purchase, he was dead."

Nico tilts his head, examining me like he wants to open up my skull and see what's going on inside. His inspection makes me nervous and I'm suddenly aware of a pulsing sensation in my toes, my hands... the *whoosh-whoosh-throb* of my blood.

"I can't imagine how hard losing a parent was for you, and I'm sorry for all you've suffered." This stuns me for a second, but Nico doesn't pause before adding, "But your father's death isn't something you can pin on me, as much as you might want to."

Angry heat scorches my insides. "If I have to listen to you deny—"

"It was a heart attack." He enunciates each word, sharpening the syllables as if he thinks they'll penetrate my delusion. *Condescending prick.* "In business, shit happens. If it was too stressful, then maybe your father oughtn't to have been playing the game."

A gasp of outrage sticks in my throat, and then the words escape in a rush. "It wasn't the stress that killed him. It was you. Your fucking choices. He wanted that deal more than anything. And Lansen was a good business. Why didn't you buy it back then? Why did you mess him around?" I pause for a beat to let Nico answer, but he doesn't, so I continue. "Dad didn't deserve it. He was a good man. A hundred times the man you'll ever be."

"Is that so?" There's something in Nico's gaze that draws me off point: the softening of his features, a gentleness to his eyes. If I had to guess, it's pity.

I will not be pitied by Nico Hawkston.

"Yes, a hundred times. A thousand times. Loyal, caring, honest. Whereas you, you... you ruined his life. You fucking *ended* it."

Nico is staring at me, utterly unmoved, whereas I'm losing my cool, which in this temperature is an impressive feat. Somewhere beneath the anger, I know I shouldn't be saying any of this. If Jack could hear me, he'd rip my head off, but I can't stop.

"Dad was going to retire. He had the whole thing planned out. Wanted to buy a boat and a house in the South of France with the money from the sale. We were going to stay with him. It was his retirement plan. We could have had years together as a family." I break off, my voice thick with grief, unable to look Nico in the eye. "Years of memories. He wanted me to bring my children there. His grandchildren. He had a future marked out, and you destroyed it. That money... the money he wanted to set aside—"

"Little K—"

"Stop saying my name like that!"

His brow furrows. "Like what?"

"Like you care."

The silence that falls is fragile and thin; a veil Nico could waft away with one hand, exposing all the long-denied emotion hiding beneath my words.

I wait for him to protest or confirm, but he says nothing.

I can't take it anymore.

"You know what? It doesn't matter." My arm flails in his direction. I'm making a fool of myself, but I don't care. Let him think whatever he wants. He's a cruel, calculating bastard, even if he does look like a Greek god.

I crush the contract in my fist and throw it on the ground. The wind catches it and it shuffles along the balcony floor towards Nico's highly polished black shoes. He lifts his foot and pins the paper in place before bending to pick it up. I don't know what he intends to do with it, but I'm not waiting around to find out.

I storm back towards the glass doors. The party is still going on inside. Everyone looks happy and relaxed, whereas I've been transported to a parallel universe where I'm experiencing the full gamut of emotions. Hatred and lust perform a riotous shuttle run through every cell in my body.

I can't be with those cheerful people now, and I absolutely cannot stay out here with Nico Hawkston.

I'll have to go home.

Just as I reach the door, a hand grips mine, firm yet gentle. "Wait."

Nico's touch sears my skin and I skid to a standstill, electricity zapping through me, raising every tiny hair.

I can't breathe. *Can't think.* Biochemical reactions explode through my body like fireworks.

He's touching me.

I'm rooted to the spot, anchored where our bodies meet. He's standing so close that I'm struck by the breadth of his shoulders and the strength that lingers beneath his suit. I could never over-power him or outrun him. His scent mingles with the cool night air, wrapping around me like the jacket I wouldn't take.

His gaze fixes on where we're joined, a puzzled expression crossing his face, like holding my hand has made his brain misfire. *Is he feeling this too?*

The expression vanishes and his gaze traces a slow path up my body to my face, dragging sparks through my flesh.

"Let go of me," I whisper, although the teenager in me is yelling, *touch me, touch me everywhere*.

Nico doesn't release me. "How much money did he want to set aside?" His voice is low; more of a vibration than a whisper, and it resonates in my bones. "For the house. The boat. For the future he never got to have with you. How much was it?"

He leans in, the warmth of his breath ghosting my cheek. My heartbeat skitters. Whether he knows it or not, I'm completely at his mercy. I want more of this. *More of him*. And I hate that I want it.

His dark eyes hold mine as he waits for an answer.

"Ten million." My voice is breathy, and I'm ashamed of how it sounds. "Nothing to someone like you, but a huge sum to my father."

Nico releases my hand, at once shattering the tension and severing the circuit running through us. He steps back, and the distance between us feels like the theft of something I didn't know I needed.

He flattens the scrunched up contract and takes a pen from the inside of his jacket, scrawls something on the paper, then neatly folds it.

He holds it out, stretching across the gulf between us.

My fight has drained away, and I find myself yielding to him as I take the contract. As soon as it leaves his grip and is safely in mine, he gives a sharp nod.

"Good night, Little K. It was good to see you again."

The dismissal is a slap in the face. I freeze as Nico steps around me and pushes open the glass doors, disappearing back into the party, leaving me alone with the realisation that my world has shifted.

I thought my attraction to Nico Hawkston was long dead.

I couldn't be more wrong.

A chill breeze ruffles the papers in my hand, and the sheets flap open. Jack was right; the price Nico's paying for the company is colossal. Multi-millions. A sum that will propel Jack right up The Rich List. It's printed in black ink at the bottom of the second page, but it's been scratched through.

Underneath, Nico has scrawled another figure.

I blink to check I'm seeing it correctly, because it looks like he's increased his offer by exactly ten million pounds. I run my finger over the neat row of zeros as I try to drag coherent thoughts through the fog Nico has left behind.

Did he really think more money would make this better?

Anger is a yoke across my collarbones, crushing the desire that surfaced only seconds ago. *That fucking bastard is trying to buy me.* Still staring at the contract, I follow in his footsteps, his name sitting on the tip of my tongue. I'll call him back and give him a piece of my mind.

"Kate?"

I jerk my head up. David Webster, my contact at Argentum, is leaning through the balcony doors, beaming at me. I've never met a happier looking man than David. Big red cheeks and a white beard. A perfect Father Christmas, if Father Christmas ran marathons, played regular tennis and had fifteen percent body fat.

At our spa meeting yesterday, he was more casually dressed. Tonight, he looks dapper: black tie suit and curly white hair brushed into a slicked-down side parting. "I thought it was you out here."

Shit. My spa project depends on this man's co-operation and I'm mentally all over the place.

I force a smile and slide the contract into my handbag. "David. Hi."

"You must be freezing," he says, holding the door open for me. "Come inside. There's someone I want you to meet."

My body responds like an automaton, marching inside on demand, but my mind is slipping in and out of focus. I fix my gaze on David, but the memory of Nico keeps pushing him out. Nico's eyes, his touch, his hand-written scrawl on the contract...

A large man lingers just inside the door, a looming presence that fills the space with a cloud of disgruntled ill-intent so thick it seems to suck all the oxygen out of the air. If David is Father Christmas, this man is the Grinch. A knot forms in my stomach when I realise he's waiting for us. He's familiar, but I can't place him.

"This is Martin Brooks," David says. "Do you remember him?"

I mentally filter through possible identities for him, but come up short. Too much of my brain power is still whirring over Nico like a clogged up hard drive.

"Your father's business partner," David explains.

The memories click into place. *Martin Brooks, of course.* But what the hell is he doing here? He never showed up to Dad's funeral, nor did he send a condolence card. I remember because Mum has never forgiven him. There is no way she would invite Martin anywhere, and I doubt Jack would because he doesn't have anything to do with him either. The man dropped out of our lives eight years ago and I haven't seen him since.

He's aged a lot. His previously dark hair is now a salt and pepper grey, and he's carrying more weight than he used to. He taps the lapels of his green tweed jacket. Jack's invitation was very clear about the dress code—black tie. So either Mr. Brooks didn't know or doesn't care, or he never received an invitation in the first place.

"Hello, Mr. Brooks."

Martin looks down his bulbous nose at me like I'm an insignificant fly in the ointment of his life. "Kate Lansen. What a pleasure."

His slow, bored drawl makes it sound anything but. The knot in my stomach tightens. I trust David, but I can make no sense of Martin's presence here.

"I didn't know you still saw Jack," I say, careful not to sound suspicious.

"I don't. Wasn't invited."

I suck an inhalation. The awkwardness in the air is palpable.

David draws back, his red cheeks blanching as a tiny frown forces the wrinkles on his forehead into high relief. "My wife couldn't make it, so I brought Martin as my plus one. I hope I haven't transgressed a boundary. Martin was very keen to see all the Lansens again."

"Figured I could crash the party very briefly and see you all," Martin says. "I didn't want to miss Gerard's son turning thirty-five. Time flies." He gestures to the balcony. "Was that Nico Hawkston you were out there with?"

The sudden mention of Nico has the butterflies in my stomach sprouting wings and soaring, but Martin's malevolent tone kills them off almost instantly. I collect myself enough to nod, but offer no further explanation. It's none of his business.

"Hmm." Martin's fingers rasp over his unshaven chin, stretching the slack skin around his jaw. "Tricky bastard, Nico Hawkston. Looks like a gentleman, but he's not. Steer well clear, Kate."

I'd rather steer clear of you. The thought pops up unbidden, like a mushroom in a dank forest.

David scratches his white beard and laughs uneasily. "Martin is our newest member on the Argentum board."

Martin chuckles, but the sound is so clogged with phlegm that it sounds more like a smoker's cough. "I'm very excited about your spa project. I remember how much your father loved that idea. Can't wait to get my hands stuck in and get dirty."

He utters the last sentence with such malice that a cold sensation ripples over my skin.

"Don't look so worried, Kate," David says, looking just as concerned himself. "Martin assures me his vision aligns with ours. Anyway, I just wanted to touch base before I head home. Wife's home with the grandkids, which is where I should be."

"About time for me to leave too." Martin drains the last of his champagne and plonks the glass down on the nearest table. "Wouldn't want to outstay my welcome. Bye, Kate. Have a good night."

I watch the two men walk away. I'm unsettled and, without thinking, I reach for the contract in my bag and look again at Nico's handwritten scrawl, and the addition of ten million pounds.

Surprisingly, staring at the neat black ink on the page no longer stirs up the same anger it did only moments ago. It's still true that an offering of cash will never take away the pain of losing my father. And yes, I still don't want Nico to think he can buy me.

But maybe the gesture wasn't all bad.

Comfort spreads through me, soothing the unease that Martin's appearance dragged up. Because if I had to choose between the two evils that are Nico Hawkston and Martin Brooks, I'd pick Nico.

Every fucking time.

7
NICO

"You overpaid." Seb kicks his feet up on my desk, sliding his hands behind his head. He looks casual, but his eyes narrow as he stares at me. "What were you thinking? I'm surprised you got it past the board."

Seb has been pestering me about this since I added the extra ten million to the purchase price of Lansen, but I've given him the same answer every time. "*It's a good business*". I keep my words to a minimum so he can't squirrel out whatever meaning he's searching for, but the fucker won't let up, especially not today, when the Lansen team is moving into our building. Jack and I managed to wrap up the deal in less than a month, and this day has careened towards me like a freight train.

I swipe my arm across the desk to knock his feet off. The shock of it nearly sends him flying out of the chair, but he grips the armrests and shoots me a death stare.

"If I didn't know you better," Seb says when he's recovered, "I'd think a pretty face and a good pair of tits had you digging deep for that company."

This irritates me. "That's not how I do business." I glance at my watch. Kate will be in the building in the next fifteen minutes.

Why am I thinking about her? It's not as though I don't have enough to occupy my mental space. It must be because the Lansen team is starting today.

But why do I feel so... *on edge*? We've done buyouts before. This isn't new.

Seb arches a brow. "I saw you out on the balcony with Kate at Jack's party. It looked heated."

I sigh, deciding to edge closer to the truth. "She was kicking her feet in. Didn't want to sell her dad's company. She would have done everything she could to stop Jack selling up. And you know how much he adores her. He might have let her sway him. I'm thinking of taking her to lunch today. See if we can sort things out."

Seb purses his lips, but before he can say anything else, his phone pings.

"Shit," he says as he reads the screen. "Matt's downstairs. He's got Charlie with him."

"Why?"

Seb scrunches his face. "Where's your head at? He's here for work experience. Matt wants him to spend the summer in the office."

I can't believe I forgot. I pull my phone out of my pocket to see seven missed calls from Matt. He's heading to New York today, and if he realises I forgot about Charlie joining us, he won't be happy.

Together, Seb and I head for the lift and take it down to the lobby.

Matt is standing off to one side, near the sofas. Charlie is lounging on one, arms spread across the back. He might be dressed in a suit, but his body language tells me he doesn't want to be here.

When he sees me and Seb crossing the lobby, he peels himself off the sofa and stands.

I'm struck by how tall and gangly he is for a fifteen-year-old. He's good-looking, but his skin is pale and speckled with acne. The blue hair is gone, leaving only a shaved head, which makes him look emaciated.

He traipses towards us. "Hey, Uncle Nico. Uncle Seb."

"Hey, big guy," Seb replies, giving Charlie a fist bump. "Good to see you're sober this time."

Charlie cringes. "Don't remember seeing you."

Seb laughs and Matt scowls.

"And the hair," I add. "Did you shave it yourself?"

"I did," Matt says.

Charlie throws his dad a resentful look, and I wonder how Matt shaving Charlie's head played out. I'm guessing it didn't involve a relaxing head massage.

Seb nudges Charlie. "Kept the tongue piercing, though?"

Charlie gives his first little smile, and it's only for Seb. He pokes his tongue out, briefly flashing the piercing. "Yup."

Matt puts his hand on Charlie's shoulder and Charlie winces a little at the contact. "Go get signed in. Get your office pass. They'll sort you out at the desk."

Charlie trudges towards the reception desk, leaving the three of us alone.

"I need you to watch him while I'm away," Matt tells me.

Uh-oh. Something's up. Matt's often abroad, but in the months I've been back in London he's never asked me to take a particular interest in Charlie. I'm not the type to babysit.

"No blue hair. No piercings. No alcohol," Matt clarifies.

"Where's Gemma?" I ask. "Shouldn't his mum be the one to watch him?"

"She's at home, in the Kensington house. But can you keep an eye out when he's in the office? I know he's young, but it'll keep him out of trouble while I'm away."

"Fine," I say, although I'm not fully concentrating. I've half a mind on the fact that Kate Lansen's going to be arriving any minute now. My gaze drifts to the entrance.

"Are you sure?" Matt asks.

I drag my eyes from the doors back to Matt, who's glaring at me like I'm the kid not listening at the back of the classroom. I collect myself instantly. "Yes. Definitely. I can do that. Watch out for Charlie in the office. Don't let him get into trouble."

Matt sighs, sounding relieved. "Good." He checks his watch. "I don't have long. Flight's in two hours."

Matt stops talking as Charlie returns. A green lanyard hangs about his neck with an office pass attached to it.

"You're with us for a couple of months, then?" I check, directing myself to Charlie.

"Yup. All summer." Charlie gives a cocky twitch of the head. "Beats hanging out with Dad. Not that he gave me a choice."

I nod, like this makes total sense, even though there's a lot about the statement that raises questions. "What are you most looking forward to?"

Charlie's gaze flicks towards the entrance. His jaw falls open and I'm pretty sure he forms the word '*wow*', although he doesn't make a sound. "Who is *that*?" he asks.

I glance over to see Kate walking into the building, and a rush of heat assaults me. She looks even better than she did at the party. How she makes a pencil skirt and white shirt so damn sexy, I have no idea. If I weren't acutely aware of Seb watching me for a reaction, I'd probably be gawking just like Charlie.

"That's Kate Lansen," Seb says coolly. "Our newest recruit."

"Oh, *that's* her?" Charlie says it like he's heard her mentioned before. It makes my hackles rise. "She is hot as—"

"Watch your mouth," I snap. "You talk like that about a colleague in the office and I'll fire your arse faster than you can say '*hot as fuck*'."

Charlie tilts away from me, eyes widening. Next to him Matt straightens, surprised by my vitriol, but then gives a tense nod to signal he agrees with my reprimand.

"Shit, Nico," Seb mutters. "The kid just got here. Cut him some slack."

Charlie shifts awkwardly on the spot, mumbling, "Dad said the same thing." He glares at Matt, his voice clearer when he adds, "You said Kate Lansen was gorgeous—"

"Enough." Matt booms, before lowering his voice. "In the office, we don't comment on people's appearance. It's a hard rule."

"Actually, I'd call it a flexi-rule," Seb interjects. "If I'm about to go into a meeting with my fly undone, you can definitely comment."

I'm not sure anyone hears Seb apart from me, because Charlie and Matt are too busy glaring at one another, which is just as well because if Charlie comments on Kate again, I'll wring his neck. I don't know why, but hearing him call her 'hot' as if she's nothing more than a teenage boy's pinup irked me.

Matt beckons one of the receptionists over. She rushes out from behind the desk and Matt instructs her to take Charlie up to his desk to meet his new team.

When they're gone, Matt turns to me and Seb. "If he acts out, or messes anything up, I'll make it up to you, I promise. But please, I need you both to swear you'll be there for him if he needs you."

Seb and I share a glance, and I'm pretty sure he's thinking the same as me. *What the hell are we signing up for?*

I want to say no, but Matt is looking so desperate that I can't deny him. "Sure."

"Absolutely," Seb agrees.

"Great. I owe you. I'll see you in a few weeks." Matt bids us farewell and heads outside, where a car is waiting to take him to the airport.

I look at Seb. "Did he sound weird to you?"

Seb pouts his lower lip. "A bit. He's been anxious about heading back to the States and leaving the kids with Gemma. Charlie's a handful, sure... but Lucie's only three. How hard can that be?"

Just as I'm wondering what's going on in Matt's private life, Seb nudges me and points at where Kate is standing, talking to her brother, Jack, who's just arrived. "Go on then."

I'm tempted to tell Seb to shut the fuck up because his knowing glances and smirks are dangerously close to teasing and that pisses me off, but it's not worth my time. There's nothing here to tease about. Kate hates me. But the least I can do is be polite.

I walk towards the Lansens with Seb at my side.

"Morning, Jack," I announce, setting a professional atmosphere from the get-go. Kate, her back to me, goes rigid.

"Nico." A wide smile spreads over Jack's face as he takes my hand and shakes it vigorously. "Didn't realise you'd be in the office in person."

"Where else would I be?" I answer casually.

Slowly, Kate turns to face me. I don't miss the way her eyes rake over me in what appears to be appreciation before she throws a frosty glare my way. It's enough to give me whiplash.

Seb greets them both with equal enthusiasm, before drawing Jack away towards the lifts.

Subtle, Seb.

Left alone, Kate and I stand in awkward silence. I'm painfully aware of the way her breasts move beneath her silk shirt with each inhalation. The neckline exposes an irresistible hint of cleavage, and I have to drag my gaze away.

It won't do me any fucking good to be staring at a woman I can't touch.

"Little K."

"Not in the office, Mr. Hawkston." Her lips curve as if she's delighted with herself at having dared to correct me.

I bow my head in apology. "Where then, Miss Lansen?"

Kate's eyes widen.

Fuck. Did that sound suggestive? I meant to say something respectful, but apparently my brain-to-mouth connection is faulty. My imagination, however, is working perfectly to create a list of alternative locations, all of which are lewd as fuck.

Kate doesn't move. Is she waiting for me to explain myself? I don't know whether to apologise or pretend I never said it, so I say nothing. I keep my expression neutral and stare at her, and she stares back.

My pulse beats in my neck like the repeated thwack of a blunt guillotine.

I have no idea how long we stand like that, or if we're standing too close. She's warping my perception of time and space. Everyone in the building could be staring at me right now, and I wouldn't have a clue. Wouldn't even care.

All of a sudden, Kate turns and marches towards the lifts without another word.

8
KATE

Where then?

The resonance of his voice rings over and over in my head. What did he mean by it? The unreadable expression on Nico's face gave nothing away. Did he mean it to be as... *suggestive* as it sounded?

I've thought about him non-stop since Jack's party and this morning I was so distracted by the strain of his muscles beneath his shirt that, *of course,* I took his words that way. I walked away from him like a stroppy teenager, and it's possible he didn't mean it like that at all.

But I had to get out of his general vicinity. The way he was looking at me... *fuck*. I don't know if he does it on purpose, but there's a raw sexuality about him, like he wears his sex drive on the outside. My entire body heated just being near him. Any longer and I'd have had sweat patches on my silk shirt.

"Big day, eh, Kate?" Jack's voice pulls me back to the present moment. He's leaning against the side of my desk, looking so comfortable you'd never know this was his first day in a new office.

I tilt my head. *Yes.*

Jack levers himself off my desk, props his hands on his hips, and looks around. "It's an improvement on the little concrete block we leased," he says. "Dad would have loved a building like this."

I can't disagree. The reception area downstairs is like a luxury hotel lobby. The ceiling must be twenty feet high, and the external walls are all glass.

My desk phone rings unexpectedly. I jump in my seat and the boy opposite, a pimply teenager with a shaved head whom I discovered earlier is Matt Hawkston's son, Charlie, snorts in amusement. I scowl at him as I lift the handset. Jack is quietly chuckling too and raises a hand in a silent wave as he saunters back to his side of the office. I watch him go, noting the way the women steal glances at him. I roll my eyes and grip the phone.

"Hello, Kate Lansen speaking."

"Miss Lansen, this is Victoria. Mr. Hawkston's PA. He's requested a meeting with you. It's off-site. A car will pick you up outside reception in fifteen minutes. He's instructed that you don't eat anything beforehand."

She hangs up before I can ask any of the questions that are running wild in my head. Off-site? Don't eat anything? Which Mr. Hawkston? It's unlikely to be Seb, seeing as we've had no dealings yet, and Charlie's already told me his dad left for the States this morning. She *must* mean Nico. Springing an off-site meeting on me out of nowhere is just his style. His way of taking control and keeping me on the back-foot.

Nerves flutter in my stomach. I tell myself it's because I'm annoyed at the brusque, impersonal invitation, and the presumption that I'll drop everything for him.

I guess I have to go. Lansen Luxury Hotels might have been swallowed up by Hawkston, but keeping this job is the only way I can hold on to my spa project. And that's my little slice of Dad's legacy.

I step out onto the street, where a sleek, black car is waiting.

The flutter of nerves in my stomach has become a horrid, bubbling sensation in my gut. I don't like surprises. This whole scenario has my anxiety sky-rocketing.

"Miss Lansen?" the chauffeur asks.

I give him a nod and he opens the door for me. Is Nico already inside? I suck in a breath as I go to get in and exhale with relief when I see the car is empty. He's not here.

I straighten again and eye the driver. "Where are we going?"

"It's confidential. I'm under instruction not to tell you."

Weird. "How long is the drive?"

"I'm not at liberty to share that information."

I hesitate, wondering if I should complain about this. It's very odd. But the driver is staring at me, holding my door open, so I cave and get in, but I'm surprised when the car leaves and I'm the only passenger. We're not waiting for Nico.

I sift through emails on my phone for a while, but as the minutes pass, I begin to feel increasingly uneasy. Where am I going? This is crazy. Maybe I need to call Jack and tell him where I am, in case I'm being kidnapped. I laugh a little at this idea. Nico might be an arsehole, but he's not psychotic.

But even so, my palms are sweating and my thighs stick to the leather of the car seat. My stomach is so unsettled that I could be sick. What is Nico playing at?

We're beyond the bounds of central London, and outside there are only green fields and trees.

Finally, the car approaches an imposing set of gates that look like they belong to a country manor, and it's then I notice the sign. *Hawkston Elite*. I immediately know where we are. It's one of only a handful of extremely high end Hawkston Country Clubs. This makes a certain type of sense, at least, but I feel no calmer about the situation.

We drive past pristine lawns on one side and a golf course on the other. An enormous stately home looms into view and we park outside.

"Here we are, Miss Lansen," the chauffeur says, opening the door for me to get out. "You're expected."

My heels crunch across the gravel and I walk into reception. It's beautiful in here, and low-level music is playing. It goes a long way to calming my nerves. Scented candles fill the space with a gorgeous floral aroma, and vast bouquets of white roses decorate the coffee tables positioned between velvet sofas at the edge of the lobby.

The word Hawkston rises over the receptionists' heads, displayed on the wall behind in silver capital letters a foot high. *Big, but not as big as Nico's inflated ego.*

A woman in a smart uniform greets me as though she's expecting me, and hands me a folded white towelling robe.

I take it from her in a daze. "There must be a mistake—"

"No mistake, Miss Lansen. You're booked in for a hot oil aromatherapy massage before lunch."

A massage? Hot oil? Aromatherapy? Before lunch? I can't process this overload of confusing information. It's madness. I thought we were having a meeting. If Nico's idea of a meeting is a couple's hot oil massage, I might die.

I'm so confused. Am I angry or flattered?

Angry. I decide to be angry. He tricked me into coming here, with not a word of warning.

I try to pass the robe back to the woman. My anger is rising, but I know she's not the one I need to take it out on. This isn't her fault. "No. I can't. I should be at work."

The woman smiles calmly. "Mr. Hawkston gave instructions we are to put you at your ease until he arrives. The entire spa area is reserved for you until lunch."

This makes no sense, but my mind clings onto one thing, and one thing only. *Nico's coming*. "The entire spa? For me? What about your other guests?"

The woman gives me a tight smile and passes me the robe, and this time I take it from her. "It's all yours for the next two hours. A massage first, followed by the sauna, steam room and plunge pools."

Wow. This could well be the best first day in a new company that I have ever experienced, and I'm not sure what I've done to deserve it.

I hug the robe. "All right. Lead the way."

I'm blissed out as I lie on a lounger by the plunge pool. My muscles have been tenderized and I've sweated in the sauna. When did I last take time to myself like this? *So relaxing*. I'm practically asleep when the door opens.

"Little K."

I lurch upright to find Nico staring at me. I thought I'd get a little warning before he showed up, and his sudden arrival has my empty stomach filling with jangling nerves.

He's wearing an immaculate white shirt beneath an expensive charcoal suit, his hair casually coiffed to perfection. We're alone for the first time since Jack's party, and he's all perfect and I'm a sweaty mess, wrapped in a hotel robe, damp hair scraped back off my sauna-baked face. I bet he did this on purpose.

He's so handsome that it hurts to look directly at him, like staring into the sun.

I squint, then force my eyes wide. I will *not* be attracted to him, even if I have to put my body on a leash to control its impulses.

Maybe I can find something repulsive about him. Something that will put a dampener on this excruciating crush.

As if he reads my thoughts, dark eyes flash at me, causing a ripple of warmth to pool at the apex of my thighs.

Nope. There is nothing physically repulsive about Nico Hawkston whatsoever. He's appealing in totality.

I imagine him pushing me back down on the lounger and ripping off my robe, and fucking me like I've never been fucked before. I'm screaming, begging for more, more, more...

The scene is so compelling that every sane thought vanishes from my mind.

This cannot be happening. *Shit.*

Sweat pearls down my back.

I strive to control my subconscious, focusing on the real, present moment Nico, still standing calmly over by the door, one hand in his pocket. Effortlessly sexy.

He runs his other hand through his hair. What would it feel like to be touched like that? To have him run his fingers over my skin... my shoulders... my breasts... my—

Get it together.

"What the hell is this, Nico?" I speak quickly in a desperate attempt to keep my mind on track, gesturing around the spa. The irritation in my voice contrasts harshly with the calming music floating from the speakers in the ceiling.

He eyes me with amusement. "So direct, Little K. No time for pleasantries?"

I stiffen. "Stop calling me that. I don't like it." His mouth fixes into a line and his chin shifts almost imperceptibly, as if he might be listening to me this time. I tighten the belt around my robe and stand. "I was freaking out in the car over here. The driver wouldn't tell me where I was going. That was cruel. Manipulative."

He appears contrite, his gaze dipping to the ground for a moment before flicking back up to me. "I'm sorry you see it that way. I wanted to clear the air after our interaction at Jack's party. It appeared to cause you significant distress."

This stuns me. "So you booked me a massage and closed the spa for me?"

Nico tilts his head in agreement. "As you see. An apology for our last interaction."

Should I thank him for this? I recall the wonderful massage and have to admit that this is the best morning I've had in ages. "You should have asked me first. Who knows I'm here? Does Jack know?"

Nico presses his lips together, and a beat passes before he says, "No."

My heart squeezes at his confession. He didn't even tell Jack he'd done this for me. Why not? Did he want to keep it secret, just between the two of us? The idea thrills me. But then I remind myself it was all arranged behind my back, just like the deal to buy our family company, and I'm annoyed again. "You can't sweep me off to a spa without telling anyone. Without telling *me*. It's insane."

He frowns. "Is it? You're running a spa project, aren't you? Consider it market research."

I cross my arms and glare at him. "There was no need for any of this."

Nico strokes his jaw. The low rasp of stubble on skin scrapes through the room. What would it feel like against my inner thighs?

Stop.

"Here's the deal, Little K. Any unresolved emotional situation puts me off my game. I'm a busy man. I can't have"—his gaze runs up and down my body. A feather-light touch that's almost physical—"distractions in the office." *I'm a distraction?* That I could affect him at all blows my mind. "It's an energetic trickle down effect. The successful operation of this company originates here." He taps his chest. "I have to maintain focus."

What a pompous ass.

"Then I should go. I wouldn't want to impede your *performance*."

Shit. I just hammered the last word with sexual innuendo and I didn't even mean to. Is this how every conversation we have is going to go? How am I supposed to handle the daily onslaught of this loathsome man's sex appeal?

The muscles around Nico's mouth tighten like he's constraining the urge to smile. "We're not done clearing the air."

As much as I hate it, his commanding tone fixes my feet to the floor, but years of suppressed anger blaze beneath my skin enabling me to speak my mind. "You can't clear this, Nico. There's too much. And you know what annoys me the most? That you did the deal without my knowledge because you knew I wouldn't like it. It was underhand, and it was unfair."

"That's not what we did."

His denial has my rage escalating and my voice is scratchy. "Don't lie! It's exactly what you did. You and Jack kept secrets from me. You treated me like a kid who can't handle the big business. I'm not a child anymore. I know I didn't own the company, but Lansen was my father's legacy. I deserved to know what you were planning for it. Jack ought to have told me, but you... fuck, Nico..." I break off, covering my face with my hands.

He steps closer, and for a second I think he's going to cross the room and take me in his arms, but he stops, and his voice is tender when he says, "Kate..."

Kate?

But not even the use of my full name is enough to penetrate my fury. I let my hands fall. "When you saw how much I didn't want this to happen, you threw money at the issue. An extra ten million." My whole body is trembling, and where my voice was scratchy before, it's raw now. "And now this?" I indicate the luxurious spa area. "Do you think you can buy me? That you can get your wallet out and I'll do exactly what you want?"

Nico's flinch is the merest crack in his veneer, instantly smoothed like it was never there. "That money wasn't an attempt to buy you. It was a gesture of goodwill."

"Save it for Jack. I don't want your goodwill. And I don't want your hot oil massages either." I sound like a total bitch, and I *really* loved that massage, but I'm not about to admit that to Nico. But he's so unmoved that I keep goading him. "If it had been up to me, I would never have sold our company to you, no matter how much cash you were willing to pay. I will not be bought."

Explode, you prick. Yell back at me. Give me some hint you feel as strongly about this as I do.

But he keeps his calm, staring at me for a moment before glancing at his watch. "It's time for lunch. We're booked in the private dining area upstairs. There's a delicious seabass dish on the menu. I recall it's your favourite, so I ordered ahead for both of us."

My mouth falls open. Is he for real? Does he think I'll sit and eat with him after everything I just said? But I do *love* seabass. I can't believe he remembered that. And I'm starving. I press a hand to my stomach, hoping it doesn't rumble.

"I don't eat fish anymore," I lie.

His expression opens with surprise. "What do you eat?" He points back at the door. "I can change your order."

"Don't. I have lunch plans," I fire back, picturing the room temperature contents of the Tupperware I stuffed in my handbag this morning.

Nico smooths his tie with one hand, staring at me like I'm a scientific exhibit he's never encountered before. Clearly, rejection is not something he's had much experience with. "I'd advise you to reconsider. It's a rare opportunity for an employee as junior as you to be invited to lunch with the CEO. In fact, it's unheard of."

The arrogance. But he has a point. A one-to-one lunch with Nico Hawkston is career gold dust, but I'm too irritated to see it that way. "You didn't invite me to lunch." I fist my hands at my sides to restrain the urge to flap them. "You ambushed me. And now you're expecting me to drop to my knees and thank you for it."

As soon as I've said the last sentence, I immediately want to shove it back inside my mouth as a hot blush burns my cheeks.

He draws back slightly, one eyebrow creeping up. "I was expecting no such thing."

Just me with the filthy mind then...

"A simple thank you would have been enough," Nico adds, his mouth twitching in amusement. "But don't let me stop you if you're more comfortable on your knees."

Holy shit. What did he just say?

He gestures to the floor like he's waiting for my kneecaps to hit the tiles.

I straighten my spine to meet his gaze head on, trying to muster as much dignity as possible while dressed in a fluffy dressing gown. He's messing with me, but there's a definite heat in those dark irises, like he knows exactly what effect his words have on me. It scorches a path down to my core. If I don't get out of this room soon, I have no idea what's going to happen, but it won't be good for my career.

I glance at the door, hoping to make an escape. "If there's nothing else, I should get back to the office."

He raises a hand to deter me from moving. "There is one more thing I wanted to discuss before you go. Your spa project—"

"No!" White-hot anger rushes through my system, propelling me to take a bold step in his direction. "You might have bought my father's company, but keep your greedy hands off my project. That was my father's dream, and I'm going to be the one to complete it. If you dare interfere, I swear to God, Nico, I will kill you myself. You already messed things up enough for Dad. I won't let you do it to me—" I'm so carried away on a crest of outrage that it takes me far too long to notice that Nico's staring at me like I've gone completely crazy.

He closes the distance between us, and his energy hits me like a wall. I'm way too worked up for him to be increasing his proximity like this. What is he doing?

He tilts his head and raises a brow. "You were saying?"

"I thought..." I frown, shake my head just a fraction.

"You don't think much of me, do you?"

The question takes me by surprise and all I can manage in response is a gulp.

"I have no intention of taking your project," he continues. "I know how capable you are. Jack's always singing your praises. And David Webster tells me you've done a stellar job thus far. The feedback is good. Great, even."

"Then what were you going to say?"

"Exactly that. I'm impressed."

Against my will, delight flashes through me. I hate how good his praise feels. If I were a dog, I'd be rolling on my back, tongue out, kicking my feet at the ceiling, and begging him to rub my belly. *Fuck, fuck, fuck.*

"I want you to have the best of Hawkston to work with," he continues. "I've picked out a team of twenty employees with skills particularly suited to your project."

This takes my breath away. Why would he bother paying this sort of attention to a project like mine? It's small scale compared to what he has to deal with. Well below his pay grade. "Thank you," I grit out.

"You deserve it. Not many people would have persevered with a project as long as you have. It's commendable."

That flash of delight repeats. More of this and I'll be licking his expensive shoes any minute now. I hope it doesn't show on my face. "I'm doing it for my dad."

"I know."

My chest constricts. His response is so direct, so simple, and yet it means more than it should. He understands why I drive myself so hard and why this isn't just another project. Nico was Dad's godson. It might have ended badly between them, but perhaps he isn't immune to that shared history. I'm certainly not.

My heart thumps and silence stretches between us before Nico speaks again.

"Stay. Have lunch with me."

I hold his gaze for a moment, and there's a softness in his eyes that's inviting. He appears to want my company, and for a second I want to say yes, want to grasp this moment alone with him. But I remind myself that Nico Hawkston is still a controlling, arrogant arse who cares more about money than people, and a few kind words and big gestures aren't enough to change my opinion of him.

"Like I said, I have plans. But there must be at least a hundred other junior employees who would jump at the opportunity to have lunch with you."

He slides his hands into his pockets. "True. But I don't want them. I want you."

My stomach bottoms out. Ten years ago, I would have died to hear those words from Nico. But now, it's too late. I steel myself and say, "The answer is still no."

He flicks a flat look my way. "You'd better have some very important plans."

A few beats of silence hang in the air. I'm not explaining myself any more than I have already.

"Will that be all?" I keep my voice as hard and cold as I can manage, which is a challenge, given the heat raging through my body.

"For now, yes. You can go."

His tone is even colder than mine. *Well, fuck him.*

I march double-speed out of the spa, pushing the door open with such force that I'm surprised I don't hear it clattering off its hinges behind me. "I'm putting my cab back to the office through expenses," I yell over my shoulder.

He doesn't reply, but even if he had, it wouldn't matter because the words *I want you* have taken up residence in my head. I can hear nothing else.

I want you, I want you, I want you.

And in spite of everything, all I want is to turn around, march back into the spa, and ask him to say it again.

9
NICO

I stand in the middle of the empty spa and drag both hands through my hair. *Fuck*. This was supposed to be an opportunity for us to get on better terms. To repair this messed up connection we have going on.

I'm more riled than I've been in weeks. Kate Lansen has a way of getting under my skin. She's like the tip of an expertly wielded needle, sliding unnoticed into a vein and emptying its poison into my bloodstream.

I close my eyes and pinch the bridge of my nose, recalling my words to her.

I don't want them. I want you.

What the fuck was I thinking? If she'd just done what anyone else would have done and had lunch with me, I wouldn't have said something like that.

Our interaction has well and truly wiped out my appetite, and I'm not going to sit alone in the restaurant now that Kate has gone.

I stalk out of the hotel, my mind a blur. I get in my car and speed back to the office. Thank God my subconscious can drive because all I can think about is Kate. The Ice Queen. Not even a sauna and a massage could soften her up.

I don't know why I bothered.

When I arrive at the office, I have almost no recollection of how I got there. I pace across reception in a fog of frustration, only to be waved down by Seb.

"Lunch didn't go well, then?" He smirks, making me regret telling him I was taking Kate for lunch. Thank fuck I didn't admit I'd booked her into the spa at the Elite.

I flip my middle finger at him as I pass. I wouldn't normally brush him off like that, but if I stop to explain, he'll only gloat, and I don't have time for his bullshit.

I stride towards the reception desk without another look in his direction, Kate's angry words rattling around in my mind like some bastardized form of torture. *You think you can buy me? That you can get your wallet out and I'll do exactly what you want?*

Was that what I thought? Was that why I did it? I don't fucking know anymore, because the moment those words sprang from her pink lips, the only thing I wanted to do was yell *Yes, please*.

I cannot focus around this woman at all.

I press my palms to my temples like I can force her out of my head.

Suddenly, I think of Charlie, and guilt hits hard. I've been so preoccupied with Kate that I haven't checked to see if he's okay on his first day. Maybe he'll be more amenable to lunch than Kate was.

I take a deep breath, grip the knot of my tie, and force a smile to my face as I approach the reception desk. The receptionist grins up at me. "How can I help, Mr. Hawkston?"

"Can you tell me where my nephew Charlie is sitting?"

I wait as she checks, observing the steady slowing of my pulse rate. I'll be all right in a moment.

"He's on the sixth floor. Matt put him with the Lansen team. In fact, he's opposite Kate Lansen."

The universe must be messing with me right now. Of all the desks in the office, Matt had to put his son next to her.

Maybe she won't be there. She said she had plans.

"Thanks," I say, and head to take the lift to the sixth floor.

―――――

When I approach Charlie's bank of desks, I see Kate immediately. She's standing at her desk holding a Tupperware box and a set of cutlery.

This is her lunch plan? What the actual fuck? She'd rather eat out of a plastic box at her desk than sit with me?

Fury rises like a tidal wave, and I quicken my pace, noticing that people are stealing glances and hunkering down, pretending to be busier than they are.

Half of them are probably worried I'll fire them on the spot. But I'm not a yeller. That's more Matt's style of management, not mine. Although right now I'm feeling pretty damn close to letting loose.

I ignore the flickering glances of other employees. Kate's the only one that holds my attention.

As I get closer to her desk, she puts her lunch down and leans over to pick something up, presenting me with a view of her arse. It's pert and perfect, and the skirt is tight, revealing the outline of her underwear beneath. I'm torn between wanting to fuck it or spank it for insubordination.

A shock of heat rushes to my cock.

Shit.

I did not come up here for this, but I keep moving towards her, unable to look away. With each step, my body temperature ratchets up a notch.

A choked gurgle of laughter distracts me. Charlie grins, his eyebrows arched like a *McDonald's* logo. He bites his bottom lip and nods at Kate, where she's still bent over, then looks at me like I'm a horny teenager who shares his amusement.

I glare at him, and the venom behind it is enough to wipe his expression clean. I'll address his lack of office decorum over lunch. That's something we have to stamp out.

"Lunch?" I question.

When Kate sees me, her face flashes with anger. "Were you not listening—"

"I was talking to Charlie." My voice is edged like a knife as I deliberately glare at the Tupperware box on her desk. "My plans fell through, so I'm taking him to lunch."

"Oh, brilliant." Charlie raises his voice so no one in the vicinity could fail to notice the preferential treatment he's getting. Now that's the type of response I'm used to. It's the most animated I've seen him.

Kate sits down, a tight smile on her face, and clicks open her Tupperware box. I can't fucking believe it. She's so brazen. I'm standing *right here,* and she's not even pretending to have plans.

She removes the lid, exposing the contents. Some kind of brown mulch with limp green leaves mixed through it. *Revolting*.

She gathers a forkful and slides it between lips parted so wide they could take my cock. She chews, then swallows, and her throat bobs exaggeratedly with the motion.

She might not be looking my way, but I'd wager my entire fortune on the fact that her awareness is fixed on me. Her tongue, her lips, her over-exaggerated swallow; it's all a performance for my benefit.

Anger simmers in my blood. She's taunting me with the contents of that plastic piece of shit like it's a lover.

Or am I so far gone for the woman already that I'm seeing sexual suggestion where there is none?

Images of Kate on her knees, taking my cock down her throat, invade my mind as heat lasers through my chest.

So much for clearing the air. There's a storm waiting to break, and there's only one way I want it to happen: with Kate Lansen wearing a lot fewer clothes than she is right now.

But first I'm going to burn that plastic box until it's a melted heap of toxic waste.

I run a finger inside my collar, which suddenly feels far too tight. Kate catches me, turning those big, honey-brown eyes up to look at me.

"Something wrong?" she asks.

I gnash my molars and let my eyes shut briefly. "No."

"Good." She fills another forkful with food, her tongue curling out to wrap around the tines as she slowly takes the whole thing into her mouth. She hums a sensual *mmm-delicious* noise and looks up at me, her eyes wide.

Fuck this. I'm not imagining it. She's practically orgasming over her Tupperware, and the sound has my cock hardening. A powerful flash of rage burns through me.

Ignoring me entirely, she pushes the Tupperware aside to type out a response to an email.

The repulsive mixture stares up at me, the Tupperware hanging off the edge of her desk, and all I want to do is launch the whole fucking thing across the office.

I need to get out of here. I can hardly see straight. Putting my hand on Charlie's shoulder, I guide him towards the lift, but my irritation hasn't subsided as I pass Kate's desk. My hip knocks against the corner of the Tupperware, toppling the whole thing into the bin. It lands with a *thunk* in a perfect drop shot.

I'm not even fucking sorry.

Kate gasps, and Charlie stares into the bin. "Geez, Uncle Nico—"

I elbow him in the ribs, cutting him off, but people are already staring.

Kate glares at me, her cheeks flaring. "My lunch—"

"How unfortunate." My voice is devoid of emotion. "I know that was an important meal." I take my wallet from my pocket, flip it open, and pull out a fifty, which I deposit on Kate's desk. "Buy yourself something else."

Charlie's eyes are saucers as I usher him away from Kate before she can start yelling again.

I can't come back down here. I do not need this sort of distraction in my life. No matter how thrilling Kate's presence might be, the sixth floor is going to have to become my personal no-fly zone. Kate Lansen is off limits, and I need to do some fucking work.

10
KATE

My phone buzzes and a text message from Elly pings in.

Elly: You'd better not be working late tonight.

I glance at my watch. It's edging up to nine o'clock on Friday evening and here I am at my computer, spreadsheets open. I was so engrossed I hadn't noticed how much time had passed. I sit back from my desk like I'm waking from a dream. There's hardly anyone here. Even Jack has left. The cleaners are moving between the desks on the other side of the office, vacuuming the carpet and dusting the surfaces.

I've been working late every day since Nico dropped that fifty quid on my desk. I wanted to burn that money. Tear it up into a million tiny pieces. Take it to Nico's office and demand an explanation. But… for what? Knocking my lunch off my desk *could* have been an accident. I suspect not, but I can't prove it.

Either way, Nico Hawkston is an arse.

I've hardly seen him since. On the few occasions I have, I've sensed him first: a slight prickling of the skin on the back of my neck, or a tingling heat in my chest. My bodily reactions are verging on obsessive, but there's nothing I can do to stop them. It's inconvenient, but that doesn't lessen the thrill.

And as much as I hate to admit it, I miss hearing his low, sexy drawl of *Little K.*

My phone buzzes again.

Elly: We're already here. Where are you?

I save my documents and power down my computer. This morning Elly roped me and our other flatmate, Marie, into agreeing to accompany her on a night out. She put our names on the guest-list for a new club called Martini Gems, which is hosting the after party for the end of Amy Moritz's World Tour.

Elly has been a huge Amy fan for years, and her most recent album—*Limelight*—has been stuck on repeat in our flat since its release. There was no way Elly was going to miss out on the opportunity to go to an exclusive club night with the one and only Amy Moritz, and when she begged me to come, she was so excited that I couldn't deny her. She'd even gone to the trouble of choosing a top secret outfit for both me and Marie and packing them into tiny backpacks. Mine has been lodged beneath my desk all day. She'd shoved it into my hands as I left the flat after breakfast, making me swear not to look inside until the last minute. Amazingly, I've resisted the temptation.

Another message flies in.

Elly: All the drinks are free! Getting the first round in. Champagne cocktail? It'll be waiting for you.

I should be at the club in half an hour and I've been so busy all day that I haven't even checked where I'm going. I bring up Google and type the name of the club into the search bar.

Shit.

It's in the basement of the Hawkston Mayfair Hotel. It's been rebranded, so that's why I didn't recognise the name. I'm not sure I want to attend a party in a Hawkston Hotel.

Another message from Elly buzzes on my phone.

Elly: OMG OMG Amy Moritz just arrived! Get down here ASAP.

Elly: I will personally murder you if you aren't here in the next hour.

Marie: Come quick. Elly's so overexcited, she's doing my head in. I need someone sane to talk to.

I chuckle at Marie's last message and push any reservations about turning up at one of Nico's hotels out of mind. I gather my stuff, shove it in my handbag, and head to the toilets, taking the tiny backpack Elly gave me this morning.

I do my makeup first, spreading blush over my cheeks, gloss on my lips and thick black eyeliner over my top lids before I add more mascara. It's the best I can do with the time I have.

I wriggle out of the black sheath dress I'm wearing, letting it drop to the floor, and kick off my shoes. They're my favourite silver heels. I pushed the corporate dress code by wearing them today, but I didn't have any meetings, and I'm pretty sure I can pair them with whatever Elly has planned for me.

I need privacy, so I lift the tiny backpack and opt for the end cubicle. I step inside and pull the door closed, locking it.

I unzip the bag. There are only two items inside it, both carefully folded. Both tiny. The first is a pair of silky black shorts. I hold them up against my hips. They're barely going to cover my bum.

Damn you, Elly. It might be warm outside, but this is indecent.

I check the time. Nine fifteen. I'm definitely going to be late.

I haul the shorts on, then shake out the second item. A top. It's got thin straps, a scooped neck and a low back, and is covered in green sequins. There's no way I can wear a bra with it.

I imagine Elly giving me her '*don't be a spoilsport*' look, and I know she'll be furious if I don't wear it. What choice do I have? It's not as though there's time to buy a different outfit. The shops are closed. Plus, knowing Elly, there is some reason for this choice.

In a few minutes, I'm fully dressed. I fluff my hair and empty my bladder and I'm ready to go.

I reach for the lock and try to spin it, but it won't turn. I put down the tiny backpack and try with both hands.

Nothing.

I wipe my hands on my shorts and try again.

Nothing.

I shoulder the door. Kick it with my foot. Then try the lock again.

Nothing. No matter what I do, there's no give in the mechanism whatsoever.

Fuck. I'll have to call someone. Maybe Jack is downstairs having drinks.

Oh, balls. I've left my phone on the side of the sink.

I try the lock again, but it doesn't budge. My body heats with panic that I'll be stuck here all night. Elly will kill me for missing our night out.

My heart drops to my stomach. If I can't get out of here, it won't be one night. It's Friday and the office will be empty until Monday morning. No one will be around to rescue me until next week.

Could I die of starvation before then? I don't think so, but I could definitely die of boredom, if panic doesn't get me first.

Then I remember the cleaners outside.

If I shout loud enough, maybe they'll hear me.

I take a deep breath and batter the door with my fists. "Hello?" I yell. "Is anyone there?"

Nothing but the silence of the empty bathroom greets me.

11
NICO

I haven't set foot on the sixth floor for the best part of a month, and yet almost every second of every day, in the background of my mind like the distant drone of traffic, I've been aware that if I wanted to find Kate, that's where she'd be.

I've resisted the siren call of her presence with admirable fortitude. But now, as I lean back in my chair on Friday evening and gaze out my office window, I succumb to the truth: I can't get her out of my head. I'm wasting too much of my time wondering what's underneath her prim and proper office attire, or what her skin feels like beneath those silk shirts, or how firm her thighs are and what they'd feel like around my neck.

Fucking pointless too, because I'm never going to find out.

I push aside the contract I've been trying to read and draft a quick email to my PA to set up welcome drinks for the Lansen team. I can't avoid Kate forever, and it's verging on unacceptable that we haven't formally welcomed them. I'm busy, sure, but it's no excuse.

A wave of irritation blasts through me as I hit send. Avoiding floors in my own building because there's one woman down there who turns me on but shouldn't is beyond ridiculous. I can control my fucking sex drive.

I'll go down to the sixth floor and talk to her right now and invite her in person to the welcome drinks.

Five minutes later, I walk out of the lift onto the sixth floor, and the silence hits me. No chatter, except for the hum of electricity whirring through a hundred computers. *Shit*. Everyone's gone. I didn't realise how late it was.

A shout distracts me. Or was it a scream? I hold my breath and listen.

It comes again. Muffled, but definitely a shout, coming from the bathroom. My mind immediately goes to Kate, a burst of pressure in my chest urging me to run. I dodge through the desks and slam my way into the bathroom.

It's empty, aside from a handbag I recognise as Kate's lying on the side of the sink. Makeup is strewn around, and a crumpled black dress lies on the floor next to a pair of silver shoes. What in God's name is she wearing if her clothes are out here?

"Hello?"

The voice is definitely Kate's. Tension seeps from my muscles. She's all right. At least, she sounds it.

"Is somebody there?" she demands.

A pounding starts. Fists on the door of the end cubicle. Then the banging stops. "This is just fucking typical."

She sounds resigned to her fate, and the frustration in her voice makes me want to laugh. *Is she on the phone?* I wait for her to speak again, but she's silent. I catch sight of her phone by the sink. Nope; she's alone.

"I know you're out there," she yells. "I heard footsteps. Help me, you motherfucker."

Motherfucker? You'd think she knows it's me out here.

"Kate?"

The noise stops entirely.

I step closer to the door. "Do you need help?"

For a few moments, she says nothing.

While I wait, I pick up one of her shoes and lean back against the sink. The shoe looks almost new. Soft leather, with supple soles. High quality. She must have splashed out on these. A present for herself, perhaps? I check the brand, only to find my friend's signature on the inside sole: *Erica Lefroy*. Her fashion line has been doing well recently, but I didn't realise Kate was into that sort of stuff.

I let the silver heel dangle from my index finger and check the size. Her feet are smaller than I would have thought.

I drop the shoe and lean my ear against the door of the bathroom stall. There's a frustrated muttering coming from the other side that draws a wry chuckle from my throat.

I'm probably the last person she wants to see.

I tap gently against the door with my knuckle. "I know it's you." More silence. "Are you stuck?"

A loud sigh burrows its way through the door. "No, Nico. I enjoy spending my Friday evenings locked in the toilet."

I snort. *She's funny*.

"The lock is jammed. Bloody stupid cubicles," Kate explains. "If you had regular toilets, I could have squeezed underneath the door."

I stand back, slide my hands in my pockets, and tamp down the urge to laugh as I imagine Kate squirming on the bathroom floor to escape her temporary prison. "What would you like me to do about it?"

"I don't know," Kate huffs. "Redesign the bathrooms? What do you think I want you to do? Get me out of here. Break the door down for all I care."

"As much as I'd love to break down the door and rescue you, I don't want to damage my property."

Kate mutters something I can't make out.

I'm silent as I examine the lock. I can't swing it from this side. I walk to another cubicle and check the mechanism on an open door. It's sticky, but it twists.

Kate's voice, less irate now, echoes around the stalls. "Are you still here?"

I return to her cubicle. "I am."

Lucky for Kate, I always carry a penknife. Strangely enough, it was a gift from her father. I pull it out of my pocket and read the inscription on the handle.

Don't kill anyone.
Love, Godfather Gerard.

I wonder if he ever imagined that one day I'd be using his gift to liberate his daughter from a locked bathroom stall.

I pull out the screwdriver option and set to work.

"Stand back," I tell her, and I hear movement on the other side.

A moment later, the lock falls away entirely. I catch it on my side, but on Kate's, it clatters to the floor.

She gasps, and for some reason the noise makes me want to haul her out and sling her over my shoulder.

I push the door open, but I'm completely unprepared for the sight that greets me.

Her makeup is more intense than normal, her already large eyes outlined in sweeps of black that make them appear bigger, sexier, than normal. Something dark and slick coats her full lips, giving them a sheen that catches the light. Her mouth looks... *moist,* and I immediately want to suck the offensive bottom lip between my own.

But it's the fact that she's more naked than clothed that snares my attention. There's so much flesh, so much skin, that I can't stop staring. She's perfect... smooth all over.

A pair of sleek black shorts reveal long, toned thighs and a shimmering green top scoops low between her breasts. A narrow expanse of stomach is visible where the top doesn't meet the shorts, the skin lightly tanned and unbearably tempting.

But her breasts... *fuck me*. If she tilted towards me, they'd fall out, and there's no way she's wearing a bra. As my gaze lingers, I swear I can see the outline of her nipples hardening. My cock twitches in response.

Kate clears her throat, calling me out. I raise my eyes to meet hers with just enough presence of mind to conceal the fact that I'm completely blown away by how fan-fucking-tastic she looks.

I lean casually against the doorframe.

Kate nods at the penknife in my hand. "What are you, a boy scout?"

I slide it back into my pocket and arch a brow, attempting to affect disdain. "What the hell are you wearing?"

She stiffens, clearly irritated. "That's none of your business. My contracted hours are over for the day. I can wear whatever I want." She steps closer to me, as if she expects me to move aside at her instigation.

I don't.

"Where are you going?" I ask.

"Also, none of your business."

Christ, this woman is infuriating. "Wear a coat when you leave."

"Worried about me getting cold again?" Her lips tilt up, and if I didn't know better, I'd think Kate Lansen was flirting with me.

"No." My gaze hovers at her full lips, then slides down her neck to her bare shoulders. Her skin is so flawless that I'm consumed by the desire to touch it. Such an intimate part of one's body, the shoulder. Rarely revealed, particularly in an office environment.

Her throat bobs, breath hitching as she watches me watch her, and tension expands like steam, engulfing us both. There's no sign of amusement or flirtation on her face, because whatever's happening right now feels much more serious than that.

Every item of clothing I'm wearing suddenly feels too small, scratching at my skin.

"Are you going to move out of my way?" she breathes.

Shit. I'm still blocking her way out.

I turn aside and she assesses the gap I've left for her to move through. Her gaze flicks up to mine, and she takes one more small, deliberate step, halting right before me. *So close.*

"Nico..." My name is a mere exhalation on her lips. It sounds... *needy*. The energy intensifies, swirling between us; a force that's trying to drag me closer to her.

As if of its own volition, my hand stretches out, fingers reaching towards the expanse of bare skin that runs between the shorts and top.

What the fuck am I doing?

Everything happens in slow motion. She watches my hand. She could stop me, but she doesn't. She's hardly breathing, but neither am I.

Our eyes lock, and I make an almost imperceptible gesture. *Can I?* Her responding nod is so small I can't be entirely sure it happened, but then she takes another tiny step closer. So close I can feel her breath on my face.

My fingertips dust against her hip, and the flesh flutters beneath. A small gasp escapes her lips, not loud enough to break me out of whatever trance her body has drawn me into, but enough to let me know my touch affects her.

Her skin is so soft, so warm, that I immediately want more. More skin, more flesh, more contact. It's all I can do not to grab her with both hands.

I hold my breath and slide my finger along the waistband of her tiny shorts; the motion feels illicit; a sin I want to commit over and over and it sends my pulse sky high. All it would take is one swift motion for my fingers to slip down...

Goosebumps scatter over Kate's skin and she lets out the tiniest moan. Heat pools deep in my groin. *Fuck me.* I don't think I've ever wanted a woman as much as I want her right now.

I'm crossing so many lines, I've burnt them all to fucking ash. I need to pull it back, and fast.

I let the waistband of her shorts snap back in place. I should stop touching her, but my hand lingers, my thumb gently stroking her hip. She hasn't acknowledged it, but tiny jerks of her body continue to echo my touch. I want to tell her how beautiful she is, how perfect. But a husky rasp comes out. "I don't want anyone else seeing you like this."

Laughter bubbles up in her throat, an almost hysterical sound that breaks me out of my stupor as she draws back just far enough that I would have to stretch to reach her again.

"I hate to disappoint you, but I'm going out," she states, her defensive mask back in place. I'm impressed by the speed of her recovery. "A lot of people are going to see me like this." She gestures at her almost naked body—the body that until seconds ago was about to dance to my fucking tune—and a salacious look ripples over her face, that all but screams, '*I'm hot and I know it, and you can't have me*'.

My shoulders tighten. The suggestion that others are going to see her this way, maybe even touch her, makes me want to burn the whole fucking world to the ground.

"A lot of men are going to see me like this," she teases, seemingly encouraged by whatever reaction she's noticed in me.

Fuck that. If she wants to play, I'm game.

"And here I thought you were getting dressed up for me." I cross my arms and lean back against the doorframe, smiling. "You cut me deep, Kate."

She flinches at the use of her full name. "Why you…" She shuts her mouth, like she's decided against whatever she was about to say. Then she stares me down until I finally shift out of her way, giving her just enough space to edge past me. Our bodies brush and the contact is electrifying, but Kate reveals no sign it affects her as it does me.

She slides on her shoes, grabs her belongings, and stuffs everything into a tiny backpack. Her shorts reveal the curved half-moons of her butt cheeks, and when she bends over, it's fucking delicious.

She paces towards the door, but just before she reaches it, she glimpses herself in the full-length mirror and slows.

She bends to fix her shoe, sliding her finger in the heel.

I slow down so we don't collide and at the same moment the main door to the bathroom swings open.

"Kate," I yell, closing the distance between us so fast I'm surprised my shoes aren't smoking. I lurch across the curve of her back, sticking my hand out so the door crashes against my palm instead of her head and bounces back towards its closed position.

I'm off balance and my momentum throws me forward. I smash into Kate, who's frozen in her half-crouched position, and I grab her with both hands.

I stumble, clinging to her, trying to find my feet so we don't collapse in a heap. I'd fucking crush her.

She swipes at me. Grabs and clings. We're a mess of tangled limbs; for a second I don't know which way is up and I'm bracing to thud against the tile floor.

Somehow, I stay upright and drag Kate up to standing beside me. Her skin is hot beneath my hands, but the alarm in her dark eyes is so beguiling that I want to scoop her up and take her home.

A silent beat passes, the two of us locked together, our noses only inches apart. The look in Kate's eyes softens, and warmth spills through my insides.

A cleaner appears on the other side of the door, all wide eyes and frizzy dark hair. Her gaze runs over our haphazard embrace and her eyebrows rise. "Oh dear. Sorry. I'll come back later, okay?"

Without waiting for a reply, she disappears. The door closes and the intimacy of the moment shatters as Kate's palms slam against my chest, pushing me away with unnecessary force.

"What are you doing? Get your hands off me."

I release her, and she trips back a few steps before righting herself. Her breaths come fast, the green sequins of her top shimmering with each shudder of her breasts. She places one steadying hand between them.

I mock-frown. "I think what you mean is 'thank you'."

"For what? Groping me in the office bathroom?"

"No. Saving you from a head injury."

She huffs out an exasperated breath. "You're an arsehole."

Frustration coils in my gut. I can't believe I came down here to invite her to drinks when all she does is swear in my face. No matter how attractive this woman is, I don't need this crap in my life.

I run a hand over my forehead and then point towards the cubicle she was stuck in. "Should've left you locked in there all night. At least then I wouldn't have to deal with your bullshit."

That harsh, dismissive laugh erupts from her mouth again. "My bullshit? You're the one quizzing me on where I'm going and what I'm wearing when it's none of your business. I'm leaving. And before you ask, I'm going to get my coat, so you don't need to worry about me getting cold. Or my near-nudity degrading the reputation of your company when I leave the building, or whatever bothers you about this outfit."

She stands tall and marches out of the room, and all I can do is watch her perfect arse saunter away.

Well, shit.

She might as well have my dick in her pocket, because there is no woman in the world right now that gets me hard like Kate Lansen.

I'm completely hers, whether she wants me or not.

12

KATE

As I descend into the belly of the club, I am determined to put Nico out of mind. I'm here to have fun with my friends, not fret about whatever that strange interaction back in the office was, or what it meant. Or that the gentlest of his touches had me almost—

Stop it.

I bring my focus back to the present. Martini Gems is elaborately decorated like an ice cave, with glittering walls and ceilings, ice sculptures on podiums and crystal light fittings overhead. It's like Disneyland—with alcohol—for wealthy adults.

Lights flicker and bodies heave in every inch of space; the music is pounding so loud that I can feel it in my kneecaps. I'm eager for a drink. I need to shed the stress of the last few weeks, not to mention the last hour.

I search for Elly and Marie, finally spying them huddled at a table in the corner. They're dressed identically to me, except Marie's top is red and Elly's is gold. I want to laugh that Elly has dressed us up like a girl band.

"Kate!" she yells, waving me over when she sees me. She grabs me and kisses the side of my face, engulfing me in her huge mop of blonde hair. It smells clean, like strawberry soap, but her breath is boozy. I suspect she's already had one too many cocktails. She points a wavering finger at me. "I knew you'd look smoking in this."

I smile at the compliment and join them at the table, which is littered with empty glasses, as well as a huge ice bucket with two champagne bottles inside.

Marie, dark hair pulled back in a ponytail so tight it tugs at her temples, looks to be enjoying herself, but I note the dark circles beneath her eyes; she's a junior doctor and works even harder than I do. It's rare we manage a night out together.

She slides a champagne cocktail in my direction. "You've got some catching up to do." Her expression contains a dare, and, not wanting to disappoint, I take the glass and down the whole thing in one go. Marie chuckles and Elly whoops. It's been far too long since I let loose, and their reactions let me know they agree. Elly wastes no time in passing me a second glass, which I gulp down just as quickly as the first.

We spend a few minutes catching up, shouting over the music, and Elly and Marie both share news of their week. But when it's my turn, I can think of nothing to say that isn't *Nico, Nico, Nico*. His face, his eyes, his voice... his hand on my hip, tenderly stroking the skin, looking at me as though he wanted me as much as I want him...

Could he want me that way?

I shake my head as if I can drop all thoughts of him out of my mind. But they're lodged deep in the crevices of my brain and all the attempt does is knock his words from earlier loose.

Should've left you locked in there all night. At least then I wouldn't have to deal with your bullshit.

No. Nico doesn't like me.

"What the hell are you thinking about? Is it that arsehole of a boss?" Marie queries as she tops up all our drinks.

"No," I lie.

"Arsehole?" Elly says. "Do you mean that hottie she works for?"

"Yeah, exactly. Nico fucking Hawkston," Marie says, employing my usual name for him. I've told them both about how he booked out the entire spa for me on my first day and demanded I have lunch with him. Elly swooned, but Marie shared my opinion that he ought to have asked me first. Not asking, she said, was a power play.

Elly directs a pointed look my way, and I let out a hopeless sigh, dropping back into my seat. "Maybe."

Marie shakes her head at me as though I've failed a test I didn't know I was taking.

"I know you hate him," Elly begins, with a brow raise that indicates she doesn't believe it. "But he *is* insanely good-looking. I'm not remotely surprised you tried to take your clothes off for him."

My body tenses. I know what Elly's referencing, but Marie has no idea.

Marie focuses on me. "You got your kit off for him?"

"Oh, shit." Elly's fingers flutter to her lips, her eyes apologetic. "Was it supposed to be a secret?"

"No. Not really. It was a long time ago..."

"Kate was in love with him when we were at school," Elly interrupts, like I just waived my right to privacy.

"I wasn't in love with him," I reply far too quickly.

Elly laughs, tilting forward in her seat to share the gossip. "You were obsessed."

I wince. Even now, energy is vibrating in every cell because we're talking about him. "Can we not talk about this?" I groan, feigning reluctance.

Elly's smile splits wide, and she points a finger at me. "Stop pretending you don't want to. You're practically drooling already."

Damn. She knows me too well. "Am not."

Thankfully, Elly doesn't push me any further before she turns to Marie. "Kate got in the hot tub and took off her bikini top. Twirled it round on her finger and tossed it in the water." Elly stands up, whirls her index finger in the air and shakes her hips in a playful version of a stripper dance. She finishes by flicking her finger, letting the imaginary bikini top fly across the dance floor.

That's not at all how it went down, but I don't want to spoil her theatrics.

Marie smirks. "Then what happened?"

I take a deep breath. Might as well tell her the whole story. "He looked at me like I'd lost my mind and told me to go back inside. And then..." I grimace at the memory and Marie raises an eyebrow.

"What?"

I press my hands over my mouth and talk through my fingers. "He covered his eyes."

Marie seals her lips, her facial muscles tightening like it's an effort not to laugh. When she relaxes enough to talk, she says, "That bad, eh?"

"That bad," I confirm. "He tried to grab my bikini top from the water without looking and give it back to me."

Elly giggles, throwing her forearm over her eyes and patting the air in front of her. "I'm blind. Little K, your tits are brighter than the sun. Stop shining them in my face."

"Little K?" Marie frowns. "That's what he calls you?"

"Yeah, he has a nickname for her. Cute, eh?" Elly says, smiling. Then her eyes light up and, if it's possible, the smile gets wider. "Did he give you that nickname before or after he saw your boobs?"

"Hey!" I cry, gesturing to my breasts, which are at least medium-sized, and definitely don't warrant the diminutive nickname.

Elly's giggling so hard now she's holding her stomach. I'm laughing too, but mostly out of shame. Marie's glancing between the two of us like we're crazy.

After a few minutes, Elly's laughter has run out of steam, and she slides back into her seat opposite me. "When was the last time you had sex?"

The change of topic throws me for a loop. "Eh?"

"I remember when." Marie picks a cube of ice out of the ice bucket and pops it into her mouth, speaking around it. "It was that chap she met in Cornwall last summer. Said it was the worst sex she'd ever had. No orgasms. Not even nearly."

"Actually, that was the summer before last," I admit.

Marie whistles. "Fuck, Kate. What's that? Two years? Your pussy must have cobwebs in it."

I give an exaggerated gasp, grab a fistful of ice and chuck it across the table at her. She raises her hands and squeals, then does the same to me. Ice skitters all over the table, and we both laugh. The alcohol is doing its work, my blood running hot with it and a wooziness dripping through my awareness, softening the edges.

"You have to spring clean. Have a proper dusting session," Elly smirks at me, but then her eyes flash over at the bar and she grabs my wrist. "Oh, my God," she hisses. "It's Michael Drayton." She's staring at a tall, blond man by the bar, dressed in a white t-shirt and low-slung blue jeans.

"Michael who?" Marie asks.

Elly quivers with excitement, so eager to get her words out that she stammers before she's able to string a sentence together properly. "Drayton. Michael Drayton. He's the lead in those new action movies. You must have seen the adverts on the side of the buses." She spreads her hands wide through the air as if she's imagining seeing the posters before her. "He's shirtless and running at the camera, a huge explosion happening behind him? One of the best bodies in Hollywood. Totally ripped."

"Oh, right, him," Marie says, looking utterly disinterested, and no wonder; she's completely besotted with her boyfriend, Kevin.

"I have an idea," Elly says, and before we can stop her, she slips away from the table and marches up to Michael Drayton and introduces herself. Marie and I watch, amazed, as Elly smiles and chatters, pointing over at us. Michael turns in our direction, shooting cut-glass cheekbones and blue-eyes in our direction.

"Wow, he *is* gorgeous," Marie whispers, turning googly-eyed.

Elly skips back towards us, a satisfied smile on her face. "He's coming over. Bringing shots."

A nervous void opens in my stomach. "What?"

She nods. "Yup. He's the one you should spring clean with." She feigns a swoon, pressing the back of one hand to her forehead. "Dreamy. What a way to break the dry spell."

Before I can object, Michael Drayton saunters over with a tray of shots, which he sets down on our table before sitting down next to me. I'm not usually one to get star-struck, but when the biggest name in Hollywood is sitting so close your thighs are touching under the table, it's hard not to react.

"Evening, ladies," he says. "Elly tells me you're all big fans."

I nearly laugh at this, but Elly shoots me a '*shut up*' look, which is somewhat justified. Who doesn't know who Michael Drayton is?

"I'm not a fan," I say, and although I mean it, it sounds like I'm flirting.

An array of emotions flit over his handsome face, finally settling on pleasantly amused. "Is that so?" He doesn't wait for a response before he hands me a shot. "Vodka," he announces.

I take it from him. "I haven't eaten."

He laughs, and I can't deny that his laugh, and the way his eyes sparkle, is very appealing. "Eating is cheating," he says, in a husky voice.

Before I know it, I'm clinking my vodka shot against his and we down them simultaneously.

He smacks his lips and sets his glass down, staring right at me when he says, "You're the green traffic light."

At first, I don't know what he's talking about, and then it clicks. *Our tops*. Marie's is red, because she has a boyfriend. Elly's is gold—or amber—and mine is absolutely green.

Horrified, I stare at Elly. "I'm a green traffic light?"

She pushes another shot into my hand, tipping my elbow to coax the glass to my lips. "Yes. You're available. You're green. *Very* green," she says emphatically, then looks at Michael and adds, "Green means go."

Michael tips back his head and laughs, and he really is handsome, but I feel none of the flutters I feel with Nico.

But Nico's not here, and I shouldn't be having any kind of feelings for him, anyway. Maybe a fling with a handsome movie star is just what I need to push Nico out of my mind for good.

"Let's drink to that," Michael says.

"Let's." I take another shot, slamming the empty glass on the table.

13
NICO

I'm at my desk, trying to get through the contract I abandoned earlier, but I can't shake the memory of Kate, all dressed up, lips plump, eyes dark. I've never seen her look like that, like she's out to—

My stomach squeezes, folding in on itself.

Fuck.

Kate Lansen is dressed up like she wants to get laid, and I'm powerless to do anything about it. I don't know where she's going, or who she's meeting.

Fuck it.

What she does with her Friday night has nothing to do with me. I grit my teeth and force my eyes to the paper in front of me.

I read the same page over and over. The minutes trickle by. Nine forty-five. Ten. Ten thirty.

I can't concentrate.

My phone rings, Seb's name flashing up on the screen.

"Nico, where the fuck are you?" He yells when I answer. There's a lot of noise in the background, and he says something that sounds a lot like, "*Double Scotch, on the rocks,*" before his voice comes back loud and clear. "It's Amy's after-party. Amy Moritz. She's asking for you. What the fuck are you doing that's more important than celebrating with her and christening Martini Gems?"

I groan, dropping my forehead into my open palm, elbow propped on the desk. I've been so distracted I completely forgot that tonight was the opening night at the new club in the basement of the Mayfair Hawkston.

"Erica Lefroy's here too," Seb continues. "Wants to know where you are. Get down here pronto. It's fucking rude not to show up and everyone wants to see you."

I let out a long sigh. The last thing I want to do is engage in small talk with the over-inflated egos of conceited celebrities. Not Amy or Erica... but the rest I could leave.

"I'll be there in twenty," I tell him before hanging up and dialing my driver.

There's a queue outside. Plenty of paps too, waiting to get a picture of Amy Moritz and anyone else who's in the club tonight. I stroll right to the front of the line, ignoring the irritated glances of the people waiting and the constant clicking and flashing of the cameras.

"Mr. Hawkston," says the doorman, nodding at me and waving me through.

The beat of music thumps through the soles of my shoes as I descend to the basement, and I'm greeted by a blast of hot air that already smells like overheated, sweaty humans. *Fuck's sake.*

I reach the bottom step and turn into the club itself. The music, louder now, assaults my ears. The place is lit like an optic migraine. A plethora of bodies writhe and grapple one another on the dance floor under the flashing overhead lights.

I'm the only person wearing a suit. I'd stand out like a sore thumb if anyone was sober enough to notice.

Velvet booths line the walls, where groups of people cluster around tables covered with champagne flutes and cocktail glasses. Everyone looks to be having a great time.

"Do you want to check your coat, sir?"

I turn to the cloakroom attendant. "No. I'll keep it on."

I'll do my duty. Give Amy my congratulations. Make sure Seb knows I've shown my face, and then I'll head home.

I jostle my way through the bar area when I catch sight of Seb. He's wearing a t-shirt and jeans. How long ago did he check out of the office? He's standing at a booth, leaning over the table, chatting animatedly with the people sitting down. I keep my eyes on him as I head in his direction and he must feel it, because he excuses himself and comes towards me, slinging his arm around my shoulders, tugging me close and yelling in my ear.

"You made it. Take your fucking coat off. You look like you're about to leave."

"I am."

He shakes his head and leads me over to the table. Several women sit around it, including Erica and Amy. There's also a male TV star I vaguely recognise, as well as one of Amy's backing dancers. Judging by the way Amy's draped over the dancer, they're either sleeping together or about to.

Amy, who's wearing a dress covered in more rhinestones than Elvis Presley's jockstrap, drags her long-lashed eyes away from him long enough to notice me. She jumps up from her seat in the middle of the booth, realises she's penned in on both sides, and climbs right over the table. Glasses and drinks go flying, and everyone tries to dodge the debris. Amy hops off the table, brushes down her dress, and throws her arms around my neck.

"You were going to miss this, you little prick," she shouts over the music. "Sit and have a drink."

I hesitate.

"Fucking sit down," Seb hisses in my ear.

"Do sit," Erica adds, extending a long, graceful arm across the table towards me. She looks more sober than the rest, exuding that supermodel elegance she's renowned for.

They all start shuffling round the table to make space for me when a flash of sparkling green catches my eye. I turn to get a closer look.

There's a woman pressed against the wall beyond the bar. She's clearly inebriated because she can hardly stand up. A guy is grinding himself against her like he's trying to have sex with his clothes on. His jeans are so loose they're hanging halfway to his knees. In contrast to her apparent inebriation, his movements are sharp, deliberate, and obviously sober.

His fingers dimple the woman's skin where he grips her bum, which is half-exposed in a pair of tiny silk shorts.

Shorts I saw only a few hours ago. Shorts I fucking *touched*.

It's Kate.

A knot forms in my chest, immediately sending spirals of heat through me. I want to rush over there and slam him against the wall until his skull shatters, but I hold back, clenched fists deep in the pockets of my overcoat. I need to know if she's into this.

Seb turns to see what I'm staring at. "That's the star of that new movie franchise. Michael Bond. James Bond. Whatever the fuck it is."

"Michael Drayton," Erica fills in. "That's his name."

I'm hardly listening, staring as Kate flicks her hair off her face, and Seb squints across the room. "Shit," he says. "Is that—"

"Yes," I reply.

A swathe of dancing B-list celebrities obscures my view, but when they clear the actor is gripping Kate's wrists, forcing them over her head with one hand. She's writhing against the wall. His other hand grabs her jaw, pinning it in place. He tilts his head, his mouth coming down fast towards hers. She twists in what looks to be an attempt to escape him. But is it? I can't be sure.

His hand slides down the column of her neck.

Fuck. Heat blazes through me, ravaging my insides, destroying every intention to hold back. I don't fucking care if she's into this or not. It's not happening.

I march towards them, Seb at my elbow. He grabs my arm, tugs me round to look at him.

"Nico," he hisses, "Don't make a scene. It's opening night, and he's an A-lister."

I cast him a dismissive glare and shrug him off. "I don't care if he's the King of fucking England."

Seb retreats, eyes wide and hands raised in surrender, and I continue my march across the dance floor. People swerve out of the way, yelling and cursing at me, but I ignore them. My focus is on Kate, and Kate alone.

Michael grabs her with both hands and yanks her into him. She's turning her face away so he can't meet her lips, but he pursues her mouth, undeterred, adjusting her body to meet his needs.

Another step and I have the guy by the collar, wrenching him towards me. "Get your hands off her."

Up close, he's unusually good looking, his sweat-slick blonde hair falling over his forehead.

Kate gawks at me, a look of horror on her face.

"What the fuck, dude? We're busy." Michael's voice is hard and sober, as expected. I'm itching to punch his handsome face, but there are people watching and I can hear Seb's warning ringing in the back of my head. *Don't make a scene.*

"I said take your hands off her. She's drunk."

As if to prove my point, Kate flops forward from where she's leaning against the wall, and Michael roughly props her back up with one hand.

"Dude, fuck off," he spits at me over his shoulder. "I'm about to get laid here."

Before I can think twice, I'm pulling back a tight fist and swinging a perfect right hook that catches him in the jaw.

Kate squeals, her hands covering her mouth as Michael bends double, clutching his face, blood gushing from his nose, or his mouth or I don't fucking know where from.

"What the fuck?" Michael groans, spitting blood through his fingers as he cups a hand over the lower half of his face. "I'll sue you. This face is worth millions."

"Go ahead," I mutter. "I'm good for it."

I signal to the security guards who are lingering discreetly at the sides of the room. They move at my command and whatever objection Michael is about to make dies on his tongue as he holds his hands up.

"Get the fuck out," I demand, and then turn my focus to the head of security who's now beside me. "Take him out the back. Clean him up. Call a doctor if he needs to see one."

The men escort Michael away, him slumped between them, all bravado vanished, and I grip Kate by the elbow. She's so unsteady on her feet, she'd be on her arse in seconds if I let go.

"You hit him," Kate slurs. At least I think that's what she says. She's drunker than I thought. "He didn't do anything to you."

"Didn't he?"

She frowns like she can't make sense of what I'm saying, then wriggles in my grip. "Let me go."

I shake my head and, keeping a firm hand on her elbow, I escort her off the dance floor, pushing through the people who paused their dancing to stare at the ruckus. Seb tries to get my attention, but I wave him off; I don't have fucking time for whatever reprimand he's going to give me. If there's a PR issue because of what I've done, we have people to sort that shit out.

Kate stumbles, and suddenly she's grabbing me to stay upright, tripping over her own feet, which are bare.

I fix my hands on her elbows, securing her in place so we're facing each other.

Even drunk, her hair damp with sweat, she's indisputably gorgeous. Her hands grip my forearms through my coat, and I wish I wasn't wearing it.

She's looking at me intently… at least as intently as a drunk person can. "Why did you do that? Why did you hit him?"

She's struggling to focus. I don't have time to answer because she lunges towards me as if she means to kiss me.

For a split second, I'm stunned, and her lips are dangerously close to mine when I put my hand out to hold her off.

She lurches into my palm, and I prop her up by the shoulder, pushing her back.

She blinks like it might help her understand what's happening, but she can't fully open her eyes when she's done. "Don't you want to kiss me?" she whines. "I thought you wanted to."

This is new. "You're too drunk to be kissing anyone."

She topples toward me again. "We don't need to tell Jack."

With one hand I hold her up, but her body is so close to mine, and she's soft and yielding and extremely tempting, but I won't take her this way. "I'm not going to kiss you."

She pulls back, trying to give me what appears to be a haughty look, but is just her wrinkling her nose. "I won't even remember it tomorrow. It'll be like it never happened—"

I press a finger to her lips, and her eyes widen. The drunken swaying of her body ceases. "Exactly. Trust me, when I kiss you, you're going to want to remember it."

"Wait." Her lips brush my skin as she murmurs against the side of my index finger. "Does that mean you *do* want to kiss me?"

A few tense beats pass. "It's all I think about."

Her breath stutters, uneven gusts of warmth hitting my finger. She holds eye contact like she's daring me to do something about it.

The heat in Kate's drunken stare is undeniable. When she realises I'm not going to make a move, her tongue slides to the edge of her mouth, peeking between her lips. I can't take my eyes off it as she runs the tip along my skin.

Warm wetness coats my finger, turning my blood thick, each beat of my pulse like a slow-motion hammer blow. She might as well have licked my dick because every fibre of my body pulses with need.

Shit. This can't happen. Not now, not here.

I fist the hand she's just licked and something like fear flashes in her eyes as my skin leaves her lips.

"Let's get out of here," I say.

She breathes a sigh of relief and then pushes away from me with drunken determination. I follow behind.

"I can't leave my shoes," she declares, wobbling about like a newborn foal as she moves from booth to booth, peering between people's feet and bumping into everything and anything. "They're my faves. My Erica Lefroy's. All sparkly and silver."

"Forget the damn shoes," I growl, hoisting her up into my arms before she can protest. "I'll buy you as many fucking pairs of shoes as you want."

She squeals and attempts to hit me, a limp fist striking my chest. "Put me down. I can still walk."

"Barely. And this floor is probably covered with alcohol and broken glass. I'm not letting you walk around in here without shoes on."

Her body relaxes and as she stares up at me, there's a look in her eye I haven't seen before, as if my actions have challenged some long-held belief.

"But I smell like tequila," she whispers into my shoulder.

"That's true," I mutter, although I don't think she hears me. I don't care either, because she's vulnerable, and seeing Kate like this tugs awkwardly at my lungs and my breathing falters. I shrug away the feeling and hold her tighter against my chest.

I carry her through the bar and up the stairs, into the main area of the hotel.

"What's your address?" I ask, but she makes no reply. "Kate?"

She gives a drowsy little snore against my chest.

Fuck it. She's fallen asleep.

"Kate?"

No response. I repeat her name, a little louder this time, but it makes no difference. She continues breathing rhythmically against my chest.

I briefly debate shaking her awake to get her address out of her, but she needs the sleep. I walk over to the reception desk and the woman behind it looks up at me, recognition flaring in her eyes.

"Mr. Hawkston," she says. "Do you need a room?"

"I do. The Penthouse."

14

NICO

Kate rouses as I reach the Penthouse door. I set her down, and she leans against the wall, eyelids drooping. I press the keycard to the lock and push into the room.

The Penthouse is a vast suite, with a bed large enough to fit an entire family, and a separate sitting and dining room with glass windows all round.

I coax her inside.

"Wow," she breathes, examining the suite, but she remains in the doorway, not moving beyond the threshold. "The penthouse? Fuck, Nico. Bold. Is there only one bed? How pres... presu... what's the word?" she asks, waving a hand at me.

"Presumptuous?"

She clicks her fingers and points at me. Her head rocks, lolling this way and that like she can't hold it straight. "Yes. That one."

"I presume nothing. We're not having sex."

She frowns, one eye drooping shut a tad. "Then what are we doing here?"

Is she disappointed?

"You need to go to sleep," I say. "You've had too much to drink."

Her eyes narrow, like she's trying to work something out, but she's too drunk to do it. "You could take me home."

"Sure. Where do you live?"

She screws her eyes closed and then her face goes totally blank. "Don't remember. Clapham. South London. Number fifty... fifty-something."

Who the fuck doesn't remember where they live?

I hold out my hand for the tiny handbag that's slung over her shoulder. "Give it."

She clutches it to her. "Why? You can't look in my handbag. It's private."

I hum a laugh but retract my outstretched hand. "Driver's license. Your address will be on it."

She opens her bag and looks through it, frowns, then snaps it shut again. "It's not there." She gives a little shrug but doesn't seem fazed at all that she's lost it. Maybe it's because she's drunk, but part of me suspects she's lying. "Guess I'd better stay after all."

I affect my most disinterested nod. "It's big enough."

She nudges the door shut with her foot, then paces towards me. Her bare feet sink into the plush pile of the carpet. When she reaches me, she pokes her finger into my chest. "You stopped me from having sex tonight. That was the plan." She gestures to her top. "I'm the green traffic light. *Green means go.*" I don't know what she's talking about, but the fact that she's mentioning sex, even if it is in a drunken, aggressive tone, doesn't strike me as a good thing. We're alone in a hotel room, mere feet from a huge bed.

"Haven't had sex for a long time," she continues. *Sex, again.* "My pussy could be full of cobwebs."

Pussy? "Cobwebs?" I ask, a smothered laugh escaping me, but Kate is so drunk she doesn't notice.

"Michael Drayton, too," she continues in a serious tone, albeit a little slurred. "You know what a big deal he is?"

Her words stoke the embers of my jealousy. I should've known she wouldn't thank me for stepping in, but I didn't expect this.

"He was taking advantage of you. He was sober and you can hardly stand up."

She attempts to stand straighter to disprove my point, but fails miserably as her shoulders involuntarily slump and her spine curves.

"Who I have sex with is none of your business, Nico fucking Hawkston." Her finger presses against my pec with each word of my name.

Before she can poke me again, I grab her wrist and she turns those big brown eyes up to meet mine. "You can thank me in the morning when you come to your senses."

She snatches her arm from my grip. "Fuck you." Then she stumbles into the bathroom and slams the door.

I wait outside, wondering if she's drunk enough to throw up. The bathroom is silent, then water begins to run.

"Kate? Do you need any help?"

"Only if you want to get in the tub with me."

She's running a bath?

"You can't bathe now. You're too drunk. You'll drown in there."

"Oh, fuck off, Nico," she says, but her tone is soft. Softer still when she adds, "Go away. I don't want you here. I hate you. I *need* to hate you."

She needs to hate me?

I press the door open slowly so she has time to object if she doesn't want me coming in, but she says nothing. She's sitting on the edge of the bath, fully clothed, her knees together. She turns off the bathwater and looks up at me through a curtain of dark hair.

"I'm not going anywhere," I tell her. "You're not well."

Scowling, she replies, "God, why do you have to be so..." Her words tail off as she waves a drunken hand at me.

I brace for her usual abuse. "So what?"

"So damn gorgeous." She breathes the words like a secret, and a curious warmth fills my chest. I've lost count of how many times someone has complimented my appearance, but this one hits differently. I want to tell her she could have me if she wanted, or that she too is gorgeous, but instead I settle for staring at her.

There's an innocence to her wide gaze that's absent in sobriety, and I'm reminded of how she used to look at me back when she was a teenager. But I'm simultaneously saddened by the fact she's so inebriated that her words and actions tonight mean very little. This isn't a shared experience we'll both remember. For Kate, this is a blackout she won't recall.

I step towards her, the soles of my leather shoes creaking against the tile floor. "How did you get this drunk? Did you eat anything?"

She shakes her head. "I was working late. Remember? And then... free drinks." She shrugs and drags a hand through her long, dark hair. Her fingers get stuck in the tangles and she glances up, catching sight of herself in the mirror. She dances her fingertips over her face as she stares at her reflection. "Shit," she mutters. "I look horrendous."

"You always look good."

Her eyes flash at me before she looks away, her hand dropping from her face to the edge of the bath, fingers curling around it tightly. "I'm really not that drunk. I can only see one of you." She closes one eye, which looks much harder to perform than it should. "I could definitely have sex like this."

I don't know if it's an observation, a joke or a suggestion. I don't want to think about it too hard, but the words alone are enough to have inappropriate images springing up in my mind.

I need to get out of here. If I have to hear Kate mention sex one more time, I'll fucking lose it.

"You should go to bed," I say, taking quick steps to the door. "Get some sleep."

"Nico..." Her tone is sultry, if a little slurred, and she lets my name dangle like an invitation. A flare of warning, sweetened at the edges by temptation, burns in the pit of my stomach as I glance over my shoulder.

"Yes?"

She flutters her eyes. "You owe me."

"Owe you what?"

"Sex."

The word knocks my heart off beat.

"And alcohol makes me horny."

I blink. *What the fuck?* I must look confused because she adds, "Will you sleep with me?"

Before I can answer, she slides the little silky shorts down to the floor and kicks them aside, leaving her in only black underwear and the skimpy green top.

I can't breathe. Toned legs, smooth skin, thighs slightly parted. My gaze runs up the length of them, coming to rest at the lace of her panties nestled at the top. I'm pretty sure I can see right through them.

My dick swells while every other part of me seizes. Her body is so fuckable. I want to bend her over the bath and pound into her until she screams my name.

I've known this woman her whole life, but she has never spoken to me like this. *Never*. Not even the incident in the hot tub comes close. Then, she was an insecure teenager who didn't know the power of her body. But now... She fucking *knows*.

Kate reaches up to tease at the strap of her top, sliding it down her arm.

"Kate…" My voice tails off. I mean it as a warning, but clearly miss the mark because she smiles as she continues undressing.

My world shrinks to this one woman, this one moment. Her movement is painfully slow, or maybe it's my distorted perception of time. But one thing I do know; in seconds her breasts are going to fall out, and if that happens I don't know what the fuck I'm going to do. I don't trust myself to resist whatever's coming next.

A host of thoughts crash through my mind. What if it wasn't me standing here? What if it was someone else? Someone who would take advantage of how drunk and vulnerable she is right now?

How close was she to going home with someone else? Fucking someone else?

Fire scorches through me, blistering my insides, spreading tendrils of hot flames through my arms and legs. My grasp on my control is so slim that I make the only decision I can. The only one that won't kill me in the morning.

I close the space between us, breathing hard as I tower over her. "Stop. Keep your fucking clothes on." The words are harsh, the tone even more so.

Shock blooms in Kate's eyes. Her shoulders curl in, her head lowers, hands cupping her nearly exposed breasts. She's a vision of shame and humiliation and I'm so fucking sorry I've done it, but it's better this than anything else.

I scan the room, grab a bathrobe from a hook on the back of the door, and give it to her. She awkwardly slips into it, tying it tight around herself while she keeps her gaze on the floor.

"Go to bed." My voice is hard; I wish I could do this with kindness, but I can't. It could slide too easily into something else, and I refuse to do that. Better she thinks I'm angry.

She walks out in front of me, heading towards the enormous emperor sized bed. She stops at the foot of it but doesn't get in.

I'm right behind her when she says, "You should go."

"Get into bed, Kate. I want to make sure you're safe."

She spins to face me, our bodies inches apart. "I'm safe. I'm fine. I can see myself to bed." When I don't move, she puts her hands on the belt of the dressing gown and begins to loosen it. "I'm going to take off all my clothes and go to sleep. Naked, Nico. I'm going to be naked. And seeing as that's such a problem for you, you should fuck off."

Her abrasive words smash my resolve and searing heat burns in my chest. I don't know if it's anger or desire, but Kate's eyes flash with recognition.

I lean in and ghost my mouth against her ear. "What is it you want? To drive me to distraction so I'll fuck you?"

Her lips part, hot breath hitting my jaw, causing a shiver to trip down my spine.

"Nico..."

The breathless way she says my name sounds like *yes*, but also like *please don't*. I can't decipher how she feels, and I remind myself how drunk she is. I draw back. "Fuck. Don't answer that. Go to bed. Please, Kate. Go to bed."

The plea hangs in the air like a poison we're too afraid to inhale. Neither of us moves for longer than I care to count.

"Okay," she whispers. Submissive. Her robe falls slightly open, revealing the curve of a breast beneath.

We share a few more tangled breaths as we come down from whatever fucking high we're on.

"Are you going to stay?" She sounds insecure, and there is none of her earlier teasing lilt in the question.

I back up, taking a few steps away from her while I run a hand through my hair to calm the fuck down. "Yes. I'll get you a bottle of water and some painkillers, then I'll sleep in the other room. I'll be there if you need me."

"Okay."

I walk towards the sitting room.

"Hey, Nico?"

I spin back to face her. "Yeah?"

"Are you going to take this"—she gestures to the enormous penthouse suite—"out of my pay?"

I bite my bottom lip, repressing a smile at the concern on her face. "No. This is all on me."

I wake early the next morning, having slept in my suit on the sofa. My body aches all over and I'm not nearly as well rested as I would like to be. I stayed awake most of the night to make sure Kate didn't throw up and choke on her own vomit.

I pad back into the bedroom. She's sleeping quietly, her clothes lying in a crumpled heap on the floor.

Temptation twists in my chest at the idea she's completely naked beneath the sheets. She's so vulnerable. Anything could have happened last night.

I stare at her beautiful face, her tangled hair spread over the pillow. I've imagined seeing her like this so many times, but I had no idea that the sight would cause a crushing squeeze around my heart. She's right here, and yet I can't have her.

I take another bottle of water from the minibar, intending to replace the now empty one I put on her bedside table last night. She'll have a terrible hangover when she wakes.

She rustles in the sheets, pulling an arm out of the covers. Her hand hangs over the edge of the bed, and something drops from her fingers, landing at my feet.

I bend to pick it up, but before I touch it, I know exactly what it is.

It's her fucking driver's license.

15

KATE

My head is pounding like a ten-inch drum, with a skin that's too tight and might split at the next beat. This is the worst hangover I've had in months, if not years.

My mouth is parched, my tongue fuzzy like it's wearing a winter glove. I'm damp and sweaty, and the sheets cling all over. Sheets that are so soft... too soft.

These aren't my sheets. *Where am I?*

Patches of memory float into my awareness. The club, losing sight of Elly and Marie, tequila shots bought by some guy I didn't know, Michael Drayton pinning me against the wall, and then...Nico.

Nico! My body flushes hot. And that's saying something because with this hangover I'm already running well over a healthy temperature.

"Oh, God," I mumble, head in hands, as more sketchy memories of Nico shift in my mind. His scent, the warmth of his body, the strength of his arms as he carried me. All the good memories shatter as his words splinter the remains of my brain.

Stop. Keep your fucking clothes on.

What is it you want? To drive me to distraction so I'll fuck you?

Go to bed. Please, Kate. Go to bed.

"Oh, my God," I wail again, as my drunken attempt to stick my lips on his flashes across my mental screen. Did I lick his finger too?

Oh, fuck. This is truly messed up.

The rush of shame is so violent I feel immediately nauseous. I tried to seduce Nico Hawkston last night, and he shot me down so hard I'm surprised I'm still alive.

What the fuck was I thinking? Clearly, I wasn't. I don't know how I'll survive this. Maybe my hangover will kill me, because if it doesn't the humiliation will.

Oh, my God. The hotel. The Penthouse.

Will you sleep with me, Nico?

Fuck. Is he still here?

I sit up, trying to ignore the pounding in my dehydrated brain, and clutch the bedsheets against me. I hold my breath, listening for any sign that someone else is in the suite. The other side of the bed is unrumpled, the sheets smooth and tucked in, so if Nico stayed, he didn't sleep in here with me.

I peer beneath the covers. Yup. I'm naked. Completely naked. At what point did I take off my clothes? Where are they?

I scan the room, but there's no sign of them. All I see is a thick white bathrobe draped over a nearby chair. A vague recollection of Nico putting the robe around my shoulders slips between the pounding of my headache.

"Nico?"

Silence.

I'm not taking any chances. I reach out of the bed and grab the robe, hauling it off the chair, which falls sideways with a bang.

I wait, but there's no response. No concerned Nico appearing from the other room. I slide into the dressing gown, intending to head towards the bathroom, when I notice a note on the table by the window.

Kate,
Gone to a meeting. Don't go anywhere. I'll be back before ten.
Nico.
P.S. Found your driver's license.

My license sits right next to his note. I pick it up and another wave of nausea rushes over me as the shameful memory bursts open: pretending not to have it so he couldn't send me home and then sleeping with it in my hand so he wouldn't know.

Fuck, fuck, fuck. Drunken me is a complete idiot.

There is no way I am waiting here for Nico to come back. Where the hell are my clothes?

A knock at the door makes me jump out of my skin. I pull the robe tighter and open the door just a crack. There's a man in Hawkston Hotel uniform outside with a trolley.

"Room service," he says. I must look completely nonplussed because he adds, "Breakfast."

I open the door wider and he pushes the trolley in, setting out an entire spread of food and a steaming pot of coffee on the table.

Then he hands me a bag and I'm too stunned to do anything but cling to it. Inside is my outfit from last night, fully dry cleaned, right down to the black panties I was wearing.

I want to die.

Could this situation be any more humiliating? I wait until the attendant is gone, then put the clothes on as fast as I can, stuff a pastry in my mouth, and down a scalding cup of coffee that burns my tongue. I need to get the fuck out of here.

But I have no shoes. I lost my favourite Erica Lefroy's. *Shit*. No time to mourn them. I'll think about it later.

The only thing I can use instead is the free bathroom slippers. White slip-ons with exposed toes and a grey HH for Hawkston Hotels embroidered across the front, beneath a silver hawk, wings spread wide in its bid for freedom.

And then I make my own dash for freedom, flip-flopping down the corridor, into the lift, and down to the lobby. Nothing says walk-of-shame like sequins, hot pants and hotel slippers. The plastic soles squeak as I walk across the marble floor.

I'm halfway to the exit, heart-thumping like I'm escaping a million dollar heist, when—

"Miss Lansen?"

I freeze. A man approaches, dressed in a black suit and flat cap. I've never seen him before. Am I about to be arrested for stealing the hotel slippers? They're free, aren't they?

I shift awkwardly on the spot and the slippers give an almighty squeal. The man's gaze dips to my feet, his brow lightly furrowing. *Damn it.*

"Yes?" I ask, striving for casual.

"Your car is outside," he announces.

"My car?"

"Mr. Hawkston said to expect you. Gave me your address. I'm here to take you home."

Fuck. My. Life.

I unlock the front door of the flat to find Elly and Marie staring at each other over their coffees, seated on either side of the kitchen table.

They both turn to look at me.

"No guesses where you spent the night," Marie says, looking pointedly at the hotel slippers.

"What happened?" Elly asks with a smirk. "Everyone saw Nico punch Michael Drayton in the face. And carry you up the stairs."

"Lucky it was a private party," Marie adds. "Otherwise you'd have been all over the tabloids this morning."

"Oh, my God," I mutter, as the last futile hope that I'd dreamt the whole thing collapses around me like a dry sandcastle. "Why didn't you do something?"

"I would have, but I was so drunk I didn't even know I had hands," Elly explains, waving said hands like they're new discoveries. "Sorry. Besides, Nico looked like he had it under control."

"So... what happened?" Marie asks, and the two of them sit there staring at me, looking hungover as hell, waiting for an explanation. I can't tell them all the details. Even if I wanted to, I'm not sure I'd be able to form the words. Embarrassment would be the glue that would stick my lips together and seal my throat.

I settle for the least of my offences. "I tried to kiss him."

"I thought you hated him?" Marie reminds me.

Elly perks up. "She doesn't hate him. She just thinks she hates him because she's too frightened to admit she's still obsessed with him." Elly fixes her attention on me. "Did he kiss you back?"

I shake my head. "No."

"Aww. Babes. I'd have kissed you back."

I roll my eyes, which makes the sockets ache. "Thanks."

"Where did Nico Hawkston come from anyway?" Marie says. "One minute you were getting it on with Michael, the next Nico appears like a fucking tornado of masculinity, determined to raze the place to the ground." She tilts her head to one side, pouting her lower lip. "It was kinda hot."

My head pounds as I struggle to comprehend what she's saying. I have no idea where Nico came from last night. He was suddenly there, pushing people around and dragging me away.

"He owns the club," I explain.

"Ah," muses Marie. "He looked pretty chummy with Amy Moritz too. I saw her climb right over the table to give him a hug."

I drop my head in my hands. "I want to crawl under my bed and die."

"Except you can't," Marie says. "Because it's your mum's summer drinks party tomorrow." Marie points to the calendar on the wall behind her where I've scrawled 'MUM PARTY' in red pen. I groan. I'd forgotten about the glamorous party she throws at the Surrey house every year. If I miss it, she'll never let me forget it. I *have* to go. "Shit."

"And your annual"—Elly makes finger quotes—"'family dinner' tonight." She grins, taking an infuriating delight in my misery.

"You can't drive like this," Marie says. "I won't allow it."

"I can. I'm fine. I drove hungover in my early twenties all the time."

"I bet you were over the limit then too," Marie continues. "But now that we're all responsible adults—"

Elly giggles, cutting Marie off, and at the same moment, my phone rings.

The contact *Massively Hot Nico* flashes on the screen.

My body goes hot, then numb, then pins and needles prickle me all over. I didn't even realise I still had his number. That's how I saved it in there a decade ago. I stare at the phone like it's about to explode.

"Does that say what I think it does?" Marie asks, staring at the screen.

"Yes," I say. "Don't answer it."

Elly presses the button to answer the call, quickly putting it on speaker before leaving the handset in the middle of the table.

"Bitch," I mouth.

"Kate?" Nico's voice is so cold I'm surprised frost doesn't spread across the kitchen table.

If he didn't hate me before, he does now.

I cover my face with my hands, speaking between my fingers. "I'm here."

"I'll pick you up at four."

"What?"

"You won't be safe to drive to Surrey."

He's coming? It's predictable, but my mind hadn't gone there. Before Dad died, Nico always came to our family events. And Mum was so taken with him at Jack's birthday party that I'm not surprised she invited him. Just like old times.

Marie is making eyes at the phone and nodding in agreement.

I groan. "I'll go tomorrow."

"Then you'll miss the family dinner tonight," he counters.

I close my eyes, feeling the headache pound behind them.

"Mum won't care," I tell him.

Nico says nothing; he knows she'll care.

His silence breaks me. "I'll take the train," I argue.

"And risk vomiting all over public transport?"

"I'm not going to be sick."

"Good. Then you can come in my car. I'll be there at 4 pm. Don't make me wait."

He hangs up, and all three of us sit in silence for a few moments.

"I think he cares about you," Elly says, her face a vision of studied sincerity.

To my annoyance, hope is soaring like a drug in my system. *Pathetic.*

Marie shoots Elly a *don't-be-an-idiot* look. "Ooh yeah. He sounded all warm and cuddly."

Marie's sarcasm neutralises that pesky hope pretty quick. Although, there is one thing that's still bothering me about last night. I glance between my friends and say, "Why do you think he hit Michael Drayton?"

"Duh," Elly says, slapping her hand across her forehead. "Because Michael was trying to make out with you. Green-eyed-monster. JELL-OH-SEE."

This is exactly the response I wanted, but I don't dare cling to it because it can't be true. I couldn't really make a man like Nico jealous, could I? "What? No..."

"Yes. That whole unrequited crush thing you had going on as a teenager? Not so unrequited now, eh?" Elly grins and strums her hands on the table like a drum roll.

There's a riot happening inside my chest. My lips itch to split into a smile, but it would reveal too much so I force them into a straight line and say, "Hmm. It's weird, and more than a little controlling."

Marie shrugs. "It's a bit weird, but probably a good thing he stepped in. You were a mess. I guarantee you'd have regretted it."

"And who cares if he's controlling? Mmm, mmm," Elly murmurs, licking her lips suggestively. "He's still unbelievably hot. He can control me any day."

At 4 pm, I'm outside the flat with my overnight bag. It's warm, so I'm in a t-shirt, faded jeans that are ripped at the knee and a pair of battered old trainers. I'm trying to look like I don't care, but I'm not sure even my casual attire is enough to hide the fact that I do. A lot.

Nico's car rolls up. It's a bottle-green Aston Martin. I don't know much about cars, but this one is special. And it's spotless. I'm betting Nico doesn't clean it himself.

He pulls up beside me and lowers the window, resting his forearm on the ledge.

He looks so handsome, so suave, that the scene looks like a cut-out from a luxury car magazine.

What was I thinking, making a move on a man like this? It was only ever going to end in my complete and utter humiliation. I want to run, but I force myself to stay put. The car ride's not long. A little over an hour. I can do this.

Lowering his sunglasses, Nico gives me the once over, his gaze lingering on my feet before roving upwards again. It's so invasive, I might as well be standing naked on the pavement.

This man sent my panties to dry-cleaning.

Crap. There is no way I'm recovering from this anytime soon.

He holds a box of painkillers out to me, letting it dangle between his index and middle fingers.

"What's this?" I ask, nodding at the packet.

"Thought you'd appreciate them more than flowers." I cringe under the weight of sarcasm in his tone. I'm tempted to tell him to shove his condescending gift up his butt crack, but with a flick of his fingers the packet flies towards me and every remaining brain cell I have is occupied with trying to catch it. Somehow, my fingers clutch around the box in midair.

"How are you feeling?" he asks, opening a water bottle and handing it out the window to me.

I shake my head. "I'm pumped full of painkillers already, but thank you, for—"

"Good." He recaps the bottle and gets out of the car, taking my bag from me and putting it in the boot.

"Thank you for this," I say, indicating the box of pills, determined not to be silenced by his abruptness. "And for breakfast. And my dry-cleaning. And the driver to take me home."

This gratitude list is longer than I realised. I'm about to add '*thank you for saving me from having stupid drunken sex with a man I don't know*,' or something to that effect when Nico slams the boot closed.

"You really shouldn't drink that much," he tells me. "Anything could have happened."

His tone irritates the hell out of me, but he might have a point. In fact, given how horribly hungover I am and how many pockets of memory blackout I have from last night, he *definitely* has a point, but I won't let him scold me like a kid.

"I'm old enough to take care of myself."

"I beg to differ."

I exhale sharply. "I'm not getting in this car if you're going to spend the entire journey treating me like an errant teenager."

Nico's eyebrow slides upwards, disapproval pulsing off him, and his words from last night crash into my mind.

Stop. Keep your fucking clothes on.

My memories might be blurry, but I definitely remember the fury in his eyes when he said that. In all the time I've known Nico Hawkston, I've never seen him look so angry.

I give an involuntary shudder and decide I don't want to piss him off, so when he opens the passenger door for me, I get in without comment. Nico walks round to the driver's side and takes his seat.

With the doors closed, the car feels too small. Nico's energy spills out everywhere, and even though he's not looking at me, let alone touching me, somehow it feels like he is. Invisible fingers stroke my skin, raising tiny hairs and sending shivers down the back of my neck. Even my toes tingle.

I feel him *everywhere*.

Nico keeps his eyes on the road and we say nothing as he drives too fast through London's narrow residential streets, but I don't feel unsafe for a second. His unwavering focus has an allure I wasn't expecting, and each time he shifts the gear stick, the movement is so natural, so smooth, so *powerful*, that it kindles heat between my legs.

His sleeves are rolled to the elbow, and I get the bizarre urge to run my fingers down the veins on his arms, following their path over the back of his hands and between his knuckles. There's no sign that he hit someone last night. He must know exactly how to throw a punch.

Butterflies dance in my stomach at the thought.

I'm so fucked.

Closing my eyes, I let my head fall against the headrest. No point denying it. I'm just as attracted to him now as I was when I was a teenager, and in the interim, my desires have taken on a far more libidinous edge.

A thick silence falls between us, and for a while, I watch the streets outside flash by. Finally, I summon the courage to address the issue that's been bothering me. "I can't believe you hit Michael Drayton."

Nico glances at me. "Is there a question in there?"

My heart is thumping uncomfortably. "Why did you do it?"

I scan Nico's face, but there's no sign he's remotely unsettled by this line of interrogation.

"He was assaulting you."

"No, he wasn't."

"Hmm. My mistake," he says casually, like hitting an A-list celebrity is no big deal, but his fingers clench a little harder around the steering wheel.

"And taking me to the penthouse?"

He shifts gear, not taking his eyes off the road as we slip onto the motorway. He slides through traffic to the fast lane. "You fell asleep. I couldn't ask you where you lived."

"You could have called Jack."

He nods without looking at me. "Next time I'll do that. Or—" He pauses so long that a nasty feeling bubbles up in the pit of my stomach. If we weren't travelling eighty miles an hour down the motorway, I'd be tempted to open my door and roll out of the car. "You could have told me your address."

My chest is tight and hot all at once; there's no way I can take a breath because my lungs have solidified.

"Couldn't remember it," I mumble, so quietly that I barely hear myself.

"Kate," Nico purrs, and the sound of my name on his tongue makes me ache. When was the last time he used my nickname? I miss the intimacy. *Little K* was his, and Kate is everyone's. "No one forgets their address. Even when you're so drunk you can't remember your own fucking name, you always get home."

I could sit here and die of embarrassment, like I've been doing every second of the day since I woke up, or I can address this head on. Maybe I'm still drunk, because I pick the latter option. "What exactly are you implying? That I deliberately pretended not to remember where I lived so that we had to share a hotel room?"

A muscle ticks in his jaw, and he taps the steering wheel with his index finger.

Shit. I don't know why raising this seemed like a good idea.

"Yes," Nico says.

The word condenses behind my breastbone. I guess we're not messing around anymore.

I cross my arms. "Well, I think you hit Michael Drayton because you didn't want him to kiss me. And you know what, Nico? You don't own me. You don't get to decide who I hook up with."

"I know that."

"So why then? Because I think you didn't want to have to watch while I hooked up with someone else. Someone who wasn't you. Am I right?"

His entire face hardens as he stares at the road, lending a dangerous—*sexy*—edge to his handsome profile.

I want him to say yes. My entire body wants him to say yes.

He takes a moment to answer, making me wonder if he's thinking up an excuse. "No. You're not right. I hit him because you were drunk and he was sober and he fucking knew it too. He was taking advantage. I couldn't stand by and let that happen."

"I had it under control," I argue, even though it's a bare-faced lie. Control was so far out of my reach last night that I didn't know what the fuck I was doing.

"So shitty drunk sex with a movie star you've never met before was what you wanted last night? That was the aim? The goal?" Nico's voice is calm, his delivery casual, but his words are carefully launched grenades and even though I know what he's doing, I explode, right on cue.

"Fuck you, Nico. Like you've never had casual sex with someone famous. Who the hell do you think you are? Some kind of vigilante white knight who saves women from making mistakes when they've had one too many tequila shots? Because if that's the case, turn the car around right now and go back to London because there are thousands of women who are gonna need your help tonight."

The car shoots forward with shocking speed as he shifts lanes, and I'm jerked back in my seat.

Fuck. I've really roused the beast now.

A displeased rumble sounds in Nico's throat. "What's with the aggression, Kate?"

For a split second, I don't know the answer. Then it roars to life and I can't help but give it voice. "I'm never going to forgive you for what you did to Dad. To Lansen. You can show up at Mum's and play the dutiful godson, or whatever the hell this is, but it will never be the same. When you killed that deal, you killed him, too."

"You don't know what you're talking about."

"Then explain it to me."

His nostrils flare as he inhales, like he's battling for control.

"You can't, can you?" I argue. "You're a ruthless businessman who only cares about your bottom line."

He slams the heel of his hand on the wheel with a bang that makes me jump. "Of course, I care about the bottom line!"

I gasp, bite my lip, and shrink into my seat. I've never heard him raise his voice before.

"But it's not just about me," he continues. "It's about my family. The company. The shareholders, the board of directors. The thousands of people we employ all over the world. Of course, I fucking care about my business. That deal no longer made sense. Now it does."

Nico's phone rings through the speaker system, slicing through the tension. Seb's name flashes up. Nico curses under his breath and answers, but before he can say a word, Seb's voice blasts out.

"You broke Michael Drayton's nose. His lawyer's been on the phone. They'll have to delay filming—"

"Make it go away," Nico barks. "I don't give a shit what it costs."

Seb tuts. "There are photos. Of you. Michael. Kate."

"Fuck," Nico curses under his breath. "Get Elliot on it."

"I already called him. He fixed it this morning. They're gone."

"Why are you calling me then?"

"To remind you that you're a fucking idiot. Have a great weekend."

The line goes dead.

Nico looks so furious that for a while I don't dare speak. Then, because I'm far too nosy to hold my tongue, I ask, "Who's Elliot?"

Nico rolls his lips. "He cleans stuff up for us. There's nothing to worry about. It'll be like last night never happened."

Like it never happened. Didn't I say something like that last night? Uncomfortable memories tug at my mind, but I can't put them together.

"That's good." I sit back in my seat, but then a thought occurs to me and I lean forward again, turning to stare at Nico. "Hold on. You have a fixer who sorts all kinds of crap out for you, but you couldn't get hold of my address last night?"

Checkmate.

My words hover in the air, as close to a direct accusation as I dare to get right now. A few moments of silence pass and then Nico mutters something under his breath that I can't make out.

We drive the rest of the way in silence.

It's only when we finally draw up outside my family home, and we both get out of the car, that the tension in my abdomen releases.

Nico opens the boot, hands me my bag, and lifts his own out, as well as several boxes I assume are gifts for Mum, which he tucks under his arm.

He clicks the boot closed and we turn at the same moment, colliding in an explosion of bags and boxes.

"Shit," he mutters, as a box falls from his pile.

The lid topples off and the contents slide halfway out. A shoe. A woman's shoe.

What?

My heartbeat ramps up. *That's not just any shoe.*

It's a pair of shoes, identical to the ones I lost last night. *Erica Lefroy's.* It can't be a coincidence. The side of the box reveals that they're my size.

But my shoes were last season's exclusive editions. I bought them in the winter sale, stored them for six months and cracked them out this summer. I'd only worn them a couple of times. *How the hell did he source another pair?*

My skin buzzes, coming alive with an emotion I can't name. I look up, but Nico's frowning at the lone shoe like he's never seen it before.

"What's that?" I ask.

He shifts the other parcels in his arms, a small crease forming between his brows. "That's for you."

As if it needs no further explanation, he steps over the box and walks straight towards the house.

16
NICO

My mind spins as I walk away from Kate. I wasn't ready to show her the shoes. I'm not sure I fully intended to do it at all. Erica already thought it was weird that I was desperate to get my hands on a pair at short notice, so I can't imagine what Kate's thinking.

Not my proudest moment either, dropping them on the gravel and stepping over them, leaving Kate to pick them up. In my defense, my hands were full, and hers were empty.

I decide to put the incident out of mind; no point worrying about it, or the way Kate looked at that shoe like it was a bomb that was about to detonate in her face.

I stand a little straighter as I head towards the Lansen family home, like my height might ward off Kate's inquisitive gaze, which I'm pretty sure is still burning holes in the back of my shirt.

This place holds a lot of pleasant memories for me. Due to our fathers' close friendship, Seb, Matt and I were over here often, but I came more than the others because I'm Jack's contemporary. We went to boarding school together, and that bond is nearly as unshakable as the one between me and my brothers.

The house itself is a little tired, but it's still impressive in the way most large commuter homes in the Home Counties are. It's red brick, with a 1930s arts and crafts feel to it; terracotta tiles decorate the walls like fish scales beneath the windows. The garden must be at least five acres, and there's a pool and tennis court in the back, and the hot tub... well, that holds one of my more enduring memories.

Mrs. Lansen greets me at the door like a long-lost son. She kisses me on both cheeks, blushing as I put the pile of gifts down on the hall table.

"Mrs. Lansen," I say. "Thank you for having me. It's been a long time."

"Debbie. Call me Debbie. My God, you get better looking every time I see you." She beams. "Just like your father. You know, if I hadn't met Gerard first, I'd have been all over your father like a rash." She lets out a girlish giggle, and I force myself to smile politely. "Don't stay away so long next time."

"I don't intend to," I reply.

Curtis, Mrs. Lansen's new partner whom I recognise from Jack's party, bounds towards me from the depths of the hallway, one hand extended. His hair is still lank and a little greasy. I suspect it's part of his look, but I doubt he's washed it since I last saw him. He's even younger than I originally thought; possibly my age or thereabouts.

"The famous Nico Hawkston." He grips my hand and his mouth splits into the type of grin I've seen many times before. When people want something from me, or think I can get them somewhere in the world, that same seedy smile appears. I repress a shudder. "I've heard so many great things about you, man. What a fucking honour."

"How do you do?" I say, trying to extricate my hand from Curtis' warm and over-enthusiastic grip. He notices my pull-back, glances at our hands, then chuckles and releases his hold.

"Sorry, mate," he says, bumping my arm with a fist. "Don't often get a chance to shake the hand of a bonafide billionaire."

Bloody hell, Debbie Lansen is dating a man-child.

Kate appears behind me, and Mrs. Lansen acknowledges her with the barest flick of her gaze before fixing on me. "You brought Kate?" She stands on tiptoes to peer beyond us to the driveway. "Oh, that car. What a fancy set of wheels you have, Nico." She lightly slaps my arm. "I dare say it's not the only one you have, is it?"

"It's not," I agree.

She laughs. "A car for every day of the week, I imagine? Well, it was very kind of you to drive Kate down. What a gent you are." She gives me a grateful smile before turning to her daughter. The smile fades as she runs her gaze down to Kate's feet. "What are those shoes you're wearing?"

Kate stares down at her worn out trainers. "What's wrong with them?"

Debbie huffs. "They look awful. I hope you're not intending to wear them tomorrow."

"Of course not."

"Oh, good." Debbie puts a hand on her heart, relief pouring off her. "What about those wonderful, sparkly ones you love?"

Kate goes rigid, like she's bracing for an attack. "I lost those—"

"Lost your shoes? Goodness, how does one lose one's shoes?" Mrs. Lansen glances over her shoulder at Curtis. "Did you hear that? Kate lost her shoes! Never grew up, this child."

"Mum, will you stop? It's not a big deal. I have other shoes." She indicates the shoe box in her hand and a warming sensation spreads through my body.

Kate stares up at me, and in her deep brown eyes I can see the question, *Why did you do this*?

My brows pinch together. *I don't know why, Kate. I really don't.*

Mrs. Lansen frowns, then shakes her head and mutters, "Can't believe you lost your shoes." Then she forgets about Kate and flaps her arms to urge us further inside. "Come in, come in. Let's not stand in the doorway. Jack's already in the pool. The weather's glorious. I hope it holds for tomorrow."

Kate doesn't follow, but stands in the hall, glancing at the walls. "Where are the paintings?"

"What, dear?" says Mrs. Lansen, her voice strained. She knows exactly what Kate's talking about.

"Dad's paintings. The art collection. Where is it?" Kate points at the grey rectangles of grime on the walls—obvious vacancies where pictures have vanished.

Kate trots down the hall, poking her head from room to room. "Where are they all?"

Mrs. Lansen taps her temple. "Oh, the art. Curtis has a fabulous art collection, which is being delivered tomorrow, before the party. We had to clear space for it, so we put your father's stuff in storage."

Kate stills, a stunned look on her face. "All of it?"

"Yes, all. It's about time for a change. Some of those pieces had been on the wall for thirty years. Curtis arranged everything. Didn't you, dear?" Curtis gives a smarmy smile, pleased with himself. "We had the men take them away yesterday."

"You didn't think to ask me if I wanted any of them?"

"Oh, Kate, don't be silly." Mrs. Lansen's mouth stretches into a condescending smile. "What would you want with any of those old paintings? You couldn't hang any of them in your flat. It's too small. And what with the insurance costs, it wouldn't be worth it. They're much better in storage. Maybe when you buy yourself a house, we can talk about it."

"What about Jack?" Kate asks.

"What about me?" Jack strides down the hall, chest bare and nothing but a sun-bleached beach towel wrapped around his waist, his hair slicked back. Ever the exhibitionist.

"Didn't you want any of Dad's art collection?" Kate asks him.

"Oh, Mum did ask me—"

"When? When did she ask you?" Her voice wavers, like she's starting to panic.

Jack scratches his head. "Maybe two weeks ago? I thought about it, but I'm redecorating and I'd only have to store them." Jack narrows his eyes at Kate, only now noticing the energy of the moment he's intruded upon. His eyes flick to his mother and back to Kate, his voice lower when he says, "Didn't she mention it to you?"

This conversation is increasingly feeling like one I shouldn't be witnessing, but I can't take my gaze off Kate.

She shakes her head and mutters under her breath before focusing on her mother. "What about my art?"

"Your art? What art?" Mrs. Lansen's confused gaze slides to the ceiling, then snaps back. "Do you mean that portrait you did of your father before he died?" A spurt of laughter pops out. "I don't think you could call that art, sweetheart. It's in your father's study, along with all your other doodles. I was going to let you see if there was anything you wanted to keep, otherwise, I'll send it to the skip on Monday."

Kate's shoulders tighten; the motion is slight and you wouldn't notice unless you were really paying attention. I shouldn't fucking notice, but I do.

"Right." Kate draws out the word, as if she's struggling to process her mother's callous comments. "You're going to throw it all away?"

Mrs. Lansen laughs. "Oh Kate, we can't keep everything. The place is cluttered enough as it is. I have to prioritise to keep things under control here. If I kept every scrap of paper, I'd be swamped."

"Yeah. Okay," Kate mutters, but there's a flash of hurt in her eyes so visceral that I feel it like a slash across my chest.

"Wonderful," Mrs. Lansen says. "Let's have a drink. Gin and tonics on the terrace?"

There are mumbles of agreement as we traipse towards the back of the house, but Kate isn't moving.

"I'll be there in a minute," she says, lifting her bag and turning towards the stairs. "I want to unpack."

I stare as Kate mounts the steps. The staircase turns halfway up, and she disappears out of sight.

Curtis and Mrs. Lansen are already heading out towards the pool. She's leaning into him, her temple resting on his shoulder, his arm around her waist. The woman is so self-involved she probably didn't notice Kate's distress.

Fuck this. I can't wait here and ignore it.

I'm about to follow Kate when a hand lands on my shoulder. "She's touchy about Dad's stuff," Jack tells me. "Give her a moment. She'll be all right later, and if she's not, I'll talk to her. She always finds it tough to be here. You know, ever since Dad died." A melancholy expression flits across Jack's face, his gaze drifting before he refocuses on me. "Come and have a swim. The water's perfect."

"We only just got here. I'm not going to let Kate stew up there. I'll bring her back down."

Jack's hand slides slowly off my shoulder and he raises an eyebrow, causing my heart to double-skip. Is he reading something into my concern? But the expression disappears, replaced with something altogether more relaxed and my rib cage drops two inches.

"Give it a go," he says. "I'll see you outside."

Jack departs, and I bolt up the stairs after Kate. She must hear me, but she doesn't turn. She's halfway to her bedroom when I grab her hand and pull her back towards me.

She snatches her fingers out of my grip. "What do you want?"

I step back. "I know you're upset."

She eyes me cautiously. I expect some snarky comment about my powers of observation, but she says simply, "I'm fine."

I don't buy it for a second. "Okay. Come back downstairs then."

Her throat bobs, and she blinks for an extended moment. *Shit.* She looks like she's about to dissolve. I want to offer comfort, but I hold back, unsure if touching her is a good idea.

"Is it the art?" I say quickly. "Your Dad's stuff?"

A little broken sound cracks from her lips as she drops her bag to the floor and covers rheumy eyes with her hand. "Can you not look at me?"

"I don't give a shit if you're going to cry."

She splutters a laugh. "So glad you're here."

"I didn't mean it like that." I smile and she smiles back, wiping her eyes, and the moment feels... tentative. Like the tiniest of shifts between us.

"Maybe I'm overreacting," she says. "But sometimes I feel like I'm the only one who cares that he's gone."

"You know that's not true."

She shrugs. "Maybe. I still feel alone in it, though."

Her gaze holds a thousand unspoken words, and even though I don't know what any of them are, they tug at my gut. I have no idea if my presence helps. Maybe I'm making it worse. A stillness creeps into the space between us.

"You're not alone," I tell her honestly. "I'm here."

"God, of all the people..." She gives a half-hearted laugh. "It has to be you."

Something twinges in my chest. "Sorry."

She sighs. "Mum didn't even ask me if I wanted anything. She just... got rid of it all."

"It's not gone. It's in storage. I'm sure we could get something out if you wanted. We could find out where they are; swing by the unit—"

"Why do you keep saying 'we'? This has nothing to do with you."

"I didn't..." I let the words fade, unable to express that I hadn't realised I was saying 'we' at all.

In the silence that follows, Kate puffs erratically, causing her breasts to shift under her t-shirt. The motion draws my gaze, and I trace the soft outline of her nipples beneath the fabric. I raise my eyes to her mouth, where agitated breaths draw through full, pink lips.

I want to kiss them, to press my mouth hard against hers. The urge to take her in my arms and fuck the hurt right out of her is all-consuming. Without thinking, I step closer and her scent spins around me, more potent now than it was in the car. Roses and vanilla, sweet and thick, dragging heat up my legs, through my hips.

"Don't," she whispers.

"Don't what?"

"Don't look at me like that."

My insides compress. "Like what?"

"Like I'm another notch you can add to your bedpost."

The air pulses like a heartbeat. "You're not a notch, Kate. You could never be a notch."

A delicate pink blush washes over her cheekbones. "Then what am I?"

Shit. This isn't how this conversation was supposed to go.

"Come back downstairs," I say, holding out my hand. She stares at it. Her fingers twitch like she wants to take it, but she doesn't. "Have a drink. A swim. You can unpack later." I nod at the discarded bag at her feet. "Let's not fight in the stairwell."

Awkward seconds pass, neither of us moving, before she jerks her chin at me. "Why don't you call me Little K anymore?"

"You said you didn't like it."

Kate accepts this explanation without comment and slides her hand into my outstretched one. The contact sends a spark of electricity up my arm. Her fingers are small and warm against mine, and so soft that I never want to let go. I lead her back down the stairs. The silence is crushing as we descend, but when we reach the bottom, she tugs on my hand.

"Nico?"

"Yeah?"

"What's going on?"

"We're going outside to join the others."

"No. That's not what I mean. I mean... between us. What's going on between us?"

My heart thumps rapidly. Despite the colour in her cheeks, Kate brazenly holds my gaze. Her expression is earnest, like she really thinks I might be more qualified than she is to answer the question. As if this situation is some kind of algebraic equation I can easily explain.

It's not, and I can't.

I sigh deeply. "You're Jack's sister. And my employee."

"That's not an answer."

"It's not a lie. But right now, I need a fucking drink."

I try to let go of her hand, but she won't release it. She tugs on it again.

I raise a brow to welcome her question, and it's all the invitation she needs.

"Last night… did you want to sleep with me?"

Fuck, this woman is direct.

This time when I try to slip my hand from hers she lets me. I roll my neck, the tension in my body suddenly unbearable.

"I would never have slept with you last night."

"Why not?"

An image of her, drunk, vulnerable, pushed up against a wall, flashes in my mind. I step closer to her. "Because you were so drunk, you'd have given yourself to anyone."

A harsh gasp sounds from deep in her mouth. We're standing so close the warmth of it hits my skin.

"When you sleep with me," I continue, "it'll be because I'm the only man you want. Because you need me more than anyone else. Because you belong to me. Not because you're drunk and lonely and any man would do. When you're mine, you'll fucking know it."

Her blush deepens. "When?" The word slips from her lips like a whisper I'm not meant to hear.

We're on the edge of a precipice, and I could push us over it with one word, one movement, one kiss.

"If," I say. "Hypothetical."

And with two words, I've hauled us back to safety. Kate's shoulders sink on a hopeless exhale. But whatever disappointment I glimpsed—*thought* I glimpsed—is gone in an instant, replaced by her impenetrable armour.

I clear my throat. "Are we done here?"

She frowns, then nods, her hand sliding from the banister as she steps fully to the ground floor.

"Great," I reply. "Because I really fucking need that drink."

17

KATE

Nico storms ahead of me, not pausing to fix himself a drink. Either he forgot he wanted one, or it was an excuse to get away from me. And he still hasn't given me an unqualified answer. Maybe I need to be clearer next time.

Do you want to fuck me, Nico? Yes or no?

I rub my palms over my face and let out a noise halfway between a groan and a sigh. What the hell am I doing, having whispered conversations with Nico in my mother's darkened hallway? The entire exchange was like a dirty secret and my body vibrates with the aftershocks.

I linger a moment in the kitchen, then follow Nico out to the pool, blinking in the sunlight. Jack's in the water again, and Mum and Curtis are sitting at the outdoor dining table, shaded beneath a yellow parasol. They're holding hands, leaning into one another, whispering and laughing like teenagers in love.

Mum's still wearing her floral summer dress, but Curtis has shed all his clothes except a pair of tiny red Speedos. He's tanned all over, suggesting he's regularly exposing himself in his skimpy attire.

His hands skim up Mum's legs and dance over her upper arms. Long fingers slide around her neck as he pulls her towards him. My stomach clenches and a little bubble of bile rises.

I don't know if I'll ever get used to Mum and her boyfriends, but Curtis strikes me as one of the worst. He's sleazy, conceited, and seems far too comfortable in this house. Like he already owns the place.

I sit on the edge of a lounger and help myself to a glass of cucumber water from a jug that's sitting on the side table.

The smell of chlorine mingles with the perfume of the jasmine plants that climb the walls of the pool house. My skin warms beneath the sun, and water rhythmically laps the sides of the pool as Jack swims. I try to imagine I'm on holiday.

The sight of the hot tub taunts me with memories of my disastrous strip tease with Nico all those years ago. It's bubbling away, but no one's in it.

As if my thoughts have summoned him, Nico walks out of the pool house wearing swimming trunks and a t-shirt.

Jack's voice cracks through the air. "Nico, get in."

Nico flashes a dazzling smile. I haven't seen him do it much recently. What I wouldn't give to see him smile like that for me.

I pull my sunglasses down to cover my eyes, thankful for the reflective lenses, just as Nico pulls his shirt over his head and throws it down on the nearest lounger.

My breath hitches.

He's absolute perfection; skin gently tanned, shoulders broad. The muscles of his chest and the ridges of his abs are beautifully defined. *Wow*. He's like a golden bar of chocolate, and I want to eat him up. When does he have time to work out? You don't get a body like that by sitting at a desk all day. A trail of dark hair runs from his navel and disappears from view beneath his trunks, creating a pathway I desperately want to follow with my fingers... my tongue—

It's been way too long since I had sex.

Every cell in my body heats as I watch Nico from behind the lenses of my glasses, careful to hold my head so it doesn't look like I'm staring at him.

There isn't an inch of fat on him. He's glorious, built like an athlete. I'm so used to seeing him formally dressed; the only skin ever revealed is his forearms and the triangle at his neck when he isn't wearing a tie.

Nico tosses his head to flick his hair off his forehead and dives into the water. It's all so effortless. The muscles in his back and shoulders ripple with the movement as he freestyles the length of the pool. When he reaches the other end, he climbs out and stands, hand on his hip, the other in his hair as he talks to Jack, who's messing about in the pool.

Jack splashes, deliberately showering Nico with water. It's so childish, so joyful, that it immediately transports me back in time. How many times have I sat right here and secretly longed for Nico to notice me?

Far too many.

Jack splashes again and yells, "Get back in," before dipping under the surface.

Nico laughs, then turns, his gaze honing in on me like he knows I haven't taken my eyes off him. One of his hands is a visor that shields his eyes from the sun and our eyes lock. My heart races until I'm nothing but scorched flesh and pulse.

Neither of us moves, tethered by an invisible force that excludes everyone else. I can't look away, can't breathe... but he's here with me in this. Locked into this storm of unspoken words and denied emotion.

His stare is so intense it strips away layers without my consent, exposing parts of me I wouldn't want anyone else to see. One truth rises harder and faster than the rest: the old longing is as real and potent as it ever was.

Does he sense it too?

My throat tightens. It doesn't matter whether Nico returns the sentiment because I *can't* have feelings for him. I simply can't. The guilt would eat me alive. It's easier to hate him, because he's still the man who screwed over my father.

And yet, it's a pull that's hard to resist.

Nico's the first to break eye contact. He dives back into the water, leaving me questioning every feeling, every thought I just experienced.

Perhaps I imagined it all.

I get up, still feeling a tad shaken, and make my way to the pool house. Inside, it's as dowdy as the rest of the place, and I cringe at the idea of Nico getting changed in here.

I failed to remember a swimsuit when I packed, so I open the large plastic box that has held various family members' swimsuits for years. I rifle through the offerings, hoping to find something suitable, when a white bikini top catches my eye.

It's *the* bikini. The same one I wore ten years ago. I pull it out. Amazingly, it looks brand new. I find the matching bottoms, testing the elastic. Miraculously, it hasn't perished.

Dare I wear it? Will it even mean anything to Nico?

I quickly get changed. It still fits; I do a lot of running, and my body shape hasn't really changed since I was in my teens.

When I walk back out, Nico and Jack are still in the water. Nico breaks his conversation to follow my movement along the side of the pool. My bare feet hit the hot stone with each step, and I hope to God this bikini looks as good as I think it does. I'm nearly naked and warm summer air scatters over my skin like the gentle brush of Nico's attention.

I drop to the sun lounger, lie back and close my eyes, listening to the noise of Nico and Jack chatting. Their deep voices and laughter float across the surface of the pool, mingling with the lapping water.

My sun lounger dips. Someone's sitting on the end. My heart tremors in the hope it's Nico, but I didn't hear anyone get out of the pool.

It can't be him.

I open my eyes and my heart plunges. Curtis is sitting next to my feet in his tiny Speedos. The back of my neck prickles and I glance over at the table where Mum was sitting, only to see she's disappeared. I scramble to sit up, pulling my legs away from Curtis.

"Nice place you've got here," he says, nodding at the house.

"Yes. We're very lucky."

He stares at me, and I really don't like the look in his eye as he drags his gaze up and down my body. My skin is crawling.

Where the fuck is mum?

"Bet Debbie looked just like you when she was young," he continues. "You're a beauty. Great body too. But you know that, don't you?"

"Erm…"

"Otherwise you wouldn't have put on that bikini and laid yourself out like this." A little oily laugh swills out his mouth. "But you know what they say. If you've got it, flaunt it, right?" He gestures to his own body, puffing out his chest. Revulsion swirls in my stomach. His hand flails in the air until he brings it down, rests it on my shin, and strokes his thumb up and down.

My body goes rigid. "Please take your hand off me."

Curtis laughs as he lifts his hand. "Ooh, sorry. I've always been touchy-feely, me. It's my love language." He squeezes my big toe.

"It's not mine." I pull my feet out of reach, tucking them beneath me. "You can keep your hands to yourself."

"Ooh. Prickly little thing, aren't you?"

A shadow falls across the lounger, and Curtis shifts backward, looking up.

"Everything all right over here?" Nico's voice is firm and powerful, and Curtis almost cowers.

Nico steps closer to me and rests his hand on my shoulder. It's a small gesture, but so protective, so dominant, that I feel completely safe. It's such a primal sensation that desire whips through my body from the point of contact.

"I was just saying what a great place this is," Curtis stammers, standing up and stepping away from my lounger and pointing back at the house.

Nico lets out a low, rumbling sound that's close to a growl. There's a force emanating from him; a silent threat. It's invisible, but most definitely real. He looks at me. "Is that what was going on?"

My eyes flick to Curtis, unsure what to say, but it's enough of a reaction that Nico's focus shifts to Curtis, who freezes, half-hunkering under the weight of Nico's ferocious glare.

"Touch her like that again and I'll hit you so hard your teeth will meet your brain." Nico's voice is full of menace; he means every word. It's fucking terrifying. Even I cower a little, but in response, Nico's large, warm hand gives my shoulder a reassuring squeeze. It's totally at odds with the violence in his tone, and a knot of tightly coiled fear deep inside me releases slowly.

Curtis frantically nods and shuffles backward. "I'll...umm... I'll go and find Debbie."

Nico nods, pool water dripping down his bare chest, every muscle on his torso shimmering in the sunlight. "You do that."

Curtis scampers off towards the house in his tiny red trunks, and only then am I able to breathe again.

Nico lifts his hand from my shoulder, and I immediately want the touch of this large, protective man against my skin again.

"You okay?" His voice is deep and gentle now. Warmth spreads through my torso, sinking low in my hips, nestling between my thighs. I've never had a man who's not my brother defend me so overtly.

"Ugh." I give a shudder, recalling the feel of Curtis' hand on me. "There's something deeply off about that man."

Jack hauls himself out of the water, coming to stand next to Nico. "What was that about?" he asks stiffly. It's clear he didn't see the entire exchange between me and Curtis, or hear Nico's threatening words, because if he had, he'd have more to say about it.

Nico's brows draw together for a fraction of a second and he glances at me, as if to check what response we're giving.

"Nothing," I tell Jack. "Everything's fine."

Jack assesses us for a moment. "Sure?"

"Absolutely."

A muscle in Nico's jaw feathers like he's biting down on the truth, but I'm not about to fill Jack in, because I don't want him going mental about it too. We still have the rest of the weekend to get through, and it's already going to be awkward now.

"All good," Nico confirms.

"Great. I'm gonna set up the barbeque," Jack announces, all casual ease again. "Nico, can you go get the meat from the fridge? Mum can show you where it is. Caterers marinated it all, so it should be ready to go."

"Sure."

Jack grabs his towel, roughly dries himself, and heads towards the barbeque, where he tears open a bag of charcoal.

When I turn back to Nico, he's staring at me, a puzzled look on his face. He takes me in as I lie on the lounger, and his appraisal couldn't feel more different to Curtis'. I could bask in Nico's attention forever, relishing the way my nerves dance beneath my skin.

As our eyes meet, his gaze turns heated. He looks away almost immediately, but I sense it's more than avoidance. Something has drawn his attention.

I follow his gaze.

He's staring at the hot tub.

When he looks back at me, there's a little furrow between his brows.

He remembers. I know he does.

18
KATE

I'm still dripping wet from the shower when I sink onto the bed in my childhood room. It's mine in name only. When I left for university, the year after Dad died, Mum redecorated, and now my bedroom is a soulless spare room.

It's like she erased me.

I try to shrug it off, which I've found to be the best way of dealing with Mum's underhand attacks. Does it really matter if my bedroom isn't really mine anymore? I'm not here that often. But Jack's room is untouched, a shrine to his perfect childhood, which makes the whole 'shrugging it off' thing a little harder.

I shove it out of my mind and get ready for dinner. I don't want to look like I've made too much effort, especially not with sleazy Curtis around, but the last time Nico saw me dressed up I was wearing hot pants and couldn't see straight.

I put on a pale blue dress and slide into the silver heels Nico bought me. Absolutely identical to the ones I lost. I vaguely recall articles linking Erica Lefroy and Nico. Did he ask her directly for them? The idea of them being that close unsettles me. Perhaps his PA sourced them. She must be brilliant if she found them at short notice.

But either way, Nico had to give the instructions. He had to explain what they looked like. What size they were. What brand. He didn't just get any sparkly pair of shoes; these are the exact same shade: a cross between silver and rose gold. He noticed all those things... My heart constricts. These shoes are the most thoughtful thing someone has bought me... well, in longer than I can remember.

Is it possible that Nico Hawkston actually cares about me?

I don't know where I stand with him, but something between us has shifted. There's a safety to his presence that I didn't feel before, or at least I haven't felt in a long time. I'm eager to be near him again, and no matter how hard I try to deny it, I like him. No, it's more than *like*. Whenever he's in the vicinity, my body tingles with delicious awareness, heat pooling in secret places.

With thoughts of Nico circling my mind, I head down to the kitchen.

I pour myself a glass of chilled white wine and make my way to the dining room, where everyone is already sitting and eating.

"You're late," Mum snaps, her fork paused halfway to her mouth. "You know we always eat at eight."

I glance at my watch. It's only five past. I swallow down the urge to protest or make excuses. It's not worth it. "Sorry," I offer.

Mum nods, satisfied, and slips her forkful into her mouth.

Enormous platters of barbecued meats rest on a warming plate on the sideboard, with potato salads and grilled vegetables in separate bowls. I grab a plate and help myself, then take a seat between Mum and Curtis at the table. I'd rather not sit next to Curtis, but there's no other place set. He busies himself with his food, sawing aggressively at a piece of meat rather than acknowledging me. Nico sits opposite us, but I don't look at him as I settle in my seat.

"This is delicious," he says, taking a bite of what looks like a chicken skewer.

"Isn't it?" agrees Mum. "I got it from the local butcher, then Jessie marinated it all." She nods back towards the kitchen as if Jessie, the catering woman, is still there. "She's back tomorrow with a team for the party. Jack cooked it beautifully, don't you think?"

There are murmurs of agreement from around the table.

"Meat on fire I can do," Jack says, deflecting the compliment with a chuckle.

"I won't have you doing yourself down. This is perfect," Mum says, eyeing the meat on her plate thoughtfully before turning a sharp gaze on me. "How's that flat of yours, Kate? Still renting like a student?"

A jerk goes through my body as I prepare to ward off an attack. "No student could afford that rent, Mum."

"It's a great house," Jack adds. It's one of his many residential holdings, which he rents to me and my friends. I love living there so much I don't care that it desperately needs renovating. "Good bones. When Kate moves out, I'll knock the flats together. It'll be a prime family home in South London."

"Hmm." Mum dabs the corner of her mouth with a linen napkin without taking her eyes off me. "I really don't understand why you insist on staying there, and with that barmaid."

"Elly's a musician. She's not a barmaid, but even if she was, what difference would it make?"

Mum gives an elaborate shrug. "Oh, there's no judgment here, darling. It's just... isn't Jack paying you well enough? Lansen has been making so much, and you're barely away from your desk since you started there. And now you're under the Hawkston umbrella—"

"I have enough."

"Kate earns a lot of money, Mum," Jack defends me, his wary glance darting between the two of us.

Mum raises her wine glass. "That's what I thought. But that's half the problem, isn't it? It's intimidating for a woman to earn as much as

Kate does. No man wants that. It's emasculating. That's why you're always single."

I bristle. "You think I'm too successful to attract a man?"

"Absolutely. You only need to look at you. Beautiful, intelligent, and haven't had a decent boyfriend since you got your first period."

She's referencing my menstrual cycle at the dinner table? My cheeks flare. But if I call her out on how inappropriate it is, she'll gaslight me. She's the queen of insults that can be passed off as compliments. I can hear her defense now, *"I said you're beautiful and intelligent, didn't I? You're being oversensitive."*

"Maybe I'm not looking for a man, Mum."

"Oh, you don't need to pretend, darling. We're all friends here, aren't we?" She gestures around the table and titters. Curtis clears his throat and hacks at another piece of meat without lifting his eyes from his plate. And thank goodness, because if that creep thinks he's entitled to voice an opinion about me, I'll lose my shit.

Jack tucks his jaw so deep into his neck he gives himself a double chin. I'm pretty sure he mutters '*fuck*' under his breath. Nico watches me intently.

"Mark my words, Kate." Mum sips her wine, making a little tutting noise when she finishes. "You'll end up alone with all your cash in the bank and nothing to show for it. And then you'll have to watch those flatmates of yours getting married and having babies, and you'll be their single middle-aged friend. Trust me, I've seen it among my girlfriends. That's always how it works out for ambitious women like you."

The warning prickle of tears hits me unexpectedly. I hate that Mum can so easily destroy my self-esteem. It's her superpower. And even though I know what she's doing, my thoughts spiral. *What if she's right?*

I swallow, and there's an audible gulping noise. They must all know I have a lump in my throat the size of a peach stone.

"Mum," Jack cuts in, his tone stern. "Give her a break. She's fine."

Mum ignores him entirely, her expression all false sympathy as she keeps her gaze locked on mine. "Don't worry, darling, I've told all my friends how difficult it's been for you to find a boyfriend. I put feelers out and asked them if they know anyone. I've got a few leads too. Sue from book club—"

"Stop! I don't want to go on a blind date with some guy Sue from book club has unearthed from God knows where."

Mum huffs and places her hands on the tabletop. "I'm only trying to help."

"Why don't you fixate on Jack instead?" I say. "He's single."

Jack opens his mouth to object when Mum flicks her hand at him and laughs. "Oh, but Jack's a catch. He doesn't need any help. The ladies are lining up for him. But you... who's going to go out with you?"

Mum's words strangle my insides, crushing my organs. A few seconds of awkward silence pass.

"I would." Nico's low drawl is almost sensual.

Fuck me.

He leans back in his chair, wineglass in hand, and takes a sip, cool as anything, like what he just said is no big deal, and the suggestive way he said it hasn't stunned us all into silence.

Jack's eyes look like marbles that are about to roll out of his head and Curtis is dabbing his napkin over his forehead.

Mum flaps her hand. "Oh, my—"

"With all due respect, Mrs. Lansen," Nico continues, cutting across whatever Mum was about to say. "Kate's an incredible woman. Any man, regardless of his income, would be lucky to have her. If she's single, then I'm sure it's because she's choosing to be. Focusing elsewhere. Like on the Knightsbridge spa project. The dedication she's shown to Gerard's final project is inspiring. We should be praising everything she's doing well, rather than criticizing her because there's one area of her life that might not look the way you think it should. And on that note, you're wrong that no one would take her on a date. Like I said, I would."

Silence blankets the table. Surely they can all hear the racing of my heart? Does Nico really mean any of it, or is he saying it for effect?

The word he used earlier—*Hypothetical*—booms through my consciousness. Of course, he's not serious. He doesn't want to actually date me. He's saying it to make a point. How could it be anything other than that? But even if it is just to shield me from Mum's interminable criticism, isn't that... *something*?

Mum waves her napkin at Nico. "What a joker you are. You'd get bored with Kate in a flash." She cackles, then taps her wineglass with her fork. "Now, who's ready for pudding?"

My chest crumples. I can't take any more. Not even Nico's kind words are enough to make up for the way my mother views me. She completely ignored everything Nico said about my dedication to the spa project, instead choosing to stick her claws into the idea that Nico might want me and ripping it apart.

You'd get bored with Kate in a flash.

I push my chair back and stand up. "I'm not hungry."

"Oh, Kate. Don't be such a sourpuss. You're overreacting." And there it is, each word a piercing pain like I'm being stuck through with needles. "I only say these things so you'll sort your life out. I'm trying to help. It pains me to see you floundering—"

"I said, I'm not hungry. Eat without me."

My throat is so swollen I only just manage to get the words out. I stare at the table, not wanting to look up, but Nico's attention draws mine. He's tilting his head at me, his brown eyes serious and so full of care that a fresh wave of sadness pulls at my heart.

"Kate," he whispers.

The compassion in his voice nearly breaks me, but I refuse to cry in front of everyone. I rush into the hall. Footsteps follow behind, and my heart leaps because *maybe* it's Nico.

Jack is suddenly beside me, leather loafers shifting on the stone floor. "You can't walk out in the middle of dinner."

"I just did. I'm not sitting in there with her."

"Ignore her. She doesn't do it deliberately. If we went back in there"—he nods back to the dining room—"and asked her what she said to you, she wouldn't even remember. It means nothing."

"Exactly."

Jack blows air out over his bottom lip. "So let it go."

All of a sudden, my brother ceases to be the comfort he's always been. There he is, awkwardly trying to get me to do the right thing. To keep the peace. A small voice rises in the back of my mind that maybe he's right, but the frustration bubbling to the surface wins out. "It's so easy for you, isn't it? You're the perfect son. She fucking worships you."

"That's not fair."

"Isn't it?" We stare at one another for a few seconds, my jaw clamped shut, Jack's head shaking slowly.

When I turn away, Jack doesn't follow and I hear his footsteps retreat to the dining room. I head straight for the sanctuary of Dad's study, but the sight that greets me isn't as comforting as I'd hoped. A thick layer of dust coats everything: a cruel reminder that he's gone, and no one cares enough to keep the room clean.

I shut the door and sink onto the small velvet sofa nestled in the bay window, hugging my knees up to my chest, wishing he was still here.

I shouldn't have come this weekend. I thought I could bear Mum and her comments, but today I wasn't ready. Maybe it's because I was out late last night and drank too much. Maybe it's the draining heat of summer. Maybe it's the fact that Dad's memory is being cleared away like old food. Or maybe it's Nico and the caring way he looked at me, like if my heart broke, his might too.

All I know is that it's too fucking much.

Tears prickle behind my eyes, but I swipe them away, furious that Mum makes me feel like this. I focus on my breathing until the wave of emotion that drove me from the dining room subsides. I stare around the study. My artwork litters the room, paintings and pencil drawings propped against the walls. In my teens, I was an avid artist. Black A3 folders that bulge with content teeter on dad's desk.

I get up and open the first folder. Sketches of my father topple out, along with various still lifes and landscapes in oil, pastel, and watercolour.

I crouch down, flicking through them. Seeing it all spread out around me is like stepping into the past, reliving each moment of creation. A documentation of my life, captured in coloured strokes. Images created out of nothing.

"These are good." Nico's deep voice sets my heart racing and I freeze, hunched on the floor, surrounded by sheets of paper.

I look up to see him leaning against the door frame, one hand in the pocket of dark linen trousers. His casual elegance is breathtaking.

"What are you doing here?" The question sounds so harsh, even to my ear, that I immediately wish I could take it back.

He straightens a little. "Do you want me to leave?"

God, no.

I don't say the words aloud, but he seems to hear them anyway, and tension seeps from him to me—or the other way around—I can't tell.

He exhales slowly, eyes trailing the room, eventually landing on the desk where there is an array of silver-framed photos of the family. There's one of Dad with me and Jack at *Disneyland*; another of Mum and Dad on their wedding day. There's one of Nico and Jack, Dad between them with an arm around them. They're all dressed in fishing gear and grinning as though they're having the time of their lives, even though it's raining and they're bedraggled and soaking.

Nico clears his throat. "I haven't been in here since—"

"Since Daddy was alive?"

Daddy. I want to stuff the word back in my mouth. I can't believe I called my dead father Daddy in front of Nico. I'm a grown woman. If he didn't still think of me as a child, I'm sure he does now.

Nico's brows pull together, and there's a hesitation in his eyes as if he wants to say something but isn't sure he should. I see no judgment in his gaze, and it gives me a surge of confidence.

"Did you mean what you said in there?" I tilt my head towards the dining room.

The muscles along Nico's jaw stand out briefly before he speaks. "Yes. I meant all of it. You are incredible. You always have been."

My blood turns to warm syrup. He makes the admission so freely, like it's nothing at all to compliment me that way, but it affects me as much as if he just confessed his undying love.

A smile threatens to break through my sadness. "Thank you."

He gives me a slow, sexy smile in response, and part of me melts. "Anytime."

He paces across the room and crouches beside me, amidst all my pictures.

"I still can't stand you," I tell him, but there's a warmth to it.

He laughs, a deep sexy chuckle that caresses my skin. "You wouldn't be worth winning over if it was that easy."

My stomach hollows, heart fluttering over the emptiness. Is he trying to win me over? If he is, he's already won. He won a long time ago.

Nico reaches for one of my pictures at the same moment I do. His hand grazes mine, sending a bolt of energy to the pit of my stomach, bringing to mind other moments we've touched: Jack's party, the club, the penthouse, by the pool.

The same raw frisson fills the air. My breath hitches, and for an extended beat our hands remain there, touching in midair. My awareness shrinks to that one point of contact and his gaze flits to our hands too, before he moves away.

He picks up a few more sketches and flicks through them until he notices the framed charcoal of my father that's propped against the sofa. "That one is fabulous. It reminds me of something. The style of it..."

"Stephen Condar; the artist. That was the intention, at least." Heat rises to my cheeks. I haven't spoken about my art to anyone for years.

"The famous recluse?"

I'm not surprised Nico knows who I mean. Some of the biggest art galleries in London have rooms where the Hawkston name is painted in gold letters over the door and Condar's art hangs on the walls.

"Yeah," I reply. "He was my dad's favourite artist, so I did his portrait in the style. Dad loved it. That's why it's framed." Grief pulls at my throat. The picture might be framed, but the glass is broken. No one cares enough to fix it now.

Nico notices my struggle, and his expression softens. "You really loved him, didn't you?"

"He was my dad. Of course I did. He was the most wonderful, loving, kind man."

Dark eyes meet my own, mirroring my emotion so perfectly that for a second I forget where I end and he begins. I'm consumed by him.

"I loved him too," he says after a beat.

My body tightens as though his words are compressing me, forcing new, deeper emotions to the surface. The whispered confession is so close to one I'd dreamed of him making to me that a fierce choking heat rises up the column of my throat. *I'm going to cry.*

I shuffle sheets of paper into piles to keep my hands busy, to have something else to focus on other than Nico. But it doesn't work. I'm painfully aware of him. His presence affects me like no one else's, and an uncomfortable swelling sensation occurs within, as though his particular form of radiation is damaging my insides.

"Kate." I keep moving the papers. "Look at me."

I grip the sheet I'm holding so tight it crumples as I turn to face him.

"You've been crying." Before I can move, his hand is on my cheek, his thumb stroking away the remains of a tear. It's such a gentle gesture that it shocks me.

"No. I didn't..."

"It's all right." He lets his fingers rest against my cheek, holding my gaze with those inescapable eyes. "I'd cry too if my mother said no one wanted to date me."

His serious expression breaks into a smile and his eyes are so bright with mischief that, even though he's mocking me, I laugh.

"Fuck you, Nico Hawkston," I reply, shaking my head. "Your mother would never say that."

His smile vanishes, plunging us into a moment that feels almost suffocating.

"Your mother is wrong." His thumb slips down and skates across my lower lip, coming to rest right in the middle, tugging it down and exposing the underside.

What is he doing? My lip throbs, pulse beating right beneath his touch. It would be so easy to suck his thumb between my lips. And God, I want to. So much. I want to taste his skin again, and have some part of him inside me, in any way I can.

He stares at my mouth, his gaze so full of longing that I can almost see it surging across the small distance between us. His teeth rake over his full bottom lip, tugging on it. It's sexy as hell.

"You tried to kiss me last night," he rasps.

A prickling heat climbs up my legs, and a strangled affirmative sounds in my throat. Nico releases my lip so I can speak. "I was drunk."

"Uh-huh," he agrees, without looking away. "You asked me to sleep with you."

"Again, drunk."

He nods once. "So you don't want those things?"

The question slides over my skin, trailing goosebumps in its wake. He leans closer, his breath warm against my cheek.

Please, kiss me.

Nico's fingers press beneath my chin. His head tilts, his eyes fixed on mine, so dark and passionate I could drown in them. *He's going to kiss me.* I know it in every part of my body. Nico Hawkston is going to kiss me.

I close my eyes and lean towards him, but his hand falls from my face, and I startle, opening my eyes to find him looking at me with concern.

"Do you want me to take you home?" he asks.

What? My insides tighten, my mind whirring to catch up to the shift in gear. "Now?"

With one word, I've exposed a host of emotion: disappointment, shock, outrage, disbelief.

Nico ignores all of it. "If you don't want to stay, I can drive you back to London. It'll be after midnight by the time we get home, though."

"I can't leave. Mum would never forgive me."

"You'd stay for her, even after how she spoke to you?"

I blow out a long-suffering sigh. "It's not new. I've had much worse from her. It's just how she is."

"It's how you let her be."

I frown, not wanting to think too deeply about the point he's making. "This party is the most important event of the year for her. I don't want to ruin it."

His slight nod is dismissive enough to make me feel like I've let him down somehow.

I stand quickly, but a sudden head rush renders me unsteady and I grab the side of the desk to keep myself up. My fingers glance against a tottering pile of my sketchbooks, which clatter to the ground. The top one falls open, spilling sheets of charcoal sketches to the floor.

"Oh, God," I cry, seeing the face that stares back at me. Nico. Over and over again. At twenty-five, twenty-six, twenty-seven. The beautiful features of his face in profile, three-quarter turn, looking up, looking away, looking straight out of the page.

Nico stares at the papers strewn around us. "Is that... me?"

I kneel, scrabbling to gather them. There are too many. I can't hide them fast enough. I grab a few more, but in doing so expose the worst one.

Nico. Idealised. Perfect. *And absolutely bollock-naked.*

My body heats like a furnace. *Shit.* I went all in on the detail on this one. Really let loose with the imagination.

Nico clears his throat, but there's laughter in the sound. "Wow. I don't remember posing for that."

I want to die. I let out a little squeak and shove the offending image into the pile, continuing my frantic attempts to conceal the lot.

Nico crouches beside me and grips my arm. "Stop."

I wrench free of his hold. "God, no, this is... it's... *fuck*." I raise a sheet to my face, sheltering behind it. "Don't say anything, please."

He teases my hand away, forcing me to meet his eye. "I had no idea," he says, his voice gentle.

"I was a teenager," I confess, as if that excuses what was clearly an unhealthy obsession. "Long time ago. Long, long time. Very long."

I stand, but my legs are shaking. This is a nightmare come to life.

Nico rises to his feet too. "And now?" he asks, taking the sheet of paper out of my hand. He's so close, he must be able to hear the gallop of my heartbeat. "What do you want right now?"

He's staring at me as though his very existence depends on my answer; I can't think straight.

"Now? Now, I hate you," I mutter, but the phrase lacks any conviction.

"You do?" he confirms, leaning so close that his mouth grazes my ear, his breath sending a ripple of desire all the way down my body.

What the fuck is going on right now?

"Yup," I choke out.

"That's a real shame, Kate." His voice is so low that the words are little more than a vibration against my skin. "Just when we were starting to get along."

One of his hands rests on my hip as his lips hover at my neck. He presses them gently, but deliberately, against my skin. I jerk like I've touched a live wire.

Did he just... *kiss* me?

Nico huffs a laugh against my throat and his lips continue to press up and down the side of my neck, trailing fire across my skin. *Yup. Definite kissing happening.* A pleasurable shiver scatters goosebumps down my arms; my body aches for more.

His hand slides around to the small of my back. Each movement drags a new swathe of desire through my body. A whimper escapes me, the sound unmistakably sexual.

Nico's lips lift. "Shall I stop?"

Desperation claws within me. If I say yes, I might never get this chance again. But if I say no... if I let this continue, I'll be betraying my father's memory. I hesitate too long and he pulls back to look at me, but I can't bear the scrutiny. I stare at the floor, where the pictures of his face lie scattered.

He presses his fingertips beneath my chin again, lifting it, forcing me to meet his gaze. Something dangerous simmers beneath the surface, and I know what I feel is mutual, returned with equal force. *I could choose Nico.*

Do I dare?

He steps back. The absence of his touch leaves me reeling. Of all the things I expected him to do, *wanted* him to do, moving away wasn't it. Did I read him wrong?

My hand reaches to my neck, my fingers ghosting over the skin where his lips had been moments before. His eyes dart to where my hand rests, and his lips pull up at the corner.

The silence that falls between us is too loud, begging to be filled with the unspoken words that hover in the air. We stand like that for I don't know how long, waves of arousal pulsing through me. I'm pretty sure I'm going to orgasm if he continues to stare like that. Finally, he lifts the picture he's holding, which, thankfully, isn't the nude. "Can I keep this?"

I shake my head, nod, shake it again. "If you want to."

"Thanks. You're very talented."

We stand opposite one another for a few beats longer, then he turns to leave.

"Wait."

He glances at me over his shoulder. "Yes?"

"I didn't say I wanted you to stop."

His smile doesn't meet his eyes. "I know."

Disappointment swirls in my gut as he leaves the room, and all I can think is, *'what does that mean?'*

19
NICO

I've got a hard on just from being in that room with Kate. I'm so pent up I'm close to exploding.

I take the stairs, two at a time. I could have kissed her, pressed her against the wall and fucked her until she came apart in my arms. I could have done anything I wanted with her. I could sense her resistance yielding.

But to kiss her in her father's office, the tears on her cheeks barely dry, and her brother and mother just down the hall... it didn't feel right. She was upset, vulnerable; the way she spoke about her father messed me up. She still worships him, and I can see why Jack thinks it would do more harm than good to tell her the truth.

But *fuck*, I want to tell her. To confess to it all so we can move forward without the ghost of her dad, the deal, and all the sordid history of it blocking the path.

But I swore an oath. Made a promise to a dying man. And I don't want to take advantage of Kate, which is exactly what would have happened if I'd stayed in that room a second longer, because she was wide open for me. She would have given me whatever I wanted to take; I could see it in her eyes.

I don't know how much longer I'll be able to hold out.

"Mate, come and have a drink," Jack calls from the dining room. "We'll be on the terrace."

"I've got to take a call," I shout back, continuing up the stairs. I enter my room, close the door, and lean back against it, glancing down at the sketch in my hand. It's beautifully drawn. I meant what I said; she really is talented. But it's the throbbing of my cock that has my attention now.

I proceed to the bathroom, tossing the sketch on the bed as I pass. I can still smell the floral scent of her perfume, like wild roses. Her skin was so soft and smooth... so supple, warm, begging to be touched. How the hell I managed to walk away from her is beyond me. There's only one place my cock wants to be, and it's buried deep inside Kate Lansen.

I have the restraint of a fucking saint, despite the fact my trousers are pitched like a circus tent.

I can't go back downstairs like this. I lean one hand against the sink, my other fumbling with my trousers, unfastening the belt, button and fly, sliding my hand into my boxers.

My cock springs free and I grab the hard length of it with one fist, the need for relief consuming me above all else. I imagine my hand is hers, and I see her beautiful lips, soft and plump, and so ready to take my dick.

I pump my fist, beating this one out like a poison I need to expel from my system. It'll only take a moment, and then I can go get that drink. Because God knows, I need it.

20
KATE

Nico's footsteps thump up the stairs, and I collect the rest of my sketches, sliding the loose sheets back into sketchbooks and piling them on the desk.

I can't believe he walked away. He didn't even wait for me to choose when he asked if he should stop touching me.

He decided. He decided *everything*. He always has.

Maybe this time, I get to decide.

I follow him upstairs. I'm not clear on exactly what I intend to say to him, but my body is on a mission I'm powerless to redirect.

When I reach his room, I grip the door handle, take a deep breath, and push the door open. I'm immediately struck by the decor. What must Nico think of this place? The carpet is worn and moth-eaten in patches and the soft furnishings are all chintz fabric from the early nineties. My sketch lies discarded in the middle of the bed, but there's no sign of him.

A noise comes from the bathroom. The door to the ensuite is wide open. What if he's taking a piss and I'm marching in here uninvited? I'll leave before he sees me.

"Kate."

Too late.

But the way he said my name... it was almost a groan. Guttural. Desperate. Does he know I'm here? Has he seen me? Maybe he's as confused as I am. Maybe he wants to talk about what just happened.

I freeze, wondering what to do when he says my name again. *Crap.* He definitely knows I'm here. No point running away now.

I step towards the bathroom, and he looms into view. His back is to me, and he's braced against the sink, the muscles of his shoulders rippling beneath the fabric of his shirt. But his trousers hang halfway down his thighs, the tail of his shirt half-covering a perfectly muscled arse.

It takes me a moment to realise that what I can't see from behind, I can see clearly reflected in the mirror.

Fuck.

He's pumping his hips, fisting his cock, driving it so hard into his hand that it looks painful. But pain isn't what I see on his face; he's approaching ecstatic bliss, and it's the sexiest goddamn thing I've ever seen.

Another deep groan rumbles from his perfect mouth, and heat pools between my legs. Nico Hawkston is about to come, and I have a front-row seat.

He grits another sound through his teeth, low and harsh with arousal. I shouldn't be here. This is a private moment. I need to get out. I need to leave.

But I can't move, because I'm tethered to Nico. Wave after wave of heady desire spills through me, so intense my entire body throbs with it. I need to witness his climax like I need my next breath.

I've got seconds to break this spell. To back away. To get the fuck out—

Nico's eyes pop open, meeting mine in the mirror.

Oh, shit.

He doesn't stop, his hand continuing to move up and down his shaft. Once, twice more, before cum spills over his fist. His mouth is wide, his jaw and throat tense as he silences his pleasure, but he doesn't look away from me for a second.

Heaviness settles between my legs, pulsing and tingling, bringing me closer to orgasm than I've ever been without being touched.

Nico breathes heavily but continues to stare, the heat in his eyes enough to give me third-degree burns.

And then something snaps—some sliver of shame ruptures my trance—and I'm free, stumbling backwards, tripping over my own feet. "Gosh. Sorry. Shit, sorry." I bump into the side of the bed and the jolt lets me break eye contact with him. My limbs feel hollow and weak. "I didn't mean to—"

"Stay and watch?" he rasps, as he turns on the tap and rinses his hands. He reaches for the towel to dry his hands before tugging up his trousers and flicking the belt in place. "I'm pretty sure you did."

How the hell is he so composed right now? My cheeks are so hot I know they're flaming red; my skin is damp all over.

"You said my name. Twice."

I can't believe I said that out loud.

He holds my eye in the mirror. "I did. Is that a problem?"

His collected confidence unnerves me. "No. Not at all."

A hint of a smile tugs at his lips. "Good. Next time we can do this the other way round."

Too many words. I can't make sense of them, and don't dare believe he means what I think he does. "What?"

He rubs two fingers over his full lips. "Do you need me to explain?"

"Yes." *What the fuck am I doing?*

"Next time, I get to watch you."

My heart stops for at least a second. Maybe longer. But the pulse in my clit is fierce and strong, never skipping a fucking beat, and from the look on Nico's face, he knows it.

My brain immediately begins processing how or why or when such a thing might happen, but before I can offer to do it for him *right now*, which is exactly what will happen if I stay here, I'm backing out of the room as fast as I can and closing the door behind me.

My head feels like it's exploding as I run down the hall. Nico Hawkston is attracted to me. I turn him on... *me*. He didn't even deny it. His dick was stiff in his hand at the time. The pleasure on his face as his orgasm spilled out... it's an image I won't ever forget.

I burst into my room and kick the door shut behind me.

"Fuck," I moan, throwing my arms into the air, thrashing them like I'm swatting at an invisible swarm of bees. There's so much energy sizzling in my body that I can't stand still. I march to one side of the room, then the other. "Fuck," I repeat.

I'm so turned on that I'm half-tempted to bring myself off right here in the middle of my bedroom. The blood pulsing to my clit is aching for sweet relief. But what would that achieve? I need more than an orgasm to sort this out, and the nervous skittering of my heart takes precedent.

I need to talk to someone.

Hands shaking, I grab my phone from where I left it on the dresser and call Elly. She answers on the second ring, and, in a rapid hushed whisper, I tell her everything that happened.

She listens, squealing occasionally, but it's only when I've finished that she goes completely silent. I check my phone in case we've been cut off. We haven't.

"Elly?" I whisper.

"Shit, Kate," she replies. "I think I'm turned on. Does this count as phone sex? Are we having phone sex right now?"

I giggle. "Please don't tease."

Elly laughs. "Sorry. But I genuinely don't know what to say."

"Me neither." I let out a groan. "He's messing with my head. He was completely composed when he noticed me staring at him. Totally calm. Not embarrassed at all. Whereas I feel like I've melted. He's probably downstairs sipping a scotch as if nothing happened."

Elly makes a *hmm* noise down the phone. "Do you want him to… you know… watch you wank?"

I clap my free hand over my mouth, give a muffled squeal, then release it. "I can't believe you just asked me that."

"You rang me. I'm trying to help." Elly's voice is high-pitched, and she gasps as though she's stifling laughter before she collects herself. "He's staying at your mum's tonight, isn't he?"

"Yeah."

"Go to his room."

Immediately, I imagine myself climbing into his bed, feeling him next to me. Touching me. Kissing me. His dick hard and—

Fuck. I'm like a dog in heat over here. Maybe this *is* phone sex. *Focus.* "What? No. I couldn't do that."

"You could. Put on that underwear you packed. Come on, this is a sign from the universe. Take it by the balls."

I rub my temples. "I feel like a teenager."

"Of course you do. You're in your family home. Scene of the bikini hot tub gate. You need to break free from the past. Teenage Kate might have run away in shame, but present day you doesn't have to.

"Go to his bedroom and outright ask him what he's playing at. You've *got* to do it. Think of it as healing old trauma." She lets out a little burst of laughter. "For what it's worth, I think you should go for it. He's gorgeous. I mean... swoon."

"Are you joking right now? I don't have the brain capacity to work out if you're serious or not."

"Deadly," she confirms. "He's into you. Do it, do it, do it. Go to his room. You won't humiliate yourself. You might even end up having hot sex and loving it." She laughs again.

"I hate how funny you're finding this."

"I might be laughing, but I'm jealous. Believe me. Look, I've got a gig to get to. Let me know how it goes. Love you."

I check the time on my phone. It's three thirty in the morning. I've tossed and turned, sleep eluding me. Damn Elly for putting this idea of corridor-creeping into my head.

I'm not going to do it. No. Definitely not. I just happen to be wearing my only set of matching lingerie because it's a warm night, and I have nothing else to sleep in. I wasn't at my most effective when I was packing.

The bra is under-wired and push-up, and my breasts spill just a little over the top of the lace cups. The matching knickers are red lace, and at the back they ride up revealing the curve of my butt cheeks. It's a killer lingerie set, but who am I kidding? It's not for sleeping in.

It very clearly states, '*I want sex*'.

My heart is racing, my palms are sweaty. Every creak the house makes—every potential footstep on the floorboards—sends my heart rate into overdrive. Because maybe, just *maybe*, one of those noises is him making his way to my room...

This is ridiculous. I can't relax enough to sleep.

I throw the covers off and stand, my body vibrating with anticipation, even though my mind is holding me back.

Don't do this. You'll make a fool of yourself.

But I'm done listening to that frightened voice in my head. This is my *I want sex* underwear, and I'm wearing it because I do want to have sex with Nico, and I'm done pretending I don't.

Before I know it, my hand is on the doorhandle and I'm pushing it open, slipping into the corridor.

Moonlight streaks through the window at the end of the hall.

This is crazy. But I keep going, one foot in front of the other. Closer and closer to the room he's staying in.

And then it hits me just how stupid this really is. What am I going to do? Knock on the door and present myself like an offering?

I'm not doing it. Elly can stuff her stupid, crazy ideas up her bum. I spin one-eighty and head back to my room, but I barely make it a step before the door opens behind me.

It's him. I know it is. The back of my neck tingles under the weight of his gaze, my skin buzzing at his proximity.

I turn towards the noise.

Nico stands, broad shoulders silhouetted in the moonlight from the window behind. He's fully dressed in chinos and a shirt, overnight bag in one hand. Unless he was planning on moving into my room, he definitely wasn't coming to see me.

Is he leaving?

But as Nico's unwavering focus latches onto my body, it renders the question insignificant. *He's not going anywhere.*

His eyes roam my legs, my hips, trailing more slowly over my breasts. Beneath his predatory glare, my skin is aflame, humming with anticipation that's dangerously close to fear. For a few seconds he continues drinking me in, gaze snagging on my lips before finally reaching my eyes.

"Is this for me?" His voice is full of gravel.

A pulse beats between my legs, slickness gathering there, seeking to welcome his touch.

Nico drops his bag and steps into my space, so close that we're breathing in each other's exhalations.

"What do you want?" he whispers, and the sound sends a ripple of liquid desire through me. "Did you like what you saw earlier? How much I want you? How fucking hard you make me?"

Yes. I want to scream it, but my mouth won't form the word. I put one hand against his chest, feeling the firmness of his pecs beneath. I don't know if I mean to push him away or draw him closer, but the raw masculinity that radiates off him sets up a flame of need within me.

I step back so I'm pressed against the wall and he follows me, caging me in with his arms. Every nerve ending sparks like I'm a box of matches and Nico's lit the entire thing at once. I never imagined it would feel like *this*. It's all I can do to resist the urge to tear at his clothes.

That someone could open a door and find us at any second only increases my sense of urgency as fear mingles with lust.

"Do you want me to fuck you? Is that what this is?" He lifts the bra strap at my shoulder, slowly running his finger under it. "You're Jack's little sister. And my employee. I shouldn't touch you at all."

"No," I whisper. "You shouldn't." My breathing is embarrassingly loud, embarrassingly *desperate*. I haven't had sex in years, and even then it was perfunctory and unsatisfying. Right now I'm so turned on I'm almost delirious.

"Touch yourself then," he growls, shifting closer to me.

His words have desire unfurling within me just as the length of his cock presses against my thigh. I gasp and bite my lip to muffle the sound. *He feels huge.* A thrill fires through me at the idea that I make him hard. My fingers itch to reach out and touch him, but panic freezes me in place.

"Let me see you come," he commands. "I'd say that's only fair."

A choked affirmative sounds in my throat, and Nico's eyes smoulder with desire. It's ten times the expression I saw in the study. "Do I make you wet?" His voice is a soft, seductive stroke in the darkness.

On cue, a gush of moisture floods between my legs. "Mmm," I murmur, but I might as well be screaming *yes, yes, yes*, because the meaning of my moan is just as clear.

"I want to hear it. I want to hear how wet you are for me."

Did he just say that? The hall is quiet, other than the sound of our breathing, which to my ears blasts loud enough to wake the dead. *This is insane*. Maybe I am dreaming...

Nico presses his forehead to mine. "You've seen what you do to me. It's your turn. Show me. Show me how much you want me."

Even if he didn't have me pinned against the wall, the coil of latent pleasure waiting to unravel in my core wouldn't let me walk away. I hold his gaze as I slide my hand into the lace of my underwear. I hesitate, my hand brushing the top of the fabric. "I've never done this... for anyone."

A deep noise rumbles in Nico's throat. "Then let me be the first." He runs his hand over the bare skin of my hip, his touch like fire as he slides my underwear down my thighs, giving me more access. I wriggle, allowing my panties to fall to the floor. I kick them to the side before Nico nudges my legs apart with his foot.

How was it this easy for him to get me here?

"God, I hate you," I hiss under my breath.

The warm breath of a chuckle hits my cheek. "Keep telling yourself that."

His confidence only increases his appeal, making me more eager to do as he asks. I edge my fingers lower, sliding them along my slit. I'm soaked. As I move my hand, the sound of my arousal fills the space, exposing my need.

Panicking, I cease the movement. This is too much. I can't do it.

"Don't stop," he murmurs, his thigh sliding between mine to spread me wider. "I want to see you come. I want to hear you moan my name."

And just like that, I'm lost once more to the thrill of his words, his voice, the intoxicating desire that pulses beneath the sound. They're all the encouragement I need, my body aching for friction, the building pressure in my clit desperate for relief.

"That's it," he coaxes as I move my fingers, sliding one inside, then another, wishing it was him doing it. His fingers, his hand, his touch. I arch my hips towards him to find some purchase against his body, but he tuts and shifts just out of reach.

"Look at me," he instructs, and I can't help but obey.

I meet his gaze as I drag my fingers forward, pulling wetness up to my clit, making circular motions over it with slick fingers. I grab his shoulder with my other hand, digging my nails into the soft cotton of his shirt, desperate for something to anchor me. A small moan leaks from my mouth as the pressure builds.

"Good girl." He grabs my thigh, bringing it to rest up on his hip. "Faster now."

"Please," I mutter between moans, "touch me."

He shakes his head and murmurs, "Not this time."

I'm nearly out of my mind with pleasure, but I cling to his words. *Not this time.* Will there be another time? Will I have Nico Hawkston like this again?

My grip on his shoulder is so hard the tips of my fingers feel numb. My forehead falls against his chest. "I'm close, so close."

His fingers dig into my hip, and he speaks through clenched teeth. "Say my name, Kate. Say my fucking name."

I let out a sound more animal than human; husky, dripping with desire. I don't recognise myself.

"My name," he growls.

Tingles at the base of my spine explode like gunpowder. "Nico. Oh, *fuck*. Nico. I'm coming."

He swears against my neck, his arms encircling me as my orgasm rocks through my body, fizzing in every cell, giving me the most intense release I've ever had. He supports me through every last tremor of pleasure until my trembling legs are so weak that I sink down onto his thigh.

Beneath me, his leg is solid, and he bears my weight easily. My wet pussy rests on the fabric of his perfectly pressed chinos, my arousal soaking through.

His breathing is as ragged as mine, and we stay tangled in one another's arms until our breaths return to normal.

"Fuck, Kate."

Kate.

The sensual tone of his voice spreading over those four letters of my full name sends another wave of arousal skittering through my overly sensitive nerve endings.

He brushes a strand of my hair off my face. "You're so beautiful. And when you come, you're exquisite."

Fire burns through me at his words. I've given him so much tonight, and we haven't even kissed yet.

Making sure I'm stable on my feet, he edges himself from between my legs and takes a step back. His shirt is a little crumpled, and there's a dark patch on his thigh, but otherwise he looks pristine. He picks up his bag and looks at me for longer than is decent. There's so much emotion in his eyes, I don't know what to take from it.

I notice the bulge at his crotch. "Do you want me—"

"I have to go. Something's come up."

He lets the statement linger without moving, as if waiting to see if I'll ask him to stay, or ask what's so urgent that he has to leave in the middle of the night. Instead, I nod at the erection straining beneath his trousers.

"I can see that."

He smiles, pinning his bottom lip in place with his teeth as he shakes his head the tiniest bit. It's so sexy that a breath stalls in my chest.

"Goodnight, Kate. Sleep well."

He brushes past me, striding towards the stairs. The air is full of his scent, wrapping itself around me like regret.

My heart thumps with every strike of his shoes on the steps. Hoping, *hoping*, he'll turn back.

Come back, you bastard.

I don't move until the front door clicks open and closed, and he crunches across the gravel. The car door slams, and the engine rumbles.

And then he drives away.

21
NICO

My cock is aching like a bitch, but I blast the air con on full and tune into the voices on the radio. Not that I'm listening to the words; it's a blur of upper-middle class British accents which is oddly soothing. Streetlights streak across the road ahead as I speed back towards London.

Kate Lansen is going to be my undoing. The attraction I thought I had locked down has opened like Pandora's box this weekend. And I couldn't even stay to see it through.

My PA called after I finally fell asleep to tell me that Charlie had been arrested. He was safe; no one was hurt, but the police were holding him.

I floor the accelerator, guilt running through me because I wasted time with Kate when I should have been on the road. But there was no way I could deny her when she was standing outside my room in that stunning underwear.

I probably shouldn't be driving this fast, but I'm agitated. The speed provides something close to the release I denied myself earlier.

I shut down thoughts of Kate, of her soft moans and the desperate way she clung to me as she came, focusing instead on the task at hand. I call my PA again from the car. It's antisocial, but fuck it, she has the details and I need to be prepared.

She stifles a yawn. "Mr. Hawkston. How can I help?"

"I'm on my way. What happened?"

"He spray-painted a vehicle. Graffitied all over it. A neighbour found him and called the police."

None of it makes sense.

"Did the police call you?"

"No. Charlie did. He was trying to get through to you."

My brain is slow to compute. "Why would he call me instead of his mother?"

"He says he doesn't want to see her."

Shit. That doesn't sound good. "Okay. Thanks. Sorry to wake you."

"No problem, Mr. Hawkston."

I'm not sure I'm any calmer by the time I park the car outside the police station—a vast concrete block on the edge of a roundabout. It's fucking ugly. How is this the culmination of my evening? It feels like a bad dream.

I take a breath, stalk up to the doors and push my way inside. The station is brightly lit and smells like bleach. There's a female police officer behind the desk, but otherwise, the place is quiet. One of the strip lights in the corner isn't working, and it flickers in my peripheral vision like the beginnings of a migraine.

"I'm here to collect Charlie Hawkston," I announce.

When she looks up at me, her eyebrows disappear into her hairline. Whatever she was expecting, I'm not it. She drops her eyes to scan through some documents in front of her.

"Nico Hawkston," she says, tapping a piece of paper. "Are you the father?"

"Uncle."

She presses a buzzer, and when a voice responds, she instructs that Charlie be brought through to the front desk.

"The owner isn't pressing charges," she tells me. "You're free to take him."

Charlie slouches out between the two officers, his head hanging low. He's wearing huge baggy jeans and an oversized t-shirt with Bart Simpson on the front. The outfit makes him look skinny and younger than his fifteen years.

"You were lucky this time," one of the officers, who looks so fresh-faced this could be his first night on the job, tells him.

Charlie shrugs and ambles towards me, not meeting my eye. I'm not equipped to deal with a teenager going through an existential crisis. Then again, I'm not sure Matt would be that much better.

"Can I stay with you?" he asks when he reaches me.

Fuck, no. I'm not living with a teenager.

"Get in the car," I say, nodding my head towards the door. "You've got some explaining to do."

Charlie slumps in the seat beside me. He hasn't spoken since we left the station. The drive to central London is quick at this time in the early morning, so I don't have long to get to the bottom of what's going on. We'll be at his house in fifteen minutes, and I need to know what I'm going to say to Gemma when we get there.

And what I'm going to tell Matt.

"Why didn't you call your mum? You can't hide this from her."

"Oh, she knows."

I frown. "Okay. So you rang her? Why isn't she the one picking you up then?"

"No. I didn't call her. Didn't need to."

"Then how do you know she knows?"

"Because he'll have told her."

"He? He who? The police officer?"

Charlie lets out a low, sad chuckle. "No. The man she's screwing."

I swallow and clench my jaw. *Shit*. A hundred questions crowd into my mind, but I settle for the one I can't ignore.

"How do you know she's doing that?"

"Because he comes to the house when Dad's away."

My chest constricts. "Maybe that's not why he comes—"

"I saw them."

I flick on the indicator, trying to focus on the road, although my mind is spiraling. I don't want to be the one to break this to Matt. "You saw them?"

"Yeah. Last week. It was late, and I came downstairs for a glass of water. They were in the kitchen." He makes a retching noise. "It was fucking disgusting."

I should reprimand his language, but it doesn't feel like the right moment.

"What did your mum say?"

"She tried to gaslight me. Said I'd imagined it, but how do you imagine your mum naked on the—"

"I don't need to know the details."

He rolls his eyes. "Anyway, she told me I'd better not tell Dad, which was as good as admitting it."

"Your dad doesn't know?"

"I'm not sure. But even if he did, he wouldn't exactly blurt it out, would he? Bit embarrassing. He's Matt Hawkston, multi-billionaire.

And Mum's off shagging some random guy. His house is tiny too. One of those terraced things. I think he's only in the top-floor flat."

I raise an eyebrow and side-eye him as best I can whilst keeping my focus on the road. "Less of the judgment."

"I'm just saying... He's not even good looking."

I let out a heavy sigh. "It was his car? The one you graffitied?"

"Yeah. It wasn't a car, though. It was a van."

"A van? What does he do?"

"No idea. When he comes to see Mum, he drives a car. That's what I really wanted to fuck up."

I sigh. "Watch your language."

Charlie stares out the window. "Anyway, the van was there instead of the car and it was white with loads of space to spray paint, so maybe it was better that way."

I'm about to laugh when I remember how serious this is. "What did you write on it?"

Charlie clears his throat. "You mother-fucking piece—"

"Okay. Enough. I get it."

A tiny smile plays on his lips. "I drew on it too."

"I'm not even going to ask."

I park outside Matt's house—a great white stuccoed mansion in one of the most exclusive areas of London. A family home.

I scrape a hand down my face. What am I going to do? Ring the doorbell and tell Gemma that Charlie's told me everything, and then force them to sleep under the same roof? "You want to stay with me?"

Excitement dances in Charlie's eyes. "Seriously?"

"Sure. Just until your dad gets back."

"Hell, yes." He slaps the dashboard, then looks at me sternly. "Just don't screw anyone in the kitchen. I don't wanna see more of that."

"I promise I won't have sex in the kitchen. Or any public spaces while you're living with me."

"Good. Not even with Kate Lansen."

"Huh?"

He smiles. "Kate, who sits next to me. I know you like her."

I grip the steering wheel hard with both hands. "I won't have sex in the kitchen, if you swear not to graffiti anyone else's car, house, whatever. No defacing anyone else's property. Deal?"

"Deal."

"And don't go talking about Kate, either. That's how rumours start, and rumours can ruin a career. She's my employee, and it would be highly unprofessional if anything were to happen between us." I'm a lying shit, but I'm not about to dump more crap on Charlie's plate.

"Okay. But you might want to be a bit more subtle next time you check out her bum in the office."

This kid.

I open the car door.

Panic flashes over Charlie's face. "Where are you going?"

"I need to tell your mum. I can't kidnap you."

"No. Please, don't do that." He sounds desperate.

"It's either that or I call your dad in New York." I bring up Matt's contact details and hold up my phone so Charlie can see I'm one touch away from dialing. "You want to tell him what you did and why?"

Charlie slumps in the seat and crosses his arms. "Fine. But don't go inside. Send Mum a message."

I rub a hand over my jaw. It bristles with stubble. "I think I need to do this face to face, even if it is the middle of the night."

Charlie presses his lips together and scowls at me. "What about Lucie? Can you get her too?"

I think of my niece. Cute as she is, I can't be responsible for her. "Don't push your luck. I'm not taking a three-year-old back to my place."

It's early the following morning when my phone rings.

Who the hell is calling at this time?

I'm exhausted after last night. It was nearly dawn when I got into bed. Half-asleep, I grab my phone to see Seb's name blinking at me. I swipe to answer.

"What?" I groan.

"You said we needed to talk. About Charlie. 'Call me ASAP'," he quotes.

Blearily, I remember leaving him a voicemail from the car last night. "What time is it?"

"It's ASAP, dick-head. What's wrong? Has something happened? Is he all right?"

I hold the phone away from my ear to glance at the time on the screen. Five past six in the morning. Seb is panting down the phone. "You're at the gym, aren't you?"

He grunts. "Yup. What do we need to talk about?"

"Charlie found his mum fucking some guy in the kitchen."

There's silence, then, "Shit. This'll destroy Matt. Shotgun not breaking the news."

"Shotgun? You're such a child."

The thing is, Seb's right. Matt would never cheat on his wife. And he won't forgive cheating either. Our father cheated constantly when we were growing up. Dad's still at it, only now the women are younger than we are.

It was an unpleasant environment to grow up in.

One time, we came home from school to find Dad in a compromising position with the housekeeper. Matt was furious. He told our mother, who screamed at him like he was the one who'd fucked up. She made us swear never to tell anyone. Never to mention it again. To let our father do what he needed, with whomever he wanted. After that, we all pretended it wasn't happening. The dirty Hawkston secret we were never allowed to share.

"I think Matt knew. Or at least suspected," I say, as I recall Matt asking us to watch Charlie before he left for New York.

"Then it won't be so hard for you to break it to him when he gets back," Seb replies.

I sigh. "I'll do it now. No time like the present."

"Now? It's the middle of the night in New York."

"Oh. Right. Later then." I pause. "I've got him staying here. Charlie, I mean."

"That sounds sensible. I thought you were at the Lansen's old place for the party?"

"I was, but I had to leave. Had to pick Charlie up from the police station in the middle of the night."

"The police station? Why?"

"He went on a bit of a vigilante rampage. Graffitied abuse all over the guy's van."

"He drives a van?" Seb snorts. "Did Gemma get tired of Matt's array of chauffeur-driven cars or what?"

I acknowledge the comment with a short huff, amused that this is what Seb chooses to focus on. "Look, I'll need you to take Charlie."

"What? No way. He's all yours."

"Come on. Just a few nights. Share the burden." My mind goes to Kate, the soft feel of her skin, the sweet smell of her neck, and the sound of her moans. My cock twitches beneath the sheets, already hard. Morning glory doesn't even cover it. I glare at it like I can shame it down, then shift my focus back to the conversation. "I can't be bringing people here when Charlie's recovering from witnessing his mum get railed on the kitchen table."

"People? Multiple people?" he laughs. "You sly dog."

The phrase makes me think of my father and I grimace, swallowing down the bile that rises in my throat. "Mind your own business. But, yeah, I want some privacy. Having a teenager in the house isn't great right now."

"What makes you think I don't need the privacy?"

"Fuck's sake. I'll take him back. Just give me a few nights."

"Okay. But not until next week. I've got '*multiple people*' staying until then." I can almost hear him grinning.

"Good for you," I deadpan, then refocus. "I'll keep him this week if you take him Saturday night."

"The weekend? You want me to take him for the weekend? Fuck off."

"One night, then I'll take him back. Come on. I'll speak to Matt if you take Charlie for Saturday night."

Seb tuts. "All right. I hope you have a bloody good Saturday night planned. You don't know what I'm giving up here."

"I hope so too," I murmur, my mind already racing with images of Kate and all the ways I'm going to make her body mine. And how to plan a date so fucking good that any lingering doubts we should be together will fucking disappear.

I hang up to the sound of Seb chuckling down the phone, throw back the covers and head to the bathroom, where I plan on jerking off to memories of Kate coming in my arms.

22
KATE

I wake up hornier than I've ever been. I'm slick between the thighs and I could have sworn I was back in the hall with Nico only a second ago. I blink, but he's not here. I'm alone.

Was last night real? A harrowing sensation floods my veins, swiftly followed by a desperate need to crawl out of my own skin. Shame... embarrassment, whatever it is, the rush is so intense my head pounds like I've got another hangover.

And yet it was everything I'd hoped for and more; the strength of Nico's arms around me, the warmth of his hard body, the sound of his voice, heavy with arousal. Fuck it, shame be damned. I want more of it. More of him... I'd do it again in a heartbeat.

I check my phone.

No messages.

But then, he's not exactly a texting kind of guy, is he? No chance of finding a '*Good morning, sweetheart. How are you? I miss you*', kind of message from Nico Hawkston.

I pull the pillow over my head and let out a long groan. A thumping on the door to my room echoes the pounding in my head. I lift the pillow. "What?"

"Kate?" Mum's voice is nearing hysterical, which isn't a good sign.

The door swings open, and Mum enters in a flurry of hair rollers and green face mask, her slim physique wrapped in a pink silk dressing gown.

"Get up. This is all your fault. Nico's run off in the night. Left a note saying he had a family emergency. But I know it was because you were so rude at dinner. Making a scene." She slaps a hand to her forehead, her curlers shaking like Medusa's snakes. "You've always been an attention-seeker, ever since you were tiny. Your father indulged you. I hold him entirely responsible for how you've turned out. No wonder Nico left."

I barely hear the insults because the sound of Nico's name repeatedly barked at me in Mum's highly strung voice has me feeling nauseous. The truth of what happened between us last night burns in my lower belly like a spoonful of arsenic.

"I'm sure Nico genuinely had somewhere he needed to be," I say, hoping Mum can't hear the uncertain tremor in my voice. If I was the one with a car, I might have fled last night too.

Maybe it *was* because of me he left, but not for the reason Mum thinks.

"Oh rubbish," she snaps. "It was you who scared him off. I've never seen such bad behaviour. If you could have at least tried to put the comfort of our guests first, held your tongue for a moment..." Mum sighs like I am the most trying child in the world and she's so hard done by purely because I exist. "If you could have been a little more accommodating, Nico might still be here."

I blush. If Mum knew exactly how accommodating I had been last night, she would be screaming at me for being a hussy.

Loose women never get the guy. That's what Mum thinks anyway, and it's hard to shrug off a mother's opinions, even when you're in your late twenties. They cling like a bad smell.

Maybe that's why I rarely get laid.

Another one of Mum's opinions rears its beastly head; *a man of that calibre would never be interested in you. Not seriously, at least.* But those eyes... the way he looked at me... The pressure of his hard cock against my thigh—

"Are you listening to me?" Mum squawks, hands on her hips.

No, I want to say. *I'm thinking of all the reasons you'd tell me the man who held me in his arms as I came last night won't want anything more to do with me.*

"Sorry," I mumble, before rolling over and pulling the duvet up to my chin.

"Oh, no you don't," Mum says, bustling across the room and yanking my covers off. "Get up. We have too much to do before the guests arrive."

The rest of the day drags as the party approaches. Mum has hardly spoken to me since she harassed me out of bed, and Curtis has been avoiding me since the incident at the pool yesterday. Jack's been so busy helping Mum get everything ready that I haven't had a chance to speak to him.

Part of me wishes I'd taken Nico up on his offer to drive me back to London, but if I'd done that, then we wouldn't have shared that crazy, intense, mind-blowing moment in the hall.

By the time the party is in full swing, I'm grateful for the distraction.

There must be a hundred people here, scattered across the lawn, all quaffing champagne and munching on canapes, which, incidentally, are delicious.

My cheeks ache from fake-smiling.

It's boiling, and my dress is sticking to my thighs. *Damn it*. I fan my face with my hand, but it makes no difference. The sky is bright blue, not a cloud to be seen, and the air smells like freshly cut grass.

Jack somehow looks composed and handsome in a linen shirt and burgundy chino shorts, a neat panama hat perched on his dark hair. He approaches across the lawn, concern etched on his face. "About last night..."

"Yes?"

"I'm sorry. Really. I didn't know what to say."

"I get it. You don't want to rock the boat. I wouldn't if I were you either. Your boat is awesome." I smile, but Jack doesn't smile back.

With one hand, he lifts his hat from the pinch and re-settles it into his thick hair, lips folded in on one another. "Mum gets these ideas in her head and they drive her mad. I think she wants grandchildren and knows I'm nowhere near ready for that shit, so she's got a bee in her bonnet about you approaching thirty and being single."

"There's always something."

Jack toes the grass with his suede loafer, observing the motion for a moment before his shrewd gaze cuts to me. "What was going on with you and Nico yesterday?"

Keep calm. Keep calm. "I don't know what you mean."

"Come on. I know he said he had a family emergency, but the timing is a bit... suspicious. You and Mum get all weird, Nico steps in... the next thing he's driving off in the middle of the night. He's not normally one to run away." Jack takes a swig of his Pimms, emptying half the glass in one go. "Did something happen?"

My body tingles with fear. I glance at him, but he's peering into his glass, fishing out a strawberry which he pops into his mouth.

"No," I lie.

"Hmm." He chews on the strawberry. "You need to be careful with Nico. He's not just a family friend anymore. He's your boss."

"Don't remind me."

Jack chuckles. "You should have seen Mum's face when she found his note. I thought she was going to have an apoplectic fit, and I'd be left mopping bits of her brain off the floor. Either that or it was going to be your brain after she killed you. She was bloody furious."

I roll my eyes. "She's always furious with me. I give up trying to please her. There's no point. Plus"—I elbow Jack—"she has you to make up for all my disappointments."

Another platter of canapes goes by and I snatch one before it disappears.

As if she knows we're talking about her, Mum rushes through the crowd towards us, her face like thunder.

I nudge Jack and nod at Mum. "Something's up."

"Bloody Curtis," she hisses. "His art collection arrived too late to go on the walls and the van's just arrived. Right in the middle of the party." She grabs Jack's arm and yanks it. "And to make matters worse, it's a great big white thing with the most awful things spray-painted all over it. Help them get the stuff out so they can drive away before the guests see. Or the neighbours." She tugs so furiously at Jack's arm that I'm surprised it stays in the socket.

"How bad can it be? What does it say?" I ask.

"Stop smirking," Mum snaps at me. "This is not funny. I'm trying to host a respectable event."

Jack's eyes light up and he stares at something over Mum's head. "It says '*you mother-fucking piece of—*'"

Mum squeaks, and I turn to see the van in question. Foul language and offensive doodles are clearly visible on the paintwork.

Curtis is on the gravel, waving his arms at the driver like some kind of traffic control officer.

"Is that... a huge, erect penis?" I say, unable to conceal my amusement.

Mum yelps, covering her face with both hands. "Oh, heaven forbid."

"Yup." Jack's belly-laughing now, pointing at the splashes spouting out from the oversized tip. "It's ejaculating."

Heads are turning, looking at the van. Someone laughs and a few of the older guests gasp and tut disapprovingly. Mum grips Jack's arm again. "Do something."

Jack shakes his head, biting his bottom lip to stop laughing. "Hold this," he says, giving me his Pimms, which I promptly finish as he runs towards Curtis and the van.

"Oh, this is awful," Mum moans, pulling at the huge pearl earring speared through her right ear. "I tried so hard to make sure everything was perfect, and then this happens. I'm going to be a laughingstock."

"You could have left Dad's art on the walls and avoided this entirely."

"Oh, you little beast." Her voice is so shrill that people nearby start looking over at us. Noticing them, she lowers her voice. "You're enjoying this, aren't you?"

"Oh, no," I say, straining to keep the laughter out of my voice as I take my phone from my handbag and snap a picture of the offensive vehicle. *Elly and Marie will love this.* "It's dreadful. Truly."

23
KATE

I haven't heard from Nico for a week. I haven't been able to focus on my work, and I've spent the days flipping violently between wanting to vomit and wanting to charge up to the twentieth floor to demand an explanation. So far, for the sake of my career, I've done neither.

There were always those rumours flying around that he never fucks the same woman twice. But we didn't even have sex, and he's already avoiding me. Maybe he regrets what happened last weekend. Or maybe it was so insignificant to him he's moved on.

Neither thought is reassuring, and my stomach bubbles nervously.

Tonight is the Lansen welcome drinks on the rooftop bar of the Hawkston building. It's a warm evening, so we're all outside. Nico's supposed to be here. I overheard his PA saying that he had a few things to attend to and would pop in later, but I'm already two glasses of prosecco down and there's been no sign of him.

I try to focus on the view across the City of London: the enormous dome of St Paul's; the huge concrete jungle of the Barbican Centre; even the Shard in the distance.

It's spectacular, but none of it is enough to assuage my nerves. If Nico walks in right now, I'm not sure I'll be able to handle it.

A blonde graduate is lingering at my side. Teresa, I think her name is. She's pretty and vivacious, with a smile that lights up her face.

She's not unpleasant company either, but she's been chewing my ear off about Nico for the past five minutes. "You know him, don't you?" she asks, grabbing a handful of nuts from the table and stuffing them in her mouth. She continues talking without waiting for a response. "I saw him in reception yesterday. I've never seen a corporate man so... hot. He looks really young too. The rest of them are all old and half-bald with huge beer guts." She pauses, glancing over at Jack. "Your brother is gorgeous too, but Nico's more my type. Is he single? Nico, I mean."

"Umm..."

"I guess it wouldn't matter if he was," Teresa plows on. "He's always got some gorgeous new woman on the go. I saw him in the Daily Mail today, pictured with that musician. You know, the one who chopped off all her hair and looks like a beautiful pixie?"

A sharp pain lances through my chest. "Amy Moritz? He was out with her?"

Teresa pulls out her phone. "Yeah. Last night. Look." She flicks her screen to show me images of Amy, laughing as she gets into the back of a cab with Nico.

I've been pining for the bastard and he's out with the music scene's biggest solo star. I'm an idiot to have thought he might want me. To think that what happened between us was anything more than an impulsive explosion of decade-long repressed desire.

Nico wasn't going to say no when I was standing outside his room in my underwear. *Red* underwear. Maybe not contacting me is his way of trying to tell me he's not interested.

"And last month it was that runway model, the one with legs that reach to her armpits. Erica Lefroy." Teresa laughs, oblivious to the effect her words are having on me. "It's not like I have a chance, but a girl can dream, right? If he wanted an office fling, I wouldn't say no."

Maybe Nico's not coming. He's probably too busy. Can I even bear to face him again?

"Excuse me," I say, putting down my drink and moving towards the exit. Teresa is so stuck on Nico I don't think she cares who's listening, and she turns away with a confused shrug, ready to prey on the next pair of ears.

I stride back inside. The glass door closes behind me, shutting out the sound of chatter. My heart is racing. Is it healthy to have an elevated heart rate for this long? Maybe I can skip the gym this weekend because my heart has already had a workout.

I'm a mess.

I storm down the corridor, intending to go home. I'm not waiting for some man who may or may not show his face. I don't want to be like Teresa and the others, desperate for some glimmer of his attention.

But first I need to check out that story. I pull out my phone and put Nico's name into the search bar. I add Amy Moritz for clarity. A dozen stories pop up, each with a variation of the picture Teresa just showed me.

Has Amy Moritz finally tamed the eternal bachelor, Nico Hawkston?

Bachelor billionaire Nico Hawkston, spotted with the music industry's brightest star.

Is Nico banging Amy?

Emotion whirls in my chest. My fingers are shaking as I scroll. I need to get out of here now, before I scream. I put my head down and hurry my steps towards the lift, slamming my hand on the button.

The lights above show it's coming up.

The lift dings to signal its arrival, and the doors open.

And there he is.

Just him; no one else. My surroundings go mute as his presence consumes my senses. That unmistakable scent, which I swear must be made of pheromones, assaults my nostrils. No matter how pissed off I am, I'm unwillingly catapulted into a state of arousal.

He's wearing a gorgeous navy suit. A pale blue silk tie hangs from his neck over a pressed white shirt. How he looks immaculate at the end of a workday, I do not know.

He tips his head to one side, full lips tilting into a close-mouthed smile. Dark eyes meet mine, shining with an irresistible mischief, as if I'm exactly the person he's looking for. And whatever he's thinking, it's not PG. My chest tightens and blood surges to the lower half of my body.

He strokes a hand down the length of his tie, not taking his eyes off me. The doors begin to close and, calm as ever, he presses the button to hold them open. "Are you getting in?"

My heart splutters. *Why does this feel so dangerous?*

I glance over my shoulder. We're completely alone.

"Aren't you going to the drinks?" I ask.

"Not if you're leaving."

My mouth dries out, and perspiration gathers under my arms. *What does that mean?*

Run. Take the stairs.

I probably ought to listen to my flight response, but my whole body is vibrating with Nico's presence. I'm powerless to resist his pull.

I step inside and stand next to him as the doors close. The right side of my body is sparking at his nearness. The air is thick, charged with the promise of sex.

There's no way he can't feel it. In fact, I'm sure he's *creating* it.

Another wave of arousal washes over me. He's not even touching me and I'm drowning in it.

Nico presses the button for the twentieth floor, and the lift descends. The back of his other hand grazes mine. It's a small point of contact, but I feel the burn of it *everywhere;* a tiny taste of what my body craves.

"I haven't heard from you," I say.

He looks down at me, his dark eyes full of heat. "Did you want to?" His tone is curious, but his voice level, as if my answer has no bearing on him.

How can he be so cool? My body temperature is skyrocketing.

I glance at the lit-up numbers shifting as we pass through the floors. How long do I have in here with him? What happens when we reach his floor?

"Are you going to answer me?" he asks.

"I don't know." I say, twisting to face him. "Are you dating Amy Moritz?"

His brow creases. "Amy? No. She's a friend. Seb wants her to sing at his birthday next year." His gaze intensifies. "Are you keeping tabs on me?" He sounds amused. Delighted, even, which is annoying, to say the least.

"I am not 'keeping tabs on you.' One of the graduates showed me an article. What about Erica Lefroy? The model?"

I need to stop talking. I'm giving myself away.

"We went on a few dates a couple of years ago, but there was no chemistry. She's a friend too." He arches a brow. "I'm single. Unattached. Is that what you want to know?"

I cross my arms, determined to say nothing else, but a moment later I find myself asking, "Why didn't you get in touch? You had my number."

"And you had mine, but you didn't use it. I thought you might regret what happened, and I didn't want to pressure you."

I narrow my eyes. "You're putting a gentlemanly spin on shitty behaviour."

He chuckles, and annoyance flares inside me. The last thing I want him to do right now is laugh at me.

I opt for a direct question. "The shoes. Why did you buy them for me?"

All signs of amusement vanish from his face. He inhales, blows out the exhale, and waits so long to respond that I wonder if he heard me. Then his eyes take on that same look from last week when he asked me to touch myself, and I couldn't look away if I wanted to.

"Why did you draw me so many times?"

The air between us crackles and static buzzes on every exposed inch of my skin. We turn to face one another like we share a centre of gravity, the inches between us shrinking until I can feel the heat of him through my shirt.

Nico lifts his hand, and I hold my breath as he reaches towards me. He rests his fingers on my neck, his thumb strumming over the dip between my collarbones. "God, Kate. You have no idea how much I've wanted you."

His words increase my aching need, and I tip my head back on a sigh, giving him more access. He leans towards me, his lips almost touching mine. The possibility of kissing him is excruciating.

"If we do this, there's no going back." His voice is hoarse with desire so palpable I feel it in between my legs.

"Do what?" I ask breathlessly.

"If I kiss you, taste you... *fuck* you, we can't undo it. Is that what you want?" He runs his lips along my jaw, lightly kissing the skin. "I need to know it's what you want."

My breathing is all over the place; my body throbbing. Every sense is heightened to excruciating precision, and when he brushes his lips to my throat, a small whimper escapes me.

He makes a low murmur of appreciation that thrums all the way to my toes. He nips my neck with his teeth, sending a jolt of energy right to my clit.

"Is it what you want?" he repeats. He grips my hip and pulls me closer until there's barely an inch between us. The thick length of his cock presses against me. *He's as turned on as I am.*

"Answer me."

Yes. Yes, yes, yes. A thousand times, yes.

But not a word of willing escapes me as my blood runs thin and fast in my veins, panic roaring through the cloud of lust that fogs my brain. Thoughts cascade, an avalanche that chills me; he didn't call for a week, Amy Moritz, my dad, the deal, Erica Lefroy...

"No."

Nico jerks backwards like my words have scalded him. He touches the tips of his fingers to his lips, his eyes roving back and forth across my face, like he's trying to find some explanation hidden in my expression.

"No?" Disbelief spreads like ice through his tone. He tugs on the tie knot at his neck, and his expression hardens. He jams his finger on the button for the sixth floor. "Then you should leave."

"What?"

"I can't have you in here right now. I can't bear another moment in your presence if I can't touch you. I'm not playing games. I won't do it. If you don't want anything to happen between us, then you need to go. Now." Neat, hard muscles stand out along his beautiful jaw. There's a darkness in his eyes that flares, barely controlled.

What happens if I don't leave? What happens if I tip Nico Hawkston over the edge?

The lift dings to alert us to our arrival on the twentieth floor. The doors open and, with one final dark-eyed questioning look at me, Nico steps out and marches down the corridor towards his office without a backward glance.

The doors stay open, gaping like the gates of hell. The office beyond is quiet and the lights are low.

No one's here.

The lift doors begin to close, and against my better judgment, I stick my hand out to stop them and slide through the gap. This is the most reckless thing I've ever done, but I'm so turned on, so wound up, that it's like I'm having an out-of-body experience.

Every reservation, every hesitation, every single reason not to, has been blown clear out of my mind by the absolute certainty that I can't let this man walk away.

I don't give myself a moment to second guess it. If I stop, I'll never be able to come back.

My heels click down the corridor, my breaths echoing in the silence.

I reach his office, my hand resting on the handle for less than a second before I push the door open.

Nico has his back to me, hands braced on the desk. His broad shoulders look tense, his head lowered between them.

Beyond him, the London skyline sparkles with lights. There might be millions of people out there, but right now, he's the only one who matters.

"Don't come in here," he warns. "I swear, if you step inside this office, I will not be held responsible—"

I kick the door closed behind me, cutting him off. He jerks his head up and his whole body stiffens.

The tension is so thick I can physically feel it. Even the palms of my hands are tingling.

Nico straightens, standing to his full height. Slowly, he turns to face me. His chest rises and falls as he fixes me with a dark gaze, equal parts resentment and desire; a toxic infusion that I can't resist. His hand finds the knot of his tie, loosening it before he undoes the top button of his shirt. "Lock it."

God, his voice. So deep and commanding.

I turn around to lock the door and the air between us prickles against my back, the pressure of *him* forcing the breath from my lungs. Nico's footsteps approach and he stops directly behind me, planting his feet on either side of mine. My heart beats out of control as one of his hands hits the door with a thump, fingers splayed to the left side of my head. Tendons and veins stand out like ribbons under his skin.

With his other hand, he shifts my ponytail and drapes it over my shoulder. The warmth of his breath hits my exposed nape and a shiver trips down my spine.

"I'm going to ask you one more time." His voice rumbles against my ear. "Do you want this?"

I gulp as I nod.

"Say it."

"Yes."

He kisses the back of my neck, a smile in his voice as he murmurs, "I always knew you were a good girl."

My breath hitches as his praise spills through me like melted butter, the heat of it trickling down to my core. His free hand skims the waistband of my skirt, his fingers sliding along it all the way to my navel, but rather than dip beneath it, he grips my hip and spins me to face him. My body is utterly pliant to his will.

He's right; there's no going back from this. Whatever happens from here, I'm forever changed. Even if this, right now, is as far as it goes between us, every cell in my being has been shaken awake, shaken *alive*, by him.

He closes his eyes, and his muttered '*fuck*,' rasps like a blade on a whetstone.

His mouth crashes against mine; warm and wet and sending spirals of heat dancing through my entire body. *He's kissing me, he's kissing me*, are the last thoughts that race through my mind before the intensity of his kiss destroys my ability to think. His tongue slides between my lips, and each sensuous swipe dominates my mouth like he's trying to force a complete surrender. The man kisses like a master, and need surges through me with dizzying force.

My hands find his shoulders and tug at his jacket, but I can't shift it. Panting heavily, Nico breaks our kiss to shrug it off himself. He drops it to the floor, releasing a fresh wave of his glorious, masculine cologne mixed with something else that's indescribably Nico.

His eyes find mine and he smiles, bites his bottom lip, and tilts his head at me as if to say, *fuck, yes. Let's do this*.

He kisses me again, a little more gently this time, like he's savouring me rather than devouring me. He slides his hands around my hips, lifting me up, and my skirt rises to my waist as I wrap my legs around him.

His erection presses against the hot centre of my arousal and I grind against him, desperately seeking friction. He growls against the side of my neck, his fingers digging into my flesh.

My shoes fall to the floor along with my inhibitions as he carries me to the sofa, sits me down on the edge, and kneels before me. His eyes blaze like a man possessed.

Hooking his fingertips into the fabric at my hips, he urges my underwear down. I rise just enough for him to slide my panties off and throw them to the floor.

"Spread your legs. I want to see you."

A bolt of electricity blasts through me, and I bite my lip to contain a moan. Powerless to resist him, I part my legs and bring my bare heels up to the edge of the sofa. My knees fall open, exposing me to him entirely.

He leans forward, his tongue swiping over his bottom lip as he eyes my exposed pussy, and my brain short circuits. I've never been inspected this way; no man has ever paid such close attention to such an intimate part of me. And now, of all the men in the world, it's Nico fucking Hawkston between my legs, staring at my cunt like he wants to devour it as his last fucking meal.

Self-consciousness shoots through me, and my thighs seek to lock him out, muscles contracting as I try to clamp them together. A warm palm grips my thigh, holding them apart, and Nico's concerned gaze meets my own.

"You okay?" he says softly.

No. Maybe. I have no idea. "Uh... what are you doing?"

He quirks a brow, then slowly grins. "Checking for cobwebs."

My hand flies to cover my eyes as my drunken words from the hotel come back to me. *My pussy could be full of cobwebs.* "Oh, God," I wail, peeking at him between my fingers. "I'm never drinking again."

He dips his head, a low chuckle escaping him. *He's gorgeous like this.* When he raises his eyes to mine, his amusement fades, replaced with a kindness that simmers with heat.

"You're perfect. Relax." His thumb gently strokes my inner thigh. "I've got you."

His sincerity eases my body's tension, and I let my hand fall from my face. My legs soften, allowing Nico to manoeuvre me so he can nestle between them.

"So beautiful," he whispers, kissing the inside of my knee, trailing his lips up my thigh. "I've waited so long for this."

How long? Before I have time to wonder, he blows out a breath that cools my wet pussy. It has me squirming against the leather and a satisfied smile pulls at one side of his lips as he drags his gaze to meet mine. He rises on his knees and cups the back of my neck, drawing me into a passionate kiss that steals the air from my lungs.

His other hand trails down my body like a comet, burning up everything in its wake, until his entire palm, hot and tantalising, rests between my thighs. I arch my back, my clit desperately seeking the friction that's just out of reach.

"So eager." Delight dances in his eyes as he slides one finger over my clit, applying a gentle pressure, but his touch is gone before it can provide any sort of relief. The quick jolt of intense pleasure that fires through me isn't enough. Not nearly enough.

His finger continues a path to my entrance and traces it lightly.

"Please," I beg, my body bowing off the sofa, my pussy seeking *more*.

"So fucking wet," he murmurs, as he drags his mouth across my jaw before nipping down on my bottom lip with his teeth. "I wanted to feel this last weekend. Wanted to do this—"

I gasp as he thrusts a finger inside me, the heel of his hand resting over my clit. He slides a second finger in, curling them, hitting that sweet spot inside with a precision that triggers a deep, insatiable roll of pleasure. I shudder, lowing deliriously.

"Jesus, Kate."

He thrusts his fingers deeper, and I tighten around him as he fucks me with them. Pressure builds between my legs, and I writhe against his palm, chasing the release of the orgasm I so desperately need.

He drags his fingers out, pulling my slickness over my clit, teasing it with his fingertips. Sparks erupt, tingling through my body as he slides his fingers inside me again, burying them knuckle deep. His thumb finds my clit, circling it over and over, faster and faster.

The sound of his fingers fucking me fills the office and I fist my hands against the sofa as I take the pleasure he's giving me.

I throw my head back as I grind against his hand like a wild animal, seeking the final bit of pressure that will tip me over the edge. Pleasure spreads from my clit, down my thighs, all the way to my toes.

My body jerks and shudders, and I moan as I pump my hips. He works me perfectly, teasing every tendril of desire into one potent point that throbs between my legs. It's more than I can bear.

My muscles go rigid, my hands desperately clenching. "Nico... fuck, Nico," I cry, repeating his name like it's the only word in the world that matters.

"So fucking hot," he praises.

I teeter on the edge, unbearably close.

"Come for me. I want to hear you scream," he commands, and my orgasm explodes. I'm lost to the sensations that flood my body. I scream in stuttering gasps, trembling and shaking against him as the force of my pleasure rips through me. It lasts longer than I've ever experienced, surging in dwindling peaks of jerking ecstasy as he continues to stroke my swollen clit.

When the last remnants of pleasure have calmed, my thighs collapse inward, resting against Nico's shoulders. He pulls his fingers out, bringing them to his mouth, where he sucks them and lets out a sigh of satisfaction. "Wanted to do that, too." His voice is thick with desire.

He leans down between my legs and kisses my clit, which is so sensitive I jerk back, and in response he chases it, sucking it into his mouth.

"Stop, God, stop," I cry, grabbing his hair with both fists to pull him off me. He relents with a rumbling chuckle that vibrates through my tailbone.

"You taste divine," he says. "Next time, I'll make you come with my mouth."

I moan at the thought of it. I can't wait.

I sit forward, sliding my hand between his legs, cupping the erection that feels far bigger than any I've ever touched before. Not that there have been many, but his cock is far and beyond the largest.

"Let me see you," I whisper, fumbling with his trousers.

He undoes the button, lowers the zip, and his cock pokes out of his boxers.

I inhale sharply. "Wow."

Nico smirks, and no wonder. It isn't even fully exposed and it looks huge. How will it fit inside me? I slide my hand into his underwear, wrapping my fingers around the base. It's warm and smooth, the rigidity cloaked in soft skin... It's perfect. Nico Hawkston has a perfect penis and an insane desire to slide right onto it rolls through me.

He hisses through his teeth as I draw my hand up the hard length of him.

A sharp knock on the door shocks us both and we turn to stare. My hand rockets off his cock as someone on the other side rattles the door handle. "Uncle Nico? Are you in there?"

Nico's face contorts, and he lets out a groan, fisting a hand into his hair and tugging it from the roots. "I'm gonna have the bluest balls in the whole of fucking London at this rate."

I can't help but giggle, especially as I'm still blissed out after the best orgasm I've ever had in my entire life. Nico stands and tucks himself in.

The knocking continues.

"It's Charlie," comes the voice from outside the office. "I'm ready to go home. I'm tired. I know you're in there. I can hear you."

I look up, alarmed, and mouth, "He can hear us?"

Nico shrugs and holds out his hand and pulls me off the sofa to my feet. "If this is what it's like to have kids, I'm getting a vasectomy."

I press my lips together to contain a burst of nervous laughter.

He tugs me flush against him, kissing me hard on the mouth, then holds me at arm's length before letting go and checking the time on his watch. "Shit, it's late. I forgot about Charlie. He's staying with me for a bit."

"Doesn't his mum live in London?"

Nico frantically tucks in his shirt, adjusts the crotch of his suit. "Yes." He doesn't explain and I don't ask. He runs his hands around the waistband of his trousers. "I need to take him home. I'm so sorry to ask, but could you... hide?"

"Are you serious?"

"Yes. Get under the desk. Please." He's moving about the room now, picking up his jacket and sliding it on, buttoning his collar and fixing his tie around his neck.

He picks up my underwear, offers it to me, then changes his mind, grins and slides it into his pocket.

I reach out for it. "Hey."

"Oh, come on," he says, pointing at his dick, which is still hard and trapped in the crotch of his trousers. "Let me have something."

I roll my lips to stop myself from breaking into a full smile. He's hard for *me*.

"Fine," I huff, faking reluctance.

Charlie thumps on the door again, and Nico shoots a look towards the noise.

"I'll open the door, but I won't let him in. Wait until we've gone, then call yourself a cab. Put it through expenses. I'm really, *really* sorry." He presses a quick kiss to my cheek. "But my dick is even sorrier."

"Are you there? Can you hear me?" Charlie's voice penetrates the room.

"I'm here," Nico answers, his tone sharp.

A tentative pause. Then, quieter, "Can we go home?"

"Go," Nico mouths, shooing me towards the desk with one hand. I roll my eyes and get on my knees, crawling beneath the desk, tucking my legs in. Nico follows, crouching so I can see him, one hand on the desktop above. My breath catches at the sight of him staring at me, so excruciatingly handsome.

"Next time, you're going to do that naked."

"You wish," I say, half-laughing.

"Oh, I do. And you will." He grins, gives me a wink, and rises to his full height.

"Nico, wait." I keep my voice low.

He crouches again. "What?"

"Am I going to have to wait another week to see you again?" I cringe at the desperation in my voice, but his smile is so warm that it instantly allays all my fears.

"You think I could stay away from you that long? What are you doing tomorrow?"

Tomorrow? "Nothing."

"I'll pick you up at ten. Pack an overnight bag and bring your passport."

My passport?

He doesn't wait for agreement before he stands again. I can only see his feet and lower legs. He approaches the door, kicks my shoes out of sight and then pulls it open.

"Charlie. Let's go."

I wait until I can no longer hear them before I crawl out from under the desk and brush myself down. What the hell just happened here? And what do I pack for a night away with Nico Hawkston?

24
KATE

There's a permanent buzz under my skin as if Nico has rewired my body. I'm in a constant state of heady excitement. The slightest brush of my underwear against my pussy and I'm plunging into a state of intense arousal. It's not sustainable; I barely slept last night.

"I can't stand being around you," Marie mutters, as she packs her bag to head to the hospital. "You're like a horny version of Pollyanna. I forgot what you're like when you're getting laid."

"I haven't got laid."

Elly giggles. "Not yet." She focuses on Marie. "Lay off her anyway. We've had grumpy Kate on our hands for too long. Next time I see Mr. Hawkston, I'm going to congratulate him on giving you such a fantastic orgasm that you've metamorphosed into a pleasant human being."

Normally, I'd have something to say about an insult like this, but today a grin threatens to split my face. I can't contain my elation. Nico's picking me up in ten minutes and I have no idea what he has planned or where we're going.

"All I'm saying is, we don't know how long this is going to last," Marie explains, with her *I'm a doctor, trust me*, expression on her face. "In fact, you don't even know what *this* is."

"You're such a killjoy," Elly argues.

"And you're the kind of romantic that encourages people to lose their heads so they can't see where they're going. Stop encouraging this. Maybe if you hadn't, this wouldn't have happened."

I'm inclined to pipe up and say that it would have. My body has a mind of its own where Nico's concerned, and I'm at the mercy of overpowering hormonal impulses. But my friends are barely pausing for breath in their back and forth, so I say nothing.

"His eyes aren't painted on. I mean, look at her. She's bloody gorgeous." Elly's eyes flash at me. "You're gorgeous. And, he's thoughtful. He bought those shoes. He definitely cares."

"Or he just wants to get his nuts off." Marie looms over us as we sit at the table. "What about kidnapping her and sending her to the spa? Demanding that she have lunch with him? That was rude."

"Or... romantic," Elly counters, pronouncing 'romantic' like it's an exciting word she's just discovered. "He was trying to seduce her with the sauna and seabass."

"Stop talking about me like I'm not here," I blurt, and the two of them turn their shocked expressions on me. "I can make up my own mind about this. And I don't need you two fighting over it."

Marie folds her arms, a severe look on her face. "What about your dad? The company? Nico's role in his death?"

A rush of unpleasant emotion swirls in my stomach. I'm putting my hormones and sex drive ahead of my dad's memory and my career for the first time, and the reminder doesn't feel good.

Marie must see the change in my expression because she winces. "Sorry."

"It was a heart attack," I say. "Not Nico."

Holy shit. I can't believe I'm saying this. But the words resonate with a truth they never held before; maybe Nico's not the villain I made him out to be.

Marie nods, like she's thought this all along. She's a doctor, after all, and the death certificate says cardiac arrest. I find myself nodding too, like a few good orgasms can erase all the resentment I've directed at Nico over the years.

"I'm just urging caution," Marie adds. "He holds all the cards here. He's rich, he's your boss. And we know he's controlling. And, to top it off, he knows you're crazy about him because you dropped all your sketches on the floor for him to see." She waves a rigid arm through the air like she's laying a rug over the ground.

"Are you trying to shit all over this?" Elly asks.

"I'm being realistic. I don't want to see Kate get hurt." Marie focuses on me, her eyes full of a pained compassion that's hard to look at. It makes me feel pathetic. "By all means, have your office fling, but don't start sketching him. That's not healthy."

"Got it," I say, keeping my voice light. "Sex is good. Drawing is bad."

Marie covers her face with both hands and groans. "Let him fuck you, but not fuck you over."

The buzzer goes before her words have time to sink in. I leap to my feet, grab my bag, utter a hurried farewell, and rush downstairs and onto the street.

A blacked out Range Rover is idling outside the flat. Nico is standing on the pavement, talking to his driver through the open car window. I take a moment to survey him, all casual and sexy in his chinos and a pale blue shirt.

When he catches sight of me, he breaks into a full smile, so dazzling that I'm glad I'm wearing sunglasses.

He stalks towards me and reaches for my bag, which he takes in one hand before drawing me to him with the other and planting a soft, chaste kiss on my lips. "Morning, beautiful."

Wow. Those are words I never expected to hear Nico Hawkston direct at me. A little happy spark ignites in my heart.

"Hi," I reply, gazing up at him.

He opens the door for me and I slide across the leather seats. He gets in after me and at some point in the process, my bag disappears. A slick transition, as I glimpse the driver holding it before he closes the door after us.

My laptop is in that bag. "My luggage—"

"You don't need it right now. It's safe. I promise."

I sit back in the leather seat, opting to trust him. I can't very well tell him I'm bringing my laptop with me on our weekend away. I'll look like a crazy workaholic.

Nico presses a button, and an opaque screen rises, separating us from his driver.

"Privacy," he mutters, watching as it closes.

As soon as the screen clicks in place, we collide. His lips are on mine, hot and unrelenting, his tongue swiping roughly against my own. I want to swallow him, take every piece of him inside me. My fingers flit over his body like they don't know where to land.

I suck his bottom lip as his hand cups my breast, kneading the flesh. His thumb grazes my nipple, turning it into a hardened peak beneath my dress.

All of a sudden, his touch disappears, stealing the warmth of his body. I open my eyes to see him shift back to his side of the car, his back hitting his seat with a thump. He tips his head back and stares up at the roof. His chest is heaving. "Fuck." He mutters the word like a prayer.

Unease spills through my insides. "What's wrong?"

He rolls the back of his head on the seat rest to look at me. "I didn't anticipate what this was going to be like. Not really."

"Meaning?"

He leans across to kiss me, nipping my lower lip with his teeth before he releases it. "I have no self control around you."

Relief curls through me. *It's mutual, at least.*

"And I like control. I need it."

"Maybe"—I slide my hand up his thigh and cup his erection over his trousers—"it's time to let someone else take charge."

He laughs, a throaty rumble that I immediately want to hear again. "Not yet." His cock twitches beneath my palm, but he lifts my wrist and places my hand in my lap.

I stare at my fingers, curled on my thighs, the skin of my wrist tingling where he touched me. "Is this your thing? Self-denial?"

He laughs again, that delicious deep sound that comes from somewhere dark and dangerous. I want to press my mouth to his and inhale it.

"No. Not at all. But I like you. I'm not going to fuck you in the back of a car. Not the first time, at least."

"And if you didn't like me, you would?"

His tongue swipes over his top lip. "Absolutely."

"Damn."

He flashes his perfect white teeth at me. "Don't tempt me."

Resting his hand on my thigh, he plays with the fabric of my summer dress. To my frustration, his fingers rise no higher and he makes no attempt to slide beneath the cotton.

Through the car's tinted windows, the streets of London flash by, and inside the darkened vehicle I start to feel sleepy. I rest my head against Nico's shoulder, feeling the pleasant warmth of his body against mine.

"You've got your passport?" His voice rouses me a little.

"Yeah. Where are we going?"

"My apartment."

"Why do I need my passport for that? I thought we were going on a date. I thought we were doing something."

"I am doing something." His eyes simmer with heat and my insides melt. "I'm doing you."

I open my mouth in mock outrage, and he chuckles. "Relax. We're going to my apartment, but not my London one."

Ah. Of course, he has more than one. "Where are we going, then?"

He takes my hand in his, sliding his fingers between mine. "Wait and see."

25
NICO

Kate's standing next to me on the tarmac, and it takes every ounce of my self-control not to touch her... stroke her... grab her and never let go. *Fuck.* I am in way too deep here, but I'm enjoying the water.

A warm breeze lifts a tendril of stray hair off the fine curve of Kate's neck, and I want to kiss the skin right there, but instead, I thread my fingers through hers and squeeze. She smiles but doesn't turn my way. She's too busy staring at the private jet and, if I'm not mistaken, trying to look unimpressed.

"Paris," she breathes. "I can't believe we're going to Paris."

"Yup. One night. Whirlwind tour." I put my arm around her to guide her to the jet.

This time, she smiles up at me. *God, what I wouldn't do to see that smile every day...* It's a damn sight better than having her scowling at me, although I didn't mind that much either. Any contact with Kate is a precious gift. I can't explain it. Normally, my tolerance for other people's bullshit is low, but Kate skirts all my previous boundaries and rules. She's a beautiful exception.

The noise of the engines rumbles as I lead her up the stairs. Her hair blows about her face, her summer skirt flapping around her knees. She uses her free hand to stop it flying up. The effect is quaint and has me wanting to scoop her up in my arms and into the jet like a groom carrying his bride over the threshold.

Kate takes a few steps inside, then halts, her gaze shifting over the interior. Wide leather seats, a corner sofa area and dining table. Gleaming wood finish. She rubs the toe of her shoe against the carpet and stares down at the plush red pile.

"Holy shit," she mutters.

I repress the urge to laugh at how her attempt to remain unimpressed has completely disintegrated.

"Never been in one of these?"

She shakes her head, running her fingers along the armrest of one of the chairs.

"Welcome aboard, Mr. Hawkston," says a smartly dressed air stewardess. "Can I get you a glass of champagne for take-off?"

Kate throws an excited glance my way. "Oh, yes—"

"No."

Kate's eyes peel wide and the stewardess's gaze flicks between us, unsure who to listen to.

I slide my arm around Kate and pull her close to whisper into her ear. "It's a short flight. Let's not waste time." I nod my head in the direction of the bedroom at the back. The door is ajar and Kate follows my gaze, her eyebrows rising when she catches sight of the huge, perfectly made bed.

"But—"

"I want to be sober when I fuck you," I whisper.

Kate's eyes widen. "*When?*"

I grin at her echo of our earlier conversation. "When," I confirm.

Kate drags her gaze to the stewardess. "No champagne."

The stewardess gives a little smile. "Can I get you anything else?"

"No, thank you. Don't disturb us until landing," I say.

I grab Kate's hand and lead her towards two large leather seats by the window where we sit down and buckle in. I'm dizzy with excitement at the prospect of having her all to myself, but she's distracted, glancing back to the open bedroom door, a quizzical look on her face.

"What?" I ask.

She brings her focus back to me. "You wouldn't fuck me in the back of the car, but you will fuck me in a private jet?"

"The fact that you're even asking that question shows we haven't spent nearly enough time together."

She laughs, but when she notices I'm not laughing, she falls silent. A cute little crease forms between her eyebrows. "Shit. We're really doing this."

"Only if you want to."

She says nothing, and for a moment I wonder if she's going to change her mind.

The jet engines roar to life and we begin the taxi for take-off.

"What's wrong?" I cant my head towards the window. The plane is gathering speed. "If you're having doubts, you're a bit late."

Her face scrunches. "Is this weird?"

"What?"

"This." She waves a hand between us. "Me and you. Together."

"We're about to take-off at two hundred miles an hour and you're worried about whether us being here is weird?"

"I'm serious, Nico. I don't know what's happening."

She drops her hands, wringing them over one another. I place my hand over her clasped ones, and beneath my touch her fingers relax.

I lean across to kiss her, but her lips are tense. Resistant. She wants an answer more than a kiss, but I don't know what the fuck to say. I still don't know what this is, but I know I want to be here, with her, with every particle of my being.

My tongue gently probes her lips until she parts them and lets me in. This kiss is soft, gentle, and conveys more than any words I might give her. I hope she understands.

We break apart, and she stares out the window as we race down the runway, the cabin shaking around us as the nose tips upward and the wheels lift off.

Kate's fingers are laced in mine as we rise through the clouds. "Is it weird for you?" she asks again. "Tell me the truth."

I chuckle. *Always after the truth.* "A bit. But not really. I knew we'd end up here after I saw you that night on the balcony at Jack's party."

At the mention of her brother's name, she flinches. At some point, if this is a serious thing, and it sure feels like it is, we'll have to tell him. I'm kicking that into the long grass for now, though.

"How did you know back then?" Her nose wrinkles as she leans towards me. "That wasn't a positive interaction. I didn't leave that night feeling good. About you, or anything."

"I'm good at reading people."

"And you read me?"

I smirk. "You're very easy to read. You want to fuck me as much as I want to fuck you."

Her mouth falls into a mockery of a shocked O, her eyes darting across my face, before her puckered lips transform into a smile.

"You're the most arrogant man—"

"You want to join the mile high club?"

"Yes, please."

26
KATE

The words are barely out of my mouth before Nico is leaning over me, unbuckling me from the huge leather chair, guiding me to standing. His eyes burn with lust and he's not even trying to hide it as he rakes them over me, making my knees weaken.

"Ready?" he asks. "No going back."

I swallow and give the barest hint of a nod, but it's enough for Nico.

He grabs my hand and leads me to the bedroom, slamming the door behind us. He wraps one arm around my waist, his other hand cupping my face. The fire of his touch burns me into submission, and when he tugs me flush against him, I fold into him until every tiny gap between our bodies ceases to exist.

We devour each other's mouths like we're starving. It's messy and hard and soft and warm and wet, with nipping of teeth and swiping of tongues. A fusion of body and breath.

I pull at his shirt, tease at his collar, fingers flitting over his neck. He slides his hands up my spine and into my hair, fisting it with a dominant tug. It's too much and not enough all at once.

"Fuck, I want you," he growls. "I'm crazy about you."

My head spins. I can't believe this is happening. His words, his hands, his touch, boiling me up from the inside. It's a dizzying dream come true. I can hardly breathe with the shock of sensations racing through my body.

But there are nagging doubts in my mind. *Can I really give myself to this man? Do I trust him?*

I push back, staring up at him. "This is mad, Nico. Paris... the private jet..."

His mouth swallows my words; his tongue, hot and wet, swipes between my lips. I push back harder and he pulls away.

His lips are wet and shining, and each breath is tortured. His eyes narrow like he can't believe I'm saying this now. "It's not mad. This is my life. What did you expect?"

"It's too much. You can't buy me, Nico."

He considers this for a moment. "I know. You've made that very clear." He draws close, the tip of his nose skating down the side of my neck. My body erupts in goosebumps. "But I don't need to buy you. This fucking chemistry..." He shakes his head against my neck and blows out a hot breath. "Do you feel it?"

Yes, I feel it.

"It's you I want. All of you, all the fucking time." He drags his teeth over his bottom lip. "If you let me, I'll give you more pleasure than you've ever known."

He pulls me close and his erection presses against me. I gasp and instinctively try to pull away, but he keeps me pinned to him, and beneath the strength of his embrace, I soften. "See what you do to me?" he whispers. "You're the hottest thing I've ever seen."

My legs weaken and suddenly he's holding more of my weight than they are. One of those lusty little moans creeps out between my teeth and at the sound, Nico chuckles.

"You don't walk away from an attraction like this," he says. "So quit questioning it. This is one in a million. I can't let you go. Not this time."

Not this time? "I'm not going anywhere."

I feel his lips part in a smile against my neck. "Not at thirty thousand feet, you aren't. For the duration of the flight, you're mine."

I want to tell him I'll be his for longer than that... that I've already been his for years. But before I can form the words, his lips find mine again. Each sweep of his tongue sends a lightning bolt of desire right between my legs. One of his hands rides up my thigh, sliding beneath my dress to my bum. He kneads the flesh, his fingertips pressing so hard I'll have bruises tomorrow.

The pain is barely enough to penetrate the haze of my arousal. I'd take more of it, *much more*, if it only meant he would touch me, harder, deeper, and more completely.

I want him to destroy me. If he doesn't, it won't be enough to satisfy the wave of desire that's rising through me. He hooks my thigh up around his hip, pressing his erection against the throbbing ache between my legs.

Like an unwanted guest, Marie's warning bounces into my head. *Don't let him fuck you over.*

Is this all a mistake? Will I ever feel at ease with Nico Hawkston? Or will my feelings always be resting on a knife edge; one slip and the blade will tear through my heart?

Nico kisses me harder, as if he knows I'm having doubts. He tastes so good I don't care if it's a mistake or not. I want him more than I fear what having him might do to me, and now, when my body is so close to getting everything it ever wanted, I'm not about to back away.

With his hands on my body, his lips on my mouth, and arousal flooding my veins, I choose uncertainty over giving in. *I choose Nico, and consequences be damned.*

The fingertips of his other hand press against my panties. They're already damp. He nudges the fabric aside, sliding his finger deep into my pussy. The slick sound of my arousal is deafening in my ears. He lets out a low chuckle that vibrates against my chest. "Mmm," he hums. "Are you mine, Kate?"

He slides a second finger in and I moan, letting my head fall back.

"I don't know. Maybe."

"Hmmm." He circles my clit with his thumb, sending shocks of pleasure through my core. "I don't like the word maybe." He thrusts his fingers deeper inside me. "Try again. Are you mine?"

I moan as he introduces a third finger, and the stretch is almost painful. He curls them against my G-spot and my body trembles with rising pleasure.

I give in. "Yes. God, yes. I'm yours."

"Good." His voice is smooth as he continues to fuck me with his fingers.

I tilt my hips, riding his hand, and fisting my hands in his hair. "Please, Nico. I want you inside me."

A noise rumbles in his chest, a look of unrestrained desire crossing his face. "Fuck, hearing you say that..." He breaks off, as if even thinking about my words will send him over the edge. He slides his fingers out and lifts me in his arms, supporting both my thighs with his hands. I tighten my legs around his hips as he walks me towards the bed, lowering me onto it.

I shuffle out of my panties and throw them across the cabin, along with the last of my willpower to resist this man.

He eases my thighs open, biting the flesh as he moves towards my wet pussy, so slick now I wonder if it's actually dripping.

Suddenly, his mouth is there, his tongue running from my arse to my clit. It feels delicious and wild all at once, and I let out a low moan. His tongue slides into my entrance before rising again to my clit. He sucks it quick and hard.

His fingers enter me again whilst he tends to my clit with his mouth.

I'm embarrassingly turned on, my hips rolling against his chin, his tongue, seeking more of him. I want him to demolish me, destroy me, devour every part of my body. I've never needed anything as much as I need this. It feels as though all the years of longing for him, waiting for him, craving him, are demanding satisfaction at once. It's driving me to distraction.

He presses his palm against my stomach and pins me to the bed as the fingers of his other hand exert pressure against that sweet, sensitive spot inside me with absolute precision. The flat of his tongue swipes up my swollen clit, and he sucks it between his teeth.

I've never been handled with such skill. I'm teetering on the edge of orgasm, angling my hips towards his mouth, forcing that desperate ache building within me against his tongue. I grab the back of his head with both hands, pushing his face harder between my legs.

"Oh, God," I groan, thrusting my head back against the pillow. Sparks ignite at the apex of my thighs, shooting through my hips.

"That's not my name—"

"Oh, shit, shit. I'm close, don't stop. I'm going to come—"

"Not yet."

He stops and I stare down at him, his lips and chin gleaming with my wetness.

"What?" I squeal. "No, please—"

He kisses me, and I can taste myself on him. His mouth shifts to my ear and he sucks on the lobe before he says, "I'm claiming you. Every inch of your body, every one of your orgasms." His lips brush my cheek as he dips his mouth to suck my neck like he wants to brand me, making electricity fizz beneath my skin. "You're. All. Mine." His voice is low and full of a lust so possessive that the sound trickles down my spine, pooling between my legs like warm molasses.

I'm only just recovering as he pulls back, flashing me the sexiest smirk that has me wanting to shed the last of my clothes. He tugs his trousers and boxers down, kicking them off before kneeling over me with his fist around the base of the biggest erection I've ever seen. A bead of pre-cum glistens on the tip.

He must see the alarm on my face, because he leans down and presses a kiss to my lips. "We can take it slow." He frowns and glances at his watch. "Not that slow."

I laugh.

"Should've taken you to Rome," he says. "Longer flight time."

"Stop talking."

"Yes, ma'am."

He moves his fist up and down his dick, and I'm mesmerized by the motion. He's so beautiful, every perfect inch of him.

"Shit. Condom." He stretches across me, opens the top drawer of the bedside table and pulls one out, ripping the packet open with his teeth. He rolls it on so fast I'd have missed it if I'd blinked.

He straddles me, lowering himself to his elbows, so he's right above me, lining himself up at my entrance.

I want to savor the moment our bodies meet. I've dreamed of it so many times, and now that it's happening I don't want a second of this ecstasy to elude me.

He slides in, just an inch. "So tight," he murmurs appreciatively, as the burn of the stretch forces me to bite my lip.

"Ready?" he asks.

I nod, and he thrusts again, filling me entirely, fusing our hips. Finally. *Finally*. A wave of joy rushes over me. It's so overwhelming, I could weep. I grab his glutes, forcing him deeper, hooking my legs up and over, my heels against his arse.

With each thrust, he simultaneously hits my clit and some deep spot inside that hasn't ever been reached before.

The filthy sound of our bodies slamming together fills the cabin. Pleasure radiates from that deep, hidden place, building and building, fogging my mind, flooding my body.

I'm moving against him, onto him, into him, seeking the release until it bursts, rolling through me in stormy waves.

I scream with each shocking jolt of pleasure, and with each of his thrusts the headboard bangs against the wall. If it wasn't nailed in place, we'd bring the flight down.

"Oh, God." I tear at him with my nails, scratching welts across the taut muscles of his arse. I could be drawing blood, I don't know.

He growls, whether in pain or pleasure I have no clue, but the noise is such a turn on I'm beside myself with ecstacy.

"My name—"

"Nico. Nico! Nico fucking Hawkston!" My head falls back, thrashing back and forth, hair flailing across the pillow. "Fuck, Nico!"

"Look at me," he commands, but my body is lost to sensation. I can't do anything but writhe beneath him.

"Look. At. Me," he repeats, and this time his tone guides me through the fog of lust until our eyes lock. His gaze grounds me in a way I've never experienced, hauling me through the pleasure and into something real. Something deep and frightening and perfect. He thrusts powerfully into me, slower now, our bodies melding together in a perfect embrace. He never looks away; it's so intense, so unrelenting, as if his gaze is physically holding me.

Thrums of pleasure dart from my clit, colliding with that deep, inner pressure until they merge in the most forceful orgasm I've ever experienced. I rock and shudder against him, my thighs quivering around his hips.

"Fuck." He groans and his cock twitches as he finishes, his glutes clenching beneath my hands. He's coming with me, the experience mind-blowingly intense as the orgasm explodes between us like we're one being.

Even as it's pulsing through me, my body dissolving, I know it's different from any other orgasm. It changes everything; blasting through my barriers and defences like a bomb. It's more than physical; it's an energy force that ties us together, binding me to him and leaving me forever changed.

We collapse on the bed, mingled in sweat and post-orgasmic bliss, our breaths heaving.

"I knew it would be fucking brilliant," he pants. "You've destroyed me."

"The feeling's mutual."

I'm still wearing my dress, although it's sweaty and rumpled up around my hips, and Nico's linen shirt looks more like a rag than an item of clothing.

He props himself up on his elbows so he's looking down at me. He starts to laugh.

"What's so funny?"

"You're an animal," he tells me, simultaneously smiling and shaking his head at me like he can't believe what he's just experienced.

I slap his naked bum. "Oi."

He winces, and I wonder if I hurt him earlier. Then he smiles widely—like I'm the best thing he's ever seen—and something inside melts and pools with warmth. "A beautiful, wild, wonderful animal. I wouldn't change it for the world." He kisses me gently and the cabin rocks with gentle turbulence, reminding me we're in the air. "Welcome to the mile high club, Little K."

I kiss him back, my heart softening as I realise I don't mind the nickname one tiny bit.

27
NICO

I've definitely lost my head over this woman. I peel off the condom and toss it in the bin. I'd rather not use one, but it's early days. We'll talk about it later. Sex without a condom feels like a serious step. I'd take it now if I didn't think she'd be rushing for the door if I move much faster than I already am.

I approach the bed again, and she tugs on the end of my crumpled shirt.

"I still haven't seen you fully naked." She bites her swollen bottom lip. *God, how desperate were our kisses to do that to her mouth?* I want to kiss her again, but the way she's staring at me, so eager to see me without my clothes, is an invitation I can't resist.

"Go ahead," I reply, spreading my arms.

She gets to her knees and crawls across the bed towards me. Her hands are soft as she runs them beneath my shirt, stroking her fingertips over my abs. Then she sets to work undoing each button, rising until she's nearly face to face with me, pushing my now open shirt off my shoulders.

She sits back and stares at me. I can tell by the widening of her eyes that she likes what she sees. It sends a warm throb to my sated dick.

I reach for her dress. "Your turn."

"Oh, no." She leans back, hands cupping her breasts. "Last time you saw my boobs, you covered your eyes. I don't think you deserve to see them again."

"When did I commit such a heinous crime?" I remember exactly when. But I'm not about to admit I recall every detail of that bizarre encounter all those years ago.

"The hot tub? At Jack's birthday party?" She searches my face for some sign that I remember. Lucky for me, I have a fantastic poker face.

"Hot tub?"

"You don't remember?" Her chest falls, and there's a flash of something in her eyes—disappointment, perhaps—that tugs at my heart. "At Mum's house. It was late and most people had gone home and you were in the hot tub and..."

"Ah. Yes."

She relaxes a little at my admission, letting her hands fall into her lap, but when she speaks, there's a wariness to her gaze. "I took off my bikini top, and you covered your eyes like I was the most hideous thing you'd ever seen."

I hold back a burst of laughter, but I know she sees the smile I'm attempting to hide. "Is that what you thought?"

"Yes. It was the most brutal rejection I had ever experienced. I nearly died. In fact"—her eyes scrunch—"it still kinda hurts to think about it."

My hand finds hers, fingers sliding together, locking in. "You're beautiful. You were beautiful then, and you're beautiful now. But you were too young. Sixteen. Seventeen?"

"Not that young. It's legal. I could have been having sex."

"It's too young to know what you want."

"I'd strongly disagree with that."

I tilt my head, frowning. "I didn't know what the fuck I was doing when I was sixteen."

"I was a very advanced teen. I knew what I wanted back then. Same thing I've always wanted." She releases my hand and strokes a fingertip down my chest, idly circling my nipple a few times before ceasing the motion and tentatively raising her gaze to meet mine. "You," she whispers.

I sit on the edge of the bed next to her. "That long, eh?"

"That long," she confirms. "Does it put you off?"

"No." I lean over and kiss her, feeling the soft heat of her lips against mine. "I'm sorry. I'd had some bad news that day. I could barely focus. And Jack was in the other room. If he'd found me ogling you, he'd have gouged out my eyes and burnt them. I like my eyes. They're useful. I wanted to keep them."

She laughs. "He wouldn't." She pauses and looks to the ceiling. "I mean, he *probably* wouldn't have."

"He'd have knocked my teeth out at least, and I kinda like those, too. And—"

"And your girlfriend came out onto the terrace. Dark-hair. All leggy. Like a race-horse."

I frown. This I don't remember. "I didn't have a girlfriend."

"You did. She walked out onto the terrace and the two of you had this awful staring contest while I was trying to get my bikini top back on. It was horrendous."

My stomach twists. "She wasn't my girlfriend."

"Who was she then?"

I rub a hand over my mouth. "The bad news." Kate says nothing, waiting for me to explain. "Her name was Lilah. She was one of our friends from uni, who took a job as Dad's PA. They were having an affair, and I found out that day."

"Oh." Her fingers tug at the bedsheets, her attention focused there. "I'm sorry."

"Don't be. I'm over it. Even back then, I was used to it... more or less. Constant affairs. A stream of younger women coming through the house. Dad didn't even bother to hide it and Mum always turned a blind eye."

"Why would she do that?"

I take a deep breath. "The money. Status. Life was better as William Hawkston's wife than his ex. She endured the shit so she could enjoy the benefits. That's still how their relationship works, even now."

Kate looks so disturbed at the idea of my father's infidelity and my mother's compliance in it that I want to scratch the entire conversation. Her father might have been a gambler and a liar, but he worshiped his wife, even though Debbie Lansen is a difficult woman. When I was younger, I couldn't get my head around it. I thought all married couples were fucked up and loathed each other.

I think of my brother, Matt, and his wife Gemma. *Miserable*. Maybe it's the Hawkston way.

"Are your parents happy?" Kate asks.

I flop back on the bed, running both hands through my hair. "Fuck, no. I don't think they know what happiness is."

"Is this why you never sleep with the same woman twice?"

I shift away from her. "Who says that?"

"The tabloids. The internet. Gossip columns. That once the sun comes up—"

"You've been researching?" I grin at her and pink splotches form on her cheekbones.

"No, it's just—"

"Don't believe everything you read. You're here, aren't you?"

She gives me a hard stare. "As good as it was, you banged me in a private jet. This isn't the cosy morning after. We haven't had one of those."

"We will."

"Good." She places her hand on my forearm and applies gentle pressure. "When was the last time you were with someone for more than one night?"

"Fuck, Kate. No. I don't want to talk about this."

She leans towards me and for a brief moment I'm not sure if the concern on her face makes me want to kiss her again or propel myself off the bed so I don't have to see it anymore.

"Nico..."

"I don't remember, okay? Not for years." *Because why the fuck would you want to have a long term relationship when they all turn to shit in the end?* "I never wanted them to stay longer than one night. But with you, I do. Every fucking night. Every morning. If you want coffee and croissants in bed, I'll do it for you. Even if you leave crumbs in the sheets."

Kate laughs and the tension in my chest eases. "Crumbs in the sheets? That's true commitment."

I stick my tongue in my cheek and shake my head. "This"—I gesture between us with one hand—"might be unusual for me. But I'm good with it. I'm fucking great with it, so can we stop talking about it?" I grab her and pull her down on top of me. "And get back to more important things?"

For a split second, she looks wary, but then she raises an eyebrow and a little smile teases her lips. "You're cute when you're flustered."

I grind my hips against hers so she can feel my erection. "I am not fucking flustered."

Her eyes widen. "You're ready to go again?"

I laugh. "Yes. But we don't—"

The tannoy crackles. "Please take your seats for landing."

"—have time. You want that champagne before we land?"

Kate sits up. "All right. But I need a shower."

I chuckle as I pull on my shirt and button it. "You'll have to wait. We have lunch reservations." I look at her sitting in her rumpled dress and I reach out and run the tip of my finger across the delicate flesh of her breast that's exposed above the scooped neckline. She gives a little shudder. I'll never get tired of Kate's body reacting to my slightest touch. "I'm leaving your breasts for later."

"Saving the best till last?"

"Something like that." She goes to get off the bed, but I hold out a hand to stop her. "Wait there."

I go to the bathroom, get a washcloth, and wet it with warm water before bringing it back. "This will have to do," I tell her, as I ease her dress up and begin to wipe her glistening pussy.

I shift the cloth away and take one last, long swipe of her pussy with my tongue, earning a few of those wonderful little jerks that ripple through her hips.

"Fuck, Nico," she moans. "Can't you put the plane in a holding position?"

"Mmm. No. We're on a tight schedule." I hold her still with both hands and lick her again. "But you are fucking delicious. I defy the Parisians to have anything that tastes better than your cunt."

She throws her head back and laughs, making a heady buzz pass through me like a reward.

"Come on, let's get dressed," I say, pulling away, but she touches my face with a fingertip.

"Nico, wait." I look up at her from between her legs. "Does this mean I belong to you?"

"I thought we covered that." I smirk and she blushes. "Why do you ask?"

"That's what you said, back at Mum's house. 'When I sleep with you'"—she does a curiously deep voice as she impersonates me—"'it'll be because I'm the only man you want. Because you need me more than anyone else. Because you belong to me.'"

The tightness in my chest loosens and I sit up, frowning. "You remember exactly what I said?"

"I remember everything you say."

An odd skittering occurs behind my ribs. Why does hearing her admit that feel so fucking good? "I wouldn't want to assume anything about the other stuff, but to answer your first question..." I crawl over and kiss her. "Yes. Of course, you belong to me. You're mine. Absolutely, indisputably, mine. And not just for the duration of the flight."

At this, she smiles wider than I've ever seen, and a curious warmth floods my lower belly.

I am completely screwed, and I don't even care.

―――

Spending time with Kate is intoxicating. I'm high off her presence, her touch, her scent. I'm trying to enjoy it rather than think about it, because if I do it'll be fucking terrifying.

We had lunch at a low-key bistro that was so romantic I'm surprised at myself. This is shit I haven't done for anyone.

Afterwards, we wander hand in hand through the balmy streets of Paris. It's idyllic. I've never had a better day than this one. Most of the time I need a goal, an objective, something to fucking aim at that feels like an achievement. But here, with Kate, I need none of that. Having her is enough.

She gives my hand a tight squeeze. "When are we going to your apartment? I smell like sex. I need to shower."

I laugh and nuzzle her hair, deliberately inhaling her scent. I don't know what she's fussing about because she smells like coconut shampoo and floral perfume. "You smell wonderful. But if you do want that shower, we only have one more stop before we can go to the apartment."

"Are you deliberately making me wait all day to get you into bed again?"

"We've got all night for that." Her enthusiasm delights me and I tap the tip of her nose. "And tomorrow."

She leans into me as we continue to walk and finally, I guide us down a side street to a small art gallery. There aren't many tourists around, but the gallery is beautifully lit, and inside there are smartly dressed people drinking champagne.

We stop outside and Kate stares through the glass windows. "What's this?"

"This is why we're in Paris." I take her hand and lead her inside. A waitress dressed in black offers us champagne and we both take a glass. Kate arches a brow, like she's giving me an opportunity to refuse it as I did on the flight.

"Drunk sex. Sober sex. I'm good with it all," I tell her, tilting my glass to hers. "As long as it's with you."

She drops my gaze like it's too heavy and takes a sip of her champagne, but her brows lift as she notices what's around us. "These are all Stephen Condar paintings."

"Yup." I force my voice to sound casual, as if I haven't been desperate to surprise her with this all day. "He's here, too." I gesture with my glass towards a grey-haired man in the corner, chatting to a couple of other guests.

"He who?"

"Stephen Condar."

Kate's jaw drops open. "I thought he never left his house? He hasn't had an exhibition since before my dad died. How on earth did you find out about this?"

She turns to look at me, wide-eyed with wonder.

"This isn't an exhibition," I say. "It's a private collection."

She rests a hand over her heart. "Oh, wow. I can't believe you brought me here. This is so thoughtful. I... I don't know what to say." She scans the paintings in admiration. "These must be worth a fortune. Who owns this many Stephen Condar paintings?"

She evidently doesn't expect an answer, or is too excited to wait for one, because she immediately spins on the spot to take in the room; each wall displays a handful of black-framed pictures. The curator's done a wonderful job. The lighting is magical, each picture illuminated in shafts of gold that fall from above.

"That one was Dad's favourite." Kate points at a painting of a beautiful young woman curled up in a window seat, reading a book. There's a candle in the forefront and moonlight streams through the window behind. It's a quaint image—old-fashioned even though the woman is wearing jeans and a t-shirt, one bare foot dangling off the seat.

I keep step with Kate until we're standing in front of it.

"He took me to see it at a gallery in Mayfair once," she continues. "Did you know it sold a few years ago for something crazy, like fourteen million dollars?"

"It was seventeen."

She falls silent, gazing once more at the picture. "Dad thought it looked like me." She tilts her head, squinting as if she's trying to see the likeness and failing. She gives a little sigh and takes another step right up to it. "Look at the brush strokes here." She points to part of the woman's shoulder. "The work in this... the skill... and the expression on her face. It's incredible."

I'm not looking at the picture. I'm looking at Kate. To see her so fascinated, so in awe, delights me.

"That one's my favourite too," I say.

"Why?"

"It reminds me of you."

She scoffs. "You're just saying that."

Her gaze drifts to the little black plaque on the wall beside it and she bends to read the text.

Bedtime Story. Stephen Condar. 2004.
On private loan from N. Hawkston.

One hand flies to her mouth. I knew this was coming, but even so my pulse is racing.

She takes her time straightening up, like whatever happens next is pivotal.

"Nico," she breathes. "You own this painting?"

"I own them all. I started collecting them after your father died."

A potent stillness fills the air.

"Why?"

I shrug, sliding one hand into my pocket. I've never told anyone about this. After Gerard died, and I was left picking up the pieces of the mess he left, it had bothered me how much he had resisted selling his art collection to pay his debts. I guess I started collecting them as a way to assuage my guilt. Maybe if I'd known how much he was struggling before the end, it might all have gone differently. We could have got him help. He might not have died.

That could all be bullshit, but collecting works by his favourite artist had a way of making me feel better. Like I hadn't let him down. It was easier to buy paintings than grieve.

"I've acquired a taste for it," I lie.

Kate frowns, and I know she doesn't buy my explanation for a second. But her brow smooths and threads of understanding silently spin across the space between us, binding us together, tightening around my chest—this is so much more than merely liking an artist's work. This is love and grief and all the things we've never shared and everything we will crystallizing into one beat of presence.

And for just a moment, I have the strangest sense that Gerard is here with us.

Kate's eyes glimmer like she feels it too. "And Stephen just happened to be here tonight?"

Her words bring the gallery crashing back into my awareness. The light. The noise. The other people. I sip my champagne and bubbles pop against my tongue. "He drives a hard bargain, but I guess if you never leave the house, you have to make it count. I flew him out a few days ago."

She gasps. "You didn't. Nico." Her fingers tremble against her lips. "You hadn't even asked me out a few days ago. You only asked me yesterday."

"Like I said, I'm very good at reading you. I knew you'd say yes."

She looks completely overwhelmed as she swipes her thumb beneath her eyes. "I thought you were ignoring me. I thought you didn't message me after Mum's house because..." She muffles a moan with her palm, then lets her hand slide away from her face. "And you were planning this? You arse," she hisses. "You let me think..." I can't help smiling at the way her face screws up as she tries to make sense of it all. Her eyes flutter shut for a second, and I don't know if she's going to smile or cry when she says, "I didn't expect anything like this. I didn't..."

I press my lips to hers and her body softens against mine. This kiss is gentle, delicate, and more like a confession of love than anything else.

And I'm not fucking sure that isn't exactly what it is.

Her lips hover millimeters from mine. "Thank you."

"You're welcome." I gently take her elbow. "Come on. Let's go and meet the great man himself."

By the time Kate has finished chatting to Stephen Condar like he's a long-lost friend, she's had three glasses of champagne and is grinning like an idiot.

"I'm starving," she announces, approaching me where I'm waiting near the entrance. She reaches up on her tiptoes and kisses me. I could get used to these frequent kisses. Her lips are soft and taste sweet from the alcohol. "Let's get some food."

"I'm taking you home for a shower. We'll call for takeout. What do you want to eat?"

"Hmm. Takeout in Paris? You spoil me. I'm in the mood for..." She puckers her lips, her gaze directed to the upper left corner of the room. When she looks back at me, her eyes are glinting as if she's up to no good. "Seabass."

I fix a stern expression on my face. "I thought you didn't eat fish?"

"I lied. I love fish. Seabass is still my favourite."

I open my mouth wide in mock outrage, but the way she's looking at me, that cute teasing grin, undoes me. I smile like a love-sick idiot. Before I can suggest that we should find her some seabass, she sticks her tongue out and dashes out of the door, disappearing into the peppery dusk of a summer's evening. The little bell overhead tinkles to signal her exit.

What the fuck?

I chase after her. She's running down the narrow cobbled street ahead of me, zig-zagging in and out of shadows, glancing over her shoulder to check I'm following. She's giggling, and if I weren't dangerously close to falling in love with her, this behavior would annoy the fuck out of me.

As it is, I'm completely entranced and find myself sprinting to catch up, heat firing through my pumping muscles, the thick, balmy heat of the Paris evening clinging to my skin like heavy perfume.

Kate takes a turn into a square we passed through earlier, me close behind. The cafes are closed now and there's no one around.

"Where are you going?" I shout.

"For a shower."

She skids to a halt in the middle of the square, where a large circular stone fountain sits. Three dolphins spout water from pouted mouths. Kate sticks her hand into the stream.

As I approach, she flicks the water at me and I duck, hands raised to stop the droplets landing. "Stop! What are you doing?"

She gives me a huge grin, kicks off her shoes, lifts up her skirt and steps into the fountain. I can't take my eyes off her. She's magnetic. Joy shines out of her like rays of fucking sunlight.

I prop my hands on my hips. "This is unsanitary. Get out." I hold out my hand to help her out, but she ignores me and begins paddling around as if it's a totally normal thing to do. Water soaks her dress; the fabric sticking to the outline of her thighs.

She's fucking irresistible. So sexy, even when she isn't trying.

"Kiss me first," she demands.

I roll my eyes but lean towards her anyway. She keeps shifting out of reach until my shins are knocking against the low stone wall, my upper body teetering forward.

She relents and lets me kiss her. Our foreheads come together. We're both breathing a little heavily from the exertion of running through the streets.

She pulls away. "You like me."

"Yes."

Something softens in her eyes. "It's more than that. You actually care about me."

"Took you three glasses of champagne to work that one out?"

Her hand slides around the back of my neck, and she pulls me closer again. "No. It's not the champagne. It's that you just ran through the streets of Paris and jumped in a fountain to be with me."

Jumped in a fountain? "No, I didn't."

Full lips split to reveal Kate's white-toothed smile, and she leaps up, her entire body weight hanging from her linked arms at the back of my neck.

She hikes her legs around my hips, using her weight against me, and I topple forward. There's a brief moment where I could withstand her attack, but I don't want to. I want her to know she's right. I do care, and if me falling in a fountain in the back-streets of Paris is what she needs to really understand that, then so be it.

The last thing I hear before we both plunge into the cold water is her laughter.

It's the best sound I've ever heard.

28
NICO

We've left a trail of damp footprints all over Paris, but the evening is warm and my sopping clothes have barely distracted me from Kate at all. She doesn't seem too fussed either. She's been chatting non-stop about the gallery, the paintings, the Eiffel Tower and the fact that Paris has never looked as beautiful as it does tonight.

I barely noticed the city because Kate held all my attention. The sweet curve of her upper lip, the slight lopsidedness of her smile, the way being near her makes me feel... like my nerves are being constantly jangled in the best way.

We trip inside the apartment, both of us dripping wet. As soon as the door clicks shut, I pin her against it.

She laughs. "Aren't you going to give me the tour?" She peers into the apartment over my shoulder.

"After." I kiss her neck, biting the skin. The faintest hint of her floral perfume hits my nostrils and I can't get enough.

"After what?"

"After you take your dress off. This is a naked zone."

"Is it indeed?"

"Mmm. Yup." My hand drifts up her thigh, but she shoves me off and pulls her dress right over her head, dropping the wet fabric to the floor. It lands on the polished parquet with a squelch.

"Where are we doing this?" she asks, the eager look in her eye killing me.

"Everywhere." I pull her back against me and kiss her neck, my hands roaming her body. "I want to fuck you in every room."

Her gaze roves over the high ceilings and paneled walls. "Looks big. Huge. How many rooms are there?"

"Not enough."

Under my fingertips, her ribs vibrate as her laughter rings out through the empty flat.

She eases out of my embrace, sashaying her way down the corridor in wet underwear and heels. The lace of her panties rides halfway up the perfect curves of her arse. So supple. So ready to be kissed. Bitten. Spanked. My dick gives a hard throb that settles to a constant ache.

Kate trails a finger along the wall as she walks. It's a slow, seductive movement that draws me along like I'm on a leash.

I'm right behind her when she spins around, eyes widening when she sees the look on my face. I must look... *ravenous*. Like I want to swallow every morsel of her soft, pink flesh.

She arches a brow. "Thought you said this was a naked zone?" She tugs at the buttons on my wet shirt, then pulls at the damp waistband of my trousers. "Get these off."

I peel my clothes off until I'm only in my boxers.

I'm already hard. Pretty sure I've been hard all evening. Kate only has to look in my direction and I've got a semi. She casts my crotch an appreciative glance.

Unable to resist, I pull her against me, pressing our bodies flush. *Fuck, she's soft*. Our mouths meet and I grab the apple of her arse, forcing her closer still. My dick presses right between her legs. Hot. Warm. And so fucking close.

If I slid her underwear to one side, I could slip right in. A groan ekes from my throat; the sound loaded with need. But I don't want to do this here. I break away, trying to ignore Kate's just-kissed lips and wild eyes, as I lead her towards the bedroom.

I'm halfway down the corridor when Kate tugs on my hand. "Fuck, Nico, how big is this flat? Are we there yet? I feel like we're walking to Scotland." She peers through one of the open doors. "I'm pretty sure I can see some suitable rooms right here."

I chuckle. "Easy, tiger." I shove the bedroom door open. The lights are off, but the shutters are open and outside Paris is lit up like a fairyland.

"Wow," Kate murmurs as she takes in the view. "It's beautiful."

"We're not stopping," I say, hauling her up in my arms. Kate squeals as I push through to the ensuite beyond, with its enormous glass shower.

Kate wriggles out of my embrace, heels clacking on the tile floor as I set her down. I turn on the shower and in moments steam fills the room. She steps towards me and places a hand against my chest. I let her push me backward until I hit the sink behind.

She pulls at my boxers, tugging them down. My cock springs free, so fucking hard I could drill for diamonds with it. Pre-cum drips from my slit.

"Naked zone," I remind her, sliding my fingertips into her panties and tugging them down. We kick our underwear to the side as she grips my cock in one hand and runs up the length of it. Heat pulses from tip to base and I hiss, bending to kiss her breasts, the soft flesh exposed above the cup of her bra.

A delightful shiver ripples down her body, and she lets out a small, helpless moan. I could listen to her noises forever; messages sent right to my cock.

I graze her right nipple with my thumb, and it hardens beneath her bra, responding to my touch. I suck it through the fabric and Kate's back bows, like she wants me to take more of her breast in my mouth. *This fucking woman*. I want her more than I can bear. It's frightening and wonderful all at once.

I slide her breast out of the bra cup and bite down on her exposed pink nipple. She yelps a little, grinding her hips against me.

I reach behind her and undo the bra with one hand. Her breasts fall free and I kiss one, then the other, sucking each nipple in turn, relishing her reactions.

I sink my teeth down on her breast and suck hard.

She lets out a guttural, lustful noise. "I'll be bruised."

"I'm making up for lost time. I don't want them to feel neglected."

She emits a delightful laugh, which cuts off with a gasp as I run a finger through her folds and slide it deep into her pussy. She clenches deliciously around my fingers.

"Oh, fuck," she breathes, hands fisting against my shoulders. Her back bows again, thrusting her sex against my hand, greedy for more. "I need to come. Make me come, Nico."

"Good things come to those who wait," I tease, sliding my fingers out and walking us both under the steaming shower.

Hot water pelts us, the steamy air warm in my nostrils. We soap one another, hands everywhere, foam sliding slick and free down our bodies. When I can resist no longer, I press Kate against the tiles. Kissing my way down her body, I lick the droplets from between her breasts, trailing my mouth down her stomach. Desperate to feel her pleasure against my tongue, I sink to my knees.

I grab her hips, pulling her closer as I feast on her, my tongue swiping inside and over her, tasting her sweet wetness. Her fingers wind into my hair as she arches her back, offering herself to me. A gift I can't resist.

I slide one finger deep inside her, then another, continuing to suck at her clit until her moans grow louder and her legs tremble.

"Please," she begs. "I want to feel you inside me."

"Condom," I mutter, not wanting to have to move away from her for a second. "Fuck."

"I'm on the pill."

I look up at her, but her eyes are half-closed, delirious with pleasure.

"Are you sure?" I continue to fuck her with my fingers. "I'm clean," I add, even though she didn't ask.

She flutters her lids open and nods. "I trust you. *Please*."

Fuck. If she's going to beg me in that desperate tone, then I definitely can't resist. I want to give this woman everything.

I stand, one hand on the tile beside her head as I guide my tip to her entrance. Kate's captivated gaze fixes on my cock, which throbs angrily in response.

A rush of pleasure engulfs me as I thrust into her, watching the way my dick disappears between her lips, filling her up. With nothing between us, I can feel every wet inch of her and I have to restrain the impulse to pummel her rough and hard until I come. *So fucking good*.

I set up a rhythm, and with each movement of my hips, I hit her clit and in response she moans, over and over again. The sound is intoxicating and I pump faster, making heat burn at the base of my spine. If I don't slow down, I won't last, but Kate's fingers dig into the back of my neck, and the pinch of pain only urges me on. She presses her head against my shoulder, then her lips, then she fucking bites me, teeth sinking right into my skin.

Lust roars in my veins, and the noise that escapes my mouth is rabid. I plunge deep into her, lifting her body so it slides against the wall.

"The bed," she cries. "The bed will be easier."

She wants me to stop? I can't fucking stop now.

"Please," she says. "My back..."

Christ, I can't deny her anything.

My cock still nestled inside her, I flick off the water and carry her out to the bedroom, and land us both on the bed, our bodies wet, slick, soaking the sheets. I grab her wrists, pinning them over her head against the pillow.

Bracing my body over hers, I fuck her hard, regaining lost ground from our move. The headboard slams against the wall, and she meets my thrusts with her own, jerking her hips off the mattress, her wrists straining against my hold.

"I'm close," she cries. "Oh, Nico. Fuck, yes, yes."

It only takes a few more deep, quick thrusts before she's screaming my name as she comes on my dick, her pussy contracting around me.

It brings me right to the edge.

When the wave of her pleasure subsides, I flip us, so she's on top. She settles onto me, the wetness between her legs sliding against my stomach before her wet cunt slides right onto my dick again. *Fuuuck.*

She rides me, her breasts heaving with each movement, hair falling free around her shoulders. Her eyes are dark, lids hooded, lost in the pleasure of her rhythm. Fire rises through me to see her so turned on. It's like my own private porno with the only woman in the world I want to see.

Pleasure builds in my cock, rising through me like a tsunami. I pinch her swollen clit and she yelps, fucking me faster. I continue to rub the sensitive point. She's so ripe, so ready, that a few seconds later her body tenses, and the series of moans she releases as the wave of her climax hits again is more than I can handle.

My muscles clench as my climax burns through me with unparalleled fury, seeming to last far longer than ever before. My hips are taut as I empty into her, filling her sweet cunt with so much cum that I can feel it leaking from her before I've even finished. *Fuck me*. I've had a lot of sex, but it has never felt like this... Like *completion,* as though spilling into her is soothing my soul.

As my orgasm fades, I continue to rub her clit, more gently now. Caressing it. Kate rests on me, loose strands of her damp hair falling across my chest. She breathes heavily against my neck.

Her eyelids flutter as she moans and climaxes one more time. When the ecstasy passes, she collapses on top of me, our sweat-slicked skin pressed together, chests heaving.

"You're the sexiest thing I've ever seen," I tell her. "Seeing you come is better than I ever imagined."

She murmurs, satisfied, almost sleepy, her breaths hot against my pecs. "You imagined?"

My lips tip up as I edge my hand between us to stroke her swollen pussy. "Yes..."

Her smile widens and she sits up a little to grant me easier access. Her clit is so engorged it's almost solid beneath the delicate skin. She grinds her hips against my hand until she quivers and comes. It's a quieter climax this time, but it affects her whole body. Every muscle trembles with it.

When it passes, she falls back against me and takes a few deep breaths and I stroke my hand over the smooth skin of her back. This moment feels so right, so perfect. I never want it to end.

I tighten my arms around her, winding her long hair in my fingers, my cock softening inside her warmth. I'm not sure life gets better than this. Out of nowhere, a loosening sensation occurs in my chest, like a brick wall being shaken free of its mortar, and it's fucking terrifying.

How can something that feels this good last? I don't deserve this.

I shut the thoughts out and focus on the beautiful woman in my bed. I kiss her temple, then gently shift her so I can lean across to get the tissues from the bedside table. I give her a few, take some myself, and slide out of her, catching the mess.

I grab more tissues and wipe her down, an immense sense of satisfaction rolling through me to see my cum leaking from between her swollen lips. Carefully, I tend to her pussy and inner thighs, and then I lean down to kiss the skin.

She squirms. "Stop. It's too sensitive."

"You'll have to make me."

I dive head first between her legs and she squeals, giggling, pulling at my hair. She drags me off her and we tussle for a moment, until my mouth finds hers and we kiss, slowly, deeply.

While she's distracted, I slide my hand through her neat pubic hair and press a finger to her clit. She bucks against me. "Stop. Nico, stop. Really, I need time to recover."

I sit back, staring at her where she lies on the bed, her breasts beautiful, nipples hardened into peaks. I resist the urge to force her down and take one in my mouth. She gives me a full, stunning smile, eliciting a stirring below my ribs.

I'm falling for Kate Lansen.

My best friend's little sister.

Jack is going to fucking kill me when he finds out.

Kate snaps her fingers in my face. "Where did you go?"

I scramble to gather my thoughts. "Huh?"

"Just then. You zoned out."

I blink. Focus. "I was thinking about how much I like you."

Kate gives a half-smile, not wholly convinced by my answer, but willing to humour me. "How much? Enough to hit a man who was trying to kiss me?"

I raise an eyebrow and she sits up, a cheeky expression on her face, like she thinks she's toeing a dangerous line.

"I didn't know you were that kind of guy," she says.

"I'm not, usually. Only when you're involved."

"So it was because you were jealous?" She squeals as if she's been desperate to prove this point for a while. "I didn't dare believe it, but my flatmate was convinced of it."

Her delight at the idea that she incited me to violence produces a dizzying wave of happiness. "Jealous? No. Protective, yes."

"Of course," she says, a smug smile tweaking her lips as she straddles me, her soft hands pushing me down by my shoulders until I'm flat on my back. Even though I'm spent, a pulse of desire throbs in my groin.

She strokes a hand over my chest. I close my eyes, relishing her fingers tickling my skin, drifting lower... lower...

Blood surges to my dick as her hand draws closer.

"Right. Shower," she says.

My eyes pop open. "What? Now?"

She rocks her hips. Her wet slit rubs against my dick, making me groan.

"Yup," she replies, making a move to leave, but I lurch forward and grab her wrist.

"Don't tease." I release her arm. "I won't be nice next time."

"Ooh, sounds tempting." She shifts backwards so she's on all fours over me, breasts heavy. It's a fucking glorious sight. It takes all my willpower not to grab her and strap her to the bed.

She levels a thoughtful gaze at me. "You have a lot of money, Nico."

I raise an eyebrow. *Where the fuck did that come from?* "Are we just stating facts here? Because you have great breasts."

A slow smile parts her lips as she runs her finger along my dick, which jerks to attention. Arousal surges through me and Kate's eyes flash with delight as my eager dick exposes the effect she has on me. "I want to know what I'm worth. How much would you pay me not to shower right now? To stay here and suck your dick instead?"

Hearing those words come from her perfect mouth has heat steaming through my veins. "I thought I couldn't buy you?"

"You can't." She cups my balls, squeezing them gently. A shudder runs through me and she grins at the involuntary movement. "But let's just say you could..."

I stroke her cheek as I contemplate her question. "They do say everyone has a price."

"How much?"

I chuckle. "I'm not telling you that."

She feigns disgruntlement. Then she darts her head down and licks the tip of my dick, which leaps in response. She looks up at me from between my legs, her eyebrow raised suggestively. "What am I worth to you, Nico?"

I grab her, roll her onto her back, and pin her down. "Are we talking the worth of a blow job here? Or the worth of you, Kate Lansen, sexiest woman I've ever been with?"

She taps her finger against her chin, making a show of contemplating the question. "The latter."

I look her over, pretending to assess her value. As I do, a hint of vulnerability appears in her gaze, and this no longer feels like a game.

"What am I worth to you, Nico?" she whispers. The arched eyebrow is gone, the taunting tone absent. The words might be the same, but the question feels different.

My heart gives an uncomfortable thud.

And then I tell her the truth. "You're worth every penny I have. Every. Single. One." I kiss her between each of the last words, but it's only when she moves her hand to the back of my neck and deepens the kiss that I realise I haven't told the full truth.

Kate Lansen is priceless.

29

KATE

Nico is sound asleep when I creep out of bed. We've been awake most of the night. It must be nearly dawn and I've lost count of how many orgasms I've had. He only has to breathe near me and I'm climaxing like a hormonal teenager.

My bag is on the bedroom floor near the door. Nico was right; I didn't need to worry about it. God knows how it got here. Some rich person private jet luggage delivery service, no doubt.

The thick carpet is soft beneath my feet as I pick up my bag and head out into the large dining room. I'm naked aside from my panties, but the flat is warm so I don't bother with the nightdress I packed.

I take a seat at one end of the dining table. It's so big, it could comfortably seat fifteen people.

I take my laptop out and open it up. I have a meeting with David Webster about the spa project next week, and I really need to work. I don't want to take my eye off the ball for a second, and God knows, Nico is enough of a distraction to derail the entire thing. I won't be able to fully relax until this spa is up and built and I can sit in the sauna and sweat in real time.

The computer boots up and I check my documents. Spreadsheets. Financial projections. Development costs. I have everything here.

I sit quietly, for I don't know how long. I get so absorbed in my work that time seems to pass at double speed.

"What are you doing?"

I turn to see Nico leaning against the doorframe. My breath steals from my lungs. He's naked. Perfect. His skin, golden, his shoulders broad, muscular torso tapering to his hips. And his dick, just there. Casual. Like this situation between us is normal. It's practically domestic.

For years, I longed for this... for him to be mine. That we might share this level of intimacy. That I could be the woman who gets to see him like this. But now that it's happening, it feels too good to be true. An ache stirs in my chest, almost akin to sadness. Like I'm afraid it won't last. Can't last.

I force the thought away.

"Working," I reply.

Nico rubs at one eye with the heel of his hand and pads across the floor towards me. "Fuck me. You're working? I thought you'd run away."

My heart squeezes at the candour in his statement, and the urge to reassure him bubbles up. "I told you, I'm not going anywhere."

He places his hand on the back of my chair and leans over me to see the screen of my laptop. "What's this?"

I scoot back so he can get a proper view and show him the 3D designs I did for the spa. It's far beyond what my role requires, but I learnt to use the software so I could fully express my vision for the project.

An expression of intense concentration settles on his face, his handsome features tinged blue by the light of the screen as he leans in. "Wow. This is great. You did these designs?"

I nod and pull out the papers I brought and hand them to him. "I sketched everything before I put it into digital format."

Nico flicks through the sheets, making the tendons at his wrists, the muscles in his forearms, tense and relax in a sensual sequence, and I watch in fascination. Seeing him focus on my work while he's completely naked makes my heart flutter.

He blows out a breath. "I'm seriously impressed. You should move into design. Interior design. Architectural design?"

"I'm not trained."

"Fuck that. We have a whole department—"

"Nico." He snaps his mouth shut. "Let me see this project through before you start micromanaging my career."

A smile tilts the corner of his lips. "Just saying. You're good. But I can't believe you brought your work with you this weekend. Anyone else would have packed lingerie. Or lube. But you've brought spreadsheets and power-point slides. Fucking hell. Come back to bed."

"This is for Monday, though."

He frowns. "Do it on Sunday night, then. When you get home."

"But—"

"Kate." He speaks over me so I don't get to finish. "I'm not going to let you work. And I'm talking as your boss right now."

I restrain the urge to smile. "Fine. But if my meeting doesn't go well…"

"It will. I'm coming."

"Huh? You want to come to a spa meeting? Don't you have better things to do?"

"Yes. And no. There's nothing better than you. Do you have any idea how sexy you look at work? I want to be near you all the fucking time." He bends down and gently bites my shoulder. Goosebumps trickle across my skin. "Is that creepy?"

"No." I tilt my head to give him more access and he kisses my neck, making my nipples tighten. I let out a dreamy moan. "Maybe a bit."

"I promise I won't interfere." He licks my shoulder, circling his tongue against my skin. "Well, no more than your average CEO attending a meeting."

"So you'll take over?"

His laugh is an amused grunt. "No. But I know this project like the back of my hand. Your files came across when we bought Lansen. I've read them all."

"All? You have a special interest in the spa?"

He reaches across me and pushes my laptop closed. "I have a special interest in you."

I laugh. "Now that is creepy."

He scoops me into his arms, and I squeal. His skin is warm against mine and I can feel the strength of his muscles. He glances towards the bedroom like he means to take me there, then changes his mind and lays me on the huge dining table.

"If you're not tired, I can think of much better things to do than work," he says, as he peels my panties off and throws them aside.

And then he climbs on the table himself, his dick already stiff.

"The table," I whisper. "We'll break it."

He gives me a slow, sexy smile, making hot flames burst in my chest. "I promise you, we won't."

"How do you know?" Maybe I don't want the answer to that.

He flicks his hair off his forehead and knocks the table with a knuckle. "I was conceived on this table."

"No!"

A deep rasp of laughter fills the room. "No," he agrees. "But I've had six grown men dance on it. Simultaneously. Me. My brothers—"

"Don't you dare say Jack."

He laughs again. "No." A beat passes, his gaze never leaving mine as it heats like a blade in a fire. "Are you going to complain about your back again?"

"Nuh-uh."

He flashes a sexy smile. "Then the table's good for it."

For a split second, I forget how to breathe. *How can one body contain this much desire for another?* Moisture gathers between my legs. I'm more than ready for him. I was wet as soon as I saw him leaning naked in the doorway, but now, splayed out on the dining table before him, I'm soaked.

As if he knows what I'm thinking, he nudges my legs apart, his gaze journeying to the apex of my thighs. One eyebrow rises.

"Your pussy is fucking glistening. Are you ever not wet?"

"Are you ever not hard?"

He chuckles. "Touché, Miss Lansen."

His eyes shutter briefly as though he's overwhelmed, like he can't believe I'm real. And then he slides into me like he belongs there and we make love until the sun rises.

30
KATE

Leaving Nico at the airport tore at my heart in a way I hadn't expected. He ordered a car to take me home and then stood on the tarmac in his suit, watching me drive away. He didn't wave. He just stood there with his hands in his pockets. So handsome. So sexy. And the further we drove, the more he felt like a dream I couldn't hold on to.

It might only have been a weekend, but it felt like so much more. And was over far too soon. My emotions are all over the place. My hormones too.

The first thing I do when I get back to the office on Monday morning is check my emails.

Nothing.

Well, not exactly nothing. There's a bunch to clear through, but nothing from Nico.

I check my phone.

Nothing.

Damn it. The post-coital glow that got me through Sunday night is well and truly over. All I have to show for it now are bruises; imprints of our over-zealous love-making. Well, bruises and the memory of Nico's raw confession: *You, Kate Lansen, are worth every penny I have.*

And God knows Nico has a lot of pennies.

Charlie slams his bag down on the desk opposite. "The tube sucks. All those people squished in together. Grim."

I'm grateful for the distraction, even if he has entered like a sweaty storm-cloud.

"How do you normally get here?"

Charlie walks around to my side of the desk. "Driver brings me in with Uncle Nico. But this morning he pushed me out the door and told me to use public transport. Said I might as well find out what it's like. '*Life lesson*'." He makes air quotes with his fingers, his face scrunching. "Learn how the other half live."

"You've never been on the tube?" I ask, unable to conceal the shock that flits over my face whilst simultaneously trying not to react to the mention of Nico's name.

"No. I nearly went on it once with my mates from school, but then we got a black cab instead."

"Oh. What did you think?"

"Awful. Truly terrible. I think I need a shower to recover." He brushes invisible filth off his jacket sleeve with the back of his opposite hand, then switches sides.

He stops mid swipe, his eyes glued to my phone, which is lying on my desk. "What's that picture?"

"Huh?"

"Your phone background?"

Elly had set it to the picture of the graffitied van that had turned up at Mum's summer party last week, when I told her and Marie the story. She thought it was so funny that it would amuse me to see it there every day.

When I'd been with Nico at the weekend, I hadn't even looked at my phone. This morning I'd meant to change it, but forgot when

Marie started quizzing me about Paris. So there it is, lighting up the phone screen for all to see.

Not professional *at all*.

"Is that a giant penis on the side of a van?" he questions, eyes wide.

My stomach drops. *Oh, God.* I snatch my phone up before Charlie can inspect it further. "No. Of course not." I quickly change the background photo to a picture of me and Jack at the drinks party.

I put it back on the desk, and Charlie peers over to look closer. Just then my phone buzzes, the name *Nico Hawkston* appearing on the screen.

My composure dissolves at the sight of his name and I grab it so fast that Charlie looks at me like I've gone mad. Thank God I changed Nico's contact details from *Massively Hot Nico*.

I wave him away and he frowns before returning to his own desk and sinking into his chair, hidden from view behind his computer screen. Thank goodness. I don't want the judgmental eyes of a fifteen-year-old on me as I open the message.

My hands are shaking, my mind flip-flopping between scenarios of Nico breaking it off to those of him bending me over his desk upstairs.

Nico: *Twentieth Floor. My office. Sunset.*

A smile breaks across my face, and then immediately falls. There's no kiss. No hint of what he wants to say or do when I get there. Five words and three full stops. No emotion.

Also, sunset? It's midsummer and it won't be sunset until after nine pm. What does he expect me to do until then?

I begin to type something, then delete. Type again, then delete. The little dots appear and disappear.

Another message pings through.

Nico: *You're killing me over here. What's on your mind?*

I reply before I've even thought it through.

Me: You.

His response comes almost instantly.

Nico: Good. I've thought of nothing but you since you left.

I read it three times. It's not a dirty message. It's not even suggestive. It's... sweet. It's reassuring, but I find myself wishing he'd sent something a little more... intense. After all, this weekend was anything but *sweet*.

Images of our time together flicker in my mind like a slideshow. Nico naked, the sheen of sweat on his abs, his chest, his perfect dick pounding into me... Heat seeps through the phone, intensifying until it's flowing through every cell in my body.

"What are you grinning at?"

Jack's voice has me spinning in my chair, dropping my phone into my lap.

"Huh?"

"You look like a kid who's just discovered the Easter Bunny is real. Who's the message from?" He nods at where my phone lies discarded on my thighs.

"Oh." I glance down as if surprised to see my phone there. "Just Elly. Something stupid. You know how she is."

A flicker of... *something* crosses his brow, and when he speaks, each word is enunciated. "I do know."

Why is he being weird?

Before I can dwell on that thought, Jack changes the subject. "Spa meeting at ten. We're all coming. The team. Looking forward to seeing what you've got."

"Can't wait."

Jack grins, slides one hand in his pocket and saunters back to his office. Even though I can only see the back of my brother's head, I know he's flashing his charming smile at every female he passes because they turn to him like sunflowers straining for the light.

I'm struck then by the difference between Nico and my brother. Jack invites the attention, whereas Nico doesn't. And for Jack, the smile of a random woman in the street or the office or a restaurant energizes him.

But Nico...

I don't want them. I want you.

He said it all those weeks ago, when he booked me into the spa on my first day. I didn't know how serious he was, but I probably should have. He's Nico Hawkston. He always gets what he wants, and my objections have well and truly fallen by the wayside because I want him, too. *All of him. All the fucking time.*

I can't hold back my smile, butterflies skittering in my stomach. How the hell am I going to survive a meeting in Nico's presence without burning up?

The meeting with Argentum is on the ground floor, in one of the larger meeting rooms. Jack and I arrive early, sitting together in the lobby waiting for David Webster to arrive. My pulse flutters like a caged bird, knowing it won't be long until I get to see Nico again.

Jack's twisting a biro round his knuckles. "When did you last speak to Nico?"

The question hits me like a bucket of ice water.

Crap. I've never been good at keeping secrets. I hate them. And I don't want to lie to Jack. It feels weird. But at the same time, I can't break it to him when I have no idea what I would say. We're fucking?

We're making love? We're having casual sex and it's really great? It's not as though Nico's my boyfriend. Are we even exclusive? If it's only sex—*let it not be only sex*—then perhaps I can keep quiet and let it fizzle out.

I almost laugh at the idea of anything between us *fizzling* out. If it's going to end, it'll be with a bang.

"Last week?" I say, keeping my response deliberately vague.

"And you're okay with him being at your meeting?" Jack leans forwards a little, as though he wants to be sure he has my full attention.

"Yes."

"Great. Progress, then."

A short burst of laughter explodes from my lips. *Progress*. If that's what you call being fucked every which way for forty-eight hours by a man I cannot stop thinking about. Jack shoots me a look like I've lost my mind. And it must seem like I have, because this reaction makes no sense to anyone but me, and maybe Nico. Thankfully, the clip of footsteps distracts us both. We jump to our feet, Jack's back ramrod straight.

Nico rounds the corner, the sight of him hollowing me out. Even if I woke up next to him every day for the rest of my life, I don't think I'd ever get used to seeing a face so ruggedly exquisite.

He's freshly shaved, his square jaw irresistibly exposed this way. None of the rough stubble that grazed my most private area remains. I lament its removal, like he's shedding memories of me.

What a stupid thought. I really am losing it. I must be.

He approaches us, his expression serious. "Jack." He takes my brother's hand in a tight grip. "This won't take long. A quick meeting to let them know we're all on board. Hawkston and Lansen all lined up. United front. That's the best way forward."

"Excellent," Jack says.

Nico turns to me, giving me a tiny professional nod. "Kate."

He's good. *So cool*. There's no indication he knows me any better than any other random member of staff, and certainly not that we spent the past couple of days naked and contorted in every possible position. I get a flash of riding his face until I screamed and heat rages through me.

Shit. Get it together.

Nico, on the other hand, is completely dispassionate; perhaps even a tad aloof. If he hadn't messaged me earlier, I'd be convinced he's indifferent.

He offers me his hand, and I shake it. The contact sends a zap of energy up my arm. I don't want to let go, but before I've even processed the thought, Nico releases me.

He didn't even squeeze. Nothing. I can hardly believe this is the same man I shared a bed with all weekend. This is his public persona; it's sexy as sin, but it's a mask he wears for the world. The fact that I've seen what's behind it—what's under that tailored suit—makes my heart race and the back of my neck heat.

He turns to the main entrance, nodding his head to indicate we follow him. *How does he make a simple head tilt so commanding?*

David Webster walks into the office, precisely on time. Father Christmas in a pinstriped suit. "What a building this is," he says as we approach, gazing up at the high lobby ceiling as if it's the night sky. "Pretty different from the old place, eh, Kate?"

I nod in agreement and we all exchange pleasantries before Nico places a hand on Mr. Webster's shoulder, directing him towards the meeting room. "Let's focus, shall we? The Knightsbridge spa project?"

When we reach the door, Nico allows me to pass before him. His fingers skate along my lower back for the briefest of seconds, but even the meagre contact has flames scorching beneath my clothes. I try to catch his eye, but he's deep in conversation with David.

Nico strides to the front of the room and begins the introduction. I'm barely listening to his words, too fascinated by the way he commands the space and holds the rapt attention of everyone who was already seated in the room when we arrived.

I tune back in just in time to hear him say, "We look forward to working with Argentum." Nico points at David Webster, who bows his head. "And now it's time for me to hand you over to Kate Lansen."

Nico gives me a professional smile. Our secret swells within me like a balloon about to pop. I bite my tongue to stop myself jumping up and yelling that we've had sex. Repeatedly. But even if I spoke the words aloud, I'm not sure anyone would believe me.

Nico takes his seat right next to me, so close I can feel the heat of him. He turns to me and whispers, "You look fantastic."

I try to repress the pleasurable shiver that rolls through me as the warm breath of his words caresses my ear.

"Kate?" David asks.

"Yes. Right." I shuffle my papers in front of me.

Something touches my thigh, and I jerk in my chair. It takes me a second to realise the touch is deliberate. I glance at Nico, but he's staring at me with an expression of complete respect, his eyes communicating *Go ahead. You've got this*.

David draws his chin in, one bushy white eyebrow arching. "Are you quite all right, Kate?"

"Yes." I place a hand on my heart and clear my throat. "Absolutely."

I begin talking, running through the projections, the details, the architectural plans for the site. David listens attentively, but I'm finding it hard to concentrate with Nico right beside me. His professional mask doesn't slip an inch, but even so, my body is tingling right beneath the surface, and I swear my underwear is wet.

All the while, Nico keeps his entire focus on David, and when David directs a question to him, Nico answers as though nothing in the world could distract him.

I focus doubly hard on what I'm here to do, managing — almost — to ignore the fact that the man I fucked all weekend is mere inches away from me.

When I finish, Jack smiles at me, silently telling me that I pulled it off.

Nico gives my thigh a reassuring squeeze, and then places both his hands on the table and interlinks his fingers.

Maybe it's the relief of my presentation being over, or Nico's general proximity, or that final touch beneath the table, but arousal floods my system like water rushing through a broken dam. Heat pools in my core, and I want nothing more than to have Nico fuck me on the table, just the way he did in Paris. I have to resist reaching out and kissing him, right here in the meeting room. As ridiculous as it sounds, I'm not that far from orgasm and my brother is sitting on my other side in complete ignorance.

I'm breathing far too heavily for a casual project meeting, and the humiliating realisation crashes down on me that *I did this to myself*. I'm so obsessed with Nico that I can't sit next to him without thinking about sex.

I press the back of my hand against my cheek. It's boiling. I glance around the table to check if anyone has noticed my lack of composure.

No one has. Thank God.

When my heartbeat calms, I tune back into the conversation.

Nico is talking to David. "Is there anything else?" Nico asks. "Do you have any questions for us?"

"Not a question as such, but an announcement of sorts." David's expression tightens. "I've faced unforeseen health issues and been advised to decrease my workload. I'm handing over the reins of Argentum and the spa project."

I frown at the suggestion of health issues. *What could be wrong?* I know you can't see every issue from the outside, but David looks healthy and trim for a man in his sixties, even with his rosy Father Christmas cheeks and white beard, and I know from our client lunches he's careful about what he eats and drinks. And he ran the London marathon this year, so he's fit too.

"I'm so sorry to hear that," Nico says. Jack echoes the sentiments.

"Nothing serious?" I ask.

David grumbles a little, clearly uncomfortable with the question. Jack throws me a look like I shouldn't have asked.

"Oh, you know, you get to a certain age and the body isn't as robust as it used to be. It'll blow over," David replies, but he keeps his eyes on the table and I immediately suspect he's not being entirely truthful. "Bit of strain on the old ticker, that's all."

Nico frowns. "So you won't be able to see the project through?"

"Not personally. I'll still be on the board. Martin Brooks is stepping in to take over. And given his experience, and his relationship with your father"—he looks at Jack and me—"I can't think of a better fit."

A dark look passes over Jack's face at the mention of my father's ex business partner.

Beside me, Nico's shoulders tense. His interlinked fingers squeeze down on the tabletop before he forcibly relaxes them and lays his palms flat.

My heart drops and all thoughts of sex and Nico fall away. *What the hell is going on?* Everyone around me is suddenly as taut as a high rope.

Nico nods, slowly. "Martin Brooks."

"I thought he had retired?" Jack clarifies.

"He had. But he wants back in. Retirement bores him." David pulls on his earlobe. "He's our newest board member at Argentum."

"What?" Jack's voice is so sharp that David draws back in his seat.

"Didn't you know?" I put my hand on Jack's arm. "He told me at your birthday drinks."

"He was at my party?" *Shit.* Jack really didn't know. "Why didn't you mention it?" He scrapes his fingers through his hair. "You could've fucking said something."

I lean away from Jack's over the top reaction, and a cramping sensation seizes my stomach.

Martin hadn't crossed my mind since the party. And, if I'm honest, the only person I was thinking about afterwards was Nico.

"Sorry. I didn't think it was relevant," I say.

Tension creeps around the table as the other people in the room deliberately avert their eyes from our awkward discussion.

David shuffles in his chair, looking anxiously at Jack. "After all the work Martin did with your father, it's only natural he'd have a fondness for the two of you," David explains, again looking at me and Jack. "And he's interested in the spa project because the idea goes back to when he and Gerard Lansen were in charge. He says he misses your dad."

"Bullshit," Jack spits.

David's hand flies to his throat as he fixes Jack with an incredulous look.

Nico's fingertips leave the desk, hands half-raised in warning at Jack; a motion that wordlessly conveys, '*Rein it in and shut the fuck up.*'

Jack glowers beneath lowered brows.

"Have you done a handover?" Nico asks David.

"Not officially. We'll do it for the board, and Hawkston too, if you like. Martin won't change anything. He knows my aims for the project. You'll hardly notice the difference, I'm sure. We're very aligned in our vision. He knows all the details. Kate can meet directly with him in the future, I assume, once it's all tidied up and passed over to him."

Nico and Jack share a sideways glance I don't understand.

"We'll have to discuss it," Nico snaps, before calling the meeting to an abrupt end, leaving me and half the team confused. He immediately rises and guides David Webster to the door, escorting him from the office.

I grab Jack's arm. "What's wrong?"

He shakes me off. "Leave it, Kate. This has nothing to do with you."

"It's my project."

Jack dismisses my objection with a look, pushes back his chair and follows Nico, leaving me to pack up my documents and trail behind them.

By the time I catch up, David is gone and Nico and Jack are leaving the building together, deep in discussion about something that they clearly have no intention of sharing with me.

I stand in the grand lobby of the Hawkston building, with the sensation that the ground is shifting beneath my feet.

Something's wrong, and I have no idea what it is.

31
NICO

"What the fuck does Martin Brooks want with the spa project?" Jack glances at the sky, where speckles of rain begin to fall in a summer haze. Petrichor fills my nostrils as we pace down the pavement. Side by side, we weave between other city office workers.

"There is no way the man has good intentions," Jack continues, his voice low. "He knows what Dad did... who he was. I don't want him anywhere near Kate."

His agitation bleeds across the space between us. Of all the people to be Kate's point of contact, Martin Brooks is far from ideal. His rage on discovering Gerard's dodgy dealings was extreme; if Gerard hadn't died soon after, I reckon Martin would've killed him.

"Calm down."

"Calm down?" Jack's eyes turn wild and his voice is a raw whisper, as though his attempt to control himself makes the words scrape his throat. "He's wrangled his way onto this project deliberately. This is Kate's project. It means a lot to her. I'd put money on it Martin wants to fuck it up for her. He was supposed to retire. To stay retired." He scrunches his face, then releases the tension. "Fuck. I have a lot wrapped up in this."

"So does Hawkston. It'll be all right."

I don't know that it will be, but I can't stand Jack looking at me like he's begging me to save him. Again. I haven't had dealings with Martin

Brooks since the original deal to buy Lansen fell through. Since I paid Martin off to keep his mouth shut, and he scurried away like a rat.

He got everything he was owed and more. So why do I have a bad feeling about this?

Jack's eyes search mine. "What do we do?"

It's raining heavily now, but neither of us has an umbrella. Nor do we have a destination, so we're walking aimlessly through driving rain.

"Nothing, yet. He'll make his demands known if he has any." My voice is calm, but inside I'm unnerved. "Do you want to tell Kate?" My stomach flips as I say her name. If we're ever going to tell her what really happened, this is the moment. I hope to God Jack says yes, because I don't want to lie to her anymore, especially not after everything that's happened between us.

"Not unless we have to," Jack answers, his frown so deep his brows almost meet in the middle. "Dad didn't want her to know—"

"He's dead." Jack looks at me aghast, but I continue, regardless. "Maybe honesty is more important than keeping a promise to a dead man."

"We can't be *honest*," Jack pleads. "None of this is fucking honest. We buried the crime. We papered over the cracks with cash."

"My cash."

"And I'm grateful. I've paid you back, haven't I? Worked all hours of the day to return every penny."

"I know."

Jack's agitation shows no signs of slowing. "Then why the fuck is Martin back? We gave him more than Dad stole from him."

"It's the spa project," I tell him. "And the fact I finally bought Lansen. We did the deal he'd wanted to do back then. It must be painful to watch from the sidelines, knowing it ought to have been him." I place a hand on Jack's arm and he stills, the two of us standing face-to-face in the rain. "Relax. There's no paper trail. No evidence. Only a series of loans that were paid back in full. Business is dirty sometimes. But this is clean. We're clean."

"Are you sure?"

"Yes. Any concerns on that front, you can put out of mind right now. Money's a curse and blessing, but if you have enough, you can clean up any mess."

Jack exhales so heavily that he shrinks a couple of inches. "Fine. Then we don't have to tell Kate. Don't breathe a fucking word to her. If there's one last thing I can do for my father, it's protect his memory. His legacy."

I flinch as images of Gerard Lansen in the hospital flash before me. Tubes and needles protruding from his body as he begged me not to tell his daughter what he'd done.

She doesn't need to know. She never needs to know.

He was a broken shell of a man by the end; he'd been covering his tracks for months, siphoning money from the company to cover his debts. He'd gambled away vast sums on the stock markets, throwing good money after bad until there was nothing left but what he could steal. The house was mortgaged to the hilt, and the bank was going to call in the loan and force the sale.

The whole thing was a mess, and Debbie Lansen was completely oblivious. Too self-centred to notice what her husband was up to. That, combined with the fact that Gerard was a skilled addict who'd hidden his vice away like a precious jewel, meant no one knew until it was too late.

"Take Kate off the project." Jack's anxious voice tears me from my memories. "Take her off the spa project. She can't be dealing with Martin Brooks. I don't know what he's up to, but I don't want him talking to her."

"I can't do that. I won't do that."

His eyes narrow. "Why not?"

I search for a reason that isn't *because I'm sleeping with her and she's completely bewitched me and I won't do anything that's going to hurt her*.

"Because she deserves to be on the project. You know that. I'm not going to rearrange everything to keep a promise we made to a man who's been dead for nearly a decade, even if that man is your father. If she finds out, she finds out."

Jack's eyes go wide, his eyebrows quirk upwards. "You have to do something."

"I'll call Martin Brooks directly. I'll deal with him. Find out what he wants."

Jack opens his mouth to speak, but at that exact moment, I see something dark flapping at me from across the other side of the street.

"Hey, Uncle Nico!" Charlie is waving a vast black golfing umbrella with Hawkston printed on the side, and yelling at the top of his voice.

I wave back, but Jack grips my hand in both of his, reclaiming my attention. "Don't say anything to Kate. Please. If someone has to break it to her, it should be me. He was our father. Please, Nico. Swear it."

Fuck. Every nerve in my body rebels, stinging my skin. I've held this back from Kate for long enough, but Jack's right. Gerard was *their* father, and this isn't my secret to tell. With a sinking sensation in the pit of my stomach, I nod, and Jack, seemingly satisfied, dashes back to the office in the pelting rain.

Charlie runs across the road, leaping over a puddle onto my side of the pavement. There's hardly anyone else around now; the rain sent everyone scurrying for cover.

He holds the umbrella up so I can fit beneath it, too. I'm already soaking, but I duck under anyway.

"What's up?" I ask.

He frowns. "There's something I wanted to tell you."

"Walk with me," I say, and we pace back towards the office together, Charlie easily matching my stride.

"I saw something weird on Kate Lansen's phone," he tells me.

My heart skips a beat. Did I send her something inappropriate that he might have seen?

"What was it?"

"She had a picture of the van I graffitied. The exact same one. The one driven by the man..." His voice hitches and my senses come into keen focus.

I put a steadying hand on his shoulder, not wanting him to have to dwell on thoughts of his mother's infidelity. "I know the one you mean. Are you sure?"

"Positive."

That is an odd coincidence. "Okay. Leave it with me." I feel his shoulder loosen under my hand. "Don't say anything to Kate about it yet, though. I'm sure your dad doesn't want it known that—"

"That he's a cuckold?"

I raise an eyebrow, hoping to hell that Charlie's not about to tell me my brother's into watching his wife be fucked by other men. The conversation would be wrong on too many levels to count. "Where did you learn that word?"

"Othello. We studied it last term."

"Ah." Plain old cheating, then. *Phew*. "Actually, I was going to say it's probably best people don't know about you drawing on the side of someone's vehicle. You could've been charged with vandalism."

"I know. Sorry."

He looks so remorseful I can't help but smile at the kid. He's softer since his arrest, as if the run-in with the police has tamed him, and rather than the angry teenager, I can see the young boy beneath, trapped in a body that's nearly a man's.

We reach the Hawkston building and take the lift. I bid Charlie goodbye at the sixth floor and continue up to my office.

"Mr. Hawkston," my PA chirrups from behind her desk.

"Victoria."

Her eyes widen as she notices I'm soaked through. She jumps up and rushes to me, helping to peel off my wet coat. "You should have sent for the car," she says, folding my coat over her arm.

I frown, flicking damp hair off my forehead with one hand. "I was preoccupied. Could you find Martin Brooks' details for me? I think he's at Argentum now. Put him through to me when you get hold of him."

I head to my office and take a seat. I don't think Jack's right to keep this from Kate. I never agreed with it, but when your dying godfather asks you to do one last thing for him, you say yes.

And then you fly to the US and bury yourself in work so you never have to think about any of it again. Until Lansen becomes a viable proposition again and your best friend wants you to think about completing that deal you never finished all those years ago.

What a fucking mess.

My phone rings.

"Mr. Brooks on line one for you," Victoria says when I answer.

"Put him through."

Victoria clicks off and Martin comes on the line.

"Mr. Hawkston," he oozes, more than a hint of menace in the greeting, and it has me clenching a fist. "Figured I'd be hearing from you sooner or later."

"I'm sorry to hear retirement didn't work out for you."

He chuckles; a sound full of phlegm and mucus that makes me want to retch. "It did get a little boring. And then I heard the news that you were back, buying the company I used to have a fifty per cent stake in. And my interest was... piqued, shall we say."

"What do you want?"

"What I've wanted for a long while. I want a bite of the spa project. That was my fucking idea." Irritation skitters up my spine at the lie. Martin might have been there, but the spa was Gerard's. "And now the Lansen kids are taking all the credit? That doesn't sit well with me, and you know how I like to keep everything fair."

I take a deep breath, restraining the desire to yell at this delusional arsehole. "So do I. And the treatment you got eight years ago was very fair. You should be off sailing the ocean or drinking cocktails on a beach somewhere. Not sticking your nose into business that has nothing to do with you anymore."

"But the Lansens never paid, did they? They didn't have to lift a finger. You tidied everything up for them. And that is most definitely not fair."

I say nothing. It's true that I did fix it all... I could've walked away, but that would have been the end of my relationship with Gerard. The man who'd been more of a father to me than my own prick of a dad. If I'd walked away, it would have ended my relationship with Jack. With Kate...

"Even Gerard did nothing but sit there in his misery," Martin continues. "Didn't lift a bloody finger to sort it out. Hardly even ashamed of how he'd destroyed our company—"

"He died, Mr. Brooks. Shame, guilt, stress... whatever you want to call it. It killed him."

Martin emits an indistinct sound that vibrates down the phone. "My reputation took a hit, you know, when you pulled out of the deal.

Like the company wasn't good enough. All sorts of rumours about what a poor job I must have done." He clears his throat. "There's no money that compensates for a destroyed reputation. I hope you know that, Mr. Hawkston."

"Is that a threat?"

"What you did was barely legal."

"I paid you back for loans. I repaid debts. With interest. There would be no Lansen without me. You would have been forced into administration. I *saved* your reputation. It was all above board. There are documents to prove it."

"Come now, Nico. There's no need to pretend among friends. You and I know that's not quite true, don't we?"

"You've got nothing on me, Mr. Brooks. And I'd advise you to drop this before I sue you for slander."

I hear the smack of wet lips down the phone as if he's cracking his mouth open and shut. "I'll take this up with Kate Lansen then. She's in charge of the spa project, isn't she?"

"Leave Kate out of this," I fire back, my voice rough. "You deal directly with me on the project. All calls come through me. Understand?"

He wheezes for a few seconds, and a dark part of my soul hopes he drops dead.

"My seat on the Argentum board is very influential, Mr. Hawkston. I have David Webster's ear on this project. And I've been having some thoughts about the direction we should take. It's possible Hawkston isn't the right partner for us anymore."

Fuck. Just how much control does Martin Brooks have over the future of Kate's project?

"David wouldn't fall for this," I argue. "He knows we're the best there is—"

"Good speaking to you again, Mr. Hawkston."

The line clicks, and the bastard is gone.

32
NICO

Several hours later, and I'm still feeling like shit. I rock back in my chair, hands behind my head. I've been salvaging deals left and right. Nothing has been going well, and I'm sure it's because the news about the Knightsbridge spa project knocked me off kilter. And then that bloody call with Martin Brooks planted a seed of anxiety that's plagued me all day.

I'm watertight. I know that. Martin has nothing on me or Jack. Or even Gerard Lansen, God rest his soul.

But what if Martin tells Kate what happened? He could reveal her father's crimes. But that's not my most pressing concern. I'm worried what Kate will do when she finds out I've been lying to her. That Jack and I have hidden it from her all this time…

My mind skirts back to that first meeting in the spa of the Hawkston Elite, when Kate wouldn't stay to have lunch with me. How furious she'd been that we hadn't told her about the sale.

You and Jack kept secrets from me. You treated me like a kid who can't handle the big business.

Isn't that exactly what we've been doing?

And of course, it's not just her finding out. It's what might happen if the story gets out. I paid everyone off, so the press didn't get hold of it and drag the Lansen name through the mud.

Martin got his money; enough to retire into a life of luxury. But he lost his company. That was the deal. I repaid everything Gerard had taken from him, allowing Jack to buy Martin out for more than market value. It was a deal Martin couldn't say no to.

So what the hell is he playing at?

I didn't want to play dirty back then... at least not truly dirty. Money was as much of a weapon as I needed to sort things out, but if Martin really is a threat, I'll have to take more drastic action. Clearly, cash isn't enough of a motivator for him anymore.

I pour myself a scotch and sit at my desk, savouring the taste, feeling the burn as it slides down my throat. It's nearly sunset, and knowing I'll see Kate soon has my pulse hammering in my neck.

Fucking her takes my mind off everything else. When she's with me, I'm present. I'm not worrying. When I'm fucking Kate, I'm not analyzing whatever else we're doing. Or whatever else is going on in my life. It's like the world is a storm and she's the lighthouse.

I finish the last of my scotch, enjoying the way the alcohol seeps into my bloodstream, slowing the pace of my mind, my body.

It stabilizes me, calms me, but not enough.

KATE

It's just past 9 pm when I knock on Nico's office door.

"Yes," he calls.

God, his voice. That one word—*yes*—has arousal spiking through me. My heart is racing. I'm so turned on that I'm not sure how I'm still standing upright.

I smooth down my skirt, pop an extra button on my shirt, and open the door.

Nico is sitting behind the desk, reclining in his chair, an empty glass—probably scotch—in one hand. There's an edge to him tonight; I feel it immediately. He doesn't look at me, but drains the last tiny drop from his glass and puts it on the desk. Only then does he acknowledge me.

His gaze is so predatory, so heated, that warmth rises within me, braising my skin from the inside.

I'm speechless, and Nico doesn't seem ready to volunteer anything either. Behind him, the sunset blazes across London. The sky lit up like a bonfire. It's spectacular, filling the room with a warm glow. I assume this is why he wanted me to come up here now, but to be honest I couldn't give a crap about the ball of fire in the sky, when Nico is right there, so much closer and far, far hotter.

"It's stunning," I say, more to fill the silence than anything else, although it's not untrue.

A small smile lifts his lips, quietly satisfied, as if the sunset is his gift to me and he's pleased it pleases me. My heart warms at the thought.

He holds eye contact, but his smile fades and he makes no move to get up from his desk or to greet me properly. Nerves writhe in my belly as I wait for him to tell me what we're doing here.

He raises the empty glass one more time, tips it up and holds it to his lips, waiting for that last singular drop to roll onto his tongue. Then he licks his lips, such a sensual, slow licking that fire rolls up my body from my toes to the crown of my head.

He puts the glass down, taking his time to get to his feet. I'm about to step towards him when he speaks. "Don't move."

I glance around the room, unsure.

"Do you trust me?" he asks.

Do I?

I don't know, but there's a pulling sensation in my torso, like he's the moon and I'm the sea and I can't resist it. Whether I trust him or not, he's controlling my tides. But why is he asking? Maybe it's the gravity of the question or the tight lines of his face, but this doesn't feel like the moment to query him. I nod.

He walks round to the front of his desk, each step so slow it pains me. I thought we'd be on one another in seconds, ripping at clothes, tearing at flesh, trying to get as much of each other as we could in as little time as possible. Greedy. Desperate.

Nico clearly has other plans, and the authoritative way he's dominating the room has heat simmering in my veins. Every nerve ending is alight, every moment intensified.

"Take off your clothes."

I stiffen. I can't help it. I'd do anything he wanted, but this I wasn't prepared for. "Nico?"

One of his brows arches at my tone, his expression severe. Like he might punish me... *spank me*... for questioning him, and a low heat kindles in my core at the thought.

Nico's gaze lowers to my mouth, alerting me to the fact I'm chewing on my bottom lip. I stop, draw the whole lip into my mouth, letting it slide back out again, wet and full. Want flares in his eyes, and in response, the warmth in my core shifts to an incessant throb.

"Take them off," he repeats.

My breaths shallow as I slowly ease each button on my shirt undone and slip it off my shoulders, dropping it to the floor. He holds my gaze the entire time, jerking his chin slightly to indicate I remove the rest.

His hungry gaze follows my hands, watching as I unfasten my skirt and let it fall to the floor, where it pools at my feet. It's hard to breathe, knowing his eyes are on me, eating up every move I make like I'm throwing scraps through the bars of a lion's cage.

As my fingers slide into my lace panties, his mouth opens a fraction like he's struggling to breathe, too. *Fuck*. He's so sexy, so gorgeous, and the idea that it's me who has him this captivated makes my blood burn and my insides singe.

"Off," he says, and the command has molten lust trickling down my spine, pooling between my thighs.

I ease the panties down, leaving me naked apart from my heels and bra. My pussy feels exposed, and so wet I wonder if it's possible to drip on the carpet.

I notice the bulge at Nico's crotch, his erection straining at his trousers, but he makes no move to release it.

He nods a little, indicating my bra, and I remove that too. Unsupported, my breasts feel heavy, nipples peaking instantly. My body hums beneath Nico's darkened gaze, the appreciation on his face barely masked. He wants me, just as much as I want him.

"On your knees."

This is different. My lungs tighten and arousal sings in my blood. Each breath is an effort as I lower myself. The carpet is rough against my skin, but I don't care.

"Crawl to me."

My palms hit the carpet and a small moan escapes me. It's lusty and sodden with desire, unlike any noise I've made before.

Nico tugs at his tie as he watches me make my way to him. He takes it off, throws it to the floor, then focuses on the top button of his shirt. But his fingers are too fast, too eager. He fumbles and has to try again to undo it, yielding me the only sign he's loosing his cool.

In seconds, I'm at his feet, his dick straining the crotch of his trousers just in front of my face.

"You want this?" he rasps, gesturing at his dick.

God, yes. My mouth dries out and my body trembles from how much I want him. I lick my lips and swallow, preparing myself. "Uh-huh," I moan.

Nico presses a finger beneath my chin, tilting my face to look up at him. He tugs on my bottom lip. "Show me," he purrs, before sliding two fingers slowly into my mouth, giving me time to object, but I don't. "Show me you deserve it."

I suck his fingers, wrapping my tongue around them, lapping at them like my life depends on it.

Looking like he's about to snap, Nico pulls his fingers from my mouth and undoes his trousers, pushing them down along with his boxers. His perfect cock springs free, and the sight of it, thick and veined, makes my pussy clench.

I inhale sharply, and Nico's eyebrow rises, an amused quirk on his lips like he's daring me to take it. I lick the tip and he hisses. I take him deep in my mouth and suck hard, swallowing him as far as I can. He's fucking big... I can't take him all, but God, I want to. The earthy musk of him fills my nostrils, assaults my tongue, and my clit throbs in response. I fist one hand around the base of his shaft and bob up and down, running the flat of my tongue up his length, teasing the tip when I reach it.

Nico's breathing grows heavy and his hands come to the back of my head, but he doesn't hold me there, doesn't exert any unwelcome pressure. He lets me lead, and the thrill that surges through me at having this kind of control over him is electrifying.

"So good. Fuuuck, Kate. Just like that."

My blood is oil that bursts into flame at his words and I continue with more vigor. He groans and thrusts a little between my lips, and I sense he wants to take control. I remove my hand from his cock and hold still, allowing the shift in power so he can take his pleasure and fuck my mouth exactly as he wants.

He surges back and forth, my teeth grazing him on the way in and out as his tip hits the back of my throat, making me almost gag and tears stream from my eyes, but I keep going. I'm so turned on my pussy feels swollen. I need relief, so I reach a hand between my legs, needing to touch myself, but Nico speaks. "No," he says. "Your pleasure is mine."

I groan and let him slip from my mouth, then stare up at him. "Then give it to me." My voice rasps, laden with desperate need.

Nico smiles, like he's been waiting for me to cave. Then he rakes a hand through his hair and closes his eyes, as though he's nearing breaking point too. "I'm calling the shots here. Not you."

He pulls up his trousers and tucks himself away. A brief flash of outrage burns through me.

"Get up."

I stand, excruciatingly aware of my nakedness, still only in my heels. I've never wanted anyone as much as I want Nico right now, and him making me wait has me teetering on the edge of an orgasm that promises to be explosive.

"Go to the window."

The window? My first step is hesitant, knees weak, but I'm willing to play whatever game this is. I steel myself, striding past Nico until I'm staring out at the city as it eases into night.

Nico's attention is an energetic field that hums against my back. Without looking, I know he's fixed entirely on me. I've never felt so desired; I'm throbbing with it.

"Hands on the glass, over your head."

My stomach flips, but I do exactly as he asks, the window cool beneath my palms. Nico's footsteps approach and my lungs constrict.

Touch me. Please, touch me.

He stands behind me, and a sensation like butterflies trapped at the window flutters beneath my skin. He dips his head to kiss my shoulder. Lips soft, gentle. A shiver trips down my body and I gasp. Nico lets out a breath with a rumbling groan.

The tip of his finger travels down my naked back, causing it to arch, and my bum grazes the linen of his suit. A coil of need spirals between my legs. He's barely touched me and I'm so turned on I could shatter at the slightest pinch.

Nico slides his hands over my arse, squeezing the cheeks for a second before his knee nudges between my legs, easing them apart. Air hits my pussy, cooling the wetness and inciting a compulsion to be filled. *God, this is so intense...*

Nico's hand hits the glass to the side of my head and he leans towards me, his shirt soft against my back. I rest my forehead on the glass, each gasping breath misting it.

"Can anyone see me?" I ask, my voice husky.

"Not all the way up here." His hand trails over my hip, pulling me against him, edging over my stomach and down between my thighs, stroking my clit.

"Are you sure?" I whisper, rolling my hips, wanting, *needing*, more. "Nico..."

"I'm sure." He kisses the back of my neck. "Would you like it if they could?"

"Maybe."

"I don't like that word. Yes or no."

I know the answer, but I hesitate. *Can I admit to it?* Nico continues to slide his fingers back and forth over my pussy lips, spreading wetness up to my clit. An ache throbs in my core and his touch draws the confession from me. "Yes. Would you?"

"No." He slaps my clit and I let out a squeal as a sharp sting of pain radiates through me, fading to an intense pleasure. My mind spins, shocked to realise *I liked it,* as another gush of wetness spills between my legs. "No one else is seeing this body, touching this skin, eating this cunt." I gasp as he thrusts a thick finger inside me, then draws it out. He shifts away from me and I glance over my shoulder to find him sucking his wet finger, eyes closed as though he's tasting a delicacy. "I want you all to myself."

Oh, God. If he doesn't fuck me soon, I'll combust.

His hand twists into my hair, tugging so my head tips back. Not painful, but a discomfort that only heightens my pleasure.

"This fucking throat," he says, letting out a groan and licking up my neck in one long swipe. "You're mine, Kate. All mine."

My moan is as needy as his. "Touch me," I whisper. "Make me come."

"You'll come when I say you can," he says gruffly.

An involuntary shudder ricochets through me, and suddenly Nico is gone. I turn to see him kneeling behind me, untying his shoes, removing his socks.

He glances up, meets my eye with his hooded gaze. "Eyes forward."

"Yes, sir," I murmur, a little smile creeping to my lips. Before I turn away, I'm almost sure I see one on his face, too.

The sound of him undressing is familiar. The snap of his waistband, the shuffle of cloth as he slides his trousers down... I don't need to look. Just the idea of him slowly exposing himself is enough to have my core aching.

A moment later, his erection brushes against me. Bare. Naked. I writhe against him, my hands still on the glass over my head. I'm right against the window now, like I'm on display.

"What if someone *can* see?" I ask, my voice breathy.

Nico's warm chest, hard with muscle, presses against my back. His lips graze the shell of my ear and he grips a handful of breast, rolling my already peaked nipple in his fingertips.

"You want to be watched, don't you?" he drawls. "Want them to see you, naked, pressed against the glass, waiting to be fucked? You want them to watch you come, hear you scream?"

His words are delicious. *God, yes, I want that.*

Nico trails his hand downwards, and my stomach quivers beneath his touch. He teases at the slim line of hair at the apex of my thighs and I moan as he slides his fingers over my swollen clit, diving further to my entrance.

"Always ready for me," he murmurs.

He thrusts his finger inside me, pushing deep. The addition of a second finger causes a pleasurable twinge. He finger-fucks me, making arousal swell and pulse with each satisfying pump.

I'm gasping, and each time I do, Nico responds with a lusty, low rumble. My body is alight for him, my skin radiating a potent heat.

"Want them to see how well I fuck you?" His voice curls around me like steam and my hands claw against the glass. I could come just listening to him. "How I can drive you to the edge and break you apart?"

"Yes. Fuck, yes."

"Every last one of them would come just watching you."

Jerks of pleasure fire through me as I imagine the eyes of the crowd on me, witnessing everything. I roll my hips against Nico's hand, grinding into his palm, eager for relief.

Nico slows the finger fucking until it's little more than an internal caress, edging me dangerously close to the abyss of my orgasm.

"Nico?" I cry desperately.

"Only I get to touch you. Only me." He draws his finger out of me and slides it in again, slowly. My pussy aches around his knuckles. "Everyone's watching you, wanting you, but only I can do this." He thrusts deep, thumb pressed hard against my clit and arousal blasts from the touch.

My body jerks and a moan erupts as I throw my head back.

"Is that what you want?"

"Yes. Yes. God, yes." I sound as unhinged as I feel.

He drags his finger out. "Then say it. Who gets to touch you?"

"Only you, only you. Fuck. Please. I need you inside me."

Finally, *finally*, I sense he's relinquishing that tightly wound control and a second later his dick is at my entrance, running along my wet slit. He presses a warm hand into my lower back and I edge up on my toes to give him better access.

He eases his tip inside, keeping his hands on my hips. I dare a glance over my shoulder, but Nico is so fixated on the point where our bodies meet that he doesn't notice.

"Fuuuuck, Kate," he groans, eyes on the ceiling, throat exposed, still holding back the satisfaction of full penetration. My breathing falters as I teeter on the edge of need. *I might die if he doesn't fill me.*

I shift backwards, as if the movement will let me swallow more of his dick, but he holds me off, hands firm.

"Beg. Beg for it."

"Nico, please. Please. *Please.*"

He hums—a delighted sound—as he enters me, slowly, inch by torturous inch. "I like you begging."

"Nico, don't—"

"Tell me what you want."

"More. I need more. I want to feel your hard cock inside me. I want you to fill me until—"

He rails into me in one deep, exquisite thrust. Air rushes from my lungs, my heart stuttering at the sting of the stretch. The pain subsides quickly as my wetness coats him, and I relish the fullness of having him buried all the way inside, his balls slapping against me. Sparks ignite where we're joined, ricocheting into every hidden part of me.

My fingers splay on the glass, his body forcing mine closer and closer to the window with each thrust until my breasts are pressed against it. Nico's skin is damp with sweat and mine too; our flesh slipping against one another's as he pounds into me.

My arousal sky-rockets and I curl and flatten my fingers against the window. I can't contain all this desire. "Oh, Nico, fuck…"

My words descend into delirious moans I can't reconcile as mine. I bang a fist against the glass, which only drives Nico to fuck me harder, deeper. Pleasure rises like a wave, higher and higher until I'm aware of nothing else.

The crest breaks and my orgasm slams into me, fireworks exploding inside my core, shooting all the way to my fingers, my toes, every fucking inch of me burning. I never, *never* want this to end.

My climax blisters through me until it wanes, leaving me gasping and boneless. My palms slide down the glass and I all but collapse, but Nico holds me in place, pistoning into me as he chases his own release.

He lets out a roar and the telltale twitching of his cock is followed by the warmth of his cum spurting into my pulsing pussy. There isn't a sound in the room but our ragged breathing and the pounding of my heart. And then, in the near silence, a thought fills my mind.

I never want to fuck another man in my life.
Nico is it. He's the one.

33

KATE

Nico's head falls to my shoulder, his heart thumping against my back.

"Good thing this is safety glass," I say, exhausted from the intensity of my orgasm. "We're a long way up."

He chuckles. "Quite the fall."

His dick softens inside of me and he eases out, the warmth of our combined juices instantly leaking down my thigh. I grab the nearest piece of clothing from the floor and use it to wipe his cum from my leg.

"Woah," he says, his eyes on his shirt. I freeze, noticing how soft and fine the fabric is.

"I would have used mine if you hadn't made me take it off at the door," I retort, but I wonder if I should be on my knees, begging forgiveness.

I like you begging.

"That's a thousand dollar shirt," he growls.

"I thought I was worth every penny you have," I joke, feeling bad about his shirt.

He smirks and only then does the tension seep from my body. He kisses me with a dominance that fades to gentleness in seconds. When he breaks away, my lips throb, cool and exposed without his to cover them.

"You are. I'm never going to wash it."

I laugh. "Please do."

He takes his shirt, using it to wipe gently up my thighs and between my legs. Then, to my amazement, he shakes it out and puts it on, leaving it unbuttoned over the defined ridges of his tanned abs. His mouth curves into a tight-lipped smile, and he closes his eyes and inhales, long and slow. "Mmm. We smell perfect together."

I laugh louder this time and slap his chest, letting my hand linger on the hard warmth of his torso. "Please have a shower when you get home."

His gaze flashes with something—*regret*?—before he says, "I'd take you with me, but Charlie's at mine again. And it's not a good idea to..." He shrugs, tugging on his trousers and fastening them.

"To what?" I ask, watching as he pulls on his socks and laces his shoes.

"To do this publicly."

"Well, no. We'd get arrested." I gesture to my naked body and a deep chuckle parts his gorgeous mouth.

"I meant letting anyone know. I don't think it would be good for your career."

My chest splinters. *Does he mean that whatever this is between us has to be a secret forever?*

If that's what he wants, then this can't ever be serious. The realisation hits and it makes me feel sick. To distract myself, I pace across the room and pick up my clothes. I start to get dressed, yanking up my skirt and buttoning my shirt, not caring that I haven't put on my underwear first.

"Kate?" Nico must have noticed the change in my demeanor because he joins me on this side of the room and pins me with both hands on my shoulders, staring intently into my eyes. "Are you all right?"

"Yeah." I roll my shoulders and his hands fall away. "Just dizzy. Maybe it's the window. The height."

He pulls back a fraction, eyes narrowing. "Are you frightened?"

"A bit."

The air pulses with a heavy beat, our eyes locked, each of us searching out something more than words. His lips tug down a fraction. *He knows what I mean.*

He hugs me, engulfing me in his essence and kissing the top of my head. "I'm sorry. I've only just got back to the UK. I'm not ready to—"

"Commit to anything?" I squirm out of his embrace and peer up at him.

He frowns, and something plummets through my centre, leaving me empty.

"No. It's not about commitment. I'm yours if you want me. It's about taking things public. I need to settle back in to being in here. Keep a low profile for a bit longer. I've got to go back to New York soon. After that, we can reassess. If you still want to, we can take it public then."

He said a lot of words, but all of it translates to one thing in my mind: rejection. It hits like a blow, and I have to physically stop myself from reeling backwards.

"A low profile?" I blurt, hating how petty and jealous I sound. "Is that what you were doing by taking Erica Lefroy out? Or Amy Moritz?"

He looks at me curiously. "Did you hear what I just said?"

His gentle tone takes me by surprise. "Huh?"

He cups my cheeks, tilting my face to his. "I'm yours, Kate. Do you want me?"

His words feel unreal. I must be dreaming. I wait for a moment, in case he's joking. Or someone's about to shake me awake.

"Kate?" His mouth breaks into a smile so devastatingly warm and gorgeous that all my doubts, all my questions, dissolve like sherbet on my tongue.

"Yes. Yes. Yes, I very much do."

"Good, because I want you every night and every morning and every fucking second in between."

I throw my arms around his neck to kiss him. My tongue steals through his parted lips, claiming him as mine; not just physically, but emotionally, too. *Nico Hawkston is all mine.*

We're breathless when I eventually drag my mouth from his. "Hey," I whisper.

His eyes flicker open. "Hey, beautiful."

"Can I ask you a question?"

He tucks my hair behind my ear. "What?"

"You're not going back to the States permanently, are you?"

"Not yet. It depends what my father's plans are for retirement, and we won't know that for a while. But I have to go back in a couple of weeks for an event. Some charity thing I said I'd make a speech at. It's been in the calendar for months."

"I'll miss you."

"I'll miss you too. I think about you all the fucking time. It's becoming a hazard in the workplace. I'm constantly distracted."

My heart gives a giddy little canter.

I feel so safe, so contained in his hold. And yet, when I walked into this room, that look in his eye... there was a fierceness lurking there, hiding beneath his desire.

"Was something wrong when I got here?" I ask.

His muscles stiffen slightly beneath my hands. "What do you mean?"

"You were... different. The crawling. The fucking at the window."

"Did you not like it?"

Under his watchful gaze, heat rises through my body until I feel slightly choked by it. "I did. But I wondered if it was about something else. If you needed me to be that way and do those things to make up for something else. You and Jack—"

"Please tell me there's a good reason you're mentioning your brother right now."

He's making light of it, but what happened this morning has been bothering me all day. The way Jack barked at me for not telling him about Martin. How Nico's shoulders had tensed, his fingers flexing against the desk.

"The spa meeting," I reply. "What was wrong? Is it Martin?"

An expression I can't place flits over Nico's features, unsettling me. "It's nothing. You don't have to worry."

"You and Jack walked out of that meeting like the world was ending."

Nico shakes his head. "I'm sorry it looked that way. We weren't expecting it. You get used to one person being in charge and it takes a moment to adjust. I haven't seen Martin Brooks for years. Not since before your father died." His tone is light, but there's a darkness in his eyes that doesn't match.

"So, nothing is wrong?" I clarify.

"Nothing is wrong."

"Don't lie to me. I can't take it. I need to be able to trust you." I suspect he's keeping something from me and uncertainty coils around my heart. "Swear to me, Nico. Please. Swear you aren't lying. You won't lie. It's the only thing I need."

He lowers his forehead to mine, resting them together. A contemplative grunt sounds from deep in his throat. I don't know if it's agreement or disagreement, or pure lust.

"I need your word," I repeat, pulling back. "Otherwise, this isn't going anywhere."

He holds my gaze. "I swear it. Nothing is wrong." His voice is so steadfast that my doubts begin to seep away.

"And just so you know," he adds, closing in and speaking against my mouth. "I'd want to see you crawl whether something was wrong or not. You're unbelievably hot on your knees."

34
NICO

"Nico. What's going on back in the UK? Still raining?" Matt bellows a laugh and my stomach twists because he's in a good mood and I'm about to destroy it.

I lean forward in my chair and prop one elbow on the desk. I've been putting this call off. And not just because I don't want to give Matt the bad news. Ever since I had sex with Kate in here, I've been consumed with guilt that I lied to her about Martin Brooks.

I glance out the window, memories of Kate pressed against it flooding my mind. I blink to focus on the glass as it is now—rain running down in rivulets.

I grit my teeth and haul my attention back to Matt. "Yes. Pissing it down. Listen." I fist my hand, press it to my lips and cough. "There's something I need to tell you."

An empty moment stretches too long before Matt speaks again. "Knew you wouldn't call for a chat. What's on the agenda?"

"Charlie. And Gemma."

"God, what happ—"

"They're fine. Everyone's alive and healthy. But this isn't good news."

"Okay," he says, elongating the K. "Hit me."

I've rehearsed this in my head, but it's harder to string the words together now Matt's listening. "I had to pick Charlie up from the police station the other night."

There's a crackle on the other end of the line, as though Matt is scrunching paper in his fist. "What happened?"

The door to my office creaks open and Seb pops his head in, eyebrows raised in a silent question. "Matt?" he mouths, pointing at the phone.

I nod and beckon him in.

"Seb's here," I explain, and click the phone to speaker as Seb takes the seat opposite me.

"Hey, Matt," Seb says, his usual cheerful tone markedly absent.

"What is this? An impromptu board meeting?" Matt asks, his voice rough. "Hurry up and tell me why my son was in a police station. What did he do?"

"He graffitied a van," I explain. "But the owner didn't press charges."

"A van? Whose van?"

Seb and I look at one another.

"Hello?" Matt barks. "What's going on?"

"Gemma's sleeping with someone else," Seb spits out, before rolling his lips together like he's trying to stop himself from saying anything else.

"I knew it," Matt roars, and a smashing sound follows, as though he's breaking things.

Seb and I sit quietly while Matt swears, calling Gemma all kinds of unrepeatable names. His voice is distant, like he's on the other side of the room from the phone.

I rub my jaw. "We should have done this in person."

"Fuck, no," Seb says, eyeing the phone like Matt might leap out of the handset and strangle him. "You want to let that beast loose in the same room as us?"

"What does Gemma fucking someone else have to do with the van?" Matt barks, his voice suddenly clear again.

Seb jerks in his chair like he's been electrocuted and begins to vomit words. "Charlie walked in on them having sex on the kitchen table and sabotaged the bloke's van as payback." As soon as he's finished, Seb slams one hand to his mouth and raises the other in a gesture of helplessness.

"Fuck," I mutter as I drop my face into my hands.

The silence on Matt's end of the line is excruciating. Finally, he speaks, his voice frighteningly calm. "I'm coming home,"

"That's not necessary," I tell him. "Everything's fine. Charlie's been staying with us."

"Been staying? How long have you known about this?"

"Since last week." *Shit.* Maybe that was a mistake. I've been so preoccupied with Kate that I didn't really think about it.

"You pair of idiots. I'm definitely coming home. Right now. Hayden!" He hollers his PA's name. "Get the fucking jet ready. I need to go to London." Matt's voice lowers, directed once more at us. "Lucie. What about Lucie?"

I look up at the ceiling while Seb clenches his fingers around the arms of his chair.

"She's still at home," I say.

"What?" Matt yells. "You left her in the house when some strange man is visiting? Who is he? What do we know about him? This is a serious lapse in judgment from both of you. Fuck's sake."

"We couldn't kidnap a three-year-old," Seb explains. "She's with her mum."

"We don't know anything about the man," I say. "Other than where he lives and that he drives a van."

"Find out about him before I get back. I'll be there tomorrow. Early."

He hangs up, leaving me and Seb blinking at one another.

Seb stands, digs his hands deep into his pockets and looks at his shoes. "I think that went quite well."

"Absolute car crash."

Seb meets my eye. "Yup." He shrugs. "I'll get Elliot Maxwell on the case. He'll be able to turn up anything we need to know about the guy."

"There is one more thing we know." I lean back in my chair and put my hands behind my head. *Casual*. "Kate has a picture of his van on her phone."

Seb's expression shifts from amazed to smug in half a second, settling into a suggestive smile. "How do you know that?"

I give him my best *'don't dare insinuate anything'* glare. "Charlie told me he saw it."

"Ah. Ask her about it then." Seb's eyes gleam with mischief as he scratches the back of his neck, like he's pondering some new way of teasing me. Whatever he's about to say is likely to be as irritating as fuck. "By the way," he begins, his grin spreading wider with each word. "You should get someone in here to clean the windows. There are smudges over there that look a lot like you had a woman pressed up against the glass."

35
KATE

It's been a few days since the night in Nico's office. I've barely seen him because he's been so busy. I don't know how he's able to work, because I have little brain power left to think about anything other than him.

He messages every day, at least twice. Sometimes it's as few words as '*Morning, beautiful*', but even that coming from Nico is enough to make my stomach flip like a pancake.

Today he sent one saying, *My apartment. Nine tonight.*

He never asks... everything is a demand. Apart from that one question, the smallest chink in his armor: *Do you want me?*

Even recalling it now has my heart fluttering. As if there was ever any chance that I would have said no. But the fact that he *asked*...it's enough to make a girl swoon, which is pretty much what I've been doing ever since.

"Hey, buddy."

The speaker sounds so similar to Nico that I have to hold back from spinning in my desk chair and greeting him with a bursting smile. But I can't feel Nico's energy, or sense his presence. I'm so attuned to him, the fall of his footsteps, the unique quality of his voice, the words he chooses, that I know the man standing behind me isn't Nico.

It's close though.

I turn to find Seb Hawkston at the side of my desk. I'm about to query him calling me 'buddy', when Charlie's clipped voice replies, "Uncle Seb. Am I staying with you again?"

Seb flashes a dashing smile. I can sense a slight movement around me, as if everyone in our vicinity is edging closer, just to be near him. Friendlier than Nico or Matt, but just as good looking, I can appreciate Seb's appeal.

"Actually, yes." Seb swings round, focusing on me rather than the teenager at the desk opposite. "Nico says he has some... *things* to take care of." One of his eyebrows creeps upward. "Needs the space."

My body inconveniently heats and I break eye contact. Fortunately, Charlie doesn't notice.

"That flat is huge," Charlie says. "I swear it has ten bedrooms. What does he need the space for? I'm not even very big. Tall, but skinny. My cubic volume is tiny."

Seb snorts a laugh, then glances sideways at me. "Privacy."

I can't help but wonder if Nico has told his brother we're sleeping together. I doubt it, especially after what he said about keeping things secret, but regardless, a fierce blush burns my cheeks. I duck my head, pretending to be focused on my computer screen. Spreadsheets have never been so interesting. Thankfully, my desk phone rings and I snatch it up. "Good morning, Kate Lansen speaking."

"Kate, this is Martin Brooks." The sound of his voice is like a ghost crossing my path, and a slight shiver goes through me. Nico might have said there was nothing to worry about, but Martin's sudden reappearance is odd and something about it still doesn't sit well with me. "How's that spa project coming along?"

"Oh, hi. Fine," I stammer. "Just fine."

"Good. When are you free to meet? I'm in town today. Could you do lunch?"

I glance at my calendar. It's clear. "Yes."

"Great. I'll meet you at Valerie's on Bread Street. Not glamorous. A sandwich. I'm short on time."

"All right. See you then."

"And Kate?"

"Yes?"

"I'm looking forward to dealing with Lansen again."

The phone goes dead and a sense of dread, the source of which I can't pinpoint, slowly unfurls in my chest.

The little sandwich bar is crammed with people, and I squeeze my way inside. The smell of coffee assaults me as I look around. There are a handful of plastic tables and Martin Brooks sits at one of them, a half-eaten sandwich in one hand, leaving me confused about why he's already started eating. *Why didn't he wait for me? What kind of client lunch is this?*

He tips his fingers in a half-wave when he notices me.

I dodge the other customers and slide into the chair opposite him.

"Got you a sandwich," he says, gesturing to the wrap on the table. "Chicken Caesar salad."

I eye the wrap, tied up neatly in white greaseproof paper. I don't touch it. "Thanks."

"I gotta come clean," he admits, and my heart dips. "When I heard the rumours Jack was selling Lansen to Hawkston, I wasn't happy."

His small, pale blue eyes are staring at me as though I've deeply offended him. An icy chill spreads through me.

"Oh," I say. "Sorry to hear that."

He huffs. "That was my deal."

The comment throws me for a loop. He's clearly intending to rake over old ground here.

"Dad was as disappointed as you were—"

His braying laugh cuts me off, and bits of half-chewed food spray from his mouth. A piece hits my cheek and I draw back, wiping my face with my fingers. I want to get away from this man, and not just because he's spitting bits of his sandwich on my face.

"Oh, Little Kate..."

Little Kate. My chest pinches at the diminutive. It's so similar to what Nico calls me that I can't help but think of him. But Martin's version is laced with so much condescension that I want to slap him.

"Still clueless?" Martin's lips twist, alerting me to the fact he's enjoying the power play of knowing something I don't. "Your dad was the one who fucked it."

Shock sparks through every nerve ending and I jerk away from him, my shoulder blades hitting the back of my chair. "What?"

He nods, then takes a large bite of his sandwich. He keeps his beady eyes on me as he chews, ruminating like a cow before finally swallowing. "Didn't they tell you?" He watches me, his eyes moving over my face as though he's desperate for me to react. When I don't, he leans in and every muscle in my body tightens. "You don't know, do you?"

"They?" I croak out, having no idea who he's talking about.

"Your brother and Nico Hawkston." My heart drops to my stomach as Martin takes another bite of his sandwich, and I pray to God he chokes because I'm certain I don't want to hear whatever he's going to say next. My palms get sweatier with every second he makes me wait. Eventually, he washes his mouthful down with a gulp of water. "Your father was a crook, Kate. Destroyed the company. Embezzled hundreds of thousands of pounds. Millions probably. Gambled it all away. Screwed me over."

My breathing shallows. Nothing that's coming out of his mouth makes sense. I blink at him.

"A criminal," he repeats slowly, like I'm a child who can't understand. He's right. I *can't* understand. I hear the words, but they mean nothing.

"He was lucky he didn't end up behind bars, but I suppose he wouldn't have lived long enough to see the inside of a cell, anyway. He got what he deserved, your dad. Better off dead, all things considered."

Pain pierces my heart, like he's thrusting daggers into my flesh and my hand jerks to my chest. Martin's lips curve up as though he's pleased to see me react. Like he's feeding off it.

"Did you never wonder why Nico Hawkston didn't pursue the acquisition all those years ago?" Martin continues. "Once they dug into the numbers, the entire pack of cards collapsed. Your dad couldn't hide it. The deal didn't stack up. He nearly lost your family home and everything in it, too."

"I don't believe you," I hiss, relieved to have found my voice. "I would've known. Someone would have said something."

"Would they?" He sits back, laying a hand on his stomach, where the buttons of his shirt strain over his girth. "You're not as important as you think, are you? Little Kate, left behind, left out. The child who can't be trusted with the truth."

My hands are shaking. I clasp them tight in my lap. *It can't be true. It can't.* "What proof do you have?"

"By all means, don't take my word for it. Ask your brother. Ask Nico Hawkston. Maybe one of them will finally tell Little Kate the truth. And you deserve the truth, don't you, little one?"

"Stop calling me that." I try to sound assertive, but my voice is weak.

Martin casually takes a bite of his sandwich like his words haven't turned my world upside down. He watches me as he chews, and when I realise he's offering nothing else, I speak.

"What do you want?"

He lowers the sandwich. "It's been hard watching you and your brother thriving; getting the payout I ought to have had. I built that company alongside your father, you know? Seeing your brother taking all the glory for the sale... well, it makes me mad." He taps the plastic tabletop with two swollen fingers that look like raw sausages wrapped in cellophane. "I'm finally taking what's mine. I'm going to take your Knightsbridge spa project elsewhere. No more glory for Lansen or Hawkston if I can help it. Your involvement will be reduced to nil."

My heart is racing, my throat feels like it's swelling up, choking me, and each inhalation is harder than the last. "You can't take the spa project," I plead, and I loathe how pathetic I sound. How helpless. I'm sliding into the unknown and it's terrifying. "What about David Webster? The Argentum board?"

"Oh, I'm not worried about any of that." Martin dismisses my questions so easily that a chill runs down my spine. What could explain his lack of concern? "And if you do anything to try to prevent it, I'll tell everyone about your father. He might be dead, but I'll destroy anything that's left. And while I'm there, I'll take down your brother and Nico Hawkston for covering up your father's crimes."

My breaths come unevenly, my brain scrambled. I try to make sense of everything he's told me, but I can't, and judging from the way Martin is looking at me, he knows it.

Martin scrunches up a paper napkin and dabs his lips before throwing it onto the table. "How does it feel to be the daughter of a criminal,

Kate? Seeing Daddy in a new light now, are we?" He stands. "I'll let you digest."

He leaves and I sit in stunned silence for a moment, the surrounding noises filtering out of my awareness until they're an incoherent buzz I barely hear.

Then, I break. Tears rush like water over a dam. I can't contain them, can't hide them. I sob like I haven't since Dad died. All the grief I pushed aside rushes up, and there's more of it than I ever thought possible. I'm weeping for everything I've ever lost, and it's ripping at my heart, tearing through my chest. I cry until I'm breathless, soaking my sleeves with the tears I don't remember wiping away.

Martin Brooks tore a hole in my world and carelessly tossed me into another reality. And I don't like this one at all. My father; the most wonderful man I've ever known. *A thief? A criminal?* Memories shatter and words I thought were true warp until I no longer recognise them.

Did Jack know?

And Nico...

The wave of pain that smashes into me shatters my heart into a million pieces as I realise that he's lied to me this entire time.

Fury rises, burning like acid.

My phone buzzes and I pull it from my handbag to read the message.

Nico: There's something we need to talk about. Tonight. I'll explain later. Don't worry, it's not a big deal.

I stare at my phone, and two words come to mind.

You bastard.

36
KATE

At exactly 9 pm, I arrive at the door to Nico's apartment. It's so high that my ears popped in the lift on the way up.

I'm exhausted, both physically and mentally. I thought my anger might dissipate, but it hasn't. Nor has the empty ache of fresh loss for the father I thought I knew. I grieved when he died, but it turns out I'd grieved for a man I didn't know. A man who didn't exist.

I feel raw, like someone has rubbed away my defenses with a scrubbing brush. Part of me knows I shouldn't be here. Nothing good is going to come from confronting Nico right now. I ought to go home. Call it off. Take time out to get my head together. But I have to know if what Martin said is true.

I want it to be lies with every fibre of my being. I want to move back to a time when I was blissfully unaware.

I want to live in a world where I know my father, trust my brother and—my heart stalls and pitches at the next thought—fall in love with Nico Hawkston. But none of them are who I thought they were. I've never felt so alone.

When Nico opens the door, he's still wearing his suit trousers and white shirt, with a tie knotted at his neck. He can't have been home long.

Standing in the doorway, I absorb his energy, feel his presence, and long to be cocooned in his arms. But there's something between us now that wasn't there before; an invisible partition, a separation that can only be *felt*.

He senses it instantly, the warmth in his face fading. "What's wrong?"

I step into the apartment, and even through the haze of anger, I can see this place is amazing. Insane. Beyond the imagining of mere mortals like me. The furniture is sleek, contemporary and expensive-looking. Steel columns rise between the sofas. The ceilings are ten feet high, the external walls sheet glass.

We're dizzyingly far from the ground, and just like the night we fucked in the office, the sunset blazes outside. Only this time I don't see it as beautiful.

This time it looks like hell.

I clutch my handbag tight to my side. Nico's eyes flick to it, and his frown deepens.

"Did someone hurt you? Because I swear, if they did—"

"You did," I grit out.

His gaze sweeps over my face, his eyes narrowing. "I don't understand."

"I spoke to Martin Brooks."

His reaction is subtle. A flicker, a bobbing of his Adam's apple as he swallows. "Kate—"

"What's that?" I cut him off, looking over his shoulder to where a framed picture is leaning against the sofa.

It's the charcoal drawing I did of my father, except it has been expensively mounted and reframed, a red ribbon tied around it.

"I had it fixed. To remember your father."

"My father?" Anger thins my voice, and the words quiver. "Who the hell was my father? Because I sure as shit don't know."

Nico's shoulders compress, and he looks at me like I'm about to break and he doesn't know whether to take cover or try to catch the pieces.

"You knew, didn't you? You knew what kind of man he was?" Fire flushes my veins, heating my body, raging through my limbs. It infuses my brain and blurs my vision.

I drop my handbag to the floor, stalk past Nico, and pick up the picture, turning it so he can see it. "Is this a joke? Is this a fucking joke?"

"No. God, no. It's a gift."

"A gift? Keep your gifts, you lying bastard!" I raise the picture over my head. Nico's features contort with alarm as he reads my intention. He steps towards me, arms outstretched.

There's a split second of clarity, where I know I could pull back, *should* pull back, but then it's gone. I've passed the limit of rational thought, and anger consumes me. With a scream that comes from somewhere dark and wounded, I slam the picture to the floor. The glass shatters; the frame breaks.

Nico stills. "What the fuck is going on?"

"My father embezzled millions from the company. He destroyed it. That's why you didn't buy it. Is it true?"

Nico's eyes are full of pain. "I couldn't make it work." There's a reluctance to his words that fuels my anger. He still doesn't want to tell me the truth.

My hand flies to my mouth and emotion swells in my throat. "It's true? You knew? All this time, you knew?"

"I did." His voice sounds apologetic.

Tears spill down my face as my words from Jack's party return to haunt me. *Dad didn't deserve it. He was a good man. A hundred times the man you'll ever be.* I yelled it in Nico's face and he barely blinked, when all the while he knew exactly what type of man Gerard Lansen was. Shame rushes through me. I've been such a fool.

Nico walks towards me, one hand outstretched.

"No." I hit at his arms. "Don't touch me."

He stops. "Kate…"

"No!" I scream. "You lied to me. You swore you wouldn't, and all this time… all these years…" I close my eyes, my hand clasped over my lips, chin trembling beneath my palm. "Why did no one tell me?"

"Your father. He asked us not to. We swore to him."

"Why? Because I wouldn't be able to understand? Because I'm too young? A child? A woman? What was it?" With each word, the pitch of my voice rises. I'm strangely detached, as if the person losing their mind isn't really me at all, but someone I'm watching from a distance.

"We did it because he asked us to. He made us swear we'd protect you."

"From what?"

"The truth."

The word silences my senses before anger screams in my veins. "You can't protect someone from the truth! You can only hide it from them."

Tears stream down my cheeks. I can't stay here. I need to get out. I grab my handbag, fix my gaze on the door and stride towards it. My heels crunch over shards of broken glass with each step.

Nico blocks my path. "Where are you going?"

"Away from you."

"Let me explain," he begs.

"Explain what? That you didn't cover up a crime? That my father didn't steal from his own company? That you aren't as much of a fucking criminal as my father was? That you didn't hide it all from me for years? That when you swore to me that you wouldn't lie to me, you knew you were lying about this?"

There's a storm of emotion in his eyes as he watches me speak, but he makes no attempt to answer me.

"Can you deny any of it?"

The silence seems to quiver with hope. Desperation. Longing for some other reality than this one.

With a pained look, Nico replies, "No."

I never knew one tiny word could be so destructive. I clutch at my chest like I can hold myself together as sobs wrack my ribs and tears drip to the floor.

"Fuck, Kate. I'm sorry."

"Sorry?" I gasp. "Do you know how painful, how humiliating it is to have your ignorance exposed by someone you barely know? Someone who comes at you with such malice? You didn't protect me *at all*. None of you. Not my father, not my brother, and certainly not..." My throat is thick, my voice shaking with emotion. "You... whatever you are to me. Whatever you *were* to me."

"Were?" Nico's voice is as unsteady as mine and the sound of it nearly brings me to my knees.

"Yes. Were. This"—I wave my hand between us—"is over."

His face blanches. "Over? You can't walk away from this. This is once in a lifetime—"

I don't let him finish. "Cut the crap, Nico." The words croak out in a pitiful shout. "This isn't once in a lifetime. This is lies and dishonesty and a dozen other red flags I should have seen a mile off. I deserve more than this. It's over. We're finished. I'm finished."

The words choke me and heartbreak looms at the periphery of my awareness. One more second in this room and it will swallow me. I pace towards the door. I don't need to look to know Nico's following me; the dominating crack of his footsteps splits the air.

He grabs my upper arm and spins me around. His handsome face twists with emotion so intense I want to shy away from the force of it.

"No." He grips my wrist in his other hand. "You're wrong. This is only the beginning. I'm falling in love with you. I *am* in love with you."

The wreckage of my chest cracks, splinters, breaks into a thousand pieces. It's beyond excruciating. "Love? It's only been weeks," I scoff, trying to pretend I wasn't feeling the same thing.

"Years, Kate. I've been in love with you for years."

I can't breathe. If Nico says *love* again, in that tone that resonates deep in my core, everything I'm made of will dissolve.

I cling to the fragments of my anger.

"Years?" I wrench my wrist free. "You haven't *loved* me for years... you've *avoided* me for years."

"Because you're the one person I didn't want to lie to." His voice is hard but with a brittle edge, as though it might fracture at any second. "And I had to lie... I fucking had to."

"You didn't." My voice breaks.

We stand, arm's breadth apart, not touching physically, but tangled up in every other way. His agony is mine, and mine is his. It coils around my throat, wrapping so tight I have to fight for air.

"I can't do this." I wrench my gaze from his and something deep inside tears wide open, the pain blindsiding me.

I can't let him see me fall apart. I pace to the door, my hand on the handle when he speaks again.

"This isn't over. If you walk out of here, part of me is going with you. Part of me will *always* be with you."

I stiffen at his words, as if I can somehow harden myself against them... But each of them is a poisoned arrow that sinks into my skin and infects my flesh. Controlling to the very last; I can't even leave without Nico declaring what happens next.

"Don't fucking manipulate me." My index finger points like the barrel of a gun. "It's always about you, isn't it? I don't know what you think love is, but it isn't ordering me not to walk away because your feelings take priority. Love is listening and respecting, and letting me go if that's what I want." I let out a painful groan, hands falling to my sides. "Fuck this. We can't work together. I'm resigning from the spa project. I don't want it anymore. It's tainted with lies and Martin *fucking* Brooks. If he wants it, let him take it. I don't give a shit anymore."

Nico walks towards me, his expression lethal, his steps so rapid I have no hope of escaping him. "You don't give a shit about the biggest spa project in London? The project that will make your career? That meant so much to your father? That you've been working on for years? You'd give it all up?"

"I would."

His jaw hardens, its already strong lines even more severe. "Then know this: people who give up never get anything they want in life. If that's the path you choose, then I can't follow because I don't *fucking* quit, and I cannot be with someone who does."

His gaze lacerates me, and I know he's not talking about the spa project anymore.

He's talking about us.

If I walk out, it's over.

But to stay? I can't. It's all too much. I don't trust a word that falls from his lips.

I turn back towards the door.

"You're leaving?" he asks, exposing the merest hint of vulnerability.

I shift the angle of my chin, defiant. "Yes."

And then I leave, knowing exactly what that means.

37
NICO

I rub my fingertips over my eyelids and sink to the sofa. I don't even get myself a drink. I'm drained, like Kate came over and sucked the fucking life out of me... and not in a good way.

I don't know how long I sit there, staring at the wall, my thoughts far away. I've made no effort to clear away the evidence of Kate's fury. Broken glass carpets the stone floor, and the red ribbon I'd tied around the picture lies amidst the debris, a mockery of what I tried to achieve.

I thought she'd love it.

If I was inclined to self-pity, I'd be dropping into an enormous hole of it right about now. As it is, I'm teetering somewhere near the edge, refusing to take that last step.

I'm falling in love with you. I am in love with you. I've been in love with you for years.

I didn't intend to say those words tonight, but now I've spoken them, I know they're true. The last few weeks have solidified the feelings that I kept locked away for all that time, because you can't hit on your best friend's sister. Resistance was easier. But denial... that's as sweet as it gets.

You can't feel pain when you're in denial. So much fucking denial. Not only about my feelings for her, but about what I'd done for her father and the impact that would have on us.

I might not have struck Gerard down with my own hand, but I played a role in events that overwhelmed him. That guilt has always tinged my grief, making it feel like a dirty thing I had to hide away.

At the funeral, I watched Kate toss dirt into the grave, and it was as if her pain subsumed my own. Hers was pure where mine was sordid. She was a broken-hearted girl whose perfect father was dead.

I didn't want to be the one to destroy her memory of him, but nor could I be around her, continually having to face the lie I'd committed to tell. When my father summoned me to the States to learn the ropes over there, I jumped at the opportunity. Buried myself in work.

And yet, when I saw her standing on that balcony at Jack's party, I knew I had to have her this time. She wasn't a teenager undressing in a hot tub, trying to seduce me; I didn't have to say no anymore. And somehow, I'd convinced myself that finally buying her father's company made everything right again. Cleaned the slate so I could start over.

Only it didn't. Not even close.

A battering starts up on my door. I jerk upright in my seat.

"Nico? Open the fucking door. Your security out here is going to kill me if you don't open up." Jack's voice rouses me from my stupor. I check the time. It's after midnight. My stomach lurches. Why the fuck is Jack here? Does he know about Kate?

"Mr. Hawkston?" The voice of one of my security team comes from outside the apartment.

I get up. "I'm coming."

I unlock the door to see Jack, red-faced and furious, his arms pinned behind his back by my head of security. Jack's a big guy, but he looks small, held captive like that.

"You can release Mr. Lansen," I tell the man.

Jack immediately lurches forward as the huge bodyguard releases him with a slight shove. Jack turns to scowl at him, brushing down the sleeves of his dark overcoat.

"What the fuck?" Jack spits. "Your men are brutes."

My bodyguard retreats and I close the door behind him. "What do you expect if you're going to show up in the middle of the night, yelling the place down?" I reply.

Jack huffs and marches past me into my apartment before coming to an abrupt stop and spinning to face me.

"Martin Brooks is going to steal the spa project." The words spill from Jack's mouth, and suddenly his foul mood and panicked arrival at my flat make sense. He tips his head to stare at the ceiling. "That bastard is going to steal it from under our noses. He's going to—"

"Jack, stop. Take a breath."

But Jack is pacing like a confused greyhound trying to win a race, first one way, then the other. "He told Kate. He fucking told her everything. She called me and let me have it. She hates me. She's never going to forgive me. This is an almighty fuck up. He told her—"

"I know."

Jack's frantic movement slows as he turns his eyes on me. Beneath his foot, something crunches. His attention drops to the floor as he raises his leather-soled shoe, revealing a crushed splinter of glass beneath it. Then, as if he's seeing the apartment for the first time since he entered, his gaze roves, following the trail of glass to the wrecked picture.

The drawing itself is still in one piece, hanging in one half of the broken frame. Gerard Lansen's serious side-profile stares into the distance, Kate's unmistakable signature in the bottom right-hand corner of the impressive charcoal sketch.

"What happened here?"

I say nothing, waiting for him to put the pieces together.

He crunches through the glass towards the picture, stopping a few feet away, toeing the red ribbon with his shoe.

My stomach dips, a knot forming in my chest. I'm too tired for this, but I brace myself for the moment of realisation.

He swings round to face me, nostrils flaring. "How do you already know that Martin Brooks told Kate? Has she been here tonight? Did she come here first? Did she come to you first?"

"Yes."

He blinks, long and slow, and he pinches the bridge of his nose for a second. "Are you screwing my sister?"

"No."

Jack's eyes track me like a missile as he gestures to the mess at his feet. "Then what's going on here?"

"I'm in love with her."

Shock warps his face, and for a moment I hope it's enough to halt his reaction. Love, after all, is a big fucking word. But then his expression condenses into something altogether more wrathful.

"Your shit doesn't fly with me, Hawkston." He ducks his head and barrels towards me, cashmere-coated arm pulled back, fist clenched.

He swings an arm in my direction, but I easily block the attack, ducking when he sends the other flying in an uncontrolled arc towards me.

I shove him and he stumbles back, knocking against a side table and toppling a tall glass vase, which shatters when it falls to the floor, adding to the debris.

Jack's phone rings, but he ignores it, letting it ring out from inside his coat as he prowls around me, both fists raised.

"You could have any woman in the entire world, you bastard," Jack curses, his brow heavy over dark eyes. "And you fuck Kate?"

He charges at me again just as the front door opens, making him draw up short. My head of security stands in the doorway. A great monolith of a man, all in black.

"Shall I remove him, sir?"

I shake my head, my focus on Jack. "Let him take his shot."

"How fucking gracious of you," Jack spits.

His phone rings again.

"Someone needs you," I say. "It's late to call."

Jack glances at his wristwatch. It must be nearly 1 am. He purses his lips, then looks back at me, before lunging.

I could duck, I could block, but this won't be over until he hits me. He's huge and powerful and it goes against every instinct in my body to slow my reactions just enough to let him strike.

His fist meets my jaw, my head whips back, and pain blasts through me like a lightning bolt. My mouth fills with the metallic tang of blood.

Jack cradles his hand, hopping on the spot. "Fuck, fuck, fuck," he groans through a grimace.

His phone rings again, and this time he fishes it out with his other hand.

I dab my mouth on the back of my hand. There's a trickle of blood, but most of it I swallow down.

I haven't been hit in the face since I was at school. I forgot how much it hurts. I make my way to the nearest chair and drop into it. I'm not going to look good tomorrow. Letting him hit me is rapidly feeling like a terrible decision.

"I think we're done here," I tell my head of security, who is still standing by the door, awaiting instruction. He nods and steps outside.

"Mum?" Jack says, still shaking his hand and flexing his fingers, wincing as he does. Then his gaze shifts from his hand to mid-distance, his head snapping up. "What? When? Calm down. All right. I'm coming. Stay put. I'll be there as soon as possible."

He hangs up, staring at the phone.

"What?" I ask.

"That bastard... Curtis. Mum's boyfriend. He took everything."

"What do you mean, he took everything? Everything what?"

"The paintings. Mum's jewellery. Everything."

My aching jaw slows my brain, and I take a moment to fumble for the right train of thought. "The paintings he was putting into storage? The Stephen Condar?"

"Yeah. Dad's art. It never went into storage. Curtis fucking took it. Nicked the lot. I knew he was a fucking dodgy arsehole. I knew it. And now he's disappeared." Jack lets out a frustrated groan as his hand scrapes his face. He collects himself and announces, "I'm going down there. Mum's in a state. She's just back from Aunt Venetia's, and the house is empty."

"Empty?"

"Cleared out. Nothing of any value left."

"And the art?"

"She was letting him deal with it. She never even knew where he was storing it." Jack curses. "She's so desperate to be taken care of she let him waltz into her life and steal the whole lot."

"I'll come with you."

Jack eyes me. "You look rough. You should probably put some ice on your face."

I raise an eyebrow, or I try to, but pain shoots down my face so I abort the attempt. "Can you drive with that hand?"

Jack looks at it, turns it over, and flexes his fingers again. I can see the pain on his face before he wipes it away. "It's late. Roads will be quiet."

"Not a good idea."

Jack mutters a curse under his breath. "Fine. Okay. I'll call a cab." He winces. "But before I go anywhere, I need some ice for my hand. What the hell is your jaw made of? Titanium?"

The urge to laugh bubbles up inside me, but even as the sound escapes an aching pain shoots through the side of my face. "Don't make me laugh. It hurts."

"Good," Jack replies. "Next time, keep your dick in your trousers."

"I meant what I said. I'm in love—"

"Please." He holds a hand up and looks at the ceiling. "Save yourself. If I know Kate, she's not forgiving either of us anytime soon. And you aren't going to win her over with a big declaration, either." He glances over at the picture. "Especially if that's anything to go by. That frame looks expensive."

I shrug. "The best."

Jack snorts and rolls his eyes. "Of course."

I push off the sofa and lead the way towards the kitchen, grab a bowl and fill it with ice from the dispenser. Jack takes it and shoves his fist in it, perching on a stool at the island.

He lets out a long sigh as his hand rests on the ice. "Can I take this in the cab?" He gestures to the bowl.

"Sure. We should get going."

Jack frowns, his focus turning inward. "I don't think it's a good idea for you to come. Kate might be there."

My stomach does an unpleasant twist at the sound of her name.

"Mum probably called her too," Jack continues. "She won't want to see either of us, but I have more reason to be there. This is family business."

My heart sinks as the irrational hope of seeing Kate vanishes. "Fine."

Jack stands, cradling the bowl of ice under his arm. "I need to go before Mum loses her mind. She's flipping out down there."

Jack dials for a cab and I try to keep my mind off the fact that, had the evening gone differently, I'd probably have my dick buried deep inside his sister right now.

It would've been a hell of a lot more pleasurable than getting hit in the mouth and fighting with my best friend.

I try to stay focused. "Did she call the police?"

"Not yet."

"Have her hold off."

Jack's eyes narrow. "Why?"

"Just do it. And keep in touch."

A few minutes later and we're standing at my front door, on the verge of parting.

"Fuck, what a mess," Jack says, agitatedly shifting from foot to foot for a moment before stopping, staring at me. "Were you serious? About Kate? That you're in love with her?"

"Absolutely."

His jaw tightens, and I await his next words like a man on the scaffold.

"I want her to be happy," he declares. "Fuck it. I'd like you both to be happy. And if there is anything real between the two of you... I don't want you to mess it all up because Dad and I had you swearing to keep secrets that weren't yours to keep. Neither of you deserves that. So as much as it pains me, if you want me to, I can put in a good word when I see her."

Jack makes it all sound so simple, and maybe it could have been... but then my anger went and got the better of me and I snapped. Told her I couldn't be with someone who quits, because that would be an insurmountable difference between us I couldn't tolerate. Is it a hill I'm willing to die on?

"I appreciate the gesture," I tell him. "But I doubt she'll listen to anything either of us has to say for a while."

"Hmm. Okay. Maybe that's for the best. Let her work out how she feels first. She's got a lot to come to terms with."

And with that, he bids me farewell, and I send up a silent prayer that I haven't pushed her too far. Kate might have given up on us, but I'm not ready to quit yet.

38
NICO

The following morning, I wake to the brutal sound of my phone ringing. I'm still on the sofa, fully clothed.

I smack my hand across the coffee table until I reach it. I don't even look at who's calling before I pick up.

"What?"

"Good morning to you too," Matt's gruff voice barks down the line. "Let me up. The security down here is nuts."

A few minutes later, Matt is standing in my apartment with one small overnight bag, which he drops to the floor. He casts a glance over the place, taking in the wreckage of last night's fight. "What the hell happened here? Have you been to bed?"

I perch on the edge of the sofa and roll the sleeves of my crumpled shirt up. "Fuck," I mutter.

Matt squints at me and lurches forward to inspect my face. "Is that a bruise? That's going to look very unprofessional. Did you have a brawl in here or what?"

"Long story." I drag a hand over my face, wincing as I skim the tender side of my jaw. "How was your flight?"

"Tedious."

"You haven't been home?"

"No. Where's Charlie?"

"With Seb."

Matt kicks a piece of broken glass with the toe of his shoe. "You cleared him out so you could have a fisticuffs session with someone?"

I groan. "Not exactly. I had something much better planned, but it didn't work out." Even the oblique reference to Kate makes the acid in my empty stomach churn. "I don't want to talk about it right now. Let's do your shit first."

Matt eyes me suspiciously. "I want to know everything you know before I see my *wife*." He snarls the last word. "I've already got the lawyer drawing up divorce papers."

"Isn't that a bit sudden?"

"No. I've been thinking about it for a while. Had him on notice. The house is bloody miserable. I don't want to raise the kids in a home where Gemma and I are constantly at each other's throats. Charlie's endured it too long already, but maybe there's still time to save Lucie from it. Give her a happier home. And you know cheating is an absolute deal-breaker for me." He inhales so deeply his already broad chest doubles in size, then blows it out in a harsh gust. "Who the fuck is the chap she's been sleeping with?"

I jump to my feet, immediately recalling that I'd meant to ask Kate about the picture on her phone of the graffitied van. How the hell did I forget? I cup the side of my face, touching my bruised jaw. Pain erupts and the chaos of last night floods back. It's no surprise I fucking forgot about it.

"I don't know," I say. "But Seb got Elliot Maxwell on the case. Let's get him up here."

"Great. I'm making coffee. You look like you need one. A shower too. Go. Get your sorry arse into the bathroom. I can't look at your miserable face any longer. You'd think you were the one whose wife was cheating on him."

By the time I get out of the shower, Matt and Elliot Maxwell are sitting at the kitchen table. Elliot greets me with an expressionless nod. We never make small talk. It's easier that way. Elliot's a law unto himself. Everything between us is on a need to know basis only. He's fucking good at what he does, and that's enough for me.

Matt has swept up the broken glass and made coffee. The picture of Gerard Lansen has been removed from the broken frame and propped up on the sofa.

Matt doesn't ask about it, thank goodness. I don't want to think about last night if I don't have to.

"You've got an epic view up here," Matt says, gazing out of the floor to ceiling glass windows as he pushes a steaming mug of coffee across the table towards me. "Makes me wish I could sell up and move into one of these bachelor pads."

Matt's eyes are unfocused, like he's imagining an alternative version of his life. He shakes his head, presses his lips into a line, and takes a sip of hot coffee.

Elliot grunts like he agrees and hunches over the table, his bulk making even Matt look small. Six foot six, and thick with muscle; wide as a barge, biceps that threaten to burst through his sleeves of his worn leather jacket. If he wasn't so huge, his rugged jaw would be the biggest thing about him. Today, it's concealed beneath a tidy, dirty blond beard.

On the table, beneath his thick, tattooed fingers, is a manila envelope.

Matt keeps eyeing it like it's a nuclear warhead about to launch.

I grab the mug of coffee Matt gave me and sit opposite them.

"This is a mighty unpleasant business," Elliot says. "I'm dead sorry about it, Mr. Hawkston."

Matt's shoulders draw closer together, body contracting. He's always struggled to accept sympathy. It's only when Elliot unclips his gun from his holster and lays it on the kitchen table that there's a glimmer of response in Matt's eyes; an alertness, as if he thinks there's a chance Elliot might turn the weapon on him. Elliot's fingers linger on the weapon, which looks out of place against the clean marble surface.

"I'll happily blow his brains out for you and clean up the mess," Elliot murmurs, so low that it's almost inaudible. "If that's what you want."

"Put the gun away," Matt replies, voice toneless. "This isn't the fucking mafia."

Elliot tilts his head in a manner that communicates, *'have it your way, but if it were up to me I'd put a bullet in his temple'* before holstering the gun again and sliding the manila envelope across to Matt. Somehow, it feels more dangerous than a loaded Glock. We fall silent as Matt flicks through the contents.

Matt sighs, his eyes flickering closed for a moment before they lock on Elliot. "How long ago was the most recent photo taken?"

"Yesterday," Elliot says.

"Even after Charlie found out, she's still seeing the guy? Un-fuck-ing-believable." Anger vibrates in his voice.

"Can I see?"

Matt shoves the pictures at me, and I flick through them. There isn't a decent image amongst them, with several being taken from outside the house through the windows.

"Pictures aren't the best," Elliot says. "The guy's on high alert; scurrying around like he's already being hunted. Made it impossible to get a clear head shot. He turned up to see Gemma in a balaclava. I'm surprised she opened the door to him."

Matt shoots me a '*what the fuck?*' look, but says nothing.

I lay the photos down and Matt pushes them back at Elliot, standing up so fast his chair nearly tips backward. "We're going round there. We're getting Lucie out of that house."

"Let's hear what Gemma has to say before we rush into anything," I suggest.

Matt's jaw hardens. "What the hell are we expecting her to say? 'Oh, the sex is good, thanks. We like to role-play with balaclavas'?"

Elliot puts the photos back in the envelope, a muffled groan sounding from deep in his throat. He keeps his eyes down, but his fingers strum the table like he's itching to pull a trigger.

"I'm urging caution," I say. "We don't want to spook her."

Matt grits out, "Fine."

He sits as Elliot begins the rundown. "His name is Daniel Hunter. At least that's who the van is registered with, and that's the name on the title deeds of the house where your son was arrested. Absolutely no social media or online presence. He appears to run a removals company. He has a couple of vans, and a few men working for him. A small outfit. Casual. Not particularly professional. His accounts aren't in order, and I suspect he takes a lot of payments in cash. Two priors. Theft and domestic burglary."

"He's a fucking criminal?" Matt raises both hands as though he wants to crush the man's head between them, and his gaze flits from me to Elliot, like he's hoping one of us might contradict him. When we don't, he lets his hands fall, and continues more resignedly, "How did he meet Gemma? How did she even get to know him?"

Elliot rolls his lips inwards, thrusting his chin out further. "Can't be sure. I haven't had enough time to observe their patterns of behaviour, but so far it looks like he comes to her. She doesn't travel to see him. She may not even know where he lives. We don't know how truthful he's been with her."

"And the van," I ask. "The one with the graffiti?"

"It's been scrubbed."

"Kate Lansen had a picture of it on her phone," I tell them.

They both look at me in mute surprise for a few seconds.

"Why?" Matt asks.

"I don't know. I meant to ask, but I didn't get a chance."

Matt's eyes narrow, and I can see by the way he's looking at me he's trying to piece this shit together, but can't quite make it fit.

"What did it look like? Was it a random photo she took on the street?" Matt probes further.

"I don't know. I didn't see it. Charlie did."

Matt winces at the mention of his son, then wipes his expression clear. "Ring her. Ask her why the hell she had a photo of the van my son scrawled all over. The van that belongs to the bloke Gemma's fucking."

Elliot's face is immovable. His repeated throat clearing is the only suggestion that he has any thoughts about this scenario. "Did she have any removals recently?" he asks. "Any cause to hire a van?"

"Yes. Her mother's boyfriend had all their paintings put into storage."

"Call Kate and ask her about it then," Matt snaps.

I grimace. "I can't do that. I can't call her."

Matt looks at me, baffled. "Eh? Why the fuck not?"

"It doesn't matter, but they're gone. All the paintings. Everything that supposedly went to storage didn't go to storage at all."

"What do you mean?" Elliot leans toward me like this is crucial information. "Where did they go?"

"We don't know. The boyfriend disappeared, along with all the art. Supposedly jewellery too. Anything of value is gone."

Suddenly an idea bursts into existence, burgeoning with so much hope it's almost painful. Maybe there's a connection between Daniel and Curtis. I direct my focus to Elliot. "Find him. The guy with the removals company. Daniel. If he's involved in some scam like this, we need to know. Dig out what he knows about a man called Curtis Bellamy. That's Mrs. Lansen's boyfriend. It's possible this guy with the van is connected with him in some way... maybe they're even working together. If we move fast, we might be able to locate the paintings. We might even be able to return all their stolen belongings." I turn to Matt. "And at the same time, get Gemma's man locked up. And whoever else is involved."

"You sure it's the old lady's boyfriend?" Elliot asks. "That makes this sound like a targeted and planned scam."

I nearly laugh at Elliot calling Debbie Lansen 'the old lady'. She'd die if she knew.

"As far as I'm aware, Curtis arranged to have the artwork removed," I confirm. "Never told Mrs. Lansen where it was being stored. She trusted him to deal with it, and now the house is empty and he's vanished. I'd say the chances of it all being connected are high."

"To pose as a boyfriend and let Mrs. Lansen believe he cares about her... That's bleak," Matt adds. "Who'd want to punish the Lansens like that?"

"These scams aren't necessarily emotional," Elliot says. "But when someone is particularly vulnerable, it's the easiest way in."

I hardly hear him because Matt's question has the back of my neck prickling. There's one man who does want to target the Lansens. "If you can find any link to Martin Brooks, I want to know about it," I tell him.

Matt stares at me, looking confused. "Martin Brooks, Gerard Lansen's old business partner?"

"Exactly. He's after the Knightsbridge spa project. Says he doesn't want the Lansens getting any more glory. He's pissed that we bought the company."

Matt pinches his chin between his thumb and forefinger. "What the hell?"

"Shall I contact the police?" Elliot asks.

"Not yet," I tell him. "If this has anything to do with Martin Brooks, I want to know before the police do. Keep me informed. I want everything done properly, so all evidence is admissible in court if needs be. Don't fuck this up."

Elliot nods and stands from the table, bids us farewell, and heads to the door.

After he's gone, I call Jack. He answers on the second ring. "Your mum hasn't called the police yet?"

"No. She's sleeping. Kate's on her way down here, too."

A pinch of a beat occurs in my heart at her name. That better stop happening some time soon or I'm going to end up with an arrhythmia.

"Let me handle it," I reassure him. "We've got a lead I want to follow up before we involve the police."

"Are you sure? I don't want you to have to get your hands dirty over this."

"Don't worry about me. I'll sort it."

"If you're sure..."

"I'm sure. One more thing. Kate had a photo on her phone of a white van. Had a load of obscenities sprayed on it."

"Oh yeah, the dick on the side of the van that dropped off Curtis' shitty art collection."

"Exactly. Was it the same van that picked up your dad's stuff?"

"No idea. Kate and I weren't there when Mum had it all collected from the house."

"Hmm. I'll find out. Just keep the police out of it until I've run a few checks. Oh, and Jack?"

"Yes?"

"Don't mention it to Kate. Not yet."

He agrees, and I hang up, feeling more settled than I have since Kate left. All the while, Matt is still sitting at the table, leaning back in his chair and staring at me. "You want to tell me what's going on with you and Kate Lansen, then?"

I bury both my hands deep in my pockets and look at the floor, running my tongue over my bottom teeth.

"Oh, my God." Matt's jaw drops wide, and then a smile contorts his mouth. "You like her. I never thought I'd see the day that someone pinned you down."

"She's not even talking to me at the moment."

"I'm sure she will. You're Nico fucking Hawkston. We Hawkstons always get what we want in the end."

39

KATE

Jack hands me a cup of tea, but I shake my head. I don't want to take anything from him. We're standing in Mum's kitchen and morning light is blistering in the window, making the faux wood veneer of the cupboards gleam offensively.

"Listen, Kate. I'm sorry I didn't tell you about Dad. Really."

"Please don't." My joints lock, body stiffening. I can't listen to his excuses. "I'm not a child. I could have managed the truth."

"Managed it how? By losing your shit and smashing stuff like you did last night?"

My stomach sinks, followed by a blast of pain that runs straight to my heart. He must have spoken to Nico.

Nico.

The pain increases, and I'm aching with the cruelest type of heartbreak. I'm suffering so much emotional agony that even standing in the same room as Jack is difficult.

I haul my awareness back into the kitchen to find him inspecting me, looking for proof of what he's implying. He must find it because he adds, "Turns out you've got secrets of your own, too."

"That's different."

"How exactly is having a relationship with my best friend and hiding it from me different?"

"Because I'm not obliged to tell you about my love life."

"So it's a love life, not a sex life?"

Love. Those four letters tear at the edges of the wounds Nico's words left last night.

I scowl at him. "It's a phrase. It doesn't mean anything. But either way, I don't need some stamp of approval from you. And the fact you're even suggesting I do brings me back to my original point. You've treated me like a kid for far too long."

We stare at one another, me trying to conceal the fact that him knowing about me and Nico is making me internally freak out, and him still holding out a mug of tea like an olive branch. I glance down at his knuckles, which are raw and bloodied.

I fix on them for just long enough that he withdraws his hand and puts the mug down on the side.

"And don't lecture me about losing my shit," I argue.

I don't need to ask who he hit. I try to ignore the uneasy swirling in my stomach at the thought of Jack smashing Nico in the face.

Maybe they both deserve it, but that thought doesn't make me feel any better. My entire body is rigid with anger and resentment, but it shifts abruptly as I begin to numb out, unable to bear the mixture of shame and heartache that the memory of last night's events dredges up.

Nico might have confessed that he loved me... or some strange version of it, and God knows I'd have given anything to hear him say that before Martin Brooks spoke to me. But I'm not sure Nico Hawkston is capable of love. Not really. Even last night, he only said those words to take control of the situation. To get me to put my anger aside because his *love* is more important.

But the thing that really stung were his words about quitting. *I don't fucking quit, and I cannot be with someone who does.* He spoke them with such certainty that it drove home his point hard and fast, skewering all of my insecurities like a piece of raw meat... the belief that I'm not good enough and I'll never be good enough, so I might as well give up.

I've always been a disappointment to Mum. And as for the company... Dad left it to Jack, not me. He shared his secrets, his failures, his fears—*all of it*—with Jack, and neither of them trusted me enough to tell me the God-damned truth, and Nico's just as bad.

I'm spiraling. I know I am. The destructive thoughts running through my mind will bring me so low I won't be able to climb out of the hole of my own making.

Not only have I walked away from Nico, the one person with whom I finally found a sense of comfort and safety, but I'm giving up everything I worked for on the spa project.

Mum enters the kitchen, her hair a mess, her face makeup free. It's shocking how old and worn out she looks. She glances between us, notes that Jack's holding a cup, whereas my hands are free, and promptly launches herself into my arms.

"Oh, Kate, darling. Oh, my goodness..." She bursts into tears, collapsing on me, her arms weak and frail around my neck. "He tricked me... he stole from me... what did I do to deserve it?" she wails.

I pat her back. "Oh, Mum..." My attempt at comfort sounds wooden, but her wailing continues regardless.

"He said he loved me. And I loved him. Oh, how can I bear this broken heart?"

Over the top of her head, I catch sight of Jack, pressing his lips together. His eyes flash to mine, and I note his gaze is full of amusement.

He's holding back laughter.

It's wrong... but as soon as I see the way he's desperately trying to keep it together, I want to giggle myself. Not because it's funny, or because I don't care... but because the whole scenario is awkward and ridiculous, and the urge to laugh is some misguided reaction beyond my control. My body cannot contain the unpleasant emotions that Mum's weeping is dragging up in me, and clearly, neither can Jack's.

It's either giggle or sob right alongside her, breaking down over my own heartbreak. And there's no space for the latter in Mum's house.

She would likely accuse me of stealing her thunder or being attention-seeking if I even alluded to the fact that I have my own crap going on at the moment.

I bite hard on the inside of my cheek to shut down the urge. Jack, meanwhile, has turned to face the cupboards, so he's not looking at me, although I'm pretty sure I can see his shoulders shaking.

"Why? Why did he do it?" she wails. "Why?"

"It's going to be all right." Another token attempt at comfort.

She tugs out of my arms. "How? How will it be all right? All our stuff is gone. Those paintings your father collected." I don't dare comment that she was all too ready to get rid of them before. "The Stephen Condar. That was a unique piece. And my jewellery. Thank goodness I was wearing my rings, but all my necklaces, my diamond brooch, my earrings... all gone. That's your inheritance... vanished."

"The police will do everything they can," I say, realising I haven't seen a single police officer. "Did you call them? Have you reported it?"

"No," replies Mum at the exact moment Jack twists to face me and says, "Yes."

I look confusedly between the two of them. "Yes or no? Which is it?"

"It's in hand," Jack affirms.

"Oh, Jack. You're so wonderful." Mum totters across the room to throw herself into his arms and I breathe a sigh of relief. "Such a capable boy."

She squashes him in a bear hug, and every hint of misplaced amusement from his face is gone. "I'm thirty-five, Mum. I'm hardly a boy."

Mum gives a girlish giggle and wipes her tears with the back of her hand, sniffling as she does. "You'll always be my baby boy," she tells him. "I'm so grateful to have you to take care of me."

My lips pinch as that familiar knot of jealousy twists my insides. So much of Mum's heart is taken up with Jack that there's nothing left for me. I'm not even sure why I'm here. She has everything she needs and wants in him.

"I'll run you a bath," I say.

She spins out of Jack's arms to stare at me. "As if a bath would fix this. You have no idea the pain I'm suffering, do you? If only I had a daughter who could really understand how hard this is." She clasps her heart with both hands. "But you've never had a decent relationship. You'll never know what this feels like. How painful this is."

Anger snaps my restraint, and I speak before I've thought it through. "Actually, Mum, I've been seeing someone."

Jack makes eyes at me again, shaking his head, urging me to stop.

Mum pulls back. "Have you?"

"Yes. Someone you know. And the sex is amazing." I speak fast, and my furious tone doesn't match my words.

Jack looks like he's about to retch.

"Good Lord, Kate," Mum whines. "I don't want to know." She pulls a disgusted face, but she can't keep it up and a moment later she's peering at me, eyes agog. "Who is it?"

"Nico. It's Nico Hawkston. So I'd appreciate it if you quit making comments about how no man is ever going to choose me, because Nico did."

Mum grabs Jack's arm like she might fall flat on her face if she doesn't. "Oh, my... oh, goodness..."

"Yes. Oh, my goodness, indeed," I say with vitriol. I allow a moment for the news to sink in before I shrug and add, "I guess I'll go and run you that bath now."

I walk away as calmly as I can, praying that I get out of the kitchen before she has the chance to ask if my relationship with Nico is still ongoing. I'm not about to give her the satisfaction of telling her it's already over, and that I do, in fact, know *exactly* how she's feeling.

Because I'm just as heartbroken as she is.

40
NICO

The air conditioning in the car is blasting. Outside, it's swelteringly hot. One of those London summer days we're not equipped to deal with. The city is melting.

I'm parked on the street outside Matt's Kensington house. Behind us, in a dark-windowed sedan, is Elliot Maxwell.

"I'm not coming in," I say. "Gemma's going to have more than enough to handle without me, too."

"Fuck's sake," Matt curses. "Come. You're the one that wants the dirt on her boyfriend and this Curtis chap."

"You should confront her about the cheating first."

Matt closes his eyes and hangs his head for a second before he rubs his temples and mutters something under his breath. "Give me five minutes, then bring Elliot in."

My niece pops into my mind. "What about Lucie? Is she home?" If there's anything a three year old kid shouldn't witness, it's whatever's about to go down between her parents.

Matt checks his watch. "Not now. She's at playgroup." He snaps into action, opening the car door and getting out. He chucks a spare key at me, slams the door and marches up to his house like he's going to war.

He disappears inside and I make a note of the time. I'll give him ten minutes, not five. Who the hell can confront their wife and say what they need to say in five? Matt's efficient, but he's not that good.

When the time is up, I use the key fob to open the iron gates and make my way to the door of the large white Palladian style house. Everything is perfect. There's not a crack in the paintwork, no weeds in the window boxes.

Behind me, I sense Elliot Maxwell's presence. He keeps his distance, but I know he's there, emanating a dark, threatening energy. He's a man I wouldn't want to cross, and I'm always pleased he's on our side. He slides like a shadow through the gate, easing it closed so it doesn't clang.

I open the front door and step into the grand hallway. It's sleek and modern in here, because Matt and Gemma ripped out the original interior when they moved in. There's a two-level basement with an indoor pool, gym, and cinema room, and a lift beyond the staircase. In case they're too tired to walk to the top floor.

It's gorgeous. Not my style, but for a family home, it's the top of the market.

Unfortunately, the pristine interior is surface level only. The yells coming from the drawing room indicate a turbulent family life. Phrases meet my ears that don't sound new; they run in well-worn grooves. They've had these arguments before.

"You're never here." Gemma's voice is high and screechy, making me grind my molars. "You don't give a shit about us. When did you last spend time with your kids?"

"This isn't about the kids. This is about you fucking another man. In my house."

Something smashes and I wince.

"Our house," Gemma yells. "And if you ever came home, maybe I wouldn't need to fuck anyone else."

"Don't you dare put this on me."

"It is on you. You're a shitty husband and a shitty father."

"I'm not the one getting caught screwing a stranger on the kitchen table by my teenage son." Matt's voice strains with the effort of holding back an unwieldy amount of rage. "That alone is going to cost a fuckload in future therapy."

Something else smashes, and a tiny splinter of white porcelain shoots out across the hall, landing near my foot.

"Therapy?" Gemma screeches. "Maybe if you'd gone to therapy once in your God-damned life, we wouldn't be here."

Shit. Ten minutes definitely wasn't enough.

Beside me, Elliot's face is completely blank, as though he can't hear the conversation at all. I'm thankful for his professionalism because this is way too personal for the staff.

"When was the last time we had sex, Matt? When was it? Can you even remember? Do you even care?" Gemma is screaming even louder now. If the house wasn't so big, I'd be concerned the neighbours could hear. "You don't want to fuck me anymore. Admit it. We don't even like one another. This marriage is fucking bullshit. "

Matt is quiet for a moment. "Something we agree on, then."

"Sir," Elliot says, his voice low as he gives me an uncertain glance. "Should we come back later?"

"No. Don't fucking go anywhere," Matt barks, striding out into the hall. His eyes are wild and his chest is heaving. This is seriously fucked up. "Get in here," he demands, pointing down the hall to the room he just came from.

Elliot marches forward as instructed, the size of his muscles causing his gait to roll.

I hang back.

"Is this the right moment?" I caution Matt.

"Do you want to get that fucker Brooks, or what?" Matt hisses, and I'm suddenly struck by Matt's capacity to remember my concerns, even in the midst of his own turmoil. His question propels me to action, and I give a terse nod before following Elliot.

The drawing room floor is littered with pieces of broken ceramic. A teal lampshade sits on the floor like a discarded hat, the stand shattered, the side table conspicuously empty.

Gemma stands in the middle of the room, still immaculate. Her hair is full, her makeup excessive for a morning at home, and she's elegantly dressed in a pale yellow linen suit. She wrings her hands, twirling her wedding band.

Matt barks at her to sit. She glances at me before obeying, as if hoping I might intervene. But she's getting nothing from me. I hate cheating as much as Matt does, and regardless of how much my brother's behaviour may be at fault, he's still exactly that. *My brother*.

Matt glares at Gemma, who's now perched on a neat armchair. "Elliot has some questions for you, about your..." Matt grits his teeth and a muscle feathers in his jaw before he adds, "Lover."

Gemma's eyes are lit with fire and she scowls at Matt like she wants to tear out his insides and watch him bleed.

"Do I need a lawyer?" she asks.

"No. But tell the truth, because we believe your little fuck-buddy"—Matt's mouth twists with disdain—"is involved in criminal activity. He may even have targeted you specifically, probably because you're married to a Hawkston."

A small gasp escapes her lips. "Oh, don't make out no one would want me unless it was about you, you piece of shit."

Matt snorts. "I'm sure you'd like to think you're irresistible, but—"

"Fuck you."

"Let's keep it civil for now," I demand, and they fall silent as I shift my focus to Elliot, motioning for him to start. He places a recording device on the coffee table. A red light blinks on it, which Gemma eyes with suspicion. I'm surprised she doesn't demand he turn it off.

I sit down, ready to observe as Elliot questions her, but just as he's about to begin, the doorbell rings.

Gemma jumps up, both hands fisting at her sides. Her alarm is disproportionate to the sound. She's expecting someone.

All three of us realise at the same moment, and we move as a unit out into the hall. Matt's closest to the door. He runs, and Elliot follows.

Gemma pushes forward too, but she hasn't a hope in hell of getting past all of us.

"Curtis!" she screams. "Run."

Curtis? What the fuck? I thought we were looking for a Daniel.

Elliot grabs Gemma, holding her back as Matt opens the door to a surprised-looking man, who's already backing down the steps.

Dark, lank hair, skinny black jeans. Gold trainers. There in front of us is Curtis Bellamy, Mrs. Lansen's boyfriend.

Fuck me.

"Shit," he cries, taking in the sight of us all standing in the doorway. Behind him in the driveway is a white van, with the ghost of an enormous penis on the side. He trips over himself to get away, but Matt grabs him, hauling him into the house by the neck of his shirt.

"Oi!" Curtis yells, staring bug-eyed, at Matt. "You can't do this. Who the fuck do you think you are?"

"Who the fuck are you, more like?" Matt booms, throwing Curtis to the floor where he skids along the polished wood floor, landing in a heap at Gemma's feet.

"Babe," Curtis pleads, only getting one word out before I step forward, and it's clear from the way his cheeks pale and his mouth gapes that he hadn't registered me until this moment.

"Curtis," I mock, watching him squirm. "Fancy seeing you here."

Gemma's chin dimples, bottom lip quivering.

Curtis curls up like a dog expecting a beating.

Elliot gets down on the floor beside him and searches him, rough hands patting down his flailing body.

"Get your hands off me," Curtis roars.

Elliot flips him so he's face down, rams a knee into his back to hold him in place, and triumphantly tugs a wallet from Curtis's back pocket. He flips it open and removes a driving licence, flashing it for us to see. "This is your man. Daniel Hunter."

Gemma's fingers are hovering over her lips. "Daniel? Who's Daniel? Curtis, what's going on?"

Matt takes the driving licence from Elliot, scans it and holds it out to his wife. "This is the guy you've fucked up our marriage for. Hope it was worth it."

Gemma begins to cry, and Matt side-eyes her dismissively.

"Start talking," he barks at Curtis, who strains to look up at Gemma from where he's pinned to the floor.

"Babe, I fucked up."

"Not to my wife," Matt snarls.

Curtis glares at him. "I don't have to tell you anything. I'll go to the police."

Elliot slams Curtis' head down on the tile floor. The skin splits and a trickle of blood runs down his forehead and drips onto the floor beneath him. "You better do what you're asked," Elliot instructs. "Or this won't end well."

"Oh, please, don't hurt him," Gemma begs, dragging her palms down her cheeks.

Matt holds up a hand, urging Elliot to back off. He shakes his head like he'd rather smash Curtis' brains out than obey Matt, but he eases his hold on Curtis, or Daniel, or whatever the fuck this con-artist's name is.

"Tell us about the art collection. Mrs. Lansen's art," I demand.

"Debbie Lansen. What a bitch." Curtis scowls, then looks at Gemma and his expression softens. "Honestly, babe, it's only you I want to bone."

Bone?

If Seb was here, he'd laugh. I grimace and Gemma bleats, her legs trembling like she's going into shock.

I glance at Matt, who looks like he's about to lose his shit, but I hold out a hand to warn him off. I want to hear this.

"When I saw you at that party, you were so sad, so beautiful," Curtis continues. "I knew I could love you... Nothing like what I had to do with Debbie. I never would've fucked her if I didn't have to."

"Debbie? Debbie Lansen?" Gemma squeaks, spots of red appearing on her cheekbones. "You've been sleeping with Debbie Lansen?" She wails and gives a full body shudder. "But she's so old."

Matt catches my gaze, his expression halfway between fury and disbelief. I can practically hear his words in my head, *What a pair of fucking idiots.*

"It's you I wanted. I only did Debbie for the cash," Curtis explains.

He was being paid? My head explodes with the admission.

"Let's not tell Mrs. Lansen that tidbit," Matt says. "At least he was fucking my wife for free."

How he can find humour in this situation, I have no idea. I suspect it's a front, more for everyone else's benefit than his own.

Gemma whimpers and hides her face in her hands.

Elliot hauls Curtis to his feet and shakes him. In Elliot's grip, Curtis looks weak and small.

"Who paid you to liaise with Debbie Lansen?" I ask.

Curtis shakes his head, his lank black hair flapping around his head. He presses his lips tightly together as though he intends to share nothing else, but there's more going on here than I had anticipated, and I'm determined to understand the connection.

"Do you know a man who goes by the name of Martin Brooks?" I say.

A flame of recognition burns in Curtis' eyes. I don't need to hear him confirm his guilt, but I have no doubt it won't be long before he breaks.

"Don't know him," Curtis says, his voice quivering now.

"You're going to tell the truth, or I'll crack your skull in my hands," Matt threatens.

"You couldn't," Curtis whimpers.

Elliot, a good three inches taller than Matt at six foot six, and much wider, steps forward, hands the size of dinner plates raised. His lips part in a menacing smile. "I could. And if that doesn't work"—Elliot flips back his leather jacket, revealing the Glock in a holster at his hip. He pulls it out and presses it to Curtis' temple—"this will."

Curtis' eyes widen, then he slumps, his body giving in.

And that's when I know we've got him. This whole charade is about to come crashing down. First, we'll nail Curtis, then we'll get Martin.

I focus on Elliot. "I need you to get every scrap of evidence that connects Martin and this scumbag." I point at Curtis.

Elliot releases an exhausted-looking Curtis, who promptly flops face-down on the floor, allowing Elliot to rest one huge booted foot on his lower back as he gives me a salute. "Yes, sir."

"And Curtis?" I say. "Or Daniel or whatever the fuck your name is?"

He groans in response.

"If you don't want to end up in jail, you're going to do exactly what I want."

Curtis peels his face off the ground and gives me a begrudging, but convincing, nod.

Forty-five minutes later, Elliot's taken Curtis off to I-don't-want-to-know-where for questioning, and I'm back in the car with Matt. His laboured breathing fills the small space as he stares out the window. We haven't moved from outside his house.

He strikes the passenger door with a clenched fist. It's on the tip of my tongue to tell him not to destroy my car, but I know the comment would sink like a tank in the ocean. He's wound so tight I don't know what to do with him.

He hisses out a long sigh and leans back in the seat, his head on the headrest, eyes closed and face tilted to the roof. "I only came back for the kids," he says. "I don't care if I never see that woman again. I fucking hate her—" He strikes the door again.

I grab his shoulder. "I'm sorry. Truly."

He shakes me off. "I tried to make it work. That's why we had another child. Lucie was supposed to save us." The muscles up his neck and along his jaw are hard ropes and his eyelids, though closed, flicker rapidly as though he barely has control over the thoughts running through his mind. "Didn't fucking work, did it?"

He forces the words out, choking on the sorrow spilling from under the bitter veneer. Never in my life have I seen Matt like this—on the cusp of breaking. He's normally angry, and that I can handle. I'm used to it. But seeing him like this feels like an invasion of his privacy. If we weren't sitting in my car, I'd give him a moment alone, but instead I offer what little support I can.

"You want to stay with me?" I offer.

He shakes his head.

"Seb, then? Charlie's there. You can see him. Talk to him."

"No." Matt opens his eyes. "Mandarin Oriental. Take me there."

"You don't want me to drop you at one of our hotels?"

"No. I need to be alone. Somewhere no one knows me."

I start the engine, relieved to be able to do something.

When we arrive, I park off Knightsbridge in a quiet residential square and get out. Matt does the same, getting his bag from the boot.

He looks completely wrecked. We stand opposite one another on the pavement and the moment swells. I don't know what to say to him.

He closes the gap and draws me into a massive hug. He holds me for a moment, squeezing tight. I don't want to leave him alone, but I know he doesn't want to be with me. He's keeping his shit together by a thread.

He slaps a hand on my back and pulls away. "Thanks. I mean it. For everything."

"Anytime."

He nods, but just before he turns away, he says, "We'll get the fuckers. You know that, right?"

I give him a half-smile because *I fucking know it.*

41
KATE

A sharp squeal pierces my dreams. My mind struggles to make sense of it before I realise I'm awake, in bed, and the strange noise is the creaking hinges of my bedroom door. I need to oil them. This flat is falling apart. I must tell Jack to sort it out.

Then, right on cue, Nico's name pops in my mind like corn in the microwave. Memories explode and multiply uncontrollably, each one another wound to my already broken heart. All concern for the rusty door-hinges vanishes.

"It's Wednesday." Elly's voice splices my thoughts.

I creak an eye open to see her moving across the room, picking her way through the scattered clothes. It's been a few days since I tidied anything away. Tissues lie balled up on the floor, soaked in tears that wouldn't stop because I've lost Nico. I'll never kiss him again. Touch him. Never be held in his arms. And to think I *chose* this.

A fresh wave of searing pain hits me and I let out a wail that I quickly muffle by covering my mouth with my hands.

Concern flashes over Elly's face, but it's only there for a second before she wipes it away and checks her watch. "11.37 am."

I groan and pull the duvet over my head just as she rips the curtains open, letting the summer heat disinfect the room.

The old sash windows groan, telling me Elly's pushing them open. The roar of traffic from the street below blasts in on a warm breeze. Distant drilling and clanging of scaffolding batters my brain.

Elly yanks the duvet down, and bright light bursts against my eyelids.

"Hey!" I try to grab it back, squinting and flapping my hands.

"I never thought I'd say this," Elly says. "But you need to get back to the office."

"I can't." Even the thought of being in the same building as Nico is too much for my system.

"You can," she coaxes. "You have to. Your brother called. He said you've got stuff to do for the spa project."

Elly's had possession of my phone for a few days. She confiscated it from me to eliminate the chances of me sending regrettable messages to Nico in the middle of the night.

"Did anyone else call?" I whisper, not sure if I want to hear her answer.

Elly throws me a compassionate look. "Nico didn't call. Did you want to hear from him? I thought you broke it off?"

I don't even know what happened. My memory of being at his flat is all messed up. I smashed that picture... I really let loose. He probably thinks I'm crazy.

"I don't want to go back to the office. I can't."

"Jack said you'd say that." She holds out the phone to me. "He's on the line."

"Eh?" I say in confusion. "The whole time you've been in here?"

"Hi Kate." Jack's voice echoes on speakerphone.

"You bitch," I mouth at Elly. "Give it here."

She shakes her head, holding it up, shooting me a '*no chance*' look. She's right; I'd hang up right away.

"Get out of bed." Jack's voice cracks like a whip. "Get to the office and start preparing the best presentation you've ever done. If we don't want Martin Brooks to take the spa project, then you need to impress the Argentum board. They're coming in. Show them what you can do. It's on Friday. 10 am."

"I don't care about the spa project. It's not mine anymore," I croak.

"Bullshit."

I hold my breath too long, as though refusing to exhale might make this all go away. "What difference will it make? Martin's in charge now. He can do what he wants." My eyes briefly shutter, pain mangling my heart. *My spa project.*

"Trust me, we have a chance to keep this. A bloody good one."

"You want me to get up and make a presentation when there's only a chance I'll get to keep the project?"

"You pursued it for years and there was only ever a chance it would come off. Don't quit now."

"Martin said if I did anything to prevent him from taking the spa project, he'd tell everyone. He'd make it public... about Dad. About—"

"Just do your best," Jack snaps. "That's all you need to do. Don't worry about anything else. Whatever happens, we want them to know how good you are."

"But what's the point if—"

"Nico has this in hand. He'll make sure the project is yours, I swear it. He knows what it means to you."

Nico? Something in my chest thaws.

A beat passes. "Are you registering this?" Jack questions. "Is she listening? Elly?"

"I'm listening," I tell him, at the same time as Elly says, "She's listening."

"Good. I'll see you in the office."

"What did the police say?" I ask before he can hang up.

Jack makes a confused grunting sound.

"The police," I repeat. "About Curtis and the paintings. All the stuff he nicked. Have they found him yet?"

"Err. No. Negative. I'm sure they will, though. Get your head in the game, Kate. Stay focused on Knightsbridge spa."

"I quit the project. I already told Nico."

"Nuh-uh. You don't get to quit a project like this. That's what they call self-sabotage. Don't let Nico—"

"It's not him," I lie.

"Fine. Me, then. Whatever. You might never forgive me, but I'm not sitting back and letting you screw up your career. Do you want it? Or do you want to hide under the duvet for the rest of your life?"

"Is this a video call?" I ask, patting the duvet I'm squirreled beneath.

"No. But Elly told me what's going on over there."

I shoot Elly a resentful glance. *Traitor.*

"So, are you giving up?" Jack's tone softens.

People who give up never get anything they want in life. If that's the path you choose, then I can't follow you. Because I don't fucking *quit, and I cannot be with someone who does.*

A pitiful sigh comes out my mouth.

"Do you want it?" Jack repeats.

My heart thumps uncomfortably in my chest. "Yes."

"Good. Then for fuck's sake, get out of bed and down to the office and prove yourself, or Martin Brooks is going to steal Dad's dream project right out of your hands." Jack pauses, a clicking sound coming down the phone like he's tutting. He's not finished.

"What?" I wait. "Spit it out, Jack."

"Shit, Kate. I'm fucking sorry, you know? Nico wanted to tell you about Dad. I made him swear not to. We promised Dad on his deathbed that we'd keep it from you—"

"I know all this." I sound as bitter and hurt as I feel.

"Then you also need to know that Nico saved the company. He didn't have to. He could've stepped away. He could've let the whole thing play out. We would have lost the house. We'd have lost everything. The only reason we still have the company at all is because Nico fucking saved it. Dad would've gone to jail if he'd even lived that long. He wasn't well. His death wasn't Nico's fault; it was his own damn fault. He lived recklessly. He'd been living with the guilt and shame and the secret of what he was doing for too long. But he was my father too, and when he begged us to do one last thing for him—to keep his damn depravity from you—we swore we would. So if you're questioning Nico's loyalty, or mine, know that we did it for Dad."

Jack is talking too fast, his voice sounding closer to breaking with each word. I've never heard him like this. The emotion coming through the phone is fast and furious and vulnerable. Listening to him makes my heart ache, and tears stab behind my eyelids.

"Just like you wanted to keep the company," Jack continues. "I wanted to keep something, too. This was the oath I kept... and I'm sorry it hurt you. But that was how Dad loved you, like you would break if you knew the truth. Maybe he couldn't really see you. Maybe he was wrong, and if so, I'm sorry I colluded in it." A ragged breath blows down the line. "But I lost Dad too. I wanted to hold on to *something*. Do *something*. Don't hate Nico for it. He would've told you if I'd let him. Christ, he pestered me about it. Kept saying we should tell you the truth, and I had no idea it was because he cared about you. I thought he was having some crisis of conscience. It was me who convinced him it was better if you thought he was in the wrong... if you thought he was the bad one, rather than our father. Nico's not disloyal... his loyalty just didn't lie with you."

I swallow hard. "Maybe it should have."

My pulse beats once, twice, three times before Jack speaks again.

"I don't know what's going on between you two," he says. "And I don't want to know. God knows, I don't approve or sanction it or whatever the hell brothers are supposed to do. But I don't want you to be miserable. So get the fuck out of bed and come down to the office before Nico fires you for pulling too many sickies in a row. We all know you're not really ill." He sighs. "So, are you?"

"Am I what? Sick?"

"No," he says, clearly exasperated. "Broken. Are you broken, now you know the truth?"

Elly has the decency to look away while I absorb Jack's words. *Broken?* A tangled mess of bedsheets suffocates my body. I haven't washed since the weekend. The room must have smelt stale and airless before Elly opened the windows. With a shock, I see myself clearly, and it doesn't look good. The realisation stokes up a fire in my heart that I thought was extinguished.

I'm not giving up. No one can make me quit. Not even my father and his lies.

I won't be controlled anymore.

"No," I reply, pleased with the conviction in my voice. "I'm not broken."

"Good."

Jack hangs up and Elly and I stare at each other.

"He's not the best at apologies, is he?" she says with a bemused shrug. "But he definitely cares."

I throw back the sheets and stand. "I have a presentation to write."

Elly breaks into her best championing grin, clenching a fist and pumping it in the air. "Go show those bastards what you're made of."

42

KATE

I check my reflection in the mirror. My shirt is ironed, but my skirt is hanging off me. Apparently, if I don't eat for a week, I shed weight fast. I'm in the ground floor bathrooms of the office. This is the first day I've been back, and my spa presentation is in less than ten minutes.

My heart is racing, and my nerves are reaching uncontrollable levels. I need to get in there and get this over with before I chicken out.

The door swings open and a woman enters, but it's the voice that follows her in from outside that freezes me to the spot, barely able to draw breath.

"Why don't you fucking have it? I need it now. Fuck's sake, Elliot."

Nico sounds furious, and he's just outside.

I thought my heart was racing before, but now it's hammering so fast, it could crack my ribs.

I'm not ready to come face to face with him.

I check my watch. The Knightsbridge spa meeting with Argentum starts in five minutes. I can't stay in here and avoid him. I have a presentation to give.

"Fuck it, Elliot. This isn't good enough. I promised—"

I exit the bathroom and Nico's voice cuts short. He stares at me, eyes wild. He looks out of control. His shirt sleeves are rolled up, which

I've never seen him do in the office. He's normally so composed that the sight of him disheveled chills me.

"I've got to go," he barks into the phone. "Call me when you have it. I'm waiting."

He shoves his phone in his pocket and looks at me like he's about to say something, but the tension in his jaw, the rage in his eyes, doesn't look inviting. Whatever's up with him, I don't want anything to do with it. I walk past before he can speak.

"Kate, wait."

My heart lurches and I turn back to face him. "What?"

His gaze darts all over me before settling on my eyes. He opens his mouth, but nothing comes out.

Nico Hawkston, speechless?

"I'm already nervous, Nico. You're making it worse."

He rubs his palm over the back of his neck, blowing air from inflated cheeks as though he's taking a moment to gather his thoughts. When he speaks, I'm sure it's not what he originally intended to say. "Good luck."

Unease slithers through me, but I don't have time to question it. I turn away and cross the lobby, entering the meeting room before I lose my nerve.

Inside, the chairs are arranged in rows. I take my place at the podium at the front and look out at the audience. Everyone at both Lansen and Hawkston who's ever worked on the Knightsbridge spa project with me, is here. Matt and Seb sit in the front row. Even Charlie is here. He meets my eye and smiles, giving me a subtle thumbs up. It's such a childish gesture, and his expression full of genuine encouragement, that I feel a flush of warmth towards him.

David Webster is also in the front row, beside Martin Brooks. Martin sits with his hands clasped over his belly, and eyes me with a horrid self-satisfied smirk that makes my skin itch. I don't know when he's planning on instigating his new plan, but if I don't want him to start shouting about Dad, or Nico and Jack, then I need to pretend everything's fine.

Nico has this in hand. He'll make sure the project is yours, I swear it. He knows what it means to you.

Jack's words spark in my mind, but they don't reassure me. The Nico I just saw outside the bathroom didn't look like he had anything in hand. He still hasn't followed me. Is he coming to this meeting? I don't know if his presence would make it better or worse, but the tiny flame of hope that he'll be here is fading.

The audience quietens down as I introduce the project.

Applause ripples through the room and the lights fade so my slides can be seen more clearly on the screen.

I've barely opened my mouth to speak again when the door opens. Nico slides in, bows his head at me, and takes the empty seat next to his brothers. He's rolled his sleeves back down, and the gold cufflinks are back in place at the wrists. It's marginally better than before, but he still looks like a man who's been stretched way too thin.

My heart rate ramps up, and suddenly I feel like I'm presenting for something much more important than a development project.

Our eyes meet in the semi-light, and his gaze touches my skin like an electric current. All his attention is on me, and he sits upright in his seat. He doesn't smile, nor does his expression reveal any emotion.

Does he really have this all in hand? Can he guarantee the project is mine?

I desperately want it to be true. I want Nico to have my back. I want him to protect me.

I want him to care.

I want to be able to trust him.

My mouth is dry, and I lift the water glass from the podium and gulp down half the contents.

And then I begin, performing as though my life is on the line. There's no one else who knows this project as well as I do, except perhaps Nico himself.

When it's finally time to stop, the applause is polite but enthusiastic.

"Thank you," I say. "And now I'd like to welcome David Webster, Managing Director of Argentum."

David gets out of his chair and paces towards me. His jaw is clenched, a marked frown deepening the wrinkles between his brows. I shake his hand, but he doesn't meet my gaze.

Something's not right.

He takes his place at the podium as I sink onto a nearby chair.

"This project has a key place in my heart," he begins. "I've been on the team since its inception, working with Lansen in the early days. I confess when Gerard Lansen, Kate's father, and Martin Brooks"—he gestures to Martin, who lifts his hand in a lazy wave—"originally proposed this idea to me, I wasn't convinced it had legs. But Kate's unceasing enthusiasm has shown me that this is a project to stand behind. Argentum has aspirations to open four sites across the UK, targeting Knightsbridge first. After that we'll open in the East End, Edinburgh and York. It's ambitious, but exciting."

He wipes his brow and takes a shaking breath. "It is, therefore, with a heavy heart that I must tell you that we have made the decision not to progress the project with the Lansen-Hawkston team."

Restless movement ripples through the audience. Murmurs begin, and confused expressions spread like a virus. *What the fuck?* My stomach plunges through the floor and my legs feel wobbly. Did David just cancel the project? Is this really happening?

I expected him to announce he was stepping down, not that the whole project was off. I anticipated it from Martin... but David? And what about Nico?

He'll make sure the project is yours.

Another fucking lie.

Betrayal and anger swell within me until it feels like my chest might burst, and tears stab behind my eyes.

I glance at Martin and there's a sparkle of amusement in his gaze like he's enjoying this, and I have to swallow around the lump that's forming in my throat. I scan the crowd for Jack, who lifts a shoulder in a half-shrug and shakes his head, like he doesn't have a clue what's happening either. I don't dare look at Nico, for fear that if I do, the tears that are pricking at my eyes will leak out.

David clears his throat and continues as if the entire room isn't reeling in shock. "Martin Brooks will be leading us as we search for a new partner. And in order to provide you all with some form of closure, he's going to speak to you now."

David slopes down from the podium, sinking into his seat. He looks dejected, defeated; an unfamiliar look for him.

An oily smile ripples across Martin's mouth as he takes David's spot at the front. "I'm deeply honoured to take over this project. It was, after all, my idea in the first place." He shoots a vicious look in my direction as if I'm the one who stole it from *him*.

"I've had to make some hard decisions. The first, and most important, is to dissolve the partnership with Hawkston. It is my belief that Hawkston is reaching beyond its area of expertise. There is a huge difference between a boutique spa and a large global corporate hotel chain, and Hawkston is not the right partner for Argentum." Martin presses a hand to his heart and an expression of sympathy so false that I want to throw up spreads over his face. "We take this moment to thank all of you for your hard work, and wish you the best for the future."

Martin takes a little bow and nods at the rest of the Argentum board members, including David, who all rise to their feet.

It's over. The whole fucking thing is over.

There's a brief moment of stunned silence from the Hawkston employees, but when it's clear there is no second act, they get up, clutching folders and notepads, whispering and casting uneasy glances at each other on their way to the exit.

I chase after David, grab his elbow, and pull him to face me. "What happened? I thought you wanted us to do this together?"

He meets my eye, compassion in his gaze as he says, "I'm sorry, Kate. There was nothing I could do." His voice is so raw it scrapes at my insides and I know he genuinely means it. "It was out of my hands."

"But your position on the board—doesn't that count for something?"

David shakes his head. "I'm sorry. Some of the members weren't happy with the Hawkston takeover of Lansen. They thought we'd lose control of the project."

"Webster." Martin calls. "Let's go."

David winces at the sound, clasping my hand. "I'm sorry, Kate." He moves off, leaving me alone in the centre of the room.

I drop into one of the empty seats, trying to absorb what's just happened. Since Martin approached me in the cafe, I knew this was what he intended. But when Jack called and said I needed to do this presentation, I really thought I had a chance. I believed him. I believed him because he said Nico was going to sort it...

Anger rises in my chest, but beneath it my heart breaks afresh because yet again Nico hasn't protected me. I place a hand over my ribs like I can contain the splintering agony beneath. Behind me, the door clicks open. I know it's Nico before I see him. I recognise the way he walks, the pattern of his footfall. Or perhaps it's some sixth sense; some part of his energy reaching out and touching mine before he even comes into view.

"Kate?"

I stand, twisting towards the door. Before I can tell him not to come near me, he's closing the space between us. I hold up my hands and he halts just out of reach.

"My project..." The words contain so much pain.

"I know," he says. "I'm so sorry." He sounds sincere, but it's not enough.

"Jack said we had a chance to save it. That you had it in hand. He said you'd make sure the project was mine." I tear both hands through my hair and a noise that sounds disturbingly like a sob escapes my throat. "What the fuck, Nico?"

His handsome face screws up and he reaches for me, but I step back and his hand falls to his side. "I will fix this," he tells me. "I just haven't yet."

"You could have stopped me," I say, desperate. "Before the presentation. I knew there was something wrong with you. But you didn't say anything. You knew what this project meant to me and you let me go out there and stand up in front of everyone..."

"And you did a brilliant job."

His arms are suddenly around me, holding so tight I can barely wriggle. I want to sink into his embrace, to be held, to let him soothe all of this away.

"I will sort this out," he whispers against my hair.

"It's too late," I reply, sobs rising up my throat now. "Too fucking late." I push away and stare up at him, that splintering ache inside almost breaking me.

Nico blinks, breathing rapidly through flared nostrils. His dark eyes burn with an emotion so intense it sears me to my core. My thoughts are swirling out of control. Part of me wants him to grab me, to force me to relinquish the anger that holds us apart. To make it all fucking disappear. Another part of me wants to slap him, to strike my palm against his cheek and feel it sting. But I won't do that. I refuse to lose my temper over this man again.

His phone rings, and he holds my gaze for a few tones before he pulls it from his pocket.

"You should take it," I tell him.

He cancels the call. "We're not done here."

I bristle. "You do not get to choose when this is over."

"Kate—"

I hold up a palm. "Please, go away. Leave me the fuck alone."

He stares like he can't believe what I've just said. The air strains with tension. I'm about to walk away when his phone rings again.

He drags his next inhalation, only breaking eye contact to check the screen. Without a word, he puts the phone to his ear and leaves the room.

43
NICO

Drizzling rain strikes the windscreen of Elliot's car as we drive through the dark streets of London. It smells like wet dog and the window wipers let out an irritating squeak with each sweep over the glass.

"You got it all?" I check.

"Everything." Elliot jerks his thumb over his shoulder to a folder sitting on the empty backseat of the car. He spins the steering wheel with one hand as we take a sharp turn. Bloody scabs cover his knuckles, but I'm sure Curtis' face looks worse. "You could put Martin Brooks away for years," he reassures me. "If that's how you want to play it."

"It's not." I tap the dashboard, running my fingertips against it again and again. Elliot side-eyes them. *Fuck.* I look twitchy as hell. I force my hand into stillness. "He'll be home alone?"

"He will. I checked. No wife. No girlfriend. No family. No cameras. Nothing. It's all clear."

I should be elated, but a black sense of doom pools in my gut. Is it already too late? I wanted to do this before the presentation to save Kate the pain of losing the project. To save her from suffering another humiliation at the hands of Martin Brooks. But we didn't have everything we needed in time. We didn't know which way David Webster was going to swing... didn't know what Martin had on him and the other members of the Argentum board. Elliot only rang me to confirm *after* the presentation finished. He worked fast, all things considered, but not fast enough.

Sod's law, but it is what it is. I'll work with it.

"Mr. Hawkston?" Elliot's voice hauls me back to the musty car as he parks up outside Martin Brooks' house.

"You don't have to come inside," Elliot says. "I can do this without you."

"I want to be there." I sound deathly calm.

He nods and grabs the folder from the backseat, handing it to me before we both get out of the car.

Martin's house looks neat and well-kept from the outside: perfect paintwork, trimmed front lawn, highly polished brass knocker on the gleaming front door. But it's no surprise, given I gave the man a veritable fortune eight years ago.

I ring the bell, Elliot's enormous bulk behind me offering protection I'm not used to needing.

A shadowy figure appears on the other side of the glass and moments later, Martin's wrinkled face appears. He's wearing a tartan dressing gown and sheepskin slippers, like he was planning a cosy evening in. The chance of that happening just slid to zero.

When he glimpses me, he tries to force the door closed again and blurts, "Oh, fuck, no."

I thrust a palm against the edge of the door, forcing it wide. "We just want to chat, Mr. Brooks."

He continues to push from the other side, but Elliot thrusts the door with such force that Martin slams against the interior wall, and Elliot and I walk inside.

Martin's face creases with pain as he sucks in a breath. Pressing a hand to his lower back, he drags his gaze up and down Elliot's vast frame. "Who's the dog, Nico?"

Elliot growls, deliberately snarling and exposing teeth. I half expect him to bark.

Martin shrinks, eyes cagey as he watches me click the door closed behind us and lock it.

"Elliot's a friend of mine," I answer. "A very good friend."

"What do you want?"

"I want you to pay for what you've done."

Martin wheezes like an asthmatic. "It's too late to save your little girlfriend's spa project." He watches me for a reaction, but I betray nothing. "I assume that's why you're here. Little Kate Lansen took your fancy, did she?"

I flinch ever so slightly, and Martin knows he's caught me out.

"You thought you'd hid it so well, eh? I saw you out on that balcony at Jack's drinks party. Couldn't take your eyes off her. Terribly inappropriate, Mr. Hawkston. Taking advantage of your employee. Keeping her as your dirty little secret. But I do understand. So pretty. Great tits." Martin cups his hands like he's holding Kate's breasts. Heat fills my chest. I want to hit the prick, but Elliot's hand gripping my arm stalls me.

"And those legs. She's the whole package. She grew up really nicely. Such a shame about her project." Martin pouts his bottom lip and shakes his head. "Really was a tough decision. And telling her about her father..." He laughs that thick, choked laugh. "The way she fell apart. She wept like Gerard had died all over again. It was—" My fist cracks his jaw, making his head snap to the side and blood fly from his mouth.

Dark laughter leaks from Elliot, who shifts from foot to foot, enthused by the ruckus and eager to get involved.

Martin doubles over and spits more blood on the carpet. Before he can straighten, I hit him again with an uppercut to the jaw that makes his teeth rattle.

This time he stumbles, nearly collapsing. He grabs a side table to steady himself and drags the back of his hand over his mouth, smearing blood across his cheek. Energy pulses through me. I'm not done, not nearly satisfied, but I hold back. I need him conscious for this.

"You like knowing secrets, don't you?" I question. "Hanging them over people's heads. Like David Webster."

Martin's eyes widen and I hold out my hand for the folder Elliot brought. He hands it to me and I pull out photos of David with a much younger woman. The fool has been cheating on his wife for years, raising a second family on the other side of London. There are photos of him with a young boy of about ten, who looks so like David that a paternity test would be redundant.

"You blackmailed him, didn't you?" I challenge, flashing photo after photo in front of Martin. "That's how you got him to push the decision across the Argentum board. Threatened to tell his wife and kids about this other family?"

"I did no such thing."

"We've spoken to him and he confirmed it."

Martin curses under his breath. "So what if I did? He's a cheat and a liar."

"Blackmail is a crime, Mr. Brooks. As is theft and conspiracy to steal."

Martin is silent for a moment, and I relish the stunned look on his face.

I stroke my jaw slowly, milking Martin's shock for a few more seconds before I speak again. "There's an important lesson I've learned after all these years in business, and it's that you're only as good as the people you employ." I tilt my head, feigning sympathy. "It's especially true if you're going to do anything illegal. I had a background check run on Daniel Hunter. Not the sharpest tool in the shed. Several previous convictions. Did you know that?"

Martin winces as I flick through the documents and images Elliot has compiled, pausing to show Martin several images taken of him with Curtis, AKA Daniel Hunter, at the storage unit in South London where they stashed Gerard's art and the Lansens' belongings.

"I don't know what you think that shows." Martin points at the picture. "I don't know that man. He stopped me in the street..."

"Stopped you in the street multiple times, on different occasions?" I let out a deep chuckle. "Perhaps. But *that man*, Daniel Hunter, has agreed to testify against you for a reduced sentence. There are witnesses who saw the two of you in South London, going in and out of that unit at night." I shrug. "Could be nothing. Could be something else entirely. But it doesn't look above board, does it? Creeping about at night with a convicted felon?"

"This is the stupidest array of bullshit. You're wasting my time."

I pull my phone out of my pocket. "I have the head of the Metropolitan police on speed dial, Mr. Brooks. I'll call this in if that's what you want." I glance at the ceiling, pretending to think. "That might be the kinder option than anything else I have in mind if you don't comply with my demands."

Martin stuffs his hands deep in his dressing gown pockets, fear crossing his face.

Beside me, Elliot puffs out his chest.

"You know the maximum sentence for blackmail? Fourteen years," I say. "And conspiracy to steal and defraud? Ten years. Theft itself? Seven. And Daniel Hunter... You exerted coercive control over him, forcing him to sleep with Debbie Lansen as well as a long list of other things he's told us about. I'm no lawyer, Mr. Brooks, but I'd say it's likely you're looking at a long run in jail. It's like a fucking wedding buffet of potential charges."

Martin blinks rapidly, and as his chin begins to quiver, I feel a surge of delight.

"You could have left the Lansens alone," I continue. "If you had, maybe we wouldn't be here now. But you got greedy, didn't you? Had to take the artwork, Debbie Lansen's jewellery, the spa project. You wanted to humiliate them all because you were bitter about what happened with Gerard and the company. If you couldn't have the kudos of selling a thriving company and leading the spa project, you didn't want the Lansens to have it either. But you didn't deserve those things, did you? If you'd cared about your business back then, you'd have seen what Gerard was doing. You would have known before it was too late. But you never paid attention, did you?"

"What do you want, Nico?" Martin drags a hand down his face.

"I want it all returned, with compensation. I'll get the details to you of the sums I expect you to repay. I want you to return the spa project to the Hawkston-Lansen team. You'll make an announcement to that effect, then you'll step down from the Argentum board. You'll retire, for good this time, and you'll fuck off out of London. Sell the house, turning over eighty-five percent of the sale money to me. Then you'll move to a quiet village in the north of England. Somewhere wet and windy and fucking cold. Elliot here will be watching you very closely. If you come back to London, we'll know about it."

"And if I say no?"

I raise my phone. "Let's find out, shall we?" I hover my thumb over the call button, letting it edge closer and closer until Martin breaks.

"Fuck you, Nico Hawkston. You're a crooked fucking bastard. I always knew it."

"Is that a yes? I don't want to misinterpret what you're saying," I say, and Elliot flips back one side of his jacket to hook a thumb in his belt loop, revealing the butt of his gun poking from the holster. Martin's eyes slide to it, then pop wide. "Because as much as I admire the Metropolitan Police Force, Elliot here could sort you out much faster. But the cleanup is a bitch. I want to be prepared."

Martin's face blanches, and there's a pleasing tremor to Martin's voice when he says, "There were no weapons last time we negotiated."

"Last time, I thought you were a reasonable man. But now I know you're not, more unreasonable measures are called for."

I put a hand in my pocket, gripping the penknife Gerard Lansen gifted me all those years ago, and the inscription on the handle comes to mind.

Don't kill anyone.

I've no intention of killing Martin, but I've never wanted to hurt someone more than I do now. He came after Kate. He took her project. He set out to tear her down, to humiliate her, to steal from her family. He fucking hurt her...I can't let that go unpunished.

Elliot takes the Glock from the holster.

Martin's eyes open wider still, until they seem like the only features on his face. He shrivels, his shoulders sinking into his robe. The sight makes a wicked laugh spill from my mouth.

"You wouldn't dare," Martin says, but his voice is weak.

Elliot takes a silencer from his pocket and screws it onto the barrel of the Glock. "Mr. Hawkston won't have to do anything." He snarls, upper lip curling away from his teeth. "In fact, he wasn't even here." A grin replaces Elliot's snarl, and he winks, as if Martin is in on the joke. The shift in Elliot's persona is so fast, he looks insane. Psychotic, even. Exactly the type of man who could blow your brains out on a whim.

Martin shudders and a guttural groan comes from his lips. "Fuck you, Nico. Take your luxury spas. And the Lansens can have their shit. Nothing decent but that Stephen Condar piece and the diamonds, anyway."

A slow sense of satisfaction spreads through me. I always knew Martin Brooks was a gutless coward.

"And you'll have to make it right with David Webster," I add. "I don't condone what he's done, but that's his shit to deal with. Really, you should have taken the cash I gave you all those years ago and made a run for it."

Elliot raises the Glock casually, not even pointing it at Martin, but the old man's hands shoot in the air. "Fine, fine. Just put the gun away."

Elliot gives a slow nod, and Martin blows out a breath, lowering his hands. "It's done. All of it. Everything you want. You have my word."

"Your word better be good. Because I won't let this rest if you don't make everything right within the week. You have until Friday. If you fail to comply..." I shrug as if this is all terribly unimportant. "I'll delegate your fate to Elliot, and he can choose what to do with you."

Martin nods furiously.

I clear my throat. "One last thing..."

Elliot stalks towards Martin with the gun in hand, pointing it this time at his head.

Martin drops to his knees, hands wavering in the air, eyes bulging like ripe plums. "Anything. Anything at all," he says, nodding furiously.

"Stay the fuck away from Kate Lansen."

"Yes. Yes. Yes," Martin blubbers.

I flip the folder closed and signal to Elliot that it's time to leave. He gives me a glance that begs permission, and I nod my consent, at which he fires a muffled bullet into the wooden floor at Martin's knees.

Martin whimpers and curls into a ball, cradling the back of his skull in his hands.

"I mean it, Martin," I state, taking no pity on the man. "Next time that bullet goes in your head."

Elliot removes the silencer and shoves his gun back in the holster, leaving a terrified Mr. Brooks sweating in a puddle on the floor. He's quivering so violently that he can't speak.

We exit the house and once we're back on the street, rain strikes my skin like it can erase everything. I could fucking drink it in.

Elliot eats up the distance to the car in seconds, moving like a muscled panther in the dark, yanking the door open and folding himself in.

I'm about to get in myself when my phone rings.

Erica Lefroy. What a moment to get a call from her. We haven't spoken since that night at Martini Gems. Feels like a fucking lifetime ago.

I answer. "Erica?"

"Nico, hi sweetie. How's things?"

I pull the car door open and get in. My hand throbs from where I hit Martin, but it's a satisfying pain.

"Good. How can I help?"

She laughs. "Always assume people want things from you when they call?"

"Yes."

There's a slight pause. "You're coming to New York for the charity gala next week, right?" She sounds mildly chastened, but not in the least deterred.

Shit. I'd forgotten about it. I'm making the welcome speech and I haven't even started writing it. The last time it crossed my mind was when I mentioned it to Kate. It was the date I'd mentally put in place for taking our relationship public.

I'm yours if you want me... I've got to go back to New York in a couple of weeks. After that we can reassess. If you still want to, we can take it public then.

A sharp pain, worse than the sting in my knuckles, lances through my chest.

"I am," I reply, no hint of the pain in my voice.

"Then I have a favour to ask you. It's not a big one, but it would really, really help me out."

"Sure. Whatever you need."

And just like that, I'm back to normal life.

44

KATE

"Your phone is ringing." Charlie stands at his desk, hands on his hips, peering over at me.

I glance at the handset. 'Mum' flashes on the screen. "I know."

"Are you gonna answer it? Because your ringtone is really annoying."

I roll my eyes and pick up the phone, standing and moving over towards the window.

"Mum. Everything okay?"

"Where's your brother? I can't get hold of him."

Typical Mum. I glance over to Jack's desk but he's not there.

"I have no idea. If I see him, I'll tell him to call you. I've got to go."

My thumb is poised over the screen to end the call when she screeches. "Wait. Don't you dare hang up on me. The darnedest thing just happened." Mum pauses and I hear men's voices in the background. *Where is she?*

"All your Dad's art just showed up," she continues. "They're unloading it now."

"Who is?"

"A lorry turned up. This great big man knocked on the door. Built like one of those men who live in the gym. Messy blond hair. Said he had instructions to unload here."

"Instructions from whom?"

"Nico."

My mind spirals. How on earth has Nico managed to recover the stolen art? I didn't even know he knew about it.

Mum's talking to someone else, squealing with excitement. I can't make out what she's saying, but suddenly her voice is loud and clear. "My diamonds! The jewellery! It's all here too. Thank you. Thank you so much."

Thank you?

"Are you talking to me?" I ask.

Mum's exasperated sigh is a harsh blast. "Of course I am."

"I didn't do anything. This has nothing to do with me."

"Honestly, Kate. You can be so stupid sometimes. When you told me you were dating Nico, it sounded so outlandish that I assumed you were lying. That you'd made it up for some bizarre reason. But this... Nico tracking Curtis down and returning everything without a word... gosh." She sighs heavily. "He's done that because of you, hasn't he?"

The pulse in my fingertips beats hard against the phone, and my body is suddenly far too hot.

"So, yes," Mum continues. "I think I do owe thanks to you. And I'm sorry I ever doubted that Nico cares about you."

I listen to Mum blathering and weeping tears of joy for a few more minutes before I hang up, but my mind is on Nico and the last thing I said to him.

You do not get to choose when this is over... leave me the fuck alone.

Why did I say it? I tell myself it's because the last thing I needed was Nico telling me more lies.

But did I mean it?

The only thing I do know is that I definitely didn't expect him to actually do what I asked. When I think back on our relationship, it's hard to remember a time when Nico asked me how I felt or what I wanted to do before going right ahead and doing what he wanted, and demanding I do that too.

Since the presentation, I've been waiting to hear something from him... anything. But there's been nothing but radio silence.

I thought it meant he didn't care. It didn't occur to me that he might, finally, be doing exactly as I'd asked him.

I leap out of my seat so suddenly that Charlie stands, too. "Everything okay?"

"Yup. I just need to..." I don't finish my sentence before I run through the office, slamming my hand on the button to call the lifts when I reach them. The doors open so slowly, I feel like I might die before they do. When they edge apart, I slip in and hit the button for the twentieth floor.

I need to see Nico, right now, before it starts to seem like a bad idea.

When the lift pings, I step out into the calm lobby. There's soft music playing and Nico's PA, with her pristine blonde hair, is tapping away at her computer behind the desk.

I rush over to her, practically slinging my upper body over the desk. She leans back, a mildly appalled look on her face. "Miss Lansen?"

"Yes. Hi. I need to see Mr. Hawkston. Nico. Now. Is he free?"

She glances at the other woman behind the desk, and I'm sure I glimpse a barely disguised eye-roll. "He's not here. He's in New York until the middle of next week."

My adrenaline high crashes so hard and fast I nearly fall to my knees. "Not here?"

"No. Like I said, he'll be back next week. Can I take a message?"

I stare at her, unable to process what she's telling me.

"Kate?"

I spin to find Matt Hawkston standing behind me. He looks so like Nico that confusion swells my brain.

"Perhaps I can help?" he offers.

I shake my head. "No. It can wait."

"Okay." He stares through narrowed lashes, like he's assessing if I'm really all right. Then his features relax. "Great news about your spa project though, eh? Bet that feels like a huge relief. Great result. Congrats."

"What about the spa project?" I ask, more confused than ever.

"You didn't hear? David Webster called in this morning. Spoke to your brother. The Argentum board had a re-vote. They were so impressed by your presentation, they overturned the previous decision. It's back on the table." He pauses. "Listen, I'm on my way out. But give Jack a call. He'll talk it through."

Matt disappears down the corridor, and for a moment I don't move, wondering how everything in my life just did a complete one-eighty.

I pull my phone from my pocket and fire off a message to Jack.

Me: Where are you? I need to talk.

He responds in less than thirty seconds.

Jack: St Paul's. Meet me on the Millennium Bridge? I have an hour before my next meeting.

The sky overhead is thick with cloud, but there's a dense heat that hangs like fog in the air. I walked here so fast I'm sweating, and my clothes stick to me in places they shouldn't. We're halfway across the bridge, St Paul's Cathedral behind us, the Tate Modern opposite.

WORTH EVERY PENNY

I lean on the railing, glancing down into the murky water of the Thames below. Jack stands beside me. There aren't many other people around, probably because of the sky overhead threatening to break the week-long heatwave we've endured.

Jack has just finished catching me up to speed, filling me in on the links between Curtis and Martin Brooks, and how the events all played out. I search my phone for the photo I took of the graffitied van at mum's drinks party. Now that I look closer, I can almost recognise the handwriting as Charlie's from all the scribbled notes he takes in meetings and leaves lying over his desk. But I could be imagining it; foisting my new knowledge onto the photo.

"It's not bad," Jack says, nodding appreciatively at the image.

I arch a brow. "It's an erect dick. It's hardly a work of art."

Jack laughs, leaning his elbows on the railing, his hands clasped. He lowers his head, still chuckling.

"You're sure he did it?" I ask. "Martin Brooks orchestrated the theft of Dad's art collection? And everything else?"

"Yeah. Irrefutable proof. He had some serious demons. Absolutely plagued by the idea that Dad never paid for his crimes, so we ought to instead. All of us. Mum, me, you, even the Hawkstons."

I can't get my head around how someone can be so bitter and twisted.

"Although..." Jack continues, drawing me from my reflections. "It was a bit unfortunate that Curtis was also sleeping with Matt's wife. That seems to have been more coincidence than anything else."

I can't keep the shock from my face. "Curtis was sleeping with Gemma Hawkston? At the same time he was sleeping with Mum?"

"Yeah. They met at my birthday party. Torrid love affair, supposedly."

"Poor Matt," I say. "He looked fine when I saw him earlier."

"He's not about to spill his heart to you in the corridor, is he?" Jack shrugs. "I think he wanted a way out for a while, to be honest. He'll file for divorce."

"What a mess."

"It's very unfortunate all round," Jack says. "Mum's devastated. She thought Curtis was the one, but all along it was a set up. Martin was paying him; they were going to split the proceeds of everything they took from the house. Had a buyer lined up for the Stephen Condar piece and everything. I'm surprised we recovered it all in time."

"About that... Mum said everything was returned today. And that Nico did it."

"He did. He sorted everything."

My throat constricts, and my chest compresses. I don't want to think about what Nico had to do to 'sort it.' "What about Martin? What happens now?"

"He's resigning from Argentum. He'd been blackmailing David Webster, among others. That's how he had them swing the vote to renege on the spa deal. I don't think we'll be hearing from him." Jack turns, leaning back against the railing. Behind him, the Thames looks dark and threatening.

"I can't believe Nico fixed it all." My heart is beating like mad, knowing there's still a question I need to ask. "Why?"

Specks of rain begin to fall and thunder rumbles overhead.

"For you. I think he did it for you."

Relief floods me; hearing it from Mum is one thing, but from Jack it means so much more. He knows Nico in a way Mum never will. "That's what Mum said as well."

"Occasionally she knows what she's talking about." His gaze drifts like he's thinking about something else, then he re-focuses on me. "I'm okay with it, you know... If you want to date Nico."

"I don't."

"Hmm." He inspects my face, I assume for any sign of a lie. I don't know what he finds there, but he concedes, "Fine." His cheeks deflate as he blows out an exhale. "I'm going to take Mum away. Not for long. But I want to take her mind off things. Do you want to come with us?"

God, the idea of nursing mum through heartbreak sounds horrendous. "Sure. I could do that."

Jack peers at me.

"What?"

"You look like I asked you to shovel shit."

I press my lips together to contain a smile. "That obvious, huh?" He tilts his head in agreement but says nothing to reprimand my reluctance. "You're too good to her," I add. "She doesn't deserve you."

Jack grimaces. "I know she can be difficult, but she's the only parent we have. People can be gone like that." He snaps his fingers, and the spark of sadness in his eyes hits me in the heart. *He's thinking about Dad*. He collects himself and says, "Try not to let her get to you. What matters is what you think, and you can be proud of everything you've achieved. I know I am, and if Mum could see beyond the end of her own nose, she would be, too." He grins, teasing me as he says, "You're an incredible woman, Kate."

I wince at the reminder of Nico's words in this context, but Jack has the decency to ignore my embarrassment.

"Look, you don't have to come," he continues. "But if you want to take some time off after everything that's happened, say the word. I'll book us all in. Somewhere plush."

"Plush?"

Jack rolls his eyes. "Oh, come on. She got robbed and duped and heartbroken all at once. I'll pay for the lot. Your own room and everything. Take her for a few massages and treatments or whatever she wants. Whatever *you* want."

"Is this you looking out for the heartbroken women in the family, then?"

His eyebrow flies up. "Are you heartbroken?"

I swallow, unable to meet his eye. "Nothing a good massage won't sort."

He looks at me like he doesn't believe me. "You know, Nico's not a bad guy. Everything he did was for us. To save the company, to protect Dad, protect you. If I'd had the money back then, I'd have bailed Dad out, but I didn't. I had to go cap in hand to Nico. And you know what? He didn't even blink before he agreed to help. It cost a lot of money to repay all those debts."

"Not a lot when you're a billionaire." Even as the words leave my mouth, I hate myself for speaking them, for being so ungrateful, so *bitter*. I don't want to be that person, holding tight to a grudge that will only eat away at me.

Suddenly, I hear Nico's voice in my mind.

I'm yours, Kate. Do you want me?

A cloying feeling stirs in my lungs, and my next breath doesn't come easy. God, how I want to go back in time, to that moment when he was mine.

"I know you don't mean that," Jack says. "It doesn't matter how much money someone has, they're never obligated to help someone out. *Never*. He didn't do it because he could, he did it because he cared." Jack stares at me, a world of emotion in his eyes when he adds, "He told me he loved you."

My heart clenches, and a lingering unease settles inside me, like a bad aftertaste on the back of my tongue. I've made a mistake. I have to make it right with Nico.

I must have been silent too long, lost in a whirl of memories, because Jack's voice crashes in like a moon-landing. I tune in just in time to hear the tail-end of the question I missed. "Do you?" he asks.

"Huh? What?"

"Nico. Do you love him?"

Do I?

I open my mouth, but the sound that escapes from between my parted lips is not a word. It's a low, pitiful, aching noise.

My pulse roars in my ears. My vision blurs and my cheeks are wet, and I don't know if it's tears or rain. Jack's arms are suddenly around me and I'm breaking my heart.

Nico did everything for me, for my family. And I screamed at him for it. I flash back to smashing the picture of my father that he had framed. Shame floods me, choking my throat and forcing yet more tears to stream down my face. But the pain of being lied to, of knowing that every time I was with him he was keeping the truth about my father from me... that *hurts*.

I cling tighter to Jack, nuzzling my tear-streaked face into his coat. After a few minutes, the sobs subside.

"Hey," he says, and I tilt my face up to look at him. "Does this mean you've forgiven me?"

I clench a fist and thump him on the chest. "God, you're a prick sometimes." I laugh through the heartache, because I do forgive him. Of course, I forgive him. And if I can forgive Jack, I can forgive Nico, too.

45
KATE

"This is madness. What on earth do you hope to achieve?" Marie asks, arms folded, the toe of one shoe tapping on the linoleum floor.

I'm standing at the door, a small roll-on suitcase at my feet, passport tucked into my handbag.

"It's not madness," Elly says, bouncing on her toes, hot chocolate slopping over the edge of her mug. "It's romantic."

Marie's lids shutter on an eye roll before her sharp gaze settles back on me. "You're going to turn up unannounced? What if he's already flying back here? Or he's seeing someone else..."

"He's not seeing someone else," I reply.

Marie sets her jaw and stares me down. "You sound very certain about that."

I'm not certain at all, but it gives me some satisfaction that my act is convincing hard-nosed Marie. Even though I've decided to pursue him, Nico's words keep swirling in my mind, threatening to send me running back to my room so I can pull the duvet over my head and hide.

I don't fucking quit, and I cannot be with someone who does.

Maybe he still feels like that... maybe me showing up at the Hawkston Building in New York won't be enough. Maybe it'll be too late.

Either way, I can't sit here and do nothing, waiting for Nico to come home. *I will not get back under that duvet.*

It might have taken me a while, but I got here in the end. I know what I want, and it's six foot three inches tall and looks drop dead gorgeous in a suit and tie, and even better naked.

"If I'm wrong, I'll get on the next flight back. No harm done," I continue. "Other than my bank balance. Last-minute tickets weren't cheap."

Marie's arched brow lets me know she's not entirely convinced by my act after all.

Elly grabs my arm, turning both of us to face off against Marie. "This is the big moment. This is Kate putting her heart on the line, risking it all for the love of her life."

"Okay, stop," I cry. "That's too much. If you keep going like that, I'll lose my nerve and stay here and watch a movie with you two."

"It's just good sex, that's all," Marie says, shrugging a shoulder.

Elly pulls my head towards hers with the arm she has wrapped around my shoulder and smacks a huge kiss on the side of my face. "Go get him, babe." Then she points at Marie and hisses, "Good sex is worth fighting for too. You should try it sometime."

Marie slaps Elly's hand away and hauls us both into a hug. "I'm just pissed because if you move in with him, I'll be left here with Elly and all her sweetness will rot my brain like a decaying tooth."

"Oi," Elly cries.

Marie steps back, bites her bottom lip and gives a half shake of the head as if she still thinks I'm crazy. "Good luck. I hope it works."

It's early evening when I find myself outside the Hawkston Building. It's taller than the London office, rising over my head like a glass-fronted obelisk. Thank God Jack didn't refuse me the last minute holiday I requested. I told him he was going to have to take Mum away without me, because I had somewhere else I needed to be. He didn't ask where, but I suspect he had an idea.

It's a warm Friday night, and the street is busy. I'm standing on the pavement outside, sweating in jeans and a t-shirt, suitcase at my feet. If Nico's here, he'll still be working. He's *always* working. But if I've timed it right, then he'll be here and everyone else will have left already.

My heart is beating so hard, I can feel my pulse in the soles of my feet. This is the craziest thing I've ever done. It's okay though—like I told my friends, if it doesn't work out, all I've really lost is the cash I've spent on tickets and accommodation.

The thought sinks heavily through my chest. It's a lie, obviously. I wouldn't be here if there weren't more at stake than a few hundred quid.

I take a deep breath, tighten my hold on my suitcase and take a step forward. It rolls noisily beside me until something catches my eye.

On the other side of the glass doors is Nico, dressed in black tie.

I freeze in the middle of the pavement, people dodging around me and cursing.

He's with someone. The door opens and they step out.

My heart pounds so forcibly it lands in my gullet, blocking my airway.

It's Erica Lefroy, dressed in a deep mauve, full length evening gown. She's beautiful; distractingly so. Better in the flesh than any photo I've ever seen of her. Nico says something, and she laughs, turns to him, and fixes his bow tie.

My heart disintegrates in a wave of pain, and my lungs collapse under the force. I choke on the emotion, unable to breathe. I need to get out of here, right now.

But I can't move. I watch as she lets her hands fall and taps her palms against the lapels of his dinner jacket, letting them rest there for an extended moment. Then she kisses his cheek. She presses her lips to his skin for barely a second, but it kills something inside me.

A car pulls up alongside the pavement, the windows dark and the hubcaps sparkling like diamonds. The body of the car is highly polished, too.

A driver gets out and opens the back door.

Erica's still talking, laughing. And Nico... he's smiling, brushing his hair off his forehead as they talk. *Are they standing suspiciously close together?* It looks that way, and one of her hands is still fingering the lapel of his jacket as if she doesn't want to let him go.

A small crowd has gathered; commuters stopping to stare. A few people have their mobiles out, trying to get a quick picture of Erica Lefroy and the unbelievably handsome man she's with.

I'm no better, standing here like a groupie. A fan. An outsider witnessing a life that will never be theirs. And it looks like a fairytale.

He's moved on. And with one of the most beautiful women in the world. She'd probably never give up on him. There's no way Erica Lefroy is a quitter. You don't get to be one of the world's top models by giving up on stuff.

Fuckity-fuck.

As I stare, there's a shift in Nico's body; a tensing or tightening that would be imperceptible if I wasn't already so attuned to his form. There's a split second where his expression alters, his attention withdrawing from the woman in front of him, moving inward to some *other* sense. Awareness sparks within me—he knows I'm here and even before he turns in my direction, I know he's going to.

S*hit*.

I want to die. I want the ground to swallow me up.

His eyes lock onto mine faster than a cat could pounce, and there's no way I can move in time to avoid it. His gaze sears my skin and solders my feet to the ground. Erica notices something's up too, and her gaze follows his. Now two pairs of beautiful eyes pin me to the spot.

Every fibre of my being is quivering with the urge, the *need*, to run. But I can't run, because I can't feel my limbs.

Nico's still staring at me, his mouth loose and slightly open, like he suspects he's imagined me. Erica looks from me to him in confusion.

This was not how I imagined our reunion would go. All the scenarios I was planning out in my head on the flight over—that he would lift me in his arms and kiss me or some variation of—are burning up like Bread Street in the Great Fire of fucking London. Reality is crashing down around me, crushing my bones and smothering my soul.

Nico's the first to move, with a long, purposeful stride in my direction. His eyes are still on me when my fight-or-flight reflex kicks in. I fix my grip on the handle of my suitcase and trundle it in the opposite direction.

"Hey!"

Oh, God. Is he shouting at me? What the fuck am I doing?

I'm panicking, that's what.

But this is ridiculous. I can't very well run through hordes of people with a carry-on bag rattling on shitty wheels behind me. I stop, and a large, heavy hand lands on my shoulder.

"Don't you dare run away now," he rasps. "Not when you're this fucking close."

The sound of his voice ripples through me, melting me to my core. God, I've missed it. But... *close to what?*

"Nico, what's going on?" The voice is British, female, with a cockney twang that contrasts with Nico's deep, upper class timbre.

His hand on my shoulder is hot and firm as his fingers encourage me to turn. The weight lifts, but only when I'm already twisting towards him.

His face, so close to mine, takes my breath away. Dark irises flicker with a desperation that tugs at my soul. "What are you doing here?" His voice is a low, urgent rumble that thrums over my skin.

"Nico?" Erica asks, drawing up alongside us before I can gather myself to answer him.

Nico smooths his expression and stands to his full height, and a warm gust of air carries his unmistakable scent as he pulls back from me. People passing on the street are watching us, bemused. Me, jet-lagged and bedraggled, pinned between two of the best-looking, most highly polished people in the world.

"Erica, this is Kate Lansen. A colleague." Nico says. The rough, commanding edge to his tone is gone. Now, there's only polite inquiry. I stiffen at the sound of it.

A colleague?

"Kate, this is Erica Lefroy," he tells me as if I wouldn't know who she is.

We nod at one another awkwardly.

Nico frowns, then leans in. "Is everything all right?" The question is so quiet that I'm not sure even Erica hears it.

I hate that my throat is closing over right now. I can hardly swallow.

Erica glances at her phone, then up at Nico. "We're going to be late."

I bow and step back, like a waiter retreating from a table at which he's lingered too long after taking an order. The wheels of my suitcase nearly take out an elderly man who yells, "Watch it," then grumbles, "Fucking tourists."

Nico stares like he's willing me to say something else, but I can't. I completely clam up under Erica's scrutinizing gaze.

"Sweetie," she says, placing a hand on my arm. "Are you okay?"

"Fine. Yes. I'll leave you to it," I say, trying to back away.

"Can we get you a cab? Where are you staying?" Erica's model-perfect face is scrunching with concern. I feel bad; she's giving herself wrinkles on my account.

And damn it, the woman is actually nice.

"Kate, why are you here?" Nico repeats, the authoritative tone blasting from each word now. I feel like a junior employee wasting his time. Which is exactly what I am.

But the intensity in his eyes, the way his dark lashes flicker over irises that burn ferociously, suggests he knows why I'm here, and needs to hear me say it.

"For you," I whisper.

His eyes widen, just a fraction, and his hand clamps around my wrist. "Where are you staying?"

I mumble out the name of a hotel, and Nico's hand slides from my wrist to my shoulder, wrapping around my back like a protective armour. I want to relax into it, but I can't. I stiffen instead, and his arm tenses in response. Even our bodies are disconnected and awkward. He ushers me towards the car. *His* car.

"I'll get a cab," I say.

"No, you won't. We will," he says, and he glances at Erica. She nods, already striding out towards the edge of the pavement and sticking her hand out into the traffic.

A cab instantly indicates and rolls towards her.

"I'm giving the opening speech at a charity gala tonight," Nico says. The words are rushed and whispered as he opens the door of the car. "I can't miss it."

He puts gentle pressure on my shoulder and I lower into the car and slide over the leather seat. I want to reach out and pull him in beside me.

On the street, the driver is already putting my suitcase in the boot. Nico barks directions to him, one hand braced on the open car door, the other on the roof. He's going to shut the door and leave me. *Fuck.* Will I even see him again, or is this his way of telling me I'm not wanted?

Desperate to get some kind of answer, I say, "Are you and Erica…"

Nico dips his head back through the car door and leans towards me, a mixture of frustration and apology in his eyes. "No. Listen, I can't talk right now. I wish you'd told me you were coming."

"I know about Martin," I blurt. "You discovered he and Curtis were working together. You saved Dad's art. I know what you did for us, for my family."

"I have to go…"

"Was it legal?" The phrase spurts from my mouth, a harried whisper. "What you did to sort everything out?"

He freezes. "It was… effective." I know what that word means. It means *No.* "Is that a problem?"

Staring at his face—his stupid, gorgeous face—I realise I don't give a fuck. As long as he isn't lying to me, I don't care what he did to Martin, because that bastard deserved whatever he had coming to him.

"No," I whisper.

And then I do the stupidest thing. I lurch forwards and kiss him. If I can even call it a kiss; it's more like a clash of lip and tooth. It's warm and hard and wet and soft; overall, it's a mess. A collision of human faces in a pattern that makes no sense.

Nico recoils, his eyes darting all over me, scanning every inch of my face and body. He mutters something under his breath.

And then he's gone, the door slamming in his wake.

46
NICO

Applause roars as I finish my speech. The rich and famous of New York are assembled before me at round tables, beneath the glittering lights of chandeliers.

Ordinarily, I'd be honoured to be here, grateful for the opportunity to speak before faces that I recognise. People I might even call friends. A congressman, a former president, editors of journals and papers, and owners of the same. But there's only one thing on my mind right now.

Kate Lansen.

She came to New York. She came to find *me*.

I can still hear that breathy whisper when I asked her why she was here.

For you.

There are three hundred pairs of eyes watching me, but none of them have the impact of that glance on the street outside the office earlier this evening. Seconds before I saw her, my skin tingled with the telltale sensation of being observed. My soul knew it was her, even before my eyes confirmed it.

I give the audience a bow before I descend from the stage. I weave through the crowd to get back to my table. I nod and smile exactly when I'm supposed to, shaking hands and greeting familiar faces. I've done this thousands of times. Not that I'd call it a pretense, but it is an act, to a certain extent.

"That was great," Erica whispers, leaning towards me as I take my seat next to her.

I lift my wine, raise a toast and nod my head in thanks before downing the entire glass in one go. Erica arches a brow at me, but makes no comment. I've been a shitty date since we bumped into Kate. I've barely said a word. I can't fucking concentrate.

Although 'date' is the wrong word; it's a favour, really. That's why she called the day I saw Martin Brooks. She has a huge advertising campaign coming out for an exclusive female fragrance, and apparently being seen with me fits the marketing profile. I had to pull a few strings to get her in this evening, but she's so famous I only had to tug lightly.

The look on Kate's face, though… I'm not sure doing the favour was worth it for the pain that marred her features. She looked less like a rabbit in the headlights and more like… road kill. She was a zombie when I helped her into the car.

An army of servers march into the room, carrying plates of prawns and mango, surrounding the tables nearest the service entry first. It'll only be a few minutes before we're surrounded by them, too.

I'm not staying for mediocre food and bad conversation (mine, obviously). I can't fault Erica. She's been remarkably forgiving, considering the situation I've put her in.

I drain the dregs of wine from my glass and lean towards her. "I'm so sorry—"

"Go. Get out of here." She flicks a wrist at me. "I'll make your excuses for you."

Shit. Am I that transparent? "Really, I—"

"You're worse company than the shellfish." I worry she's annoyed, but then her features soften. "Go do your thing, with the girl from the office." I am that transparent, then. "If the press runs a story that you stood me up, you'll owe me."

"Thank you," I say, and in a matter of minutes I'm outside, calling the car.

The hotel is a solid four star in midtown, close to Rockefeller centre. Dark green paint covers the walls and jazz music hums from invisible speakers. I'm not easily intimidated, but I can feel the unfamiliar bubbling of nerves in my stomach as I cross the lobby. Kate's here, in this building. Somewhere. I can sense her.

Doubt creeps in at the edges of my mind. Perhaps I misheard that one whispered phrase. Maybe it wasn't *'for you'*. Maybe she's not here for me at all. Perhaps she's legitimately taking a well-earned mini break.

And happened to stop by the Hawkston building? I know she loves her work, but does she love it that much?

I shove the thought away and approach the desk. A smartly dressed receptionist sits behind it, quietly tapping on a keyboard. The concierge, who's murmuring into the phone, sits next to her.

The receptionist looks up and gives me a breezy smile. "How can I help?"

"I'm here to meet Kate Lansen. Could you call her room for me?"

"Can I take your name, sir?"

"Nico." I'm not blasting my surname across the hotel lobby.

She nods and dials a room number. I can hear the dull ringing on her end of the phone. We wait a few moments.

"I'm sorry, sir, but Miss Lansen isn't answering. Would you like to leave a message? I'll make sure she gets it when she returns."

"No. I'll wait."

I cross the lobby and take a seat.

I'll wait all bloody night if I have to.

KATE

"Table for one please," I say as I approach the maître d'. I'm so distracted, he's little more than a blur of features I would never be able to recognise in a line-up.

I've showered and changed into a light cotton dress, but I'm still feeling groggy, jet lagged and inherently unstable after that humiliating encounter with Nico and Erica Lefroy.

He was out with another woman, and I threw myself at him. The memory of that horrendous kiss-attack won't go away. He said he wasn't with her though, didn't he? Or did I mishear that?

I try to remember our exact exchange, but I think I'd partially left my body by that point. I definitely wasn't thinking straight.

"Do you have a reservation?" the maître d' asks, dragging me back to the real world.

"No."

He scans the list in front of him. "We have one by the window. Come this way."

As I follow him through the dimly lit restaurant, I wonder if I ought to have gone out for dinner. Maybe walking the streets would have cleared my head, but I couldn't face it. The hotel restaurant felt safer. I can run and hide in my room if the sudden urge to break down in tears overwhelms me.

To think I came all the way here, only to find that Nico's spending the evening with Erica Lefroy.

I push the thought away as hard as I can, locking it up. Otherwise I'll be weeping at the table.

I take my seat and a moment later a server appears and clears away the place setting opposite me. Great. Now there's not even a pretense that anyone else is coming. My aloneness is exposed for all to see.

"Would you like to see the wine menu?" asks a smartly dressed sommelier who has appeared at the side of my table as stealthily as a ghost.

"No. But I'll take a bottle of your best Sauvignon."

He clutches the wine menu to his chest like a shield, and the slight widening of his eyes is the only judgment he offers.

Yes, I'm alone. Yes, I mean to drink the entire bottle myself. Is it a good idea? No. Do I care? Also no.

"Wait," I say. "How much is your best Sauvignon?"

His eyebrows rise fully now, and when he speaks, his voice is little more than a whisper. "Three hundred and forty-five dollars, Ma'am."

I bite back the gasp. I might have a horde of cash in my bank account, but spending freely is a habit I'll have to learn. That sounds like a big number for a bottle of wine and this trip has already cost a small fortune. Perhaps I ought not splurge on an entire bottle if all I'll have to show for it is a hangover.

"Let's go for something mid-range," I say. "And maybe just a glass, for now." I give him the most dazzling smile I can manage in my exhausted state, and he responds with a tight-lipped smile of his own, giving me a little bow before he departs.

Alone again at the table, I lament that I haven't brought a book. I can't sit here looking at my phone for the entire time. I ought to have ordered room service.

I scan the menu. There are typical dishes, like a high end burger with truffle sauce and parmesan potatoes, or something simpler like tagliatelle with a wild boar ragu.

"I hear the seabass is excellent."

I still at the sound of that deep, sensuous voice. I'd know it anywhere. But here, now? I'm hallucinating. Must be.

Finally, I look up.

Definitely not hallucinating.

Nico Hawkston is standing on the other side of my table, the streetlights from the window behind casting a golden glow over his skin. His square jaw is tight, and the intensity in his dark eyes is like stepping into a blazing fire; my body is kindling beneath its glare.

He's still wearing full black tie, and here I am in a casual summer dress. *He's devastating in a tux.* The bow tie at his neck is undone and it drapes around his collar, hanging loose. The top two buttons of his shirt are open, revealing that familiar triangle of skin that begs to be touched... or kissed.

He rubs a hand over the dark scruff that covers his jaw. It suits him, making him look a little more dangerous than normal.

"You're here," I whisper.

A beat passes before he answers. "I didn't want you to be alone."

The words warm my chest like he's placed his palms against my breasts, and the strain around my heart eases just a smidge. I fiddle with my fork, straightening it unnecessarily on the tablecloth. "You're ambushing me again."

Amusement dances in his eyes. "And turning up at my office an ocean away isn't an ambush?"

"No. That was war."

He huffs out a raw burst of laughter. "Assuming this is an ambush, is it unwelcome?"

My gaze snags on his lips as he speaks, and I'm assaulted by memories of them moving over my body; my neck, my breasts, my thighs... the innermost part of me that already knows the answer to his question.

Not unwelcome at all.

He lifts a brow, inviting my verdict. His large hand rests on the back of the empty chair opposite me, but he doesn't pull it back or indicate that he intends to sit. For a few seconds neither of us moves, then Nico cants his head, alerting me to the presence of a server hovering nearby. Her upper body tilts forwards as she looks between us, but her feet stay firmly planted further from the table than looks comfortable. She must sense the tension, too. "Should I bring an extra place setting?"

A subtle alteration in the angle of Nico's chin communicates that he's deferring the decision to me.

I wait, letting him worry for a moment. Not that he looks worried *at all*. He's all cool poise and confidence. Only a tiny flicker of his eyelids reveals that he's remotely concerned about my answer.

"Sit," I say.

A muscle in his jaw tenses and relaxes as he pulls out the chair and sits down. The server buzzes around him, laying out cutlery and glasses.

He unfolds the starched white napkin and places it on his lap, then his gaze fixes on mine. We breathe in tandem across the table; two people fused by the weight of unspoken words.

Finally, he breaks the silence. "I owe you an apology."

47
NICO

I take a deep breath. I can hardly believe Kate is sitting before me. My muscles are fatigued with tension. I'm expecting her to up and leave at any moment.

She's as beautiful as ever, dark hair falling around her shoulders, a simple yellow dress hugging her curves. It's warmer in New York than London, but the air con in the hotel is cool, and her nipples know it. I note their outline through the material, and an electric pulse rips through me.

I'm here to grovel, but the effect this woman has on me is insane. I drag my eyes back to her face and keep them there. I can't look anywhere else, not without undermining what I'm about to say. Coming to her hotel was a risk, but not as big as the one Kate took to be here. I've got to respect that because, what's life without a little risk-taking?

I inhale, filling my lungs deeply, but as I open my mouth, Kate speaks.

"I owe you an apology, too."

I close my mouth and press my lips. That's not what I expected her to say. My brows flex together, and then we speak at the same time.

"If you'll let me—"

"I felt so dreadful—"

We stop, and for the first time, a hint of a smile touches her face and lights her eyes. She lifts her napkin and dabs the side of her mouth, even though she hasn't touched a bite of food.

She nods to give me the go-ahead and the words tumble out. "I should have told you about your father as soon as anything happened between us. This was never casual for me. The way I feel about you..." I shake my head, letting out a sigh. "I've never felt like this for anyone. I know trusting me might be difficult, but I want you to know that, going forward, I'll put you first. My loyalty will be to you, and you alone. I'll make no oaths or bonds that require me to lie to you. Nothing will come before you. And I will never, ever keep the truth from you again."

She hangs her head, fiddles with her cutlery, shifting both knife and fork until they're exactly parallel to the plate.

"It hurt, you know," she whispers.

I wait, sensing she's not finished. She's still not looking at me, and seeing her pain makes my heart ache.

"Martin Brooks humiliated me, and he enjoyed it," she says. "He tore me apart that day at lunch. It felt like you'd thrown me to the wolves, left me out in the cold completely undefended. And you could have given me that protection. You could have told me the truth."

I pause, weighing her words before I speak. "Can you forgive me?"

Kate rolls the edge of her napkin back and forth on the table, curling it up and letting it unfold. My heartbeat swells until it feels like I might explode if she doesn't speak.

"In an ideal world," I continue, "I would have told you. But I swore I wouldn't. And that duty, that honour, is important to me. Jack... your father—"

She holds up a hand, and I shut my mouth. Swallow. Clench my teeth so hard the muscles in my jaw ache.

"I understand why you did it." Unshed tears rim her eyes, trembling on her lower lids. "And I can forgive you. I do forgive you, with my whole heart. But I wish it hadn't been like that."

She forgives me. "Like I said, going forward—"

"You sound like you're negotiating a business deal."

I slowly lever my upper body away from the table until it hits the chair behind, keeping my palms flat on the tablecloth. I'm doing this wrong. *Fuck.*

"What I'm trying to say is that I'm not entirely sure what you're negotiating for," Kate clarifies. "You're making suggestions about what you plan to do as we 'go forward'"—she air quotes with her fingertips—"but you haven't asked me anything. I don't know what your idea of 'going forward' is."

Her comment silences me as I realize how presumptuous I've been. I run my tongue over my teeth as I decide what to say next.

"Why did you come to New York? I know the Hawkston building is pretty impressive, but it's hardly up there on the top ten list of things to see when you visit."

She purses her lips, suppressing a smile that doesn't reach her eyes. "I've thought about everything that happened, and the things you said when I found out about my father, Lansen and Martin Brooks."

"What things?"

"You said you couldn't be with someone who would give up so easily. Who wouldn't fight for what they want. That's why I came here." She stops, her lips opening and closing as she heaves in a couple of uneven breaths. "To fight for you. For us. Because once I came to terms with everything, and understood what you'd done for Mum, for Jack, for all of us, I realised I'd been... rash.

"That doesn't mean I agree with what you did, but once I'd thought about it, it wasn't enough of a reason to give up on us. I couldn't wait for you to come back. I had to know if there was any chance..." Her chin quivers and her teeth dig into her bottom lip, pinning it in place. "But then I saw you with Erica."

"I told you before, Erica and I don't have a romantic relationship. We never have."

"It didn't look that way." She traces circles on the white linen tablecloth with one finger, watching the movement. She stills and raises her gaze to mine. "What do you want? What's your idea of 'going forward'?"

I take a deep breath. "You and me. Together. I haven't stopped thinking about you since that night on the balcony at Jack's birthday all those months ago. And if I'm entirely honest, since before that, too. That's why seeing all your sketches of me"—a blush rises to her cheeks—"was a relief. A surprise, sure, but mostly a relief because it allowed me to admit what I've always known."

She cups her hand over her mouth, elbow propped on the table. A tear trickles from her lashes, trailing a path down her cheek. "Which is?"

"That you're the one. You've always been the one. The only one. I might not have drawn any pictures, but if I had even half your talent I would have sketched you a million times over. I would have drawn nothing but you. You amaze me. Your talent, your dedication, your strength. You're incredible, Kate." My heart has never beaten this fast before. I run a hand through my hair to calm myself and hold her gaze. "I love you. I'm completely, utterly, obsessively, in love with you."

Her face crumples, tears flowing more freely now. She sniffles, aggressively wiping them away with the back of her hand. "If we do this, do we have to keep it secret?"

"Fuck, no." I reach across the table and she puts her hand in mine. God, it feels good to touch her. Her fingers tighten against my palm.

"No more secrets. If you want to be with me, I'll tell the whole fucking world about it."

KATE

We're barely out of the lift and he's stalking me down the corridor, so close behind that if I slow for a second, we'll collide.

We talked everything through over dinner. Not that I could eat much. Nico's proximity sent my body into a frenzy, humming with anticipation, knowing I would likely find myself here, outside my hotel room, with his body pressed up against mine before midnight.

The tension from the beginning of the evening has returned in full force, but there's a distinct quality to it now... less awkward, more explosive. It's not as though we haven't slept together before, but this feels way more potent... like we're on a precipice. And once we go over the edge, everything will be different.

As long as he's still walking behind me, I can handle it. But if he were to stop for even a second, the lurking fear he's going to disappear might break me. He might slip through my fingers like the fragments of a dream in early morning. If we can just get inside the room...

I stop at the door, fumbling to get the card out of my pocket. I can't find it. Where is it? I flip open my shoulder bag, rifling through it, too nervous to search in any way that's effective.

Nico's large hand braces against the door by my head. "Having second thoughts?"

The scent of him intensifies; I can feel the warmth of his body against my back, the gentle touch of his breath on my neck.

My body pulses with need. If I can't get this door open, we're doing it against it. I reach my arm into my bag up to the elbow, fingers scrabbling amidst the contents. If I don't find the key this time, I'm chucking the bag on the floor.

"Absolutely not."

"Thank fuck," he mutters into my nape before pressing a kiss there. Electricity warps my spine and I arch into him, my arse grazing against his erection. Anticipation I can barely contain bubbles beneath my skin. "Because if I have to live another second of my life with that face-smash in the cab as the last time we kissed, it'll fucking kill me."

A laugh escapes me as I finally clasp the key card and slam it against the reader, waiting for the light to turn green and the mechanical lock to click.

We fall into the room in a tangle of limbs. I drop my bag and kick the door closed. He pins me against it, one hand on my hip. His fingers are unforgiving as they dig into my flesh. His mouth crashes onto mine, his tongue eagerly sweeping through my lips. There is nothing awkward about this kiss. It's raw, wild and lights my body up from head to toe: he's the torch to my taper, and every cell in my body bursts into flame.

I have never wanted anyone the way I want him. I claw at his jacket, desperate to feel the warmth of his skin against mine, to run my fingers over the hard edges of his muscles. Nico shrugs out of it without breaking our kiss. I'm aware of nothing but the pull of his body to mine, and the desperation that blisters between us.

I tear at the buttons on his shirt and one pops off and rolls across the floor. He growls into my mouth, and I pull back. We stare at the button, our breathing jagged and hot in the air.

"Thousand dollar shirt?"

"Yup," he says, barely pausing for breath before he's on me again, hands sliding under my thighs, hiking me up.

I link my arms around his neck, legs around his hips. His fingers slip all the way until he's cupping my arse, holding my entire bodyweight. His hard cock nestles against the tender spot between my legs, the friction sending a heady rush of lust through my system and a gush of wetness into my underwear.

He drops me on the bed before ripping off his own shirt. More buttons pop and I can't help but laugh. He grins wolfishly as he stands at the end of the bed, his glorious chest exposed, the ridges of his abs perfectly defined.

"Sew them on for me later?" he asks.

I lurch across the wide bed and grab the free hotel sewing kit from the bedside table. "Sew your own buttons," I say, chucking it at him.

He ducks, emits a growl and lunges towards me, eyes flashing equal parts amusement and heat. I squeal, delighted, and crawl up the bed, but I don't get far before his hands clamp round my ankles and drag me back down.

He flips me onto my back and kneels at the end of the bed, his palms spread on my thighs, pinning me in place.

Chest heaving, I raise my eyes to his and I swear the contact burns. Keeping his eyes on me, he slides his hand up my thigh, grazing the lace of my underwear. He pushes the gusset aside, stroking my wet pussy with his thumb.

Closing his eyes, he inhales through his nose. "You are going to be the death of me." He wrenches my panties off and the fabric rips. He smirks. "But what a way to go."

I laugh as he eases the remnants out from under me and tosses them to the floor. At this rate, neither of us is going to have anything to wear tomorrow.

He removes the rest of his clothes in record time, and stands at the end of the bed, his dick huge and angry-looking. I raise an eyebrow and bite my lip as I eye it.

"Forgot what it looks like?" he murmurs.

"Kinda."

He leans over the bed, leveraging himself on braced forearms. He's holding himself over me, entirely naked, lining up our bodies. "Let me remind you," he says, his tip gliding across my stomach, through my pubic hair and down to my entrance before pushing into me with one hard thrust.

Air escapes my lips in a gasp, but I'm wet enough to welcome him with a delicious stretch that eases from pain to pleasure in seconds. He grabs at my dress, pulling it up and over my head, and I wriggle out of it. I unhook my bra and ease out of that, too. There's nothing between us now, his skin soft and warm, but firm with muscle beneath. He stares greedily at my breasts, before sucking my nipple into his mouth, first one, then the other, teasing them into hardened points. When his lips are gone, my nipples tingle, the air in the room cold against the tender skin.

He withdraws slowly and thrusts into me again so hard that my teeth chatter.

Fuck.

I pull him deep within me and hold him there, my hands on his arse as his cock reaches the deepest parts, a potent swelling sensation building in my core. *He's mine. This man is all mine.* The thought expands, and a ball of emotion forms in my throat.

"God, I've missed you," he mutters, a tinge of awe in his voice like he's been sharing my thoughts.

I reach my arms around his neck, pulling our bodies closer together, hiking my knees up over his hips to give him better access. My arousal surges with each of his rough grunts against my neck. His hips grind against my clit and a thrilling pressure builds between my thighs, melding with that deeper vibration. Desperate, I roll my hips against his, seeking more and more friction as I head towards orgasm.

He shifts my legs over his shoulders and drives deeper. His gaze, fixed on mine with an unwavering focus, feels like a promise, binding cords around my heart. His fingers press into my flesh like he'll never let go and each brutal thrust feels raw, like together we're forging a new version of us.

I can't get enough of him, and when my climax bursts like a fountain, it showers every part of my body with sparks of electricity.

"Oh, Nico, God, don't stop. Don't let go," I say as I come undone around him, my world fracturing into little more than light and energy and Nico Hawkston between my thighs, shuddering to his own orgasm.

We lie, a mess of sweat-slicked skin and uneven breaths. He braces himself on an elbow, brushes a strand of hair from my face, and presses a kiss to my bare shoulder. "If I did nothing but worship you for the rest of my life, I would die happy."

The smile on his face sends warmth to my soul. I trail my fingers down his back. "Oh yeah? What about business?"

"You're my business now."

My cheeks ache from smiling. "I'm not nearly as profitable as the Hawkston Hotels. Your share price would plummet."

He chuckles. "Ah, but it would be worth it. Because you're worth every single penny. And more."

"More?"

His eyes dance, his face beautiful, full of immeasurable joy. The fact that it's me he's looking at will never cease to blow my mind.

"Of course, more. The most. Because there's only one you, and I love you. I fucking love you, Kate Lansen. You're one in a million. One in a billion. One in—"

I press a finger to his lips. His eyes widen for a second, but when I smile, amusement surges through his dark irises again. "I love you too," I whisper. "Always."

EPILOGUE

"A little to the left," Mum directs Jack as he stands on a chair, a pencil between his teeth. He has one of Dad's favourite paintings against the wall, moving it millimeter by millimeter until Mum is happy. "That's it. There."

Jack snorts, his sweat-damp hair clinging to his forehead. The house is muggy, despite the back doors to the pool being wide open. There's barely a breeze outside.

A few weeks after we got back from New York, we headed down to Mum's for the weekend to help with unpacking Dad's art collection. Seeing as she hasn't found a new boyfriend yet, or decided to move anyone else into the house, we're putting them all back up. Curtis' supposed art collection was nothing more than a load of cheap posters. Jack suggested we donate them to charity, but Mum's intent on burning the lot on a bonfire in the field next door after sunset. It's symbolic, or so she says.

I hold the painting at one edge, taking some of the weight so Jack can make a pencil line on the top. Then he sticks the pencil behind his ear and climbs down, propping the picture against the wall.

Jack scans his work down the hall, where a few of the pictures already hang. They're not entirely level and the sight makes me giggle.

"What?" Jack says.

"They're wonky."

Jack scratches the back of his neck. "Are not."

"Actually, darling, they are a little uneven," Mum says. "Maybe you should start again."

Jack swears and throws the pencil to the floor. "Fuck's sake. I need a drink. Anyone else?"

"I don't know why you didn't pay someone to do this for you," Nico drawls. He's leaning against the opposite wall, a glass of scotch in his hand. "Or asked me to help."

"I didn't think it would be this bloody hard," Jack says. "I bet you've never hung a picture in your life."

Nico pushes off the wall. "Actually, I hung one last night. In Kate's apartment."

His lips part in a gorgeous smile, which never fails to take my breath away. He's wearing swim trunks and a t-shirt, a pair of sunglasses pushed back in his thick dark hair.

He brought the reframed charcoal sketch of Dad over last night and proceeded to get out the toolbox and hang it in the sitting room. I know it was just a hammer and a nail, but there was something undeniably sexy about him rolling his sleeves up and setting about doing the job himself. Even Marie was late to her shift as she stopped to watch him work.

Elly was worried that my dad looking down on our sitting room would upset me on a daily basis, but I like to think I've done enough healing to look at his face and remember the man who loved me, not the one who lied to me. I know he's both, but they're two halves that make a more genuine whole.

"Why don't you fix these for me then, instead of standing there grinning like an idiot?" Jack argues.

Nico smiles, raising his glass in a mocking toast to Jack before taking a sip. "I'll sort it."

Jack scowls, flips him the middle finger, and stomps off to the kitchen. Cupboard doors creak open and slam, and ice clinks aggressively in a glass.

"You shouldn't wind him up," I reprimand.

Nico pulls out his phone, presses a few buttons and fires off a quick message.

"What are you doing?"

"I've got a couple of my guys on standby to come and hang the pictures. Jack was never going to be able to do it all himself." He pulls me towards him, pressing my body against his. "And with you dressed in this"—he tugs at the turquoise beach dress that flows loosely over my body, covering a white bikini beneath—"I can think of other ways I'd prefer to spend the afternoon."

"My goodness, you two. I'm blushing," Mum cries, hands pressed to her cheeks.

I'd forgotten she was still there, and from the widening of Nico's eyes as he steps back, so had he.

"Sorry, Mrs Lansen," he says before glancing at me and winking. "But you have the most irresistible daughter."

"Oh, Nico." Mum giggles, flapping a limp-wristed hand at him. "She gets that from me, of course. I was quite the beauty in my youth."

Nico suppresses a smile, and I hide mine behind a cupped hand.

His phone buzzes and he glances at the screen. "They'll be here in half an hour."

"Saving our asses once again?" Jack says, reappearing from the kitchen, drink in hand.

"He's very competent," Mum says. "I always knew Kate would pick a winner in the end."

I resist rolling my eyes and Jack meets my gaze with an amused smirk.

"Now we've got Kate all loved up, what are we going to do about you, darling?" Mum fixes her eyes on Jack. "I don't think there's a woman in the whole of England who's good enough—"

"I'll sort myself, thanks Mum," Jack interrupts.

"Well, fine. But Aunt Venetia has a neighbour who has a daughter—"

Jack slaps his hands together. "Nope."

Mum's lips pucker, and we all laugh.

"Seeing as Nico's got this all under control," Jack says, "I'm going to shower." Then he saunters up the stairs, a dark V of sweat down the spine of his t-shirt.

Mum checks her wristwatch. "I've got to collect some dishes from Pam down the road. She's made a queen of puddings and a bread and butter pudding for the barbecue tonight, but she can't bring them because she's got a migraine. I'll run out now and fetch them."

"I can go," Nico says, putting his half drunk scotch on the side table.

"No, no, you stay here. Finish your drink. Keep Kate company. I'm sure she'd much rather you than me, anyway."

And with that, Mum totters off down the corridor on a pair of perilously high espadrille heels and lets herself out the front door. Gravel crunches as she crosses the front drive, jangling her keys in one hand.

When she's out of sight, Nico pulls me into him with one arm. "Are you going to take this off?" He fingers the beach cover up. "I want to see you in that bikini," he says, tugging at the strap around the back of my neck.

I slip out of his grip, still holding one of his hands. "You want to see, do you?"

He nods, the desire flashing in his eyes so raw that a pulse sets up in my clit. I don't think I'll ever get enough of the way he looks at me, like I'm the only woman in the world he'll ever want. I lead him out through the kitchen and into the back garden, where the hot tub is bubbling.

"Get in," I say.

He gives me a knowing look. "You want me in the hot tub?"

"I do."

With a bemused smirk, he pulls off his t-shirt and steps into the water.

When he sits down, his eyes trained on me like a searchlight, I tug off my dress and drop it to the floor, standing before him in only a white bikini. It's the same one I wore all those years ago, and the last time we were here. The day we finally crossed the line, and I came in his arms. I see the moment he realises it too.

"You delight in teasing me, Miss Lansen," he says, a dark chuckle rippling across the water towards me as I step into the tub, the warm water bubbling against my shins.

I reach up to the knot at the back of my neck, but I don't undo the bikini strings. I pause and Nico's eyebrow quirks.

"This time," I say, "You're not allowed to look away."

He bites his bottom lip and then huffs a laugh. "If you think I'd ever look away from you now, then you've lost your mind." He surges forward in a wave of bubbles and grabs my hips, staring up at me from his knees. "I don't want to look anywhere else, ever. I'd get on my knees for you every day, Kate Lansen."

The moment he's spoken the words, he stiffens.

"What?" I ask.

"This feels like that moment where I should ask you to marry me."

I laugh nervously. "God, no. Seriously, Nico. It's been a few weeks. I am totally okay with not getting married. Or engaged. Or any of that stuff."

"Really?"

I kneel opposite him, the bubbles surrounding us. "Yes. Just promise me we'll have loads of sex."

He grins, pulling me flush against him in the water. "I promise." Then his eyes turn serious. "But Kate..."

"Yes?"

"You're it for me. I might not be proposing, but I know I want to. Not today, but one day. I don't want to live my life without you by my side. I want to wake up beside you every morning and fall asleep beside you every night. I want to share everything with you."

A warm, fizzing sensation swells in my chest, up my throat. "I want that too," I say softly.

His smile is warm and kind and sexy all at once. "Great. Now, where were we..."

"We were promising to have lots of sex."

"Oh, yes." His hand eases inside my bikini bottoms so fast that I can only laugh, even as desire spikes through me hotter than the water. He kisses the side of my neck. "May as well begin as we mean to go on."

His fingers slide inside me, right where I want them, but I'm wary.

"Jack's in the house," I remind him, eyes flicking towards the back door. "Mum's going to be back any moment..."

The heel of Nico's hand presses against my clit and I stop talking.

"This will only take a minute." His whisper is hoarse against my throat.

I pull back, my arms still around his neck. "Oh, yeah?"

"Mmm-hmmm," he says, as his other hand snakes around the back of my neck and loosens the halter tie on my bikini so it slides off my breasts and into the water.

I glance back at the house. "Nico—"

But my voice catches in my throat as he takes one of my nipples in his mouth, slowly pumping his fingers in and out of me, drawing the crest of my pleasure closer and closer to the surface.

I dig my fingernails into his bare shoulders. "Oh, fuck—"

"Thought you might want to make new memories in here," he says. "Better memories."

He plays my body like an instrument, drawing out the sweetest tune as the tightly coiled pleasure at the base of my spine unwinds, rippling out through every part of my body like a slow rolling clap of thunder.

Riding the waves of my orgasm, I cling to Nico like he's going to save me from drowning. As my breathing returns to normal, he chuckles against my neck. "Told you it would only take a minute."

I lean back and splash water in his face, and his laugh rolls out like a stream of pure joy. I reach behind my neck to fix the strings of the bikini in place.

He grabs my hand to stop me. "Wait."

I still beneath his grip, one strap of the halter neck pinched between my fingers, my breasts exposed above the water level. And then he looks at me. Really fucking looks, his stare grazing over every inch of exposed skin. It's exactly what I wanted him to do all those years ago when I stupidly tried to seduce him right here in my parents' back garden.

He nods slowly. "It took a while, but you're worth every second of the wait. I'd give you the whole world if I could. Now"—he gives me a serious look, but his lips tilt in a smile—"put your fucking clothes back on."

Laughing, I fix my bikini back in place and stand. As I get out, Nico grabs my hand again. "Hey, Kate?"

"Yes?"

"I love you."

I look down at his face, so indescribably gorgeous that it makes my next breath catch. "I know."

"Forever," he adds.

"Yes," I agree, my heart bursting with emotion. "I love you too. Forever."

THE END

Want More Nico and Kate?

She wants to be watched.
He wants to give her everything.
Want to know what happens?
You can find the bonus scene here:
https://dl.bookfunnel.com/f2fpmo3wcf

Worth Every Game

If you want more from the Hawkston Billionaires, you can preorder the ebook of Book 2, Worth Every Game, using the QR code below. I love this story and can't wait to share it with you. It releases December 16th 2024. Paperbacks will be available then, too.

Afterword

Thank you so much for reading Worth Every Penny. I truly appreciate the time you have taken to read my book and I hope you've enjoyed the experience. Putting creative work out into the world is always nerve-wracking, so I'm incredibly grateful for your support.

If you have a moment to leave a review, I'd really appreciate it. Or just shout about the book at the top of your lungs (preferably on social media, but to be honest I'm not fussy just so long as you are loud).

Joking aside, I always love to hear from readers so feel free to reach out to me at any of the places listed on the following page, or join my mailing list here:

KEEP IN TOUCH WITH RAE

Join my Facebook reader group, **Rae's Romantics**, where you can discuss my books, characters, and get information about upcoming releases.

You can also find me at my website
www.raeryder.com
And on Instagram & Tiktok
@raeryderauthor

Acknowledgements

There are so many people to thank, all of whom contributed to turning my messy first draft into the book you've just read. The first eyes on it were those of my wonderful Book Coach and Developmental Editor, Emily Tamayo Mayer, who pushed me HARD to improve the plot, the characters, and the scenes. Sometimes, she'd give me feedback and I'd dismiss it, only to take a break from my manuscript and return later to find that I agreed entirely with what she'd said.

Sido Bouvier (the talented fantasy author S. E. Bouvier) who probably had no idea when she introduced herself to me at the Self Publishing Show back in 2022 that her phone number would become the most used in my contact list. Over the last two years I have peppered her with messages about book boyfriends, sentence structure, editing queries and much, much more. Thank you so much for helping me write my first Romance, and for taking the solitary edge out of this whole writing gig.

Then there were my beta readers (you know who you are) who squealed at the good bits, but told me when I'd made Nico too mean or Kate too aggressive. They helped me kick those characters into shape, making them much more likeable.

My Editor, Sarah Baker, who improved the book more than I had anticipated. She chopped out so much that I contacted her the moment I got my edits back to make sure the word count was correct.

And my ARC Team! Absolute champs, all of you. Your enthusiasm gave me so much joy, I can't thank you enough. You helped me realise that even if no one ever buys this book, the fulfilment I gained from knowing you all had a good time reading it is enough to keep me writing for the rest of my life. You also saved this book from going out into the world with Kate wearing a t-shit. *Phew*.

Also to TL Swan and her Cygnets, for being my inspiration and for responding to all my romance and publishing queries. The Cygnets is a wonderfully supportive group and I honestly believe the universe led me to that little corner of Facebook.

Thanks also to my husband, who was once saved in someone's contacts as Massively Hot Tom, but who doesn't dare read this book. Maybe one day. But in the meantime, I will never forget the look of horror on your face when you picked one of my printed pages off the floor and saw what was on it. Despite that, your unwavering faith that I'll pull this author thing off is beautiful. I'm so grateful for your love and patience.

And to my wonderful children, who came to stand by my desk many times during the writing of this book, causing me to minimize my documents faster than Nico Hawkston can put on a condom.

And a huge thanks to the MVP. Me. Because I worked my arse off and gave up nightly Netflix on the sofa with my husband to write this book. I also gave up the gym, but I miss that less.

Finally, I owe thanks to all of you out there who took a chance on this book. I am forever grateful.

Rae x

Printed in Great Britain
by Amazon